REUNION

Eric Williams

MINERVA PRESS
LONDON
ATLANTA MONTREUX SYDNEY

REUNION
Copyright © Eric Williams 1998

All Rights Reserved

No part of this book may be reproduced in any form,
by photocopying or by any electronic or mechanical means,
including information storage or retrieval systems,
without permission in writing from both the copyright
owner and the publisher of this book.

ISBN 1 86106 805 0

First Published 1998 by
MINERVA PRESS
195 Knightsbridge
London SW7 1RE

Printed in Great Britain for Minerva Press

REUNION

Reunion
is dedicated to Rosemary,
with thanks

About the Author

Eric Williams began writing technical articles and books while working with a large, international engineering company. Qualified initially as a Physicist, he became a Professional Engineer and, in the course of his work, travelled widely through many areas of the world. His feature articles have appeared frequently in the leisure press, technical magazines and trade journals.

The novel, *Reunion*, represents his first venture into fiction and introduces the exploits of a Swedish family – the Tillkvists.

Acknowledgements

The research and writing of *Reunion* has taken several months but, in reality, the story distils knowledge gained over many years and drawn from minds and experiences more expansive than my own. In the course of my preparations, I have visited many sights, in several countries, and also turned to the writings of others more adroitly versed than I in historical detail.

Thanks must go to Gunnar Jacobsson who first awakened my interest in Sweden, its history and its people, and to Hans Sundberg for his efforts in chauffeuring me around and patiently answering my many questions during one of my visits to Sweden. I acknowledge, too, the help received from Soren Soderholm who gave of his own time to forage among the shelves of the library in Vasteras in order to dig out salient pieces of information and subsequently provide translation. I am grateful, too, to Catharina von Schinkel, joint owner of the Tido Slott, for assisting me with an insight into the castle and background on Axel Oxenstierna.

I am particularly indebted to Hubert Toenjes of British Columbia who first introduced me to the building and shooting of flintlock rifles. And to Dr De Witt Bailey of the Tower of London who, along with members of the Southern Counties Patched Ball Group, has furthered my interest in the armaments of the eighteenth century.

Thanks also to Maurice Taylor, late of Sheffield, now resident in New Zealand, who taught me the finer points of firemaking using a primitive flint and steel.

Undoubtedly, my deepest gratitude is reserved for Vilhelm Moberg, alas now deceased, for his inspirational series of books, translated into English, on the early lifestyles of the Swedish people. Without such a finely woven, descriptive tapestry of words, my knowledge of the subject would have been severely lacking.

No small amount of thanks is due to my son, Jeremy, who assisted painstakingly with proofing and preparation of the final manuscript.

Finally, I was fortunate to have, in my wife, a woman well blessed with patience and an unflagging spirit of encouragement. She unselfishly allowed me the undisturbed time to research and write this book.

Eric Williams

Preface

Based on a true incident, an unusual discovery on a remote farm in southern Sweden begins a quest that retraces Sweden's history – and the history of a proud and resourceful family. From the tribal Svear who gave the country its name, through a vast canvas that introduces some of the men and women who made Sweden a highly respected international state, to a final reunion of family, antiquity and territory, the intimate – sometimes treacherous and violent – saga of the Tillkvist family unfolds. The uncompromising Svear; Gustav Vasa and Queen Kristina; the young regent, Axel Oxenstierna; the scientists, Anders Celsius and Alfred Nobel; these, and others, mingle with generations of a family striving for recognition... and survival.

Jokkmokk
Mora
Lake Siljan
SWEDEN
Stockholm
Lake Mälaren
Norrköping
Götheborg
Falkenberg
Växjö
Kalmar
Nybro
Halmstad
Karlskrona
Ronneby
Hälsingborg
Malmö
ØRESUND
BALTIC SEA

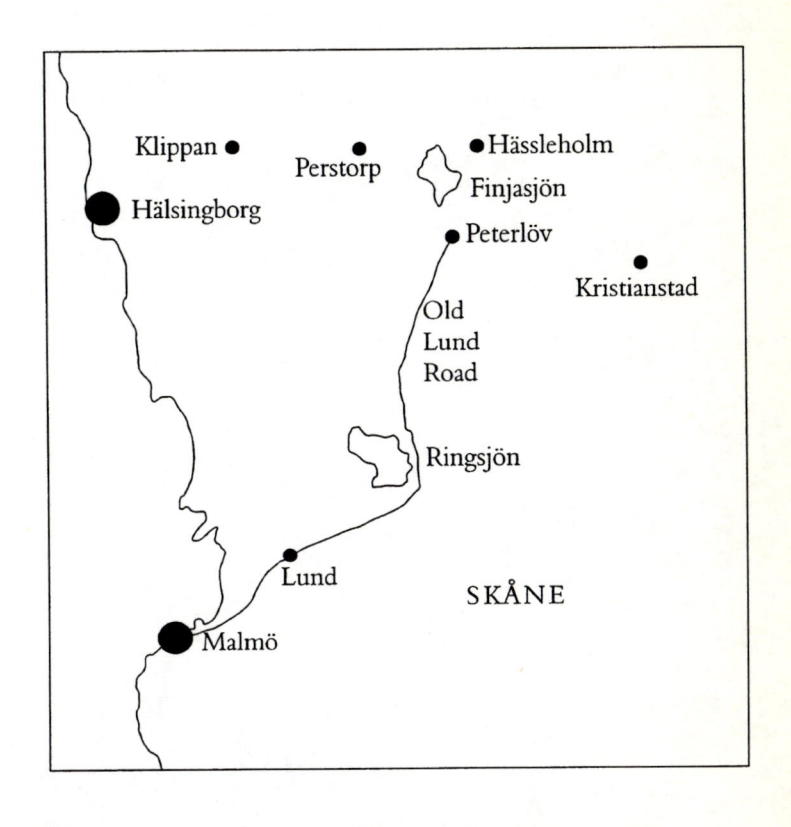

Contents

Prologue	xv
The Invitation	21
The Survivors	67
The Warriors	153
The Artisan	237
The Emigrants	337
The Inheritors	427
The Reconciliations	519
The Incident	579

Prologue

This is a novel and pretends to be none other. The Tillkvist family and many of the key characters are products of the author's own imagination. Fact and fiction freely intermingle in a style some have labelled *faction*, bringing to life real, historical situations and people but with modest licence given to the dialogue between historical characters. Wherever contemporary writings have made it possible to determine the particular disposition of characters, the author has endeavoured to keep their speeches consistent with the characters' recorded manner so that their words appear much as they would have been spoken at the time.

Considerable field and desk researches were undertaken in preparing this novel, with a view to achieving an accurate portrayal of Sweden's history and people. Here and there, small liberties have been taken with regard to chronology in the belief that it has contributed to producing smoother fiction without recourse to long and detailed explanations.

The Swedish alphabet contains three vowels that are not found in English and some modes of these produce pronunciations that don't fall easily on the ear of the English speaker. For this reason, the vowels å, ä and ö have been rendered in the text without accents but, the author believes, without detriment to the understanding of the words concerned. Most often, these occur in the names of characters or places.

The story of *Reunion* spans several centuries, during which time various forms of currency, weights and measures were in use. Within each era in the narrative, the system of measures and values appropriate to the period has been used. For example: in the late twentieth century parts of the story, distances are given in kilometres; in earlier times, distances are given in miles.

The key elements of fact and fiction in each chapter are as follows:

The Invitation

The main characters are fictitious, however, most locations are accurately described. CHP is fictitious and, therefore, has never occupied Crown House, which is real. The motel near Hässleholm was relocated for convenience. The village of Peterlöv is fictitious but the lifestyles of the characters accurately reflect those found in similar farming communities within the region today.

Guns of the type discovered on the farm were known to have originated from Germany and a similar style may well have been produced by local artisans. The Bergengrens were well-known silversmiths and articles of their creation exist in museum collections.

The Survivors

Recent archaeological excavations have confirmed the existence of small villages around the shores of Lake Mälaren, similar to that described. Although the title of 'oldest Swedish town' is claimed by Birka on the Lake Mälaren island of Bjorko, just to the west of Stockholm, there is thought to have been a significant population at the much older Helgo nearby. Helgo is one of the major finds in recent years.

The Svear were real people who lived much as detailed. Their wars with the Gotar people from what is now the southern part of Sweden were legion, however, the Svear emerged as the stronger and survived in tribal form until around AD 900.

The Warriors

The various family members of the Swedish, Danish and Polish nobility are historical. The painter, Ulrich, is fictitious. Lützen and the several other battles mentioned, including the sacking of Krzyztopor, are faithfully recorded.

The Treaty of Roskilde is a pivotal point in Swedish history and the lead-up events took place as stated. Axel Oxenstierna remains one of Sweden's greatest ever statesmen and his castle home at Tido Slott is now a popular tourist venue.

The Artisan

The main characters are fictitious, but Louis de Geer was real. The lifestyles depicted in Skåne are realistic to that era, as are the activities of the Skånian guerrillas. The Tornstroms worked in Karlskrona as depicted and, within the period, many carpenters and other craftsmen lived in the small cottages described.

Even today, the Sami people of the north are often disadvantaged and the characteristics exhibited by the fictitious Anta Utsi are typical of the Lapplanders' spirit and tenacity. Norrholm is fictitious, however the township and mill described are typical of those to be found in the region at that time. Whilst parallels may be found in other Swedish and Finnish timber operations, the Utsi mills and their eventual formation into a major forest products company are of the author's own design.

The Emigrants

The mass emigration actually took place, although it did not reach its peak until after 1880, and some shipping companies did employ agents as described.

The events concerning the Harper's Ferry raid are well known and, during the *War Between the States*, the occupation of the town see-sawed between the armies of North and South. Many minor confrontations between Union and Confederate forces took place but have found no lasting memory in the shadow of that sad war's greater conflicts. The term 'nigger' continued in use for many years after Abraham Lincoln's Declaration of Emancipation and former slaves and freemen alike suffered from ingrained discriminatory attitudes.

The main locations of the emigrants' homes are geographically correct, but Cayuga Flats did not exist as a ranch. Fort Frederick exists as described and is now open to the public. The Smithsonian Institution is one of Washington's famous landmarks.

The Inheritors

Whilst the Utsi Company is fictitious, similar labour unrest took place in the industry elsewhere at around this time. The Landsorganisation and the Swedish Employers Confederation are real. The Suffragette Movement is described accurately and within context.

Alfred Nobel is, of course, a world-renowned figure.

His background, both family and personal, is well known.

Ronneby is, even today, a centre for many conferences and symposia and is home to a popular cultural heritage museum.

The Reconciliations

The Øresund bridge project is real and accurately described. The author believes that its importance to both Scandinavia and to Europe as a whole cannot be overstated.

The particular private collection of antiques described is fictitious, however, such collections do exist, especially within some of Sweden's old, established families who characteristically often hold the same strong views on heritage and family links as did the Tillkvists.

Klippan has been, for many years, home to a thriving fine paper mill.

The Incident

The story included here is the basis for the central storyline of *Reunion* and actually took place as described.

The Families

All characters are products of the author's own imagination and relate to no known persons, living or dead.

Part One
The Invitation

For Bertil and Berthe

The best-laid schemes o' mice an' men
　Gang oft a-gley...

　　　　　　　　　　　Robert Burns

It was just after 8.30 and I knew the post had arrived. There's nothing else quite like the sound of a bundle of mail, elastic-banded together, thwacking on to the hardwood floor of the porch from a waist-high letterbox. *National Geographic* I recognised at once by its recycled yellow cover sleeve. A polythene-bound catalogue from a Dutch bulb grower and a large envelope announcing *Good News for Tax-free Savers* did little to fuel any scant inner glow I may have generated. But the last and by far the smallest item, a regular-sized white envelope, brought a conscious uplift in my spirit when I noticed the franking mark. The heraldic CHP logo with its underlying strapline declaring *Books for Learning, Living and Leisure* betraying its source as Crown House Publishing. It was formally addressed: Dr W. Kirkland.

I was at the same time excited and intrigued, but I could never have foreseen how the contents of the envelope I was holding would usurp my routinely patterned lifestyle; inculcate my thinking with new horizons and stimulate me to a wider and deeper appreciation of the changing face of Europe. My emotions would be exposed; my loyalties challenged and my diplomacy tested to the hilt.

A letter from the CHP people was not one to be read in the hallway. If it was anything like the usual communications I received from the Morden, South London office, it had to be digested and savoured from a position of comfort, generally indicating that I should retreat to my recliner in the lounge. After all, Crown House had just published the fourth of my books on historic firearms and the initial response had been promising. It majored on the finely crafted guns produced in Lancaster County during the late 1700s by Jacob Dickert and was part of an ongoing *Arms & Armour* series much sought after by collectors, enactment groups and antique gun enthusiasts. Indeed, the third book in the series, *Guns of the Colonial Trade*, was in its second printing. Quite respectable for a specialist subject.

The letter read:

My dear Walt,

As you may recall, I'm off on my travels again this week and don't expect to be back in the office for at least a month. For that reason I'm writing to you with some urgency following some interesting information sent in by one of our associates in Sweden.

Now that your Dickert work has been put to bed I'm sure you won't decline the offer of a little diversion. This sounds just your kind of thing and I believe it's worth following up.

Kerstin Berg, working for our Overseas Developments Department in Sweden, has been writing some of the lead articles for one of our trade journals, Forestry and Construction, and has met someone who has unearthed what appears to be an early Greek gun in apparently near mint condition. There seems to be a bit of a story attached to this. Perhaps you'd like to check on it and let me know what you find out when I get back.

Walt, I suggest you call my secretary, Sandra, during the next few days to get a bit more of the background on this. She will arrange your travel on the usual

basis should you decide to take this up. Also, Miss Berg has offered to provide assistance in Sweden if you need it. Sandra has her contact details.
Please excuse the hasty note. I have lots to do before I fly out.

Very best regards
Don Wade

A gun of unknown vintage and of Greek origin turning up in Sweden. That could be something or nothing. I wasn't very well up on Grecian arms although I'd read Considine's book on the subject. It was the Swedish connection that was most puzzling. Even so, I still couldn't see what had got Don so fired up that he felt he had to get this checked out. Admittedly, Greek involvement in medieval Sweden was not something that readily came to mind, although it was nearly forty years since I'd studied Scandinavian history in high school. But was it really that important? On the other hand, that was one of the things I'd most admired in Don Wade. He was so spontaneous. And so energetic. If his looks belied his age, his dynamism most certainly did. Of medium build, his almost full head of hair blending grey with black and his face carrying a year-round tan, he looked every inch the retired beachcomber. This was a man who worked regular ten hour days and carried the hopes of a growing publishing house on his shoulders. I respected him a lot. Over the years I'd learned to trust him, too. If Don said it, I believed it.

Sandra Watkins was the epitome of the modern female executive. In her early thirties, I'd say, and on the tall side; with her dark hair neatly bobbed, she wore a minimum of make-up and dressed in clothes that smacked of quality if not designer label. Her eye and body language spoke volumes, including such titles as bright, broad-minded, confident and streetwise.

'Tea? Coffee?' she offered, as I sat in the familiar office, once more taking in the collage of book jackets which formed one wall.

'Yes, thank you. Black coffee will be just fine. No sugar.'

She ordered our drinks by phone and sat back once more behind the heavy mahogany desk.

'So! What do you think of our little find? Does it sound interesting?' Her eyes twinkled as she pushed in front of me the copy of a fax. Two of the paragraphs had been circled in pink highlighter with the words 'for Walt Kirkland??' slanting their way along one margin. The page was only one part of the fax and I presumed it had originated from the Miss Berg that Don had mentioned. I scanned the marked paragraphs, adding to my knowledge of the find so far only that it had been discovered secreted in a hollow tree on an isolated farm and was marked with an assortment of Greek lettering.

'Three things puzzle me, Sandra. First, how did it get there? Second, why was it hidden so carefully? And third, why does Don think it's so important?'

'We've discussed it only briefly,' she said, handing me one of the two coffees which had been brought in along with a small plate of biscuits, 'but your first two questions are exactly what excited him. He feels the background could be interesting. It may need a bit of researching but would possibly make a good leader for our New Year edition of the *Arms and Armour Supplement* which has a significant subscription worldwide. According to Don, if this truly is a relic of some bygone Greek intrusion, he sees the story as an ideal scene-setter for this special edition.'

'It's possible. Then again, it may be no more than a souvenir brought back from a trading voyage. During the eighteenth century, many Swedish vessels plied their trade between Göteborg and Canton. It's possible they could have stopped off in Piraeus on occasion and traded with the locals.'

We speculated from a number of standpoints over the next ten or so minutes when, seemingly at an impasse, Sandra met my eyes and smiled. 'So, you think it's worth the trip?'

Before I'd ventured an answer, she had quickly thumbed through a large black desk diary: 'How about week twenty-eight?'

'Week twenty-eight? What's that in normalspeak?'

Almost exactly fifty minutes after I'd arrived at the CHP offices, I was climbing back into my car. I'd agreed to go. The plane tickets would be delivered to my home later that week and a fax was already on its way to Miss Berg stating that I'd meet her in Malmö.

For me, this would be a new kind of challenge. Although, over the years, my research and writing had centred on antique weapons of one form or another, most of my information had been garnered from sifting through museum papers, assisting with cataloguing and through discussion with private collectors. This would be quite different. I'd have to start from almost zero data; might possibly have to research the military or naval background and, quite conceivably, could finish up trekking around the Macedonian hill country. As I turned it over in my mind, I wasn't sure right then that I was up to the task. I was, at the same time, excited at the prospect. Approaching my fifty-third birthday; widowed almost nine years; and with my only daughter, Sophie, now a Mrs Warhurst living in Hamilton, Ontario, perhaps I needed an overseas trip again and something new to stretch the mind.

★

The descent into Copenhagen's Kastrup airport marked the end of a pleasant and uneventful flight. The Boeing's wheels eked out a grip on the runway with a slight swerve and wobble reminiscent of my first experience of driving on an icy road. Soon we were nosing into position alongside an overhead ramp. This first stage of my journey was over.

It's a strange disparity that applies to a journey like this: in around a hundred minutes I'd travelled from Birmingham to Copenhagen; it would now take half as long again to cover the remaining fourteen miles. Two of those hours would be spent in the duty-free shopping zone whilst awaiting my Jet Cat connection to Malmö City, the inevitable discontinuity incurred in making connections on any non-direct international flight.

It was now evening as the big Cat skipped across the docile waters past low-lying Saltholm Island and on into Malmö harbour. The huge frame of the Kockums crane echoed a past heritage of great ships that were built and repaired here. Now dormant, the massive steel rectangle loomed into the evening sky like some giant gantry awaiting the arrival of its next space shuttle.

I discovered that, in Sweden, practically everyone speaks English to some degree. Conversation with the taxi driver was low key but not unrewarding. I had my first lesson in Swedish. *Tack*. Short, delivered with a staccato abruptness, it means 'thank you'. The six minute cab ride terminated in Stora Nygatan at the St Jorgen Hotel. At the check-in desk I was handed a message which read:

For the attention of Doctor Kirkland.
Will meet you in the bar at 7.30.
Kerstin Berg

The number seven was crossed through the downstroke, declaring its origin as 'Not Made in Britain'.

With a little less than an hour to freshen up in readiness for my rendezvous with Miss Berg, I surveyed my new surroundings whilst unpacking my things. Don Wade's Miss Watkins certainly could be complimented on her organisation and choice of hotel for this first night's stopover. So far, everything had worked out as planned. The view from my window was somewhat obstructed by an adjoining lead-sheeted roof, but the room itself was delightful. The Scandinavians certainly have a way with interior design which is both inventive yet restful. Take the armchair with its high backrest that looked like a yacht sail. So asymmetrical yet somehow still in balance with good taste. It looked comfortable even before I sat in it. The experience of doing so brought theory and practice together in a matrimony of mind that must have pre-existed with its designer. The dark wood furnishings, too, lent a character to the room that surpassed the merely functional.

Monday night was obviously not the high point of the week in Swedish social life, judging by the number and dress of people in the hotel bar. The numbers were few; the dress was informal, almost to a Saturday-morning-in-the-backyard level. I ordered a Starkol beer and charged it to my room. The cost was frightening when I translated the kronor back into sterling. At least finding a quiet and unsequestered corner of the lounge was not difficult, so I settled back into a deeply upholstered leather chair, glanced at the mirror-tiled ceiling and took my first sip of Swedish beer. Not bad, though much lighter than its German counterpart. The handwritten wall signs provided a mild diversion as I waited, but my blissful solitude was short lived.

'Doctor Kirkland?'

I felt as Livingstone must have done on being addressed by Stanley in the middle of Africa: a paradoxical mixture of homeliness and distant isolation.

'That's right! Walt Kirkland.'

'Hi! I'm Sherstin Berg.'

That was my second Swedish lesson of the day. A 'K' before a soft vowel becomes a 'sh' and not the hard K as in kettle that I'd used in mentally addressing the young woman who now took her seat directly opposite me. Noticing my just-begun drink and catching the eye of a passing waiter, she ordered likewise.

'So. How was your journey? No problems?' She spoke English in a very confident manner with a trace of a North American accent that suggested she'd spent some time in that part of the world.

'No. No problems. Everything went quite smoothly although the last part, from Copenhagen to here, was rather drawn out.'

'Yes, that's always been a problem for people coming to south Sweden. Once the bridge has been completed it will make a real difference to this place.'

'The bridge?'

'Yeah, they're linking Copenhagen with Malmö by a

bridge-tunnel similar to the one crossing Chesapeake Bay. You know it?'

I replied that I did and agreed with her that such a link should, indeed, reduce the journey time considerably. In the few moments she took to sign her bill, from which I gathered that she was staying in the hotel, I studied my new acquaintance. Kerstin was not at all as I'd imagined she might be. Probably in her late twenties, she wore her honey-blonde hair in a style that divided her tresses unequally between, on the left side, a straight fall to the shoulders and, on the right, a high sweep behind her ear, revealing a dangling ethnic-style earring in dark blue which complemented her two-tone blue jacket and pencil skirt. Her skin was lightly freckled and she smiled a lot, her pink lipstick framing a set of near-perfect teeth. She had, undeniably, a personality that exuded warmth and, on first meeting, sold herself well as a woman who knew bow from stern and would not spend long on her own on any dance floor or at the bar of an English pub. She would be an ideal companion for any one-night stopover let alone the four weeks that Crown's had allowed me to cover my present commission. Her eyes were huge and seemed to billboard an inner message: 'I'm here to listen to *you*.' I instantly liked her.

She reached into her handbag and drew out a packet of Marlboro. 'Smoke?' she asked, offering me the opened packet.

'No thanks. I've long since given it up.'

'Sorry. I'm afraid I do. Do you mind?'

'No, Kerstin, *you* don't smoke. It's the cigarette that smokes. You're just the sucker.' We both laughed. My line had been neither profound nor original but it served to break any last vestiges of thin ice that lingered between us.

We launched immediately into a discussion of the subject that had brought me to Skåne, this southernmost province of Sweden.

It was almost nine o'clock when we left the bar and headed towards a small restaurant just off the Stortorget, the city's main square. On this mild July evening we strolled at a dallying pace, stopping briefly at one of the most comical sculptures I'd seen in a long time. Almost as if marching out of the Stortorget itself stood a line of bandsmen wrought in iron, their moment of stride and various instruments poised for ever as if captured by some futuristic three-dimensional photographic technology. Even their steely facial expressions suggested a determination to keep in step right through to Gustav Adolf's Square in the centre of town. Amusing, but at the same time quite charming, and so indicative of this native art form that I would come to recognise in the weeks ahead.

We had already explored the coincidental links in the chain of events that had led to Kerstin's learning about the find on the Tillkvists' farm. Of how she'd met Martin Chelford, a design engineer from Knutsford, in Cheshire, who was working on the construction project that she was writing about. Of how he'd married Annika Tillkvist, whose brother Mats had actually brought down the old hollow oak to reveal the gun that had brought me to Sweden.

'Yes, it was quite embarrassing,' she told me, 'I'd seen the word "Knutsford" written down on a fax before I'd heard it spoken and at first I pronounced it "kanootsford" as we would in Sweden. Martin still reminds me of it when I see him.' She gave a girlish chuckle and I smiled, thinking instantly of one or two similar *faux pas* that I'd made myself when I first visited Scotland many years ago.

Our current topic of conversation was Swedish food, prompted initially by the gourmet smells emanating from a cafe we'd passed on the way. From what Kerstin had told me, I was quite sure that I would cope. The pea or bean soup, traditionally served on Thursdays, didn't exactly set my taste buds tingling but, in general, the Scandinavian diet didn't sound too different from what I'd become used to back home in Lichfield.

The restaurant was no more crowded than had been the bar back at the St Jorgen. Consequently, we were able to find a table in a corner spot that was partly shielded by a pine planter full of long grasses and the light from the long-drop lamp with its bright red shade was just sufficient to illuminate the table yet create an aura of intimacy. The menu was in Swedish, of course, but I was able to hazard a guess at a number of the dishes without having to continuously call across the table for help in translation. I almost made it through the list of main courses unaided.

'What's ren?' I asked.

'Oh, that's reindeer steak. Very nice. A bit like beef but a bit more, how can I describe it?' She paused, searching: 'Gamey, perhaps.'

'You mean like venison? Deer?'

'Yeah, pretty close.'

That decided it. I would have the ren. Kerstin was sticking with the more conservative trio of lamb cutlets.

'You speak very good English. I guess you've been to England many times.'

'Only twice, to visit CHP. But I lived in Vancouver for six years and studied forestry at the University of British Columbia. My parents emigrated there when I was sixteen. They're still there, living in a small town called Abbotsford. It's in the Fraser Valley, not far from Vancouver.'

'Right. That must account for your slight North American accent.'

'Probably. Although I didn't realise that I had any accent... apart from Swedish maybe.'

She went on to tell me that she had visited her parents twice in the last four years and that her brother was also in Canada, working for a hydroelectric company.

'By the way, are you also staying at the hotel?' I asked, already knowing the answer but using it as a way of leading into clarifying our plans for the next day.

'Yes. I thought it would be best. My apartment is in Lund, about thirty kilometres from here, but I thought it would be easier if we were together. We must leave at about eight tomorrow because Mats will not be free in the afternoon so we must make the best of the time we have. He is living with his girlfriend Mia in Hälsingborg; only his parents are living on the farm. It's near Hässleholm, just a bit inland. It's not so far away and Mats would like to meet us there. Old Bertil, his father, can be a bit of a difficult man so I think it's better that Mats shows us the gun himself.'

My first impressions of this self-assured young lady had obviously been fairly accurate. She was beginning to show me that she really had done her homework. And it was clear that that included politics and diplomacy, too.

The meal was delightful and finished off with a local version of aquavit, named after the province and reputed to be among the best. I was, at last, now feeling the effects of my early morning rise, coupled with travel weariness, excitement and my recent intake of alcohol. The walk back to Stora Nygatan put the seal on a perfect insurance policy for a good night's sleep. Tomorrow would be another day.

We met in the breakfast room as planned. For me, the

breakfast was not so much a starter meal; it was more of an 'experience'. Forsaking the items normally associated with a meal at this time of the day in England, I took the avant-garde route – with a mixture of exotic fruits, cheeses and sliced meats. Quite different from my usual orange juice, muesli and a slice of toast, but this was something I could certainly get used to. We rounded off with coffee.

'We'll need to check out now,' Kerstin informed me as she ground out her cigarette, 'I've booked you into a motel closer to Hässleholm from tonight. Unfortunately, I must be back in Lund on Thursday and Friday to do some interviews but there are plenty of taxis and I'll catch up with you again on Saturday if you decide to stay on in the area. I know, of course, that it all depends on what you manage to find out from Mats. I have my car here in the basement garage, so will meet you outside the front door in, say, twenty minutes?'

'Yes, that'll be fine.'

The dark blue Saab pulled into the pillared turning area. I put my bags in the back and slid into the passenger seat. We turned into Amiralsgatan and were soon headed out of the city, the big stores and high buildings giving way to an open view on both sides. We skirted around Lund and Kerstin waved vaguely in the direction of her apartment, saying that it was about three minutes drive from where we were. I was surprised at how flat the landscape appeared. Not unlike Holland. Soon after that, or so it seemed, we were crossing the Ringsjön lake – with water almost all around us. I commented on the strangeness, to my English way of thinking, of the Swedish language, prompted by a sign for the town of Hoor. We passed a number of smaller lakes, some of which were surrounded by stands of both conifer and broad-leaved trees of several different varieties, promoting the setting as an idyll of tranquillity amidst a sea of green fields stretching towards the horizon. From time to time Kerstin commented on various landmarks we passed, elaborating on the agriculture, industry and economy of the region. I took the opportunity to find out a little bit more about her.

'Are you married?'

'No, I'm not. I lived with a guy for almost two years but it didn't work out. He was so lazy and expected too much of me. I'm afraid I'm not in any hurry to find anyone else right now. Perhaps one day.'

'That's too bad. But I guess your work keeps you busy. I understand you write mostly about forestry and construction developments.'

'Yeah, mostly. I've been researching a new forestry management programme at STFI. That's the Swedish Forest Products Institute. But that was before I moved to Lund to write this series of articles on the bridge project.'

'So, how long do you expect to be in Lund?'

'I'm not sure, maybe until next summer. You see I'm also doing some work directly for STFI as well as the various commissions I get from Don Wade.'

By now we'd left the main road and, according to the last signpost, were headed towards Perstorp, threading our way past fields and small farmhouses. It was over an hour since we left Malmö and, during the lull in our conversation, I began to feel an air of excited anticipation as I probed: 'How much further do you reckon?' and then, before she could answer: 'I assume you've been out here before?'

She answered my double question in reverse: 'Yeah, I've been over to the Tillkvists' a couple of times. It's between five and ten minutes from where we are now.'

If the final stretch of road leading to the farm smacked of back of beyond, the entrance to the winding driveway was equally unpretentious, being no more than a stoutly posted opening in the line of fencing. There was a red-painted mailbox on a post, but no gate and just a dilapidated old sign. How the Tillkvists ever got their mail must be one of the wonders of the Swedish postal system. Kerstin broke into my train of thought, 'That's good. Mats is already here. That's his car,' indicating a small red Volvo parked beside the two storey wooden-clad building, the upper floor being evident only by two small forwards-facing windowed dormers. As Kerstin manoeuvred alongside Mats' car, a tall, blond-haired man, whom I would have judged to have been in his early thirties, ambled towards us.

'Hi! Mats Tillkvist,' he smiled openly, extending his hand, 'Good to see you.' And to Kerstin, 'You, too. Come right in.'

We were soon seated in the light, sunny lounge, its rear wall comprised almost totally of window, side to side and floor to ceiling. The house could not be truthfully described as large, but its interior vividly contrasted with my first impressions of the outside: the former bright and airy, the latter somewhat dull and plain. We'd barely seated ourselves when an older woman entered the room. She was stocky, her face weathered and her hair grey, and she was wiping both sides of her hands on her apron. 'My mother,' said Mats, 'Doctor Kirkland from England and, of course, Kerstin you've met before.' She gave a shy smile and a half curtsy as we shook hands. She was clearly on the reserved side and it was Mats who ventured, 'Something to drink?' We agreed on coffees all round although the smell of fresh baking wafting through from the kitchen telegraphed a message to my inner man along the lines of, 'Breakfast was *hours* ago!' Mrs Tillkvist excused herself politely and retreated to the kitchen. So far, there was no sign of Mr Tillkvist senior.

Having dismissed the usual introductory small talk over coffee, and with my having the greatest of difficulty in mentally framing a suitable way of breaking into the subject of the unusual treasure I'd come to examine without creating an ambience of over-anxiety, it was Mats who took the initiative once again, enunciating the English words in a soft, lilting way that, somehow, made my own native tongue sound quite musical. 'Doctor Kirkland, please, would you like to see the old hunting gun now?'

I nodded towards him and flashed a quick smile at Kerstin, my eyes glancing back to follow Mats as he moved across the room to a pine-fronted, full height cupboard. Slowly, and seemingly with the fastidious care one would take on removing some delicate ornament from its display cabinet, he withdrew a long, dark leather gun cover, its slender form clearly indicating its contents, at least in size and shape if not in specific detail. The broad end of the cover had been flapped over and tied closed with a thick leather thong. He untied it and pulled back the flap, swinging the piece through a semicircle to rest the butt end on the shag-pile carpet and slipped the cover over the muzzle end of the gun, revealing its rich brown stock, dull steel barrel and buttplate. He hefted the weapon to a horizontal position and presented it to me, laying it across my knees and supported by my outstretched hands.

The drawn-out silence which accompanied my initial examination of the expert workmanship of this fine old gun was paralleled by an equally drawn-out mental exclamation equivalent to 'w-o-w!' It was a beauty and no mistake. And in beautiful condition, too, with its metal parts showing a genuine patina that confirmed it as being 'quite old'.

'I'll bet this can tell a story or two,' I remarked, turning it over and admiring its graceful lines.

'Yes, I think it comes from the country of Greece,' Mats said, 'See the letters. Here and here,' indicating some Greek characters marked on both the lockplate and on the chamber-end of the barrel.

I began to laugh quietly and, engaging Mats' gaze, just looked into his eyes for a moment or two, then began, 'No. I don't think so. I could be wrong, of course, and will need to do some more checking, but I'd say it's from either North Germany or, more likely, from right here in Sweden. I have one of the best reference books compiled on Greek guns, by a chap called Considine, but nothing he describes comes even close to this style.'

Both Kerstin and Mats looked at me in surprise, voicing almost in unison: 'Really?'

'Yep. Even at this stage I'm ninety per cent certain. It's an evolution of an early German hunting rifle known as a Jaeger, although I can't explain the "pi delta" markings, other than the possibility that it could be a maker's code. There's no other evidence to suggest who might have made it.'

We spent almost two hours – and two more coffees – speculating on its pedigree. The barrel was rifled with six deep grooves, indicating that it had fired a patched ball rather than a bullet. The firing mechanism was conventional flintlock and both the frizzen or striking face and the lockplate itself were quite large, suggesting that it dated from sometime in the 1700s. Whoever had built this rifle had been a craftsman of the highest order; the wood-to-metal fit was, in all places, close to perfection. And the sliding wooden patchbox cover on the side of the butt was elegantly carved and it still worked as it would have done all those years ago. The various springs appeared to be in good flexing order and, when I dropped my little bore-light down the barrel, I was surprised at how little use it seemed to have had. My calliper gauge showed a muzzle calibre of around 0.62 of an inch, almost 16 millimetres. The wooden stock was fitted full to the muzzle and appeared to be of some straight-grained wood, possibly beech.

Mats had already announced that he was due to begin his shift at the paper mill where he worked in Klippan at two o'clock and would have to leave very soon. I'd taken a number of close-up photographs of various parts of the rifle and some full length ones with Mats holding it. We agreed that that was probably enough for now and were preparing to leave. Mats was returning the gun to its leather sling case when we heard voices from the kitchen. Into the room came a man I took to be Mats' father. He was quite frail looking, with sallowed skin and just a few wisps of sandy hair.

'Good day. I suppose you are the professor?' His voice was low pitched, quiet and slightly rough.

Mats, still holding the gun and its case, said, 'This is Bertil, my father.'

I shook hands. 'Walt Kirkland. I'm very pleased to meet you.'

'You're not taking my gun are you?' this directed at me and with a detectable emphasis on the possessive article.

'No, father, we've just been looking at it. Doctor Kirkland has taken some photographs.'

'That's all right. I have known you were to be here to look at it. But the gun must not go. Here it stays.' His English was not as good as any I'd become used to over the past twenty-four hours in the country, but was certainly better than my Swedish. And he was making himself understood in no uncertain terms. He obviously considered the trophy to be *his* and was making sure that all three of us knew it.

'No problem, Mr Tillkvist,' I said defensively, 'But I would like to come back another time to look at it again once I've checked on a few facts. I'd also like to see the tree where it was found, if that's possible.'

'You can come back Friday. I'll be here. The tree is where it is fallen still. I will show you Friday.'

'Fine. Thank you for your hospitality. And Mrs Tillkvist, too.'

As we made our way out, Kerstin slipped her hand into mine and gently squeezed it, raising her eyebrows and giving me a look that said, 'Sorry about that.'

*

The Gyllene Ratten was a small motel poised at the end of a small hamlet on the outskirts of Hässleholm. Its name meant 'Golden Wheel', though I failed to identify any connection. It was clean, comfortable and with an adequate menu. I'd settled into a routine of reading and making notes, from time to time scanning slowly through the photographs I'd had developed in a one-hour film processing shop in the village. I walked around some of the local streets and in a small park each afternoon to introduce some variety into my day; lingered over my meals; typed up my notes in the evenings on my portable word processor... and went to bed at a respectable hour. Even so, I was conscious that the time was dragging. I was looking forward to Friday, but with a little less than full enthusiasm since Mats had told me as we left the farm that he would be working all of that day. I'd have to get a taxi, which was no real obstacle, but I'd also have to deal with Bertil Tillkvist on my own and I was beginning to think of that as being a bigger challenge.

The more I read, compared notes and photographs, recalled my past research and thought about it, the more I became convinced that this was no Greek gun. I may as well ship back home the magazine clippings, journals and the Considine book right now, for all the worth they would be to me. They'd done their job and helped me throw out this red herring of an idea. Why, then, should I continue? I'd seen lots of fine antique rifles in my time. It's hard to explain. But I just *knew* there was a bit more to the Tillkvist find than met the eye. And I still hadn't found an answer to two of the three questions I'd posed back at Crown House: how did it get there? and why was it hidden? I could now add a more contemporary question: did it really matter anyway?

Next morning, I headed back to the farm. The cab driver found the place without difficulty, following my memorised directions. It was just after nine thirty as I knocked on the already open door. 'Hello! Are you at home?' My question was both rhetorical and redundant since the arrangement had been firmly made and the open door suggested my arrival had been expected. It was Bertil who answered.

'Hello, professor. Come in, come in.'

After exchanging greetings I was conscious that I was laughing a little as I advised my host, 'I'm not really a professor, you know. I'm an author and researcher. I write books. Do you understand?'

Bertil said nothing, but nodded slowly.

'And I'd much prefer if you just called me Walt.' He seemed to take a moment to let it sink in.

'Ja, ja. Walt. It's a short name, ja?'

I noticed that he didn't reciprocate my offer and, whilst I already knew his name, I felt it safer to continue to address him as Mr Tillkvist. Likewise, I had learned from Kerstin that his wife's name was Berthe but she, too, I would address in the formal manner for the time being. Without much further ado, he motioned towards the sofa at the front of the room.

'The gun is here. Please sit down.'

He'd already taken it from its cover and it stood propped against a small bookcase.

'Thank you.' I unbuttoned my jacket and sat down. 'You know, your son Mats believes it to be from Greece, but I'm afraid I think—'

I was not allowed to complete my phrase as he cut in abruptly, 'I know, I know. And you are correct. Berthe told me. She speaks little bit of English but she can understand more. She heard you discuss with Mats.'

'And you agree with me?'

'Ja, Ja. I know all this about the gun. The boy knows nothing.'

His general attitude, his verbal treatment of Mats, and the rather disgusted way with which he voiced his latest remark, made me begin to suspect that all was not well between father and son.

'The Greek letters are like the code you said. The first one, "pi", from circles,' he said, waving one hand with his index finger extended to demonstrate his meaning, 'is from two times "t". It is for Tomas Tillkvist, the same name as my father, and was his sign. He is of our family from eight generations. My grandfather told me about him.'

At first, I was completely thrown and didn't immediately catch on. Then it dawned. The sign on the gun represented the maker's initials, TT, stylised to look like the Greek letter *pi*.

'Old Tomas used this sign on many things. But the next letter I don't know.'

Bertil talked about his forebears at some length, especially about Mats, his grandfather, after whom he'd named his own son. He told me, too, that the farm had been abandoned for over a hundred years, but the ownership deeds had been discovered around the end of last century and it was restored to the family. My interest was steadily progressing to take in more than just the 'Greek gun' I'd originally come to evaluate. I was becoming quite intrigued by the whole saga of events and background that were beginning to unfold, particularly with the implication that the gun must surely have been concealed in the tree during old Tomas's time of residence, before the farm had lain dormant. Just why the farm had been abandoned he didn't know, except that Tomas had moved to Karlskrona to make guns for the navy. I should have guessed that this commission would hold more than had first appeared. Don Wade has a nose for a good story.

I began to shift the emphasis of the subject, 'You haven't told me about the tree where the gun was found. Do you have any idea of why it was hidden?'

'No. I can show you the tree. It was hidden, for sure, and the tree is very old. I have counted the rings. It is growing for more than three hundred years.'

'That fits,' I thought aloud, 'Tomas would have been here around the middle 1700s. Just about right for the style of gun, too.' Bertil obviously didn't follow my reasoning. He merely grunted, took a small tin from his pocket and, with what appeared to be a flattened plastic tube, poked around in the tin then pushed the tube up and under his top lip. I guessed this was snuff, though I'd only ever heard about it and had never encountered its use in real life. Bertil must have noticed the puzzled look I gave him: 'Nicotine. It's good. You want to try?'

'No thanks, not for me.'

He smiled at me then turned towards the kitchen door. 'Come. We go to the tree.'

The farm, which I'd found out from Mats during our first meeting, covered around eighty hectares, about two hundred acres, grew mostly sugar beet which was sold through an agency to be processed eventually in the large mill at Arlov, not far from Malmö. As we walked across the open ground towards the edge of the nearest field, several large white Embden geese and around twenty or so Blue Swedish ducks scattered to let us pass. The chunky blue-backed, white-breasted ducks charged like a winged army towards a small pond, creating a cacophony of sound that rent the morning air.

'It's about five hundred metres,' Bertil advised as he strode ahead of me. I wondered how such a slightly built man coped with the upkeep of a working farm. We were just then walking along the edge of a large field and, although he seemed short of breath on occasion, I had difficulty in keeping up with him.

'We have a good chance with this farm,' he half shouted over his shoulder. 'It is good land.' He stopped suddenly and, turning to face directly across the field we were skirting, waved his arm towards the horizon. 'I told to Mats that he has a good chance here but he doesn't listen. He has big ideas for business. Sometimes he is stupid.' Then, almost as an afterthought, he added: 'And his girl is no good.' With that, he spat out his snuff. Whether in anger or because it no longer satisfied him I couldn't tell.

'It's here,' he said in the gruff monotone that I'd come to accept as his normal mode of speech.

We climbed over a low rail fence and were soon standing alongside the fallen oak. How sad, it struck me, to see this huge monarch of the forest now impotent, devastated for ever, the base of its hollow core exposed and cleanly severed from the stump that had, for centuries, fed it life-giving sap. Bertil interrupted my respectful silence: 'See! It was a clever idea. The big branch was closed together in the hole.'

It was a moment or two before I took in fully what he was showing me. Then the penny dropped. The trunk had been split open at one point to reveal that the tree was hollow, but then someone had forced a large low branch up into the breach to seal it up again. Over the years, with the branch growing at a faster rate than the trunk, it had literally fused together again to form a perfect seal. The tree could not have been detected as being hollow until it was sawn through and that's exactly what had happened. Mats had cut down the tree, noticed first that it was hollowed out on the inside, then spotted the end of the mysterious package.

*

I had washed, shaved, dressed and was just preparing to leave my room to have breakfast when the telephone rang. It was Kerstin. Having ascertained that I was, after all, still at the motel on this Saturday morning, she asked if she could join me for lunch. We settled on twelve o'clock. She would pick me up and we'd go into Hässleholm to a restaurant she'd been to many times before. That left me with plenty of time to jot down a few more questions I'd thought to ask her. And to get the motel receptionist to help me get hold of some telephone numbers I needed in Stockholm, Göteborg and Karlskrona to do a bit more checking on Tomas Tillkvist, one-time gunsmith.

We met as planned and the lunch was excellent. My first experience of downtown Hässleholm was not. Some local festival was taking place and the streets were busy. Some were cordoned off and we had to detour on what seemed a very long way around. We concurred that this wasn't our scene and headed back out of town and into the country.

'So. You really do think there's an interesting story behind all of this?'

'Yep. I've got a "gut feel" there's more to it than we know so far. And at the rate I'm going at the moment I'll have used up my allowance from CHP before getting anything that's anywhere near complete. I might just have to dip into my own pocket on this one; let's see what happens over the next few days.'

'How long do you think you'll pursue this?'

'Well, Don wants a report when he gets back from the USA week after next, but I reckon he figured on my having a reasonable rough-out by then. It's just that it's all turning out to be a bit different from what we thought when we first got your report.'

Kerstin seemed to be in another world as she drove on, gazing straight ahead: 'Yeah. I know what you mean.'

We'd been driving for over an hour, going nowhere in particular it seemed to me, when she pulled into a large car park alongside what appeared to be some kind of garden centre.

'Do you like flowers?' she asked, out of the blue: 'They

have lots here at this time of year. And big goldfish, too. Maybe we should get some nice flowers for Berthe since you're going there tomorrow.'

'Mmm, that sounds like a good idea. She seems to be just a slave; always in the kitchen. Can't be much of a life stuck out there with a guy like Bertil. He's such a grump.'

My last remark brought a smile and she added, 'I agree.'

I learned little more from my Sunday afternoon with the Tillkvists. In fact we talked mostly about the farm. I also noticed that Mats' name was hardly mentioned but they did show me some photographs taken at Bertil's sixtieth birthday, three years ago, together with some of their daughter Annika, now Mrs Chelford of course; and of Martin having his first skiing lesson.

The week began badly. I'd called most of the numbers I'd managed to get hold of but drew a blank from each conversation. The repetitive spelling out of my request was becoming decidedly wearing but I knew that, as always, I just had to persevere. So far, there were just two possibilities that seemed to hold any slim thread of promise. Unfortunately, their sources lay in opposite directions, at Karlskrona to the south east, and near Göteborg to the north west. But Kerstin was a real star. She'd set the week aside to help me get around. Almost like a personal tour guide. She dismissed out of hand the possibility that I hire a car and drive myself. On Tuesday we drove all the way over to Karlskrona; on Wednesday we had an even longer day, leaving the motel at seven thirty and spending the day visiting two museums in Göteborg, arriving back in time for dinner. Two days and eight hundred kilometres, and all to no avail.

The first positive progress of the week came midway through Thursday afternoon when, eventually, I managed to get hold of the curator at the Royal Armoury on the phone. He at least recognised the era I was concerned with and told me about a small, private collection of antique guns he'd once seen in Kristianstad, only forty kilometres from here. Even from his brief description, this suddenly began to sound like we were on the right track. And that was how I met Siegfried Wersel, German by name and distant origin, but his family had lived in the Kristianstad area for nearly four hundred years.

Siegfried had not been able to accommodate our visit on Friday, so we arranged to go on Saturday morning. His home was on the west side of the town, not far off the main E22 highway and was very easy to find. The journey took only fifty minutes. We drove into the yard and I was immediately impressed by the house; the more so once Siegfried had greeted us and invited us in. Like the Tillkvists', it was wooden-clad, with a steeply pitched shingle roof, but stood on a concrete lower portion that formed a basement so that, to reach the front door, there was a wide flight of stairs which reminded me of some of the old colonial buildings I'd seen in many parts of the former British Empire – an architectural carry-over from the late eighteenth and early nineteenth centuries. Then, from the level of the entry porch, another flight of stairs led off to one side, descending to the basement which was half above and half below ground level. The concrete walls of this semi-underground dwelling seemed to be around half a metre thick. I noticed, too, that all of the windows were triple glazed, with the more usual sealed-unit double-glazing panels backed up by tertiary panels set three fingers' breadth further inboard. It was just after ten thirty this Saturday morning and already the outside temperature was somewhere in the region of twenty-two Celsius. It was hard to believe right then that putting a minus sign in front during the worst of winters was the reason for this extent of investment in thermal protection.

The basement of the Wersel home was like an Aladdin's Cave to anyone with an interest in antiques, particularly in wood carvings, furniture, coins or weapons. In the corner, facing the bottom of the stairs, stood a complete suit of armour and the panelled walls were only here and there visible beyond an array of cabinets, shelves and display cases which could have graced an antique emporium almost anywhere in the world and done the owner proud. This heirloom of ancestral collections, accumulated over several generations, must have had an unthinkable market value – and would require no ordinary premium to insure it.

Siegfried, a dapper little man with neatly trimmed moustache, reminded me of a librarian I once knew. Breaking the spell that had had me bound from the moment my eyes took in their first glimpses of this treasure trove, Siegfried said, 'You are interested most of all in the gun collection, is that correct?'

'That's right. As I told you on the phone, I'm particularly keen to have a look at the eighteenth century rifles you have.'

'Then you must come this way.' We followed him down a short corridor to a smaller room, its door held open by a block of wood from which protruded what looked like a Viking axe, its studded handle rising to above waist height.

'You're free to look. But, please, do ask if you need to know something.'

'Thank you. I will.'

This was incredible. His collection was beautifully laid out in glass-fronted floor-to-ceiling cases illuminated internally by fluorescent strip lights. From where we'd entered, the display began with seventeenth century snaphaunce guns which, according to the card that Kerstin translated for me, had been used by Skåne's guerrilla forces in the war with Denmark in 1675. Some of these were beautiful examples, not unlike the types used in the English Civil War, with large club-like butts ornately carved and, in two instances, finely decorated. I could imagine some of the Sealed Knot re-enactment group members contemplating raising the necessary mortgage to purchase one of these were they given the opportunity. I was on the point of asking about the origins of a very long, rather handsome piece when, just then, my eye caught sight of something that, for a moment, completely took my breath away. Near the centre of the second case was an upright row of flintlock rifles practically identical to the one at Bertil Tillkvist's. Had they been mounted in a slightly different orientation my initial overture of surprise would have risen to orgasmic heights for, on closer examination, each one bore the hallmark of Greek symbolism with which I'd so recently become familiar as the maker's mark of one Tomas Tillkvist. There were five guns in all in this grouping.

'Eureka! Kerstin, look at these!' I exclaimed, not realising fully until we were driving back just how contextually correct, Greek for Greek, my explosive utterance had been. I asked Siegfried if it would be possible to inspect these particular guns more closely and he was only too pleased to disable the alarm and unlock the cabinet.

It was almost as if I was present in body but absent in spirit. As I looked at first one then, in turn, each of the other lockplates, I could discern a sequence from the second Greek character engraved alongside the 'pi' in each case. They formed the first six letters of the Greek alphabet: alpha, beta, gamma, then epsilon and zeta. Only delta was missing – and I knew where that one was. Kerstin gave no indication that she also had spotted the significance and I felt constrained to say nothing about it. This was something that, just for the moment, I would keep to myself.

'Would you mind if I just took a few photographs?'

'Well – for what purpose?'

'Only for private study, I can assure you.'

'Then it's okay. But please, I don't want any publicity about the collection. It's only because you mentioned your connection with Torbjorn at the Armoury that I let you come.'

'You have my word. They will not be circulated *anywhere*.' I emphasised the last word, hoping to convince him of my integrity, and at the same time pulled a business card from the top pocket of my jacket. 'I'm only too grateful that you've given me this viewing. Have no hesitation in calling me if ever there's a problem from any of this.' I set about checking the light level and thinking about the best angles to use, but I could hear Kerstin and Siegfried discussing something in Swedish that seemed to have some bearing on what I was doing. 'Everything all right?' I asked, feeling there was some uncertainty after all.

'It's just the name,' Kerstin said, pointing to the card on the back wall: 'There seems to be some mistake.' Below three lines of Swedish which, of course, I didn't understand, it read:

T. Tilderkvist
Peterlöv: 1753

'I see what you mean. I hadn't noticed. It's obviously "Old Tomas" but do you think it's just a transcription error?'

'Apparently not.'

At this, Siegfried broke in: 'Our Tilderkvist collection was purchased by my grandfather from the Bergengren family, from right here in Kristianstad. For generations they have been in the silverware business and were apparently very closely connected with the Tilderkvists from Peterlöv. See! I have a small sugar bowl here and some silver plates.'

We walked back into the main room and he pointed to a small wall-mounted cabinet. The silverware took up two of the glass shelves and the information card which accompanied the items he pointed out stated that they had been made by a J. Bergengren in 1762.

The drive back to the Gyllene Ratten seemed to take only fifteen minutes rather than fifty, probably because we didn't stop talking throughout the journey. So many pieces of the jigsaw were falling into place; but some pieces seemed to be missing completely. Like the difference in names; the reason for the concealment and – where on earth was Peterlöv? We resolved none of these issues but Kerstin did remark at one point: 'I'm not really sure that "Tillkvist" is a proper Swedish name, at least not a common one, but "Tilderkvist" certainly is. The first time I ever heard of "Tillkvist" was when I met Annika Chelford and her brother Mats. Maybe it has been corrupted over the years.'

'Maybe. There's a lot to think about in getting to the bottom of it all.'

One thing was completely clear: my original reason for being here – to discover if there *was* any medieval link between Sweden and Greece – had been totally blown away. Whatever article CHP was going to get out of this for its *Annual Supplement*, it wasn't going to be anything like the one Don had so enthusiastically envisaged before he left for the States. At this stage it was unclear whether or not the line of investigation I was now following would yield a story worthy of the lead article in the New Year publication. Time would tell, perhaps, but without a realistic advance from CHP to follow each lead exhaustively, I would have to terminate my efforts some way short of any real conclusion. In five more days I would be back in Malmö, preparing to return to England.

*

This, the last Sunday that I expected to be spending in Sweden, at least during my present excursion, was to be truly a 'Sabbath day's rest'. I was on my own. Kerstin had made arrangements to meet some of the Øresund Contractors in Malmö on Monday and Tuesday and, knowing that she would be away, had apologised profusely that she would be unable to entertain me. She just *had* to catch up on a backlog of washing, ironing and other household chores before the weekend was over. I didn't mind at all. I'd used up a lot of adrenaline over the past two weeks and my mind seemed to have been on double time. The chance of taking it easy was most welcome, but I had to undergo a kind of 'mental enema' in order to ensure that I didn't drift back into thinking of all the conflicting scenarios I'd had presented to me since leaving Lichfield, back in dear old England. No. Today would be different. I really *would* just unwind and was fortunate to tune in to a radio station that was playing classical music. I'd already had breakfast, hung the 'Do not disturb' sign on the hallway-side of my door handle and lay on top of the newly made bed as the notes of Beethoven's Sonata in C sharp minor augmented my spirit of relaxation. The second movement, the Allegretto, was being played – with its gentle poise and clever syncopation – and lulled me close to the point of dropping off to sleep once again. It was from this drowsy, half-awake state that the dramatic opening chords of Concerto No. 5 in E flat major brought me back to the realisation that here I was, at 10.48 on a Sunday morning, in Room 7 of the Gyllene Ratten. Regardless of the sustained high quality of the music, my eyes did, at last, succumb to the pull of the dreamworld that exists uniquely within our sleep domain. The digital clock at my bedside showed 14.22 when I awoke. The pattern for what yet remained of the day had been set. I excused my lethargy and consoled myself with the honest appraisal that 'it didn't happen very often'.

Kerstin, ever the organiser, had asked Mats if he would pick me up on Monday morning. He was on 'shift rotation' which meant that he had three days free. He arrived just after quarter to nine and I was still in the breakfast room. He joined me for coffee.

'So. You have some information about the old gun?'

'Well, I think I'm beginning to piece a few things together. There's still a lot that I don't know. It seems that I was right on one thing, though; that gun *was* made right here in Sweden. Didn't your father tell you that before?'

'No, he didn't. How does he know that? Have you spoken to him recently?'

'He already knew. It was he who told *me*, first of all.'

'Well, he doesn't tell me very much. I don't know what's

wrong with him these days. One thing I wanted to ask you, but didn't want to ask in front of my father. Do you know how much the old gun is worth? How many SEK?'

'What do you mean?'

'SEK? Oh, Swedish Kronor.'

'No. I couldn't really put a figure on it with any accuracy at this stage but I'd guess it could be anywhere between a hundred and a hundred and fifty thousand.'

'A hundred and—' he gasped, 'You really believe that? Who would pay that kind of money?'

I was on the point of blurting out Siegfried's name but something, it's hard to explain how or what, held me back.

'Museums, collectors, who knows? I'd have to know the market here a bit more before I could really be sure.'

'I could do quite a bit with that sort of money,' he said reflectively, 'but please, Doctor Kirkland, I would be happy if you didn't tell any of this to my father.'

It was mid-morning when we drove once again into the Tillkvists' winding driveway. Before getting out of the car, Mats leaned towards me and, in a low voice almost as if he was tipping me off about some odds-on favourite at the local racetrack, said, 'Remember. Say nothing about what you have told me. How much you think the gun is worth.'

I nodded, undid my seat belt, and followed him into the house. Bertil was not there but, almost predictably, Berthe was in the kitchen. I began to wonder if it was her obsession or simply coincidental with the timing of my visits.

'Where's father?'

She replied that he'd told her he was going to check the beets in the bottom field, the one farthest from the house. Mats said nothing in response, but made a clicking sound with his tongue and beckoned me to follow him. Once outside the back door, he turned to me and said, 'Father is down in the bottom field, so let's go to the top, where the tree is.'

I had no reason to object but, likewise, saw no benefit in reviewing the fallen oak once again. I followed closely behind Mats for some way along the narrow path, then felt constrained to suggest, 'You don't like farming much, do you?'

'No, I don't. It's too backward. Too old-fashioned. And in Sweden you'll never be rich being a farmer.'

We reached the point where we'd have to climb over the wooden fence when Mats turned completely around and, grasping me by the shoulders, turned me to join his gaze back down the gentle slope to where we could see the small tractor bumping its way along the edge of a large field.

'Look! You really think I want to be here for the rest of my life? Just fields, bushes and trees. It's just not for me, even though father says I "should be proud, it's a family heritage". Just look at him. This place is killing him. I feel so sorry for my mother.'

We leant against the fence and talked for more than an hour. Mats told me that he and Mia, his partner over the past seven years, had hoped to set up their own business. At present he was working in the paper mill and she was hairdressing, but they visualised a chain of boutiques specialising in 'green' goods, such as herbal and 'cruelty free' products, aimed at the young executive market. There remained only the question of raising the start-up capital before *Miamat Enterprises* hit the malls in Sweden's major cities and towns, spreading north, south and west from its birthing in Hälsingborg.

'You're not going to get married and settle down to have a family then?'

'What's the point. Mia and me, we're working out okay. And we don't want kids. They'd only tie us down.'

'Isn't that a bit selfish? After all, your own parents were prepared to give you a real chance with the farm here.'

'Listen, Doctor Kirkland, it's a tough world now. The only way we can make it work is to be committed to building a better future for ourselves. For us! Not for another generation that will treat us as "dead wood".'

I just shrugged my shoulders and turned away. His callous point of view left me cold. I couldn't imagine Mark and Sophie thinking this way about me, even although they were off on their own in Canada.

We'd seen the tractor make its way back to the barn behind the house. Bertil had stopped to take some lunch.

'We had hoped that father would have retired by now. Then we would press him to sell off and let us have the seven hundred and fifty thousand we need to get started. In fact, we have almost half of what we need from our own savings which is why I'm very interested in the numbers you were talking about at the motel this morning.'

'But, of course, even if the gun was to be sold, your father would have first claim to the proceeds since the gun was found on his land – you know the law.'

Either knowledge of the hard facts or the way I'd phrased things really set Mats on edge. He raised his voice and became quite agitated. 'That's the problem. He holds on to the farm; he holds on to the gun; he doesn't care if I have to go to the mill in the evenings when Mia is at home alone. He is so pig-headed about keeping things in the family. He's hung up on this "heritage" thing. What a load of crap!'

Apart from the sing-song lilt of his delivery, Mats' command of English was so natural that I'd almost forgotten it was not his mother tongue, however the venom in his last phrase made me wince. Like the glare from a traffic light on red, approached at speed, I got a clear message: 'STOP. Back off, Kirkland. Getting involved in family feuds is right outside your comfort zone.'

We walked slowly back to the house in stony silence.

'Hei, Doctor Walt. How are you?'

'Very well, thank you. And how is your crop doing?'

'Ja. It's well also. It would be better if we had more. You have seen we have many fields but not so much beets. If we could get more help here it would be a fine farm.'

I took this last remark to be directed at Mats, although there was no response from him – he was already sitting at the heavy wooden table at the wider end of the kitchen, spreading butter on some bread. Bertil stood by the door, using a wooden device shaped like a long-legged letter 'h' to remove his boots. Mats had told me about his father's two labourers, Lennart and his brother, who helped with the beet harvest and did odd jobs at other times. Neither was very bright and so could not be trusted with any job unless it was very simple or could be supervised by Bertil himself. It was no wonder Bertil looked so thin, tired and worn out. It seemed, as Mats had said, that the workload was too much for him, even though he still strode around the place like a much younger man and tried to give the impression that he was well on top of everything.

'You know any more about the gun, eh?' Bertil asked, without turning from the basin where he was now washing his hands.

'Yes. A little bit more. And I have some questions to ask you, too.'

'Ja?'

'Yes. Mats has invited me to join you for lunch so

perhaps we can discuss it while we eat. I guess you'll be going back out on the farm?'

'Ja, Ja, but no hurry. What have you to know?'

'Well, let's see. For a start, have you ever heard of a place called Peterlöv?'

Bertil looked across to Berthe and they both began to laugh. It was the most animated expression I'd seen from Mrs Tillkvist since I'd met her. Mats merely glanced up from pouring his glass of milk.

'It's here! Here is Peterlöv!' Bertil exclaimed. And again they both laughed. 'Since many years, this was Peterlöv. It was the village for all over here.' He waved his arms expansively, his hands undulating like waves on the sea as if indicating a circle of small, humpy hills: 'Now only the farm is here. There is no more Peterlöv now.'

'I see. So Tomas Tilderkvist lived right here?'

'Tomas *Tillkvist*,' he said, emphasising the difference in name, 'We are *Tillkvist*, not *Tilderkvist*. It is another name here in Sweden.'

'Sorry, my mistake.' I was not certain that it *was* a mistake, remembering my discussions with both Siegfried Wersel and Kerstin, but his quick defence of the family name restrained me from pressing the point. It was obvious that, whatever legends had been handed down from previous generations, Bertil was not aware of any corruption of the original family name. If, indeed, the Wersels and the Bergengrens had got it right in the first place.

Lunchtime passed. Mats brought the old rifle out of the cupboard; Bertil had reinstalled his feet in his boots and gone trudging off; Berthe had gone upstairs – and I once more began to examine what I now knew to be the fourth of a group of six nearly identical flintlock rifles made by Tomas Til-something around the middle of the eighteenth century. A number of thoughts were buzzing around in my mind as I looked again along the 'two cubit' barrel and sighted it just above a wall lamp in the corner of the room. There's no doubt about it, I'd become hooked on finding out something of the history of this family and its long-ago roots in gunmaking. Mats ran his fingers along the wooden stock and, in turn, we looked at the engraved signs with the aid of my small brass folding magnifier. I was just about to focus on the lockplate marks. That's when it happened: the shriek from the upper floor, followed by Berthe's drumming footsteps on the wooden stairs.

'Mats! Mats!' she screamed: 'It's Bertil! Something's wrong with him. Go quickly!'

We evacuated the room as if sucked through the back door by some enormous vacuum and I was right on Mats' heels as he tore across the yard, scattering the ducks, to where we could see Bertil slumped over against the hub of one of the tractor's rear wheels. It was almost as if he'd been frozen in time, like the lava-clothed bodies recovered from Pompeii, with his hands balled into fists and aiming a punch at his stomach. It was obvious that he was in serious trouble – and a lot of pain. He drew in the air across his teeth in a low whistle and made a series of short grunting sounds as he exhaled.

Mats shook my shoulder and said firmly: 'Stay with him! I'll get the car!' He shouted something to Berthe as she came towards us. She'd been barefoot when she saw Bertil's distress from the bedroom's side window; a large window set in the gable which overlooked much of the lower part of the farm. She'd stopped to find some shoes, but now turned instantly back to the house. I guess Mats had asked her to phone the hospital in Hälsingborg to forewarn them.

'Let's get him into the back,' Mats said, throwing open the car door: 'I'll take most of the weight. Just keep the door full open.'

We got him into an upright position and fastened the seat belt. I ran around the car and got in beside him, propping him by putting one arm around his shoulders and the other across his thigh. There was no way I could use my own seat belt, but this was an emergency. Bertil screwed his eyes tight closed. He strained to double up again and I moved my lower arm to support him under, rather than over, his legs. Mats practically bundled Berthe into the passenger seat and within seconds the car's wheels were spinning in the gravel as the little Volvo roared past the mailbox and out on to the country road that ran past the farm.

Poor Bertil. In that moment of time when he stretched upwards to grasp the handle to pull himself into the seat of the tractor that had become an integral part of his life, that life had suddenly changed. No more was he the stubborn little Skånian farmer who ruled, in his own majestic way, the realm that had once been a part of a thriving village. His was now a broken spirit, entombed as it was within a wasting body. He was kept in the hospital at Hälsingborg only that night, his transfer to Malmö being effected early next morning. He was under heavy sedation and, in those early hours of his confinement, knew little of the nature or progress of the tests that were being conducted on him by the best of medical expertise the region could currently boast.

When we'd first arrived at the hospital in Hälsingborg,

Mats had managed to contact Kerstin on her mobile phone and had, of course, spoken with Mia who was still at work in the little salon on the other side of town. It had been a shock to us all.

Looking back on it now, I can't really account for what I did. It was just one of those spontaneous things that sometimes we do, but without reasoned judgement to support the decision. Through the many years that I'd been writing, it could never be said that I qualified, in any respect, for the perhaps dubious honour of being described as a journalist. Yet I'd brushed shoulders, in a professional sense, with many men and women who had been eminently recognised in this craft. One thing I'd learned from the most successful of them: that the best stories arose almost inevitably from their tenacious and unswerving following of that seemingly naive inner prompting which had, since time out of mind, become the guiding star to both journalists and detectives alike: the hunch. It was on the strength of those same subjective feelings that I cancelled my flights and decided to stay on in Sweden indefinitely. I had the motel receptionist telefax a message to Sandra Watkins at CHP to say that I would be forwarding a more detailed report by what many in the business were now referring to as 'snail mail', the denigrating slur meant to indicate the normal postal system's inferiority to the more time-efficient e-mail. A growing plethora of electronic bulletin boards and other by-products of the worldwide information network would, in time, become the mainstay of my communications but, for now, bundles of printed hard copy, directed through the conventional postal system, would suffice.

There was one member of the Tillkvist family I had not yet met – Bertil's sister, Britt. She was four years his junior, had never married, and was presently living in Ystad where she ran the purchasing department of a small ceramics company. On hearing of the news, Britt said she would meet up with us in Malmö to visit Bertil in hospital. These were not easy times for the Tillkvist family. Bertil was to remain in hospital for eight days, the diagnosis of his problems still, as yet, uncertain and the daily round trip to Malmö was beginning to take its toll. Kerstin Berg was a source of great encouragement. She helped solve the travel problem on more than one occasion when Mats was back on shift work at the mill later that week, and her buoyant yet sensitive personality at times lifted the spirits of both Berthe and Britt.

I would have done well to have secured some shares in the local taxi firm on account of the path I was now beating between motel and farm. As we waited for a more definitive diagnosis of Bertil's problems I got to know Berthe so much better. She was a woman of great fortitude, with a keen recollective mind, who was beginning to make an increasingly greater impression on me. I sat with her during several afternoons and she shared with me a great deal from her knowledge of the Tillkvist family over the years. There were many gaps, of course, and much that she didn't know. Certainly, her coverage of the generations of even the last century was by no means complete. From the simple act of cutting down one tree, a whole series of events had been put in motion that would cause me to reflect on the history of this family. Their remarkable story would not be short in the telling, Berthe prophesied.

It was on the following Monday evening, during a routine visit to the hospital, that the full extent of Bertil's illness became known. He had been diagnosed as having inoperable cancer. A mature growth had been detected in his colon and it was expected that he would be unlikely to survive for longer than a few weeks. Two months at most. Understandably, we were all devastated. He was released from hospital the next day but, just looking at him, it was clear that another chapter in the life of the Tillkvists was about to close. I would find out, ultimately, the reason for this dogged patriarch's uncompromising love of family traditions – and, too, the reasons for his unforgiving attitude towards his own son. Berthe had warned me: it would be a long story. I didn't know it then, but I would have to dig deep – and go back a long way to get at the roots of this proud family. Their heritage, their mindset was closely entwined with the origins of their forebears. And with the origins of Sweden itself.

Part Two
The Survivors

For Lippe and Fride

Sometimes 'tis hard to live – always, to die!
William Houghton

It was cold. Bitterly cold. Only by the four layers of hide and fleece that swathed his body could Odal know that it was 'four-cold'. That was his own way of knowing how deep the winter had become. When it became three-cold, then two-cold, he would know that soon the ice should melt away and he could then trap fish in the streams once more. Until then, he would have to hunt the land beasts; the bear, the elk, the boar and the ubiquitous reindeer. It would be more than two thousand years before some future hunter would give this cold a name that all men would recognise. He would call it 'sub-zero'.

Leaning against the tree that shielded him from the wary eyes of a female elk as she nuzzled the frozen bark of a small birch, Odal carefully balanced his spear in his right hand while, with his left, he reached around his spear-hand side of the tree to quietly grasp a waist-high branch in his fur-gloved hand. His eyes narrowed as he drew the cold air into his lungs with a slow and measured control. He froze, like a coiled spring awaiting the instant of release of the latch that imprisoned its kinetic power. The elk lapped at her thigh, then pushed her mouth back to the tree. Wrenched forwards by his explosive pull on the branch, Odal unleashed the spear and gasped out the lungful of air that ballooned his chest. The elk's head swung round in his direction in the instant before the edgestone tip of the spear lodged in her side, burying part of the spruce shaft under her flesh; her alarm-filled eyes catching, too late, the movement that would have allowed her to take evasive action. She obeyed her instinct to turn from her adversary and run but, as she did so, the trailing spear prevented her from passing to the side of the birch tree that might have made escape possible. The pain coursed through her body and she faltered, momentarily, then made to round the tree on the opposite side. Odal was running towards her at full tilt when, now at almost point-blank range, he hefted his second spear and caught her square on the chest. She charged past him, her rear legs thrashing in the snow as blood spurted from her nostrils in a bubbling froth and her forelegs began to buckle. Today, Kael and young Oden would have fresh meat.

The cave was little more than a hollowing-out of the rocky hillock; one among many in the low outcrops that looked down upon the large, island-strewn lake that later peoples would call Mälaren. Stout tree branches had been thrust horizontally into the ground above the opening and were lashed with sinew to equally stout upright branches which had the effect of extending the cave forwards, more than doubling its size. Brushwood, together with clay from the lake united in an almost homogenous broadcloth of roofing and siding, providing shielding from the wind, rain and driving snow so prevalent in this rugged land. Odal, his woman Kael and their boy Oden occupied one dwelling. Five similar shelters were shared by the eighteen others in the clan, each living place marked by its smoke-blackened ceiling and walls for, once started, the small fires were never allowed to go out, so arduous and skilled was the art of making fire at each beginning. It was over these glowing fire pits, their borders lined with rounded stones each about the size of a man's head, that Odal's kill now turned on spits to be enjoyed by the little band as they huddled in their furs and skins against the biting cold.

For almost half of his twenty-four summers, Odal had lived by the lake with Kael, two summers his junior. Oden was yet a mere six summers and was the only one of the pair's offspring now surviving. Twice, infant mortality had delayed Kael's promotion to motherhood. To live through more than forty summers was to be old in this kingdom of the Svear people. The one they called Old Kuelin, the God Man, had seen more than forty-six. He was white-haired and his skin cracked and wrinkled through exposure to the wind and icy snow. He lived alone and communed with the Asa, the clan gods. His holy aura held these primitive Svear in his power. His word was law.

In time, the Svear people would give their name to this land – Sverige, or Sweden. For a little more than ten thousand years the retreating ice cap had been releasing more and more of the land to, first, its animal inhabitants and, latterly, its humans. Sweden's first human residents were nomadic hunters who arrived from north-eastern lands. Their roving lifestyle left little of substance to identify their passing. But these Svear were different. They established their communities around an embryo farming culture, living in extended families and small bands on a communal basis.

At a time when Roman galleys, armed with fireball-hurling ballistas and sailed by armour-suited men wielding short swords of beaten iron, were subjugating the navies of Central Europe, the men and women of Mälaren's shores were content to exalt edgestone, or flint, as the essence of their tools for hunting, agriculture, art and, through barter, for trade with other Svear communities. A few implements and adornments of bronze had filtered through to these tiny communities at the western end of the lake, but they were generally of poor utility compared with the naturally occurring flint that could be made to serve all manner of purposes.

They learned the skill of knapping; of flaking the edges of the flint by pressing a point of antler into the contour lines that a practised eye could 'read' and, with fastidious care, fashioned razor-sharp blades for arrowheads, knives, spear-points, hide-scrapers and plough-tips. Large nodules of flint were split down, knapped to form a double-edged axe-head, and were forced into splits in beech or birch trees to remain for a future generation. In years to come, the 'axe-trees' would be harvested like some rare, specially cultivated delicacy. The young growing tree would, given time, wrap itself in an ever increasingly tighter embrace of the flint to form an intimate bond more secure and permanent than could be achieved by shrinking or binding with sinew. When cut to the desired length, the resulting fusion of flint and wood produced an axe of great strength whose length of shaft could be matched to its intended use and shaped to give the right weight and balance for comfort in handling.

Odal excelled in his ability to catch and trap fish. He was also an excellent hunter and, during several hard winters, almost single-handedly maintained the survival of Old Kuelin's band. When fishing was restricted due to icing-over of the lake and other streams, the Svear relied on successful hunting of the larger meat animals, together with staples gleaned from their simple forms of agriculture. Barley was the main crop and the tribe's womenfolk grew root vegetables in rows close to their dwellings. One of the secrets of winter endurance was a reliance upon a properly maintained cache of crops and vegetables stored before the snow months came, whilst it was no more than 'two cold'.

The ground was softer then, too. Even so, it was only with great effort that the menfolk dug out the deep, narrow cache pits that were to be their lifeline. The man-high store pits were lined first with stones and then layers of twigs, mosses and lichen; the whole of the base and each of the sides finished with the broad, sword-like leaves of irises, flags and other waterside plants before the cache of food was lowered in reed baskets, to be sealed in this natural refrigerator until the onset of winter's hunger brought its opening.

On this four-cold day, Odal's elk meat formed the basis of a veritable feast for, when the staples from the already opened cache were added, the meal became a satisfying and well-rounded repast.

'Oden! Run to Tuma's lodge and tell him to come and share our food. Bring Talna and the girls. One cookfire is enough for all of us,' Kael shouted, her long fair hair tossed by the wind to enshroud the upper third of her gaunt, five foot frame. Odal was of little bigger build but he had, seemingly, the strength of an ox as he lifted the hindquarter of meat from where it was skewered and slung over the fire. The remaining three quarters were likewise being roasted in three other dwellings. Tuma's lodge would share Odal's meal; the others also ate together in little groups. Only Kuelin did not join in the feast. The wiry old priest continued fasting, his food intake limited to little more than dried berries and sips of his holy water.

'May the gods always guide your spear, Odal,' Tuma said, lifting a piece of meat to his mouth, the juices running over the back of his hand: 'The elk is good, hei.'

Kael and Talna used sticks to lift hot stones into a wooden bowl part-filled with a grainmash made from pounded barley, turnip and wild mushrooms mixed with water. The gruel sizzled as it met the heat of the stones, spitting a protest at the sudden increase in temperature.

'The mash smells good, too. Bring the bowls,' Odal gestured towards Oden. In a moment the boy returned with two small, hollowed-out wooden bowls in each hand. He offered them to his father and Tuma who, in turn, dipped them into the cauldron of watery grainmash, each passing one to his woman. It was an understood protocol among the Svear that a man should tend to his woman first, his children next, followed by any surviving parent before, finally, he satisfied his own desires.

Apart from its offal, one part of the elk did not become an ingredient in this meal. For, when Odal downed his prey, he first of all slit its throat with his short flint knife, turning the carcass so that the blood drained from it, staining the snow in a great pool but ensuring that the meat would be sweet. Then, as he opened the complete underbody in three swift strokes of the edgestone, he obeyed a ritual that Kuelin had instilled, over many years, into each hunter in the band. He carefully removed the heart, wrapping it in an almost square piece of soft, brain-tanned hide, uttering as he did so a prayer to the Asa in thanksgiving for yielding this source of life to his spear. The heart, still wrapped in its shroud, now lay on the sacrificial stone in front of Kuelin's lodge. It would be the sacrament in a ritual of greater significance once darkness had fallen.

'Father, may we play fourstones now?' Oden inquired, the almost imperceptible nod in reply giving him licence to leave with Tuma and Talna's two girls to join with Kilde's boy, Lippe, in this simple game which, time out of mind, had been played by generations of the Svear youngsters. Lippe was more than twice Oden's age, but he still enjoyed the carefree fun of running in a gang with the others.

Tuma smiled through his haystack of a beard: 'Remember when we were young, Odal? The summers seemed longer then, and the winters not so cold. Wagh! It's a hard life for us now.'

'And for us, too,' Kael interjected, 'Always fetching wood for the fires, preparing the skins, looking to the crops and—'

'Having a man looking to you!' Tuma said, suggestively, putting one arm around his neighbour's woman.

The banter peaked and troughed throughout the afternoon. It was always so when full stomachs lifted the spirits and introduced an abandon that, sometimes, became over-familiar. Not that the Svear were prudish – there was little privacy in the hut-fronted hollows to preserve propriety – but, in a close-knit clan, the bond of unity was an unspoken precept which ensured that friction within the band was minimal, although not non-existent.

As natural light gave out, fires were built a little higher and the fat-smeared bulrush torches were lit; the blood groups coming once more together to assemble in their own caves. There was no formal marriage among the Svear but, when a man had taken a woman to his lodge for three consecutive nights, she became his mate in the eyes of the clan. So it was that blood groups perpetuated their line. This night was, moreover, a special night. A night when the High Priest would lead his people in giving thanks for their sustenance. All males and females above four summers would prepare for the ritual that lay ahead by scrubbing their hands and arms with moist clay dug from beneath the snow and adorning themselves with 'good medicine' handed down from their forebears. Crow feathers, pieces of horn and strips of buckskin stained with natural dyes would be hung from neck and waist so that they were free to swing in an arc that would waft the Spirits of Life around these two areas of the body that signified temporal increase; the private parts that imparted life; and the throat that took the food to sustain it.

Kuelin lifted the horn to his mouth and blew two long blasts, the indefinably eerie sound reverberating around the hillocks as he blew, but cutting off short when he stopped, the sound deadened by the snow. There were no hills high enough to create an echo. It was as if a tight-sealing lid had been slammed down on a potful of bubbling sound just as it came to the boil. The Holy Man – this old seer and priest who bore the spiritual well-being of his people like a mantle around his shoulders – had transformed himself into a spectacle of gruesome greatness that belied his meagre physical stature. Smears of blood from the elk's heart were daubed on his chin and cheeks; his voluminous bearskin coat drooped under the weight of skulls of past kills and, on his head, a reindeer hide was tied to form a cap with trailing ribbons of fur cascading down his back – the whole surmounted by a pair of antlers, possibly from the same beast. He symbolised an awesome mediator between man and his deity. His flowing white beard mingled with his necklace of bird skulls and in his left hand he held a wooden staff which steadied his stance and reached almost to his eye level, the top crowned with a seagull's skull, sun-bleached and stained a bright yellow.

They stood in a circle, twenty souls in all if the moons old child in a reed basket was discounted. Kuelin raised his staff above his head and, with both arms outstretched, railed in a tongue that none present could understand, his voice rising in a crescendo while he shook the staff violently. Most of the men in the circle carried torches and the flickering light reflected from the whiteness of Kuelin's beard and grotesque ornaments to add to his spectre-like appearance. All eyes were trained skywards, oblivious to the light wisps of snow which began falling, as the chant continued. Then, as suddenly as he began, the High Priest shouted an abrupt 'Hei-ja-ja' and fell silent. The worshippers dropped their gaze to look upon their God Man once more as he advanced slowly to the sacrificial stone and, laying his staff to one side, brought from within the folds of his cloak a horn that had been plugged at its larger end with wood to form a vessel now containing the 'holy water' that he alone produced from some secret formula. He removed the wooden stopper and poured some of the clear liquid over the piece of meat then, calling forward Kilde, took his torch and waved it close to the heart. Bluish flames leapt from the stone and, in an instant, were extinguished. The offering was not consumed, only a faint odour marking any change in its condition. Returning the flaming brand to its owner, Kuelin picked up the elk's heart in both hands, bringing it up in front of his face and repeating, more or less, the whole evocation. This done, he offered the shiny, lifeless blood-pump to each of the men, women and children in order and, as they bit from it a small piece, to be swallowed whole without chewing, he brought some word of acknowledgement, as if from the gods themselves. This blessing would be an encouragement to both individuals and the whole band, endowing them with promises of future well-being.

The Svear were not a particularly demonstrative people. At no time was this more evident than during their celebratory dances although the limited repertoire of dance routines did, at times, become quite energetic. This was of appreciable bodily benefit when they chose to perform these rituals on such a chilling night as this. The accompaniment was simple, provided by a rhythmic beating of dried bones, one on another. On this night it was Kilde who took the moose thighbones, one end of each having been bound in strips of hide to form rude handles, the leather extending to loops that passed around the wrist to retain these simple drumsticks in the hands of the beater. Despite the chill of the night air, the little circle of dancers moved enthusiastically in a clockwise direction around the fire that had been built in more or less the centre of the village. With one hand extended to touch the person in front, the circle progressed to the sound of Kilde's clack-clack beat with a shuffling, sidestepping style that was broken at regular intervals by a staccato high kick as the troupe turned towards the centre, facing each other across the flames that licked hungrily at the logs piled on to the fire. With bodies swaying in time to the sidestepping motion, a trance-like reverence at times fell upon the dancers, to be broken by the chants that accompanied the high kick every so often. Men, women and children alike formed the circle, in no particular order. Kuelin remained by his own fire pit and Kilde sat cross-legged on a fleece before the main fire, within the circle, and thrashed out the beat, his steady rhythm embellished with rattling flourishes to coincide with the high kicks. The pace quickened, gradually at first, but then with a crescendo that ended in a triple hand clap. Several dances were begun and ended, very little variation in their component steps or routines being apparent to any who looked on and were not completely familiar with whichever dance had been called by Kilde as he started his drumming once more. As limbs worked with decreasing inhibition, so body temperatures rose and some discarded their outer layers of buckskin or fleece to perspire more freely and move with greater abandon. The flickering tongues of flame illuminated faces that projected a range of expressions: from concentrated effort to an exuding of pleasure. This was the Svear in celebration.

That night, as he clung to Kael beneath his fleecy bedrobes, Odal felt inebriated; filled with spiritual emotion and a feeling of benevolence knowing that he had once more this day provided meat for the clan. He put his arms around his woman and turned her towards him, feeling the swelling of her breasts against his chest. She responded warmly and he was conscious of her lips playing on his neck. The woodsmoke drifted over them in wispy billows that came and went as the wind surged and relaxed in its passage across the mouth of the cave. To Odal, it seemed as if he was in a land of clouds. And it evoked a new passion within him. With one hand he squeezed Kael's cheek as his lips sought hers; with the other he gently parted her legs as he moved his body towards her. As the ecstasy welled up within him he took her with a tenderness that made her murmur and clasp him to her. This further affirmation of their love for each other gave way to the heaviness of sleep and they settled once more below the robes that would ensure their warmth throughout this winter's night. Oden did not stir from his youthful slumber. It had been a good day.

*

Five moons had come and gone. The days were lengthening and the four-cold days of winter were all but erased from memory by the sun's warming rays, even at this early hour when the great red-gold orb had barely climbed clear of the hazy horizon's clinging grip. Outside the brushwood overhang of Odal's lodge stood Fride and

Bodil, the daughters of Talna. Their excited words to Oden sent him scampering back into the far corner of the cave where Kael was bending over a 'stretcher', a rectangular frame upon which strands of sinew were stretched and straightened. He tugged at the hide-scraper hanging from her waist and asked: 'Mother, may I go in Tuma's canoe on the lake?'

'No! I've told you before, you're too little. Maybe after one more summer.'

'But Lippe is also going. He has been many times. And Fride is strong enough to paddle a long way.'

With a sigh, Kael straightened up and looked at him resignedly, then walked to where the girls waited and, looking left and right said, 'Is this true? Is Lippe taking your father's canoe on the lake?'

'Yes, he is,' the sisters replied, practically in unison. 'Father says it's all right as long as we don't go too far. Can Oden come with us?'

'Where's Lippe now?' Kael inquired: 'I don't see him.'

'He's already putting the canoe in the water,' answered Fride, the older of the two. She had seen ten summers; her sister, nine.

'Oh, go on then. But don't lean over the side, and you must do what Lippe tells you. Understand?'

'Yes, yes, yes,' young Oden replied, not in an insolent way but, rather, as his father would have done when Kael had just asked him to do something quite obvious. The lad was overjoyed. He'd watched as the tree had been hollowed out and had looked on from the shore as others had paddled off to do some fishing or to explore one of the closer islands. This was an opportunity he'd thought would have been longer in the coming. He ran with the girls towards the spot where Tuma had embedded the large tree trunks upon which he supported the upturned vessel during the snow months.

'It's afloat. You can get in now but I need to fetch one more paddle. Don't let it drift away, Fride, will you?' Lippe half shouted, running back towards his parents' lodge.

Soon, the four young Svear were nosing the canoe, so heavy on land yet so light on the water, out into the lake.

The commune's menfolk were seated on a large log to one side of Kilde's lodge and were reminiscing over fishing experiences of times past, their hands busily fashioning fish-hooks from minute pieces of bone. Their nimble fingers worked almost automatically as they talked. The womenfolk, meanwhile, set about the myriad tasks that needed to be carried out in order to keep community life on an even keel. By the time the sun had risen halfway to its highest point, Kael had finished stretching and separating her store of sinew strands. It was a beautiful morning and she was happy in the knowledge that, inside her womb, she carried Odal's seed. It had been growing there for three moons now but, as yet, she hadn't told him and he'd given her no inkling that he was aware of her condition. She would choose her moment, all in good time. But right now, she had to fetch some water and so, with a hide-lined wooden pitcher in each hand, she strolled in carefree fashion towards the shore.

Kael was never to be the same again. With one pitcher filled and set aside on the bank, she stooped to fill the second one. As she lifted it clear of the glittering water, the stabbing pain in her back made her gasp as she staggered forwards, letting the container fall. In that instant before she pitched into the water, she must have seen the cruel shape that emerged from her stomach, spraying blood on to the gently lapping waves. She never would have seen anything like it before and could not have known that the spearhead was made of something called iron. As the water covered her head and sand began to fill her still-open mouth a heavy foot kicked down on her buttock and the metal blade was tugged backwards through her lifeless body.

Elsewhere in the village similar atrocities were being enacted. The row of men, one moment happily recalling past achievements were, in the next moment, writhing on the ground as their lives ebbed away, some with smashed skulls, others with fatal spear wounds. No greater mercy was shown to the women, nor to the one remaining child, a mere baby. Powerful hands swung it by its tiny ankles, dashing out its brains against the rocky side of the hollow that would have brought it comfort and security had these marauding giants, each a good hand's breadth taller than the Svear, not come stealthily out of the east to visit their evil on this innocent commune. Only Kuelin was still alive, his fate as yet undecided as he knelt before a leather-helmeted warrior, a spearhead prodding him between the shoulder blades.

The dwellings were ransacked. No corner was left untouched as this war party cut, hacked and prodded at anything that was likely to harbour another living soul. Robes, ornaments, tools, implements and remains of food were unceremoniously dumped into piles in front of each lodge, the sinew strappings slashed and the supporting poles of each overhang kicked aside to leave the brushwood shelters in a trampled carnage. All attention now turned to the old priest, his gods apparently no longer in communion with his spirit in this hour of need.

'In his lodge we found *these* things,' one warrior screeched, almost spitting out the penultimate word as he threw an assortment of charms in front of the old man. 'He is obviously the seer. What shall we do with him?'

The question provoked an agitated response as several of the men thrust towards him with wild gesticulations and unseemly gestures. One, who appeared to be the leader, raised his hand in an unspoken call to order. They could not converse with Kuelin other than by sign language for they spoke a different tongue, but this chief pointed out the charms and made signs to imply that he was asking if they belonged to the old man. Kuelin gave no response, either verbally or by sign, but merely lifted his head skywards, his eyes fixed on some heavenly horizon.

'The wooden sword! Give him the wooden sword!' exclaimed the man who had thrown down the accoutrements of religion. The cry was taken up by the others who, within moments, were becoming frenzied. Only the chief's silent authority restrained them. He tried once more to communicate with Kuelin, but to no avail. As with most rabble-rousing bands, the democratic view prevailed. His fate had been proclaimed. He was stripped naked, his arms pinioned and his wrists tied behind his back. The half-blind, almost toothless old man looked a pitiable sight.

The 'wooden sword' was being prepared. If Kuelin's powers of discernment had still operated he would now be screaming for mercy. In the event, he remained silent. He could not have known what was to befall him for the chosen means of ending his life could have been born only of the most barbaric of imaginations. The 'sword' was a sharpened stake, its hilt-end wedged into the fork of the very log that had been used as a seat by the bantering fishermen only a short while before. It was held in place by a boulder taken from one of the now redundant fire pits.

Two men lifted the old priest into a standing position and held him upright on the log momentarily, before kicking his heels from behind to bring his full body weight down on the stake as it thrust up through his anus, skewering him in a sitting position across the log. Forever.

The scream that tore from Kuelin's throat was loud, piercing, and had an unearthly sound that seemed to last an age; like a host of demonic beings in torment, determined to extract every last discordant breath from the extremities of their dissipating spirits. As his blood ran in rivulets over the rough bark, the intruders turned away, showing no sign of emotion. Instead, they methodically collected up the spoils from the piles they'd stacked earlier and slowly made their way out of the devastated village.

It was young Bodil who first heard it. The far-distant sound from the village diffused into anonymity as it pulsed across the waters of the lake.

'Stop paddling a moment. I think someone's shouting. Maybe they're calling to us. We'd best go back.'

'Yes, I can hear someone shouting, too,' said Lippe, 'I think you're right, Bodil, we should go back now.'

As they turned the canoe towards the direction of home, the small island before them obscured any distant view the children might have had of the trophy-laden Barbarians trudging westwards over the last outcrop of the now silent cul-de-sac of hillocks that had formed the periphery of the village. Now orphans all, they were not aware of that fact even as they beached the little craft close to the spot where Lippe had launched it just over three hours ago. It was only when Fride raced over the crest of the bank ahead of the others and rounded a little clump of bushes that the first awareness of something wrong shocked her to an open-mouthed standstill. Her parents' lodge had lain closest to the shoreline. But now, with its former brush-and-clay overhang strewn around and no signs of any activity, it was becoming obvious to her that some grave catastrophe had occurred. At first, no one spoke. Four silent figures surveyed the scene of carnage, their eyes falling on Tulna's bloodied body, half hidden in the tangle of brushwood. Bodil screamed and Oden began to cry noisily. Fride sobbed in great gasps. All three were transfixed by their horrific discovery.

Only Lippe walked further into the remains of the village, his eyes flitting uneasily from place to place, the hair on the nape of his neck standing out as fear gripped him. It was almost impossible to take in the appalling extent of the tragedy as more and more prostrate bodies came into view, each one so obviously violated and showing no sign of life. It was when he saw Kuelin, naked, sitting on a log with his head bowed as if in prayer, that Lippe's hopes were temporarily raised.

Running towards the High Priest, Lippe called out: 'Kuelin! Kuelin! What has happened? Why are you...' His question trailed off as he began to realise that Kuelin was not merely asleep; nor was he deep in communion with the Asa. From his position in front of the old man, Lippe could see neither the pool of blood nor the base of the wooden stake, but the flies buzzing around the sedentary figure telegraphed the message that all was not what it seemed. Lippe cursed, venting his hatred on whoever had done this. Then, as he stepped over the log towards other bodies that lay strewn on the ground he took in the full explanation for Kuelin's erect posture. The boy was helpless to prevent the contents of his stomach spewing on to the grass. He stood, bent forward, hands on knees and, with tears now beginning to stream from his eyes, continued to retch for some moments, his vision blurred and his senses reeling. His ordeal had only just begun for, almost as soon as he was able to stand upright once more and draw the back of his hand across his eyes, he recognised the form of his father and the others. Shocked beyond belief and with the adrenaline pumping through his body, Lippe turned back towards his young charges and, with his own legs gathering speed, called in panic: 'Get back in the canoe! Quickly! Run!'

Without hesitation, the three obeyed him, fleeing in a blind fear back to the lake shore to clamber aboard the hollowed-out log that, not many minutes before, had known their laughter.

'Push, Fride, push,' Lippe exhorted, as they paddled furiously out into the open water. The bizarre scene they had witnessed somehow produced a superhuman strength in their young shoulders and arms. Not until they were once more back in the vicinity of the spot from which Bodil had first detected Kuelin's shriek did Lippe leave his paddle in the baffle position to slow the progress of the canoe. Fride followed suit and they hove to close to the small island which, once more, all but hid the village shoreline from their view.

Five minutes is not a long time. It's about as long as it takes to say: 'a bull moose and a bull moose and a bull moose' one hundred times. But to these four young Svear, it seemed an eternity – and then some. That was, more or less, the duration of their silence. No words were exchanged. Above the normally soporific sound of the waves gently lapping on the shingled beach of the small islet, only the syncopated sobbing of one, two and, at times, three disoriented young beings bore testimony to any human presence on the lake. By contrast, Lippe knelt in the stern and stared, ashen-faced, back towards the distant hillocks as the canoe drifted aimlessly backwards, to allow increasingly more of the bereft village to come within sight once again. Mounting bitterness welled up within him; but it did not rule his mind. It was a bitterness wrought from a deep sadness, not from a vengeful heart. It served only to steel his determination not to give way to the grief that swamped him and was being played out before his eyes, a mere paddle's length towards the bow of the canoe. Paradoxically, Lippe began to scheme in a different way: he began rationalising his thoughts and harnessing his powers of concentration to begin resolving their current predicament in the light of their immediate future. He would be to these younger, weaker comrades what his father had been to him when his mother died, four winters past. Dipping his paddle deep and with slow, steady strokes, Lippe turned the little craft back toward the open water and, setting his course in the direction from which the sun had risen that morning, although it felt like a thousand years ago, he called forward reassuringly: 'Come on, now. We've got each other to look out for. And we need to be brave for each of us. Help me paddle, Fride.'

'Wh-where are we going? What are we going to do?' she answered, laconically sweeping the paddle lightly along the side of the canoe.

'We'll find one of the bigger islands. There may be another community there. And besides, we'll be safer on an island.'

'How can you say that,' Bodil protested, her temper shortened by her still jangling nerves: 'They may come back for us.'

'No. They won't. They have no boat. They must have come overland or we'd have seen their canoes.'

The logic seemed to bring its own reassurance. Bodil and Oden became calm, almost normal, once more and Fride began to make a more purposeful contribution to the propulsion of the vessel.

Lake Mälaren is a beautifully serene place. Almost big enough to be classed as an inland sea, its archipelago is composed of myriad islands and islets. As the fugitive-laden canoe slowly slugged its way past some of the smaller of these low-lying upthrusts, a number of which were little more than oversized rocks, the warm, early summer sun cast short shadows to the left side of the canoe, for it was not yet the middle of the afternoon. Driven by an inner force that contradicted their youthful stature, the two paddlers stuck to their task of putting ever greater distance between themselves and any likelihood of pursuit. After what may have been an hour of intermittent effort, Lippe elected to direct the craft towards the more sheltered passage between a large island and the southern mainland. So large was the island that, to the voyagers, it seemed as if they were entering the mouth of a large river. There was almost no wind, the water was calm and the sun began to transfer its great heat more effectively than it had done earlier in the day. The lake water satisfied both thirst and sweating limbs, but there was nothing on board to satisfy the stomach.

'When will we go ashore? My belly's aching,' Oden complained, breaking Lippe's concentration on paddling as he turned to reply: 'What's it aching with? You need to use the pit?'

'No! I'm hungry.'

'I am, too,' said Lippe, 'but we'll have to keep going until we can find some place where we might find berries close to the shore.'

'I'm not only hungry,' Fride added to the conversation: 'My arms feel like they're dropping off and my shoulders, hips and ankles ache. In fact I feel like just one big ache!' For the first time since that morning, a lighter mood broke across the would-be sailors as Fride's comment brought shallow smiles from each of her three comrades.

The little bay they had found had been kind to them. Not only did they discover some early summer fruits that were eminently edible, but they chanced upon a patchy crop of the small, white, wild turnips that grew so well untended but were always disappointingly tiny whenever any attempt had been made to cultivate them. The limited, but by no means meagre, diet eased the immediate hunger pangs. The gathering of fruit, berries and turnips had also occupied their minds and the task had taken them until the late afternoon to accomplish. Lippe's thoughts were now turning to preparations for an overnight stay. They would need some kind of shelter.

A young man of thirteen summers, Lippe had become, within a matter of hours, the father figure of the group, assuming responsibility for their welfare. Alone, he would make the decisions that determined their routines and lifestyle. Alone, he would endeavour to ensure their safety. He began now to organise the assembling of the rudiments for a simple shelter. Without tools or any form of binding, he would have to fashion something that might, if the breeze remained low, provide some means of keeping them warm.

From deadfall branches, brushwood and ferns, the small

lean-to lodge began to take shape. By the time darkness began to close in, Fride and the others had collected a large bundle of bracken which would serve as bedcovers, both under and over. The shelter was by no means insulated against the wind should it rise to any great extent, nor to the ingress of water should it rain. Their hope was that the settled weather would hold. It did. But the night was not a happy one. Forlorn, and without the joyful spirit that a 'wilderness adventure' might conjure, Oden began to shiver uncontrollably as his nightmare became more real, his pulsating body reverberating through those huddled on either side, disturbing the deep sleep which the day's exhaustion had brought on. With legs pumping and arms scattering the fronds that served as a cover, his nightmare erupted into a physical melee that terminated in a wild scream. Fride hugged him close to her and kissed his forehead, interjecting the calming words that Talna had once spoken to her. She was to repeat her counsel twice more before the sun's rays heralded a new day.

Lippe faced a dilemma. Should he dare to return alone to the destroyed village in the hope of finding any remaining tools, implements and weapons as well as vegetables from the rows the women had so patiently planted almost two moons ago? Could he withstand the sight of the desecration? Besides, it would require some Herculean effort to paddle both ways on his own. Should they take what food their new-found surroundings allowed and strike out for another bay, with the chance of coming across another community? Or should they stay put for a while, perfecting their little lean-to and exploring the island further? His mind began to fill with visions of the neatly planted rows of vegetables and of the grove of trees where knapped flint blades had been slowly going through their metamorphosis into axes.

'Fride, I'll be back in a while. Look after the others. I must think clearly what is best for us to do,' Lippe confided, before leaving his companions to climb to the highest point of the island within their view. He wished he'd understood more of the ways of the Asa. At a time like this a man needed his gods. But for him, this would be no Moses' journey to the mountain top to 'wait upon the Lord'. This would be an exercise in pragmatism, guided by his own best instincts. The hill was hardly worthy of the name, but the air seemed somehow fresher on the summit and the climb was enough to renew the aching in Lippe's ankles, reminding him of just how far they'd paddled the day before. He sat on a large rock and pondered their predicament. With a young girl, herself hardly more than a child, and the two younger ones to look after; little food of sustaining value; no weapons; no tools. It was impossible. The sun was well clear of the horizon as he made his way once more towards the little lodge. The others had gone in search of berries and he could see them not far off. He shouted and waved, and they acknowledged him in the same manner before making their way towards where he stood.

'Come,' he said, 'I have decided what we must do.'

'Are we staying here?' Bodil enquired: 'I don't like this place.'

'No. We must leave as soon as we can. There is nothing here for us,' replied Lippe: 'We will take as much food as we can carry, but we must go that way,' he said, pointing towards the rising sun.

'But what if we meet more—'

'We won't,' Lippe stated firmly, cutting off Fride's half-formed question. He knew exactly what was on her mind. 'We will stay clear of the big land and look for another island.'

'Who will look after us?' Oden asked, his eyes like grimy-edged saucers, betraying a plethora of fears and doubts that intensified his general air of bewilderment.

It was Fride who answered, putting one arm around his narrow shoulders, 'We must find more of our people, like Lippe says.'

The boy looked up into her eyes, questioningly, tilted his head towards her breast, but said no more.

Lippe continued, 'Let's carry what we can to the canoe. We must leave soon.'

There may have been no specifically acknowledged Divine Providence regarding Lippe's decision, but good fortune, nonetheless, smiled upon them. For close on two hours they'd paddled, even Bodil taking over from her older sister for a brief spell. At times they drifted, drawing from their pathetic store of food to fortify themselves, at least psychologically. They'd passed a number of islets without once detecting any notion of occupancy when, from the leeward side of the largest island they'd seen that morning, another canoe appeared, its passengers both male but not immediately discernible as Svear. Apprehensive at first, the refugees strained to identify the strangers. As the two vessels drew closer, a new wave of hope began to rise. These were Svear.

'Hei! hei!' Lippe called, through cupped hands. The two girls began to wave furiously.

'Kneel down, Bodil, you'll upset the canoe,' Fride warned.

The two fishermen were, indeed, of the Svear people and they raised their paddles in acknowledgement. Soon the two canoes were alongside one another and Lippe acted as spokesman, distilling into a few moments of conversation the traumatic events of the previous day.

'I am Ake. This is Han. Can you follow us?'

'We've paddled this far,' said Lippe, smiling at last, 'A little farther will not kill us.'

'Ha! He's a brave one, that one!' Ake called over Han's shoulder as they manoeuvred their craft adeptly until they were once more headed back towards the shore. In what seemed no time at all, the little flotilla was pulling into a shallow cove. Two women and a boy of about Lippe's age looked up from where they were fetching water near the shoreline.

The community was even smaller than Kuelin's had been. Only four shelters declared their tenancy and one of these was without a cooking fire. It was being used as a communal store for the various appurtenances of Svear village life. The three blood groups comprised eleven persons in all, the youngest only three moons old and still in a reeded basket.

'This is Helge and this is...' The round of introductions was embellished with the story of the refugees' disaster.

'We will make a place for you here,' Ake said, indicating the store shelter, 'and soon we can have a fire, then you must share our food.'

Lippe was quickly in conversation with Ilf, the boy they'd first seen at the shore. He was the son of Han and Helge. Oona, Ake's woman, took the others to her shelter. Soon, a third man appeared. He was Sten and he joined Han and Ake as they asked Lippe to recount the detail of the tragedy once more. Sten asked about the village and whether Lippe thought there might be something of worth remaining. When he mentioned the axe-trees, he held the full attention of all three men. They told Lippe that they had come to the island only five summers ago and had no axe-trees yet mature enough to cut. There was the implied suggestion that they return to Kuelin's village to retrieve what they could. The point was more openly expressed by Ake: 'If you could show us the way to the village we could find them. You would not have to come, but stay with the canoe until we have searched.'

Lippe agreed, but warned them that the Barbarians might return. The men, of course, had already weighed up this possibility but, since Lippe had seemed certain that they were on foot, it was suggested that a cautious approach be made from the lake, overshooting the bay at first and returning to it if no one could be seen.

'If you are able, we will go at next sun-up,' Ake said with an air of authority. It was clear to Lippe that he was, in some sense, the leader of this small clan. So far, he had seen no signs of a seer or Holy Man.

The first night at Ake's village was a distinct improvement on the refugees' experiences of the night before. All slept soundly, the soft hide coverings bringing a level of comfort they had missed. The sun had not yet risen when Han gently rocked Lippe until he woke.

'Come. We go now. The canoe is ready.'

Hide-covered parcels of food, spears and clubs were already stowed, along with flint knives and the only two axes the community now possessed. The canoe was a little longer than Tuma's and the other two men were by the water's edge ready to depart. Throwing his wrap around himself and tying it securely, Lippe followed Han to join them. No words were exchanged, only a nodding of heads all round and the party pushed off through the light morning mist on to the lake. What had taken Lippe and Fride two half days to cover was executed in little more than two hours. They went by an outer route, bypassing on the other side the island on which the little band had stopped two nights previously.

Lippe felt at one with these men as he paddled. It was good to be with menfolk again. The responsibilities he'd borne so recently made him feel, in every way, a grown man. He was, indeed, a fine specimen of Svear youth. Of only average height, he was stocky and muscular, with long, light-brown hair and made quite a contrast to Fride who, although younger, was slightly taller, of slim build and with very fair hair. He dug his paddle deep on each stroke and shrugged off the onset of the aches that began to creep into his limbs once again. Familiar landmarks soon became recognisable to Lippe and he was, at the same time, feeling the growing bitterness he had known in those moments after discovery of the carnage which had represented his world. As they steered to within three body-lengths from the shoreline, no signs of life were apparent.

'Psst. Just over there is the village.'

Han and Ake turned towards the boy to follow the indication of his outstretched paddle. Sten, kneeling behind him, had already acknowledged it with a low grunt. They baffled the canoe and, in low tones, Ake outlined his intentions of going a little farther up the shoreline then circling back if no other sign of human presence was detected. A peculiar smell hung in the otherwise still air as they beached close to where Tuma had dragged the two large trunks he'd used as a rest for his canoe during times when there had been too much ice on the lake to allow easy passage for fishing.

Ake met Lippe's eyes and, in a voice that was firm but not harsh, commanded, 'You will wait with the canoe. We three will go ashore.' Then, exchanging paddles for weapons, the three men crouched forward as they began to ascend the small beach. Almost as if it was an afterthought, Ake trotted back to the canoe. 'Which way are the axe-trees?'

Lippe pointed and told him how to find the path.

'Good. Keep your eyes busy. If you see anything, whistle as loudly as you can.'

A nod to each other signified complete understanding and Ake sprinted to join his comrades near the top of the rise that led into the little semicircle of hillocks that had been Lippe's home.

Soon, the three men were in the midst of the ghastly scene. As they looked from one to another their eyes spoke a common thought: 'We did right not to let the boy return.' The stench itself was unpleasant enough, but two days of raiding by wolves and other carrion-seekers had left the remains of the bodies in grotesque form. Kuelin's legs were almost devoid of flesh; both feet were missing and the bones were twisted into unnatural postures. The wooden spike that impaled him was so firmly fixed that his upper torso had barely moved, even though his hands, too, had all but disappeared to the scavengers. Other victims had fared no better.

Lippe's mind sieved myriad thoughts as he sat alone, his eyes flitting up and down the tops of the hillocks and along the shoreline. His vigil seemed endless and, from time to time, he thought of pushing off from his beached position to hold the canoe some way out in the bay to increase the panorama of his view. Should the men have need of a quick retreat, however, he would then be in poor position to help them. He remained at his post, growing more ill at ease as time passed.

It was the hewing down of the axe-trees that had delayed the men. Han was first to appear over the brow of the rise, carrying two hide sackloads of vegetables.

'No sign?'

'No. Everything is still. But I could hear you chopping at the trees,' Lippe replied.

'Ja. We will be coming back in a little while. We have found only some fish-hooks and a knife, but will bring the best of the axes and some more of the vegetables.'

Had the little party had the ability to project themselves to the level of the clouds, they would have seen, perhaps, that the mischievous plunderers were nowhere in the vicinity. They had continued their marauding march westwards and had put some distance between themselves and the stricken village. However noisily Ake and his men chopped at the branches of the axe-trees, it would have occasioned no interest from another human soul. None was within earshot. The survey complete and, too, the retrieval of the little of consequence that had been left, with the exception of the vegetables and axes, the canoe was once more making its way out on to the lake. It was only after they'd been paddling for some time that Ake called a halt and, as they drifted idly, turned to Lippe and handed him something loosely wrapped in a large piece of hide. 'We found this. Maybe you would like to have it.'

Lippe took the parcel and unwound the hide covering. His eyes fell upon the horn that old Kuelin had once worn around his waist. It no longer contained the holy water that the old seer had secretly concocted, but its smooth surface bore the marks of the gods that Kuelin had put there long before Lippe had been born. He smiled his gratitude to the three faces that studied his, awaiting some reaction. The men smiled in return and, shipping their paddles, began to break out the little bundles of dried fish they'd brought with them.

*

None of the remnant of Kuelin's band was ever to return to the scene of the disaster. Their feelings of desolation would, over time, become no more than a fading memory. But they would never forget the bond that this tragedy had caused to be formed among them. Lippe and Fride, in particular, shared an emotional chemistry that yoked them in a common harness. A yoke that would be tested many times over the next five summers.

This band of Svear lived in a different way to Kuelin's band. Being island-dwellers, their main source of food lay not with the meat-bearing animals; they relied almost entirely on fish, either fresh or dried. The three men of the community had devised several ways of catching fish, depending upon season. When the time was right, the most productive involved team effort. It centred around a false channel that had been built up from rocks and smaller stones stacked to form two walls that extended a good dozen body-lengths out into the lake, broadening as they went and curving towards the eastern end of the island. The men would stand on the end rocks and look for shoals of fish. Once they'd spotted even a small congregation of fish, all three would jump into the water and swim around the outside of the shoal, encouraging it to enter the channel. When this had been accomplished, all hell broke loose as the men thrashed behind the shoal to find a level where they could reach bottom and advance on foot; kicking, splashing the surface and yelling at the top of their voices to scare the fish to a point of no return, congested in the shallows at the narrowest part of the decoy. The harvest was assured by pulling down from the top of the rocks, brushwood that had been laid there in readiness. With one or two branches in each hand, two of the men would present at least a visual barrier to any notion of exit from the snare whilst the third would rely on his quickness of reaction to scoop individual fish out of the shallow water and up on to the beach in a series of fluid strokes of the arm.

The refugees had been with Ake's people for two summers already and were only two moons away from completing a third. Their integration into the band had been achieved without any great recognition by either party. They were generally accepted as an extension of Ake and Oona's blood group although, of course, that they could never truly be. Fride, her sister Bodil and Oden now shared Ake's lodge. Only Lippe had remained in the store-shelter, sharing it over these many moons with an assortment of items held in common by this little fishing community. Ilf had been a stabilising presence in the early days, befriending both Lippe and Fride, whilst Bodil and Oden enjoyed the company of others close to their own ages respectively. But on this warm, almost cloudless day, Lippe found himself alone. As he whittled away with his flint knife at the wooden plank that would become his new paddle, his two companions had risen early and were making their way along a secluded pathway, heading inland along the floor of a shallow fold between the low hills. On the previous evening, Ilf had promised Fride that he would show her something that was never spoken about in the village. It was something Han had first shown him when he was ten summers old.

'There it is. Over there. This is what I want to show you.'

'Where? I can't see anything. What is it?'

'Here, behind the rocks.'

They slowed as they stepped down into the hollow and turned to face an ancient runic marker.

'What a strange stone. What is it?'

'It's the Stone of the Gods,' Ilf answered, standing before the flat-faced rock on which numerous symbols had been cut. 'It is told that the fingers of the gods wrote these messages on the stone to guide the first Svear who came to this island.'

Fride gave a low whistle as she gazed at the strange runes, their lines weather-worn and, in some places, quite indistinct. 'But the clan here is so small. Why would the gods care to bring such special messages to so few people?'

There was no way she could have known that, in a little over eighty years hence, people would be echoing these same words in connection with an event that would take place in a little back-of-beyond hamlet called Bethlehem, over a thousand miles to the south-east of where they now stood.

'We were not always so few,' Ilf countered, 'Many moons ago, even before Ake was in a basket, a large group of our people left here in canoes to find the 'Island of Plenty' somewhere towards where the summer sun rises.

That's what the message told them but we have no one left who can decipher the symbols so we don't know where to find this land.'

'Then why is the stone so secret? Why does no one speak of it?'

'It's because we are afraid. Our elders believe that because we have no Holy Man who can read the runes we are doomed here. Our life will go on only until the gods are ready to deal with us for not following the others.'

'But that's unfair. You said it was a long time ago, before we were even born.'

'Yes, but it's our destiny. That's the way of the gods. We cannot change our destiny.'

Fride bit her lip, her eyes dropping to prevent Ilf from seeing the tears that began to form at the corners. The young man sensed that she was overawed by his words and moved towards her, gingerly snaking his arm around her waist and pulling her gently to him. Shyly, but tenderly, he kissed her cheek. She tilted her head towards him, snuggling into the crook of his neck.

For some moments they stood in this pose, neither voicing the thoughts that ran through their minds.

Had they done so, each would have brought an entirely different perspective to the situation. For some time now, Ilf had been feeling an increasing attraction to this tall, willowy girl. Although he was a finger's breadth shorter than the object of his desires, he was a good-looking youth. Dark of skin, hair and eyes, he was well built and, generally, exuded a confident air. He'd longed for the opportunity to be alone with Fride and, now that the circumstance prevailed, wanted to show her in a demonstrable way the affection he felt for her.

For her part, Fride was finding it difficult to come to terms with the acceptance of their insularity by the elders of this small Svear clan. Even as she pressed her blonde head intimately into Ilf's neck, her vision was of those long-ago sailors making their way to a new land in the east. She remembered summer days in years gone by when her father Tuma had taken her on fishing trips across the lake. How magical it had seemed to sit in the prow of the canoe as it glided through the crystal, sun-sparkled waters with the only sounds coming from the morning birdsong and the regular 'blap' of Tuma's paddle-strokes. How she wished...

'A pebble for your thoughts,' cut in Ilf, breaking the silence of their romantic moment.

'I was just dreaming, really. Enjoying the stillness. Thinking about canoes out on the water.'

'Mmm, beautiful isn't it,' Ilf said in barely more than a whisper, his voice slightly husky. 'Perhaps you will come with me out on the lake. I will ask my father, Han, if I can take the canoe.' As he spoke, Ilf lifted Fride's chin gently and kissed her on the lips.

'No, Ilf, you mustn't,' she retorted in response to his gesture.

The instant feeling of rejection bit at him and, for one moment, he was caught between two courses of action. One was to turn his back on Fride and walk away. He chose the other. Grabbing at her shoulders with both hands he pulled her close to him. 'Fride, I want you! I really want you!' So saying, he cupped her cheeks in his hands and kissed her again, this time with greater passion. She looked startled, caught unawares, and made no move to resist him. But as he released his hold and drew back to look into her eyes there was only blankness. Fride showed no elation; no anger; no recognition of any impact his action might have made upon her. There was just a pregnant gap of uncertainty. She looked away, letting her gaze wander across the hollow.

'Thank you, Ilf, for bringing me here and showing me the stone. Let's go back now.'

He smiled and made to take hold of her hand but she gave a little hop-step that placed her ahead of him as she made her way up out of the depression in which the apocalyptic stone was sited, leaving him to follow her through the grove of trees that had landmarked their approach that morning.

As they wandered, side by side, into the village, it was Helge who greeted them. They'd been gone for some time and she gave them a knowing look which, although unjustified, may have carried more of an air of hopeful optimism for she was quite aware that, soon, it would be right for her son to build his own lodge and take a woman.

Lippe was bent over a small fire in front of his shelter, his full attention concentrated on the blade of his paddle which he was flaming to burn back the sharp edges made by his flint knife-cuts. Carefully, he allowed the wood to burn just enough to consume the surface fibres, before extinguishing the smoky flame by rubbing it on the grass he'd kept wet by occasional dousings with lake water. He used a fist-sized stone to rub at the burnt edges to perfect the shape of the paddle-blade. When the blade end was honed to his satisfaction, he wrapped the handle in strips of soft, but tough hide and bound them into a permanent hand-grip with lengths of sinew. He'd already shaped and smoothed the butt, fitting it to his palm until it rolled like a close-tolerance ball joint within his half-closed hand. The whole paddle was a testimony to Lippe's fastidious workmanship. It was light, comfortable in the hold and exhibited a perfect balance. He now had two good paddles. The older one he'd inherited from Sten, but had modified it to suit his own handling.

It was what took place two days later that made Fride think of Ilf in a different way. On two or three occasions he'd reiterated his invitation for her to join him on a trip across the lake. She agreed to go with him and, as on the morning when they'd ventured out to the Stone of the Gods, they planned to leave soon after first light.

The time had come. Fride chewed on the handful of shredded turnip and drew her wrap around her slim body before leaving the lodge to meet Ilf near the shoreline. As she drew close enough to appreciate his demeanour, she sensed that he no longer entertained his bright mood of the previous evening when he'd walked with her around the perimeter of the village before accompanying her to Ake's shelter. He seemed irritated, even as he casually raised one hand in a 'good morning' greeting.

'What's wrong? Do you no longer wish to go?' Fride inquired.

'Sten and my father have taken the canoe for fishing. But we'll take Lippe's canoe. He even has a new paddle you can use.'

Fride recoiled at the suggestion. 'No! We cannot take Lippe's canoe when he is asleep. He will be very angry with us.'

'Bah! He may be angry for a little while but what does it matter. Come! I have brought some food for us and on the other shore we can pick some berries. We will have a good day.'

'I will not go with you. Not in Lippe's canoe.'

'Listen to me, Fride, it's our only chance. Father and Sten will be gone for half of the day.'

'Then we must wait until Lippe is awake so that we may ask him.'

'Are you stupid? Lippe would hardly agree for me to take you out by yourself.'

'Then it's wrong to take his canoe, Ilf. We will have to wait until your father returns and then, perhaps, we can make a shorter trip.'

Ilf's reaction was both violent and unexpected. He stamped his foot hard on the ground, threw the parcel of food at Fride's feet, uttered a Svear curse and turned smartly towards the shore. Without so much as a backwards glance, he pushed Lippe's canoe down into the water and leapt aboard, ignoring Fride's pleadings.

As Fride had predicted, Lippe became very angry when she explained the disappearance of his canoe. She begged him to restrain his feelings before their thoughtless and ungracious companion returned. Her feelings towards Ilf, which had been becoming more romantic, dissipated entirely. She saw him now only as a scheming, self-centred and inconsiderate oaf.

Her mental assessment was disrupted by Lippe, 'Maybe it's time I spoke with you more earnestly, Fride. Something has been on my mind for many moons but I have not thought it the right time to tell you before.'

'Tell me what, Lippe? What is it?'

'Let's walk a little way out of the village.'

Lippe got to his feet and led the way, marching briskly. No sooner had they got out of sight of the lodges than, almost naturally, Lippe took Fride's hand in his and, together, they slowed their pace to a leisurely walk. A quick glance behind him told Lippe that they were now alone. Even so, he kept his voice low as he began, 'I've been thinking for some time about our situation here. Oden and Bodil are like Oona's own offspring, but you and I are different. I don't know what it is. Maybe it's just that we talk together more. But Ilf I don't trust anymore. For almost the last two moons he's been acting strangely. He's not like he was in the beginning. I think perhaps it is time for me to leave here. But I would miss you, Fride.' He paused, long enough for his companion to interject, 'You're right about Ilf. Let me tell you what happened two days ago – when you were busy making your new paddle.'

Painstakingly, Fride recounted the events that took place at the stone. In doing so, of course, she had to confide in Lippe about the Stone of the Gods and about the earlier migration of the Svear band to the Island of Plenty. Even as Fride continued her monologue while they walked, Lippe wrestled with conflicting emotions. It was to some extent, perhaps, a measure of jealousy that deepened his anger towards Ilf. But at the same time he felt increasingly more protective towards this girl, now a young woman, whom he'd known since childhood and who had long been his companion. Had he had the benefit of a few more years of life itself and the wisdom it brings he would, long since, have recognised that male–female triangles have little basis for long-term stability. But it was Fride who voiced the initiative in concluding her tale: 'Lippe, I think you're right when you say it's time to leave here. Would you take me with you?'

'But Fride, I have no real plans for leaving. I don't yet know where I will go, nor when.'

'Then I do. But I could not go alone. I would like to find this Island of Plenty.'

To Lippe, right then, it was as if he'd been struck by the jagged fire-flashes that sometimes accompanied the winter storms. For a moment he remained dumbstruck then, slowly, a smile began to traverse his broad face.

'Why not. When we were younger we found this place. It should be no more difficult now to make, perhaps, a longer journey. Since we have been here we have forgotten the Asa but I don't believe that the gods would have us be prisoners on one small island when others may be prospering elsewhere.'

For more than two hours they walked, talked and shared their dreams, then Fride asked: 'Would you like me to show you the stone?'

'No. I don't believe the story that goes with it. Whatever is scratched on that piece of stone is not for me. Not for us. We must make our own destiny. That is what Kilde always taught me.' The mention of his father stirred flashes of memories within Fride's mind and, as if compelled by some unseen force, she embraced this young man who seemed twice her age in knowledge and agility of mind. Lippe's kiss was not the harsh, almost brute, mauling she'd experienced two days earlier. In that instant, the care, compassion, respect and platonic friendship they'd shared throughout their youth and early adolescence became encapsulated in an embryo of love and unspoken commitment. They stood and kissed for some minutes, but neither made any move to increase their passion through any more intimate expression.

'We must go back now,' Lippe announced, 'Maybe Ilf will have returned.'

'I hope so. But I don't really want to talk to him.'

'I can understand how you feel. I'm very angry with

him, too, but I will not fight him. It's best that we make our plans to leave soon but first I must dry some more fish and it would be best if you could bring some vegetables to my lodge at night and I will hide them.'

When they re-entered the small encirclement of lodges it was clear that Ilf had not yet returned. Neither had Han and Sten. The womenfolk were busy around their respective cooking fires and Ake sat cross-legged in front of his shelter fashioning an awl from a piece of bone.

The moods that prevailed amongst the band that evening were disparately divided between the young and the old. The day's fishing had been a good one for the men and each lodge had reason to be happy. In contrast, the ill-feeling between Lippe and Ilf had not yet subsided. When Han's wayward son had beached the borrowed canoe midway through the afternoon, Lippe had berated him for his inconsiderate action in a noisy vocal exchange that fell only minutely short of coming to blows. Once the issue became known to others Han, likewise, railed at his boy. Ilf sulked off and kept to himself throughout the remainder of the day.

Fride busied herself helping Oona make some new torches, but in Lippe's lodge there was an air of sadness as he enlightened Bodil of the plans he and her sister were making.

'We think it best this way. In time, we will come back for you, but you must remain here and keep an eye out for Oden.'

'I know. I'm not unhappy here, but I will miss you both. Will you build a shelter and take Fride as your woman?'

'Yes, when we reach the Island of Plenty.'

'That's good. But do you know how to find it?'

'Not exactly. Maybe the place we find will be *our* Island of Plenty. A place where the Asa are respected.'

'When will you leave?'

'Tomorrow, in the night.'

In a strange, compromising way, Bodil accepted her sister's planned departure, although sadness filled her as she thought ahead to the moment of parting.

Oden was not made aware of the pair's venture, nor was anyone else. Bodil had hugged her sister tightly and had pressed a small charm into her hand before she bedded down that night. For Bodil, the night brought no sleep. But she did not betray her anxieties. Silently, Lippe and Fride loaded the canoe and pushed off into the water with utmost stealth. At best, perhaps, it would be six hours before their absence was discovered. Even then, the elders might possibly conclude that they were somewhere near at hand and merely romancing. They relied upon Bodil to remain loyal. And upon the Asa to guide them. Old Kuelin's horn was tucked into Lippe's belt.

*

From end to end, Lake Mälaren stretches to around seventy miles. But for the unbelievably naive and fate-filled concept of life held by Ake and his small community they, too, could have made the day long canoe journey to join the descendants of those adventuring Svear who, more than a generation ago, had set out to discover the fabled Island of Plenty. For that was how long it had taken Lippe and Fride – little more than ten hours of paddling – before they came within sight of a large village. Judging by the many lodges they could make out nestling among the low, rolling hillocks and by the number of people they could see dotted here and there around the shore, this was, indeed, a large community. To support so many blood groups, the land before them was surely the Island of Plenty. Unlike on their previous escapade, they made no effort on this occasion to hail any one of the several canoes and rafts in the bay. They paddled unmolested, although not unnoticed, towards the shore. Only when they began to haul the canoe on to the beach did they become aware that their approach had been closely monitored for, as they turned landwards, three men armed with clubs approached them.

'Hei! You are strangers here. Only two?' The language they understood, but were unaccustomed to the dialect that fell upon their ears.

Lippe hesitated before replying, re-running the words through his mind and coming to terms with the slightly different sound.

'Yes. We are only two. From a band further along the lake.'

They were clearly young Svear and unarmed, so the men showed no aggression towards them. Introductions were made by both parties, then Lippe asked, 'What place is this?'

In reply, one of the men whose name, coincidentally, was Ake, said proudly, 'We call it Helgo. We are more than one hundred persons. Come, we will show you our village.'

Having lived all of their lives in only small gatherings, the number, size and scale of things at Helgo astounded Lippe and Fride. Moreover, they saw something they'd never seen before – lodges made of stones, bound together by a mortar of clay and with roofs upon which mosses grew. This village was different from anything the pair had ever seen before. The lodges were laid out, more or less, in lines. The organisation and structure bestowed a certain orderliness that pleased the eye, yet they drew comfort from recognising many of the familiar trappings of Svear life. Even in this seemingly advanced civilisation, the women still wore the characteristic broad hide belt, weighted down with all manner of implements dangling from it. Yet even these common tools of domestic life were made of materials they'd never seen before. None were of bone, few of flint. Mostly, they were made from bronze and iron.

Here was a mix of three 'ages' of civilisation: stone, bronze and iron, although the Svear had had really no separately identifiable Bronze Age as in Southern Europe. The prevalence of articles of bronze coincided with the discovery of iron in the peat bogs. These many marks of advancement left Lippe feeling bewildered, but also made him realise how cocooned his life had been.

During their voyage, Lippe had broached the subject of what their situation might be once they reached their destination. He told Fride directly what he'd already confided to her sister, that he would like to take her to be his woman but, to avoid any further complication, he suggested that they act as if that was already their status. Fride had agreed. And so it was when they introduced themselves to the people of Helgo. On that first night at the big village they made do with a makeshift shelter but, next day, several of the men helped them choose a site and assisted Lippe in gathering the materials he would need to begin constructing a more permanent lodge. At first, the structure was much as his father had used but, over the next seven or eight days, he followed the advice given by Ake, Ottar and Frarad who, together, helped him build a low wall of boulders, surmounted by timbers. He was introduced to the use of nails, the iron pins being pounded into the timbers which formed the base of the new shelter's roof which was then overlaid with thick blocks of peat. Ten days after their arrival at Helgo, Lippe and Fride spent the night in their superior shelter. Ten days had brought them even closer together. They were now, truly, as one. It was on that night that their love was consummated.

The process of acculturation continued for Lippe and his woman. In time, they became an integral part of Helgo's day-to-day existence. Lippe's skill with wood and tools became much admired throughout the clan and Fride had inherited her mother's ability to cultivate fine crops, so making her an appreciated member of the farming community. In time, too, their frequent lovemaking bore its own fruits. Fride became pregnant.

Naming of offspring among the Svear people was never considered too important. After all, the names changed with both time and geography. Here, at Helgo, for instance, Ilf had more commonly become Ulf, and Han expanded to Hans. Odal was both changed and extended to Odils and, later, became Adils. Even the village, over a prolonged period, would relocate to another island and would see its name become Birka.

Lippe and Fride had already agreed that, should they have a son, they would name him Oden but, if it turned out to be a girl, they would name her Bodil – in memory of the survivors of Kuelin's band.

It was early spring when Fride's time came. By then, Lippe had so enlarged their lodge that it comprised three rooms. The wing section he'd added gave space for a separate sleeping area, enabling them to bed down away from the encumbrances of daily living. A further portion of the same extension provided a storeroom for, amongst other things, the nets Ottar had taught Lippe to make during the winter. The roof had also been extended to provide a common cover to all three apartments, maintaining the ridgeline and form of the original roof which always looked so sleek when the lodge was approached from the top end of the street. The low stone walls were now two cubits higher and extended in a broad arc around the front of the lodge to enclose the fire pit and give shelter from the crosswinds to anyone seated on the two driftwood logs which had been dragged into position on each side of the fire. It was in the sleeping area that Fride now lay, her contractions coming more frequently and producing in Lippe a heightening of excitement as he ran to fetch Els who would act as midwife, a task she'd undertaken many times among the Helgon Svear. Water was already being heated. No longer was it necessary to heat stones in the heart of the fire for dropping into water pots to warm the water; containers of beaten iron were filled with water and sat directly on top of the fire. Els came into the lodge carrying a hide wrapper that enclosed the various accoutrements of her role in the village, from small pinches of herbs to knives of three different shapes and sizes. She and Fride made a good match, for Els was a large woman who waddled slightly as she walked. Her big, round face beamed from below the dark hair that she always wore bunched in ties behind her neck. In these final stages of labour, Fride appeared to be almost as large as the midwife as she lay like a basking seal on the hides that normally served as under-robes on the couple's bed.

Lippe was facing a dichotomy in the choice between

staying with his woman during this most important time of birth and fleeing to some far corner of the village where he would be removed from the urge to break in upon Els, disrupting the process of bringing his first progeny into the world. In the event, he chose the latter option and sought out the man who had become his mentor over these past moons, Ottar the netmaker.

'Hah! I know how you feel. I was the same the first time.'

'I hope she'll be all right. She's so young.'

'Oh, that's never a problem. Not for Els. My Gritte was only fifteen summers for the first. She screamed a lot and I wanted to run to her but there was no need. Sometimes, of course, it can be difficult but, most times, it works out fine.'

'Do they suffer great pain?'

'Mmm. It's tough birthing. Even a little runt has bigger shoulders than the hole they have to go through. But I'm here and you're here and the women who birthed us made it through, didn't they?'

Although, understandably, Lippe remained apprehensive, Ottar's words brought some degree of reassurance. At the older man's instigation, they began to walk slowly back towards Lippe's lodge. The lad winced as Fride's cries lanced through the morning air to penetrate the whole of his being. Ottar threw an arm around the young man's shoulder, so encouraging him to continue their walk. They could hear Els rallying Fride with loud exhortations as a piercing yell erupted from the throat of the young mother-to-be. Lippe's eyes screwed involuntarily and Ottar squeezed his shoulder in lieu of apt words that refused to form in his mind. It was over, they knew. A moment's silence terminated with the unmistakable cry of an infant. Lippe burst from the yoke of Ottar's arm and bounded towards the door of the lodge. In the relative dimness of the sleeping chamber he first laid eyes on his son.

'The Asa be honoured!' he bellowed at the top of his voice and, as Els cleanly cut the umbilical cord from the placenta and tied its end, he bent over with outstretched arms to receive the little bundle of life, no bigger nor any heavier than a good-sized lake fish. Cradling Oden between his palms he raised the baby towards the roof timbers and repeated his praise to the deities then, without further utterance, gently placed the infant beside Fride. As their eyes met, he smiled at his woman and kissed her tenderly on the forehead.

'Will you leave us now for a time,' Els said, softly but with a firmness that amply conveyed the notion that she was offering him no option.

Ottar had seated himself on one of the logs alongside the cooking fire and, almost casually it seemed, looked up as Lippe emerged from the shadowy interior, raising one eyebrow in silent questioning.

'It's a boy!' Lippe beamed proudly, 'And Fride is well, but she is still bleeding.'

'Don't be afraid for that. It's usual. So! you have a son. That's good. The Asa have treated you well, Lippe.'

Ottar had become a father figure to the young Svear. The older man's twinkling eyes shone from his browned, weather-beaten face, the curls of silver-tinged hair bobbing around his ear lobes as he began to laugh heartily with his hands coming together rhythmically, the fist of his right balling into the cupped palm of his left for, although he had no genealogical link with this emerging blood group, he felt truly grandfatherly happy.

*

Lippe was now a man of twenty summers. Thus far, he and Fride had had no cause to commemorate the latter's sister Bodil by perpetuating her name through their own daughter. They'd had three sons. The second boy was named for Lippe's own father and the third for his 'adopted' father, Ottar. It was upon Ottar's birth that it was brought home to them so markedly. Realising that, once again, the gods had, in their infinite wisdom, denied them the daughter they both now so much sought, they remembered, more vividly than at any time since their arrival at Helgo, Fride's younger sister and her fellow orphan, Oden.

'Life has been good to us here,' Lippe said. 'But we must go back for Bodil and Oden. I promised Bodil that, remember?'

'Yes. I have never spoken to you about it but I knew that, one day, the time would come. Will you talk with the elders or with Ewulf?'

On many occasions they'd consulted Ewulf, the seer. They valued his counsel for they knew that he, like Kuelin of long ago, communed directly with the clan gods.

'I think we both must talk with Ewulf, for it concerns us both,' Lippe continued, 'Perhaps I will suggest to him that we take two of the large canoes. If we put four of our men in each canoe we will make good time but we will also have more than enough space to bring the others back with us.'

Ewulf heard them out then, as was his way, asked them to leave and return the following day at midday. In turn, he would discuss the matter with Frarad, now the senior elder of the band, and would then submit the issue to the gods.

Whatever rigmarole had been transacted between the

Holy Man and the deities in the intervening time, his conclusions were almost totally in line with Lippe's original suggestions. That afternoon, the plan was disclosed to a handpicked group of men, mixing youth with experience in each canoe. They all agreed that the expedition would leave at sun-up next day.

The morning of embarkation was overcast, the sky a palette of dull greys. A light rain fell and, from time to time, the wind blew in short, gasping gusts. Undeterred, the two wooden craft launched on to the lake, the deeply dug paddle-strokes carrying them quickly out into the channel that led to the open waters. As the voyage progressed, Lippe was reminded of his efforts of four years earlier. To fishermen who rarely took their little vessels out of sight of their island home, the hour upon hour of paddling tested muscles that were unaccustomed to the prolonged activity. Shoulders, hips and ankles ached. Hands began to blister. Almost perversely, the physical onslaught brought a smile to Lippe's face as he recalled these once familiar feelings. By early afternoon the weather had improved and spirits were lifted; the more so when Lippe advised the two crews that they were within sight of their objective. No outpost warned of their approach but it was not long before the eight figures, milling around as they made safe their canoes, attracted some attention from the tiny, sleepy enclave.

It was inevitable that, at some stage, Lippe would come face to face with Ilf. The moment came sooner than he expected and the reception given to these men from Helgo was not a warm one.

Almost as if drawn in lines for battle, the members of the two communities faced one another. Lippe raised his hand in greeting to Bodil yet, whilst she acknowledged his sign, each was somehow constrained from moving any closer than the respective disposition of their clan lines. As Lippe scanned the row of faces that represented his former transitory home, he detected that both Han and Sten were absent; that Oden stood almost as tall as Ake, next to him; that Ilf's arm rested on Bodil's shoulder in a familiar way and that the total number of faces now peering towards him showed no increase in the adult population of the little band since his departure. The bedraggled group of fisherfolk seemed a forlorn caravan compared with the auspicious and blossoming village at Helgo.

It was Ilf who spoke first: 'Why have you come back? You are not welcome here.'

'I have come because I promised Bodil that I would.'

Removing his arm from Bodil's shoulder and giving her a sideways glance before addressing himself to his peer once more, Ilf replied: 'Bodil is my woman now. She will remain here with me.'

'Maybe so, but I would like to talk with her.' Then, directly to Bodil, 'Fride sends her greetings and longs to see you. Won't you come back with us. The gods have treated us well and we live—'

'No! I have told you! She stays here!' Ilf cut in, his voice rude and exhibiting an obvious irritation.

'Have you no voice, Bodil? What do you say?' asked Lippe, again directly to his own woman's sister.

'I will remain here with Ilf. Always.'

A pregnant pause followed, during which Lippe stared at the ground. He hadn't been prepared for this.

'And you, Oden? How about you?'

The tall youth shifted his weight uneasily from one foot to the other then replied, 'I too, will stay here. I am needed for trapping fish. Since Ilf's father and Sten were drowned below the ice—'

Lippe's head shot round on hearing this news, his outburst interrupting Oden's explanation: 'They're dead? Both dead? How long?'

'Yes. Both gone. Last winter.'

'That's bad. How do you eat?'

It was old Ake who joined the conversation, 'We still fish. My legs are not so good now, but with Ilf and Oden, together we catch many fish.'

It was clear from their expressions and the unspoken, mysterious language of the body that Ake and Oden were as father and son. That Oden should make a life of his own choosing was to be expected, but how would Fride react should they return without Bodil? Lippe found her apparent determination to remain with Ake's band hard to accept, but that she should have become the woman of the spiteful Ilf was beyond all reason. In desperation, Lippe made one last gamble, 'Here on this island there is a stone on which the gods wrote to your forebears. They told of a land of plenty and many left here in a great act of faith to find it. We, before you, have come from that place. Fride and me, we found it by chance. There, the village is very large and contains many things you have not seen before. We have seen that you have some canoes and we have brought large ones. Why don't you leave this place, all of you, and come with us?'

Several of the listeners slowly shook their heads and Ilf, once again, took the spokesman's role: 'No, Lippe, we will not come with you. We live here, we will die here. We are not as you are. Now go. Leave us at once.'

'But we have travelled all day, may we spend the night here?'

'I have already told you. You are not welcome here. Go!'

Resignedly, Lippe looked around his companions,

shrugged his shoulders and waved them back towards the two stowed canoes. From his backwards glance at Bodil he thought he detected a distant sadness in her eyes, but then she was gone.

Lippe's fellow boatmen shared his disappointment and sadly, watched by Ake, Ilf and Oden, the canoes pushed off once again on to the lake.

After her first tearful moments, Fride's reaction to the news of her sister was entirely philosophical.

'I don't think Ilf is a good man for her, but she was always different from me in everything. If they are happy together in their ancient little world then so be it. We have our own lives to live and we must build a good life for our boys.'

'I suppose you are right,' Lippe acquiesced, 'It doesn't help to look backwards. Even so, it's very strange to think that it's because of Ilf that we are here. The gods work in mysterious ways.'

The voyage back to Ake's commune, non-event as it appeared at the time, became the springboard that launched a new vision in both Lippe and Fride and became the catalyst that forever changed their contribution to life at Helgo. If their renewed vision could be thought the catalyst, the reagent in this reaction taking place within the community was, undoubtedly, the continual influx of new inhabitants. Over the four years the couple had spent at Helgo, the village's population had almost doubled. It was becoming a sizeable town. And new arrivals needed homes. The calls upon Lippe's talents were becoming overwhelming and many were the days when he saw little of Fride or his growing boys. Such was the explosion in creating new lodges, expanding or improving existing ones that Lippe had had to find other able craftsmen to join him in the enterprise. His team of lodge builders now numbered six, himself included. It was not so much any special charisma that marked him out as a natural leader, it was his uncanny aptitude to assimilate new ideas. Four years ago he had never even heard of 'metal', yet already he had become the most highly regarded iron worker in the community. As a consequence, Lippe's bartering ensured that Fride and her brood were well fed, well clothed and wanted for little. As time passed, the little blood group established itself as a major influence in all that really mattered within the elementary politics enacted in the settlement.

It was as if every new situation became a challenge to Lippe. Just one more thing to be mastered. Through the influence of one of the more recent newcomers, he was experimenting with a windsail. He had traded for some tough, woven material that came from the east and suspended it from a frame attached to two canoes that he'd lashed together. The dark-skinned man from whom he'd obtained the cloth gave him the initial clues and, from time to time, suggested some improvements. Lippe's strange craft was a talking point throughout the town, but after several mishaps he'd set the idea on one side. Latterly, he'd discovered something of more practical interest to the common man of the Svear community: a simpler way to make fire.

Like many discoveries, it had occurred by accident. In fact, by two separate accidents that took place several days apart. The first concerned a piece of the sailcloth that had been cut from the large sheet which now canopied Lippe's canoes. Young Oden had taken it to the lake shore, wrapped around a stick, in an over-optimistic attempt to emulate his father's efforts at producing an effective sail. It had become wet and was being dried by the fire when a gust of wind caught it and sent it flopping into the fire pit. On hearing Fride's cry of alarm, Lippe dashed from behind the lodge, where he had been preparing his tools, and pulled the valuable cloth from the fire, stamping at its smouldering edge to extinguish the fire that had just begun to devour it. The glow at its frayed edge was stubborn and, several times, seemed to re-light itself. To most people, this would merely have signalled the need for greater effort in subduing it but, to Lippe, this became a matter for study. He ceased beating at the cloth and watched the burnt edge more acutely, intrigued by the way the already charred cloth seemed to hold its glow and did not yield to his efforts in the way dry grass would have done. Eventually, he played god and crushed the last throbs of life from the glowing fibres.

'We must be more careful in future,' he remarked to Fride, 'Perhaps it is better if the wind dries it.' He returned to his task and, for the moment, the glowing cloth was forgotten.

The second accidental discovery happened at the home of Ottar and Gritte. They had had two daughters, neither of whom had lived to see four summers. To Ottar, Lippe was the son he never had and the young craftsman often gave freely of his time to help the older man improve his dwelling. The current project was an unusual one in that Ottar wanted to build a high-standing fireplace *inside* his lodge, with a form of chimney extending from a hole in the ridge to within three cubits of where the fire would burn. By having the fire raised and this flue device supported on narrow pillars above it, little smoke should hang in layers around the room to burn the eyes. Lippe was fitting large stones together to form the base and was using one of the most useful, yet simplest, of tools he'd devised to help him. It was an iron wedge that he drove into any slight crevice that was appropriately positioned to split the stones into the sizes or shapes he needed. The iron rang as he clouted it, time after time, to reduce each boulder. Ottar mixed the clay and mortared the chosen pieces in place. However, one of the boulders was not stone: it was a nodule of flint and, as the wedge struck it, a small shower of sparks flew from the tip of the tool, to disappear in mid-air as if snuffed out by some invisible hand. Lippe stopped and examined the flint more closely. In splitting apart the nodule, the wedge had left the greater part of the flint with a long, curving edge and, as the metal scraped down over it, sparks were created. Again and again he tried it and, more often than not, the action of metal scraping flint produced sparks.

It was their short-lived duration that prompted the link to Oden's cloth that had fallen into the cooking fire a few days earlier. Lippe's creative mind stirred into action. If he could guide the sparks on to a piece of previously charred cloth, the tiny brands might just have enough intensity to catch the blackened fibres and remain aflame. This was the beginning of the Helgo 'strike-a-light'.

'Ottar!' he exclaimed, his eyes wide with the excitement of the potential he sensed, 'I think I've just found something very interesting.'

'What's that? Another of your little "tricks of the trade" eh?' replied Ottar.

'No. It's more than that. At least I think it could be, if this works. But I need to get back to the lodge to get some cloth.'

'Cloth? Ah, there's no need. Gritte has lots of cloth. How big a piece do you need?'

'Thanks all the same, but I need to find a particular piece

of cloth. I'll be right back.' So saying, Lippe was gone, his legs pumping as he ran the quarter mile back to his own residence, there to retrieve the partly burnt piece of cloth that Fride had hung over a high pole in one corner of their main apartment.

'This is what I needed, Ottar. Can you see? It's been charred along these edges and I think that may be the key to keeping sparks alive. If so, then we'll have a new way of starting fire. Here. Hold this edge taut whilst I strike the flint again.'

Closer and closer to the falling sparks, Ottar held the charred cloth until, at last, a tiny brand landed on it and the fibres suddenly began to glow. As Lippe blew gently on to it the ember glowed more fiercely, eating up the edge of the cloth.

'Hei! We have it!' the younger man exclaimed.

'That's amazing!' countered the older.

'Let's try it with some dried grasses,' suggested Lippe and Ottar nodded, handed him the piece of cloth, and went to a small basket to fetch some of the sun-dried tinder.

'This time, let me try it a different way,' Lippe proposed: 'I'll cut off a small piece and hold it in place against the flint near to the edge.'

As Lippe prepared to strike the flint once again, Ottar bunched the tinder grass on the floor beneath him in anticipation of another success in getting the charcloth alight. His optimism was rewarded as, within three or four strokes, a bright spray of sparks frizzled on to the charcloth and it began to glow. Casting the flint and wedge aside, Lippe dropped the glowing fragment of cloth into the nest of dried grass and both men crouched to blow across it. Without any prior indication of its intentions, the whole bundle suddenly burst into flame.

Once their initial elation had subsided, the project work continued. But that night, Lippe just couldn't sleep. As he shared the knowledge of his discovery with Fride, they lay awake and talked. Lippe would make more of his hard-tipped wedges; Fride would seek out good-sized nodules of flint. Together, they would carefully prepare the important charcloth that made the whole technique possible. Now every blood group in Helgo would have its own simple way of starting their fires. The enterprise would add further to the scope of Lippe's bartering and his strike-a-light firestarter would remain in use for almost two thousand years. Although the basic idea would be modified through the passage of time to take advantage of spring-driven mechanical striking devices, it would not be until Gustav Pasch, another Swede, invented the safety match late in the nineteenth century that the flint-and-steel firestarter would be rendered obsolete.

Three more summers passed. Among the Svear, Helgo was, indeed, a place of plenty. Not only did visiting traders and travellers introduce the idea of the sail: they also acquainted these people with hounds – and their uses both for hunting and haulage. And the domestication of goats, for both their milk and wool. It was this latter extension to agrarian life that so interested Fride and she had, over the past two summers, assembled a small flock of goats which she kept on a stockaded piece of ground not far from her lodge. It was, she claimed, to the regular consumption of goat's milk that Lippe's little blood group owed its good health, resilience and, in particular, its resistance to the epidemic that now appeared to be invading the community. Just how it began, no one knew. But, here and there, people first of all began sneezing and finding difficulty in nasal breathing, followed by the appearance of a red-spotted rash on the body accompanied by a fever. The ancient herbal remedies, so often effective against common ailments, held no sway with this strength-sapping attack. The older people were worst hit, many ultimately succumbing to the illness. Most ominously, Ewulf was the first to die and many thought that the little township was under some kind of curse. That the Holy Man should be taken first had an undermining and demoralising effect upon the community.

Early one morning, Lippe and Fride were awakened by an anguished cry at the doorway of their lodge. It was Gritte.

'Please help us! It's Ottar! He has caught the sickness.'

Dressing quickly, they left the boys asleep and hurried with Gritte to Ottar's bedside.

The elder made no move to rise as the trio entered the large sleeping room. Gritte advised him: 'See, I have brought Lippe and Fride.' Then, turning to the younger couple she begged, 'Is there anything you can do for him?'

Ottar groaned, 'Ugh. Thank the gods that you have come. I fear I have the sickness. All day yesterday I began to feel worse and during the night my throat felt so dry. Now I'm beginning to feel the fever.'

Fride spread her arms to prevent Gritte and Lippe from advancing: 'We should not touch you, Ottar, lest we all should catch it. We will fetch some water from the lake to cool you and I will bring you some goat's milk.'

Throughout the day they came and went while Gritte maintained a constant vigil. Ottar's fever was worsening and he felt death summoning him. He called out to Gritte, 'Fetch Lippe! Quickly!' With tears beginning to well up at the corners of her eyes she burst from the room and had passed only two other lodges when she met Lippe approaching. Waving wildly, she urged him to follow her.

Ottar looked up from beneath drooping eyelids and spoke softly: 'Lippe. Come close, but don't touch me. Already I can hear the Asa calling me to their kingdom. It will be hard for Gritte when I am gone. Will you take care of her?'

Lippe nodded, unable to speak as his throat gagged on saliva.

The dying man continued, 'You have been like a son to me, Lippe. Please take all that I have as yours. And Gritte, too.'

Ottar paused, screwing his eyes shut, then said, 'I would like my staff. Gritte, would you bring it to me.'

Now sobbing loudly, she left the room, to return moments later with the ornately carved staff which she handed to her man.

'No. Don't let it go,' he said, 'Keep hold of it.' She grasped the plain end and Lippe clasped his hand on top of hers. Ottar gave a half smile.

'I wished this day would never come. You have been the dearest people to me. I hope the sickness does not touch you as it has me.'

Ottar's voice became fainter and the two people he'd loved most in life watched as his breathing slowed and finally gave out. Ottar had died.

In all, twenty-seven out of the two hundred and sixty-one who could be counted residents of Helgo at that time were taken by the mysterious epidemic. In a matter of fifteen sunrises, the town had lost its seer, three of its senior elders and eighteen other men and women of more than fifteen summers.

*

Gritte survived Ottar by eight summers then she, too, passed away. For the most part, the time when she'd been grandmother to Fride's maturing sons had been one of happiness as the grey-haired old woman shared with them the stories of her own childhood. It was only through this handing down of life and legend that the Svear knew of their heritage. Their runic scrolls had not yet begun to be written.

Lippe was now one of the chief elders of the clan, their numbers having grown to more than four hundred. No longer did he spend his time in lodge building. Nor did Fride tend her animals, the goats having been supplemented by sheep. It was Kilde, the middle boy, who took on that task. More and more, Lippe's days were spent in the council house, making laws and discussing the welfare of the town with the other elders. Fride had learned the art of sewing, using fine iron needles to thread together the cloths that she traded from travellers from the east. The boys were quickly becoming young men and Oden, in particular, had a yen to travel. He was encouraged in this by the many tales he heard from the itinerant traders and by his father's one real idle-time activity: sailing.

Having perfected the use of the sail on his twin canoes, Lippe had commissioned Per and Ulf, the leading craftsmen from his lodge-building team, to construct a bigger vessel, with proportionally larger mast and sail. And, instead of having to steer always with his paddle, he designed a fixed paddle that could be swivelled to accomplish the same task more easily. The early trials with the new craft indicated that the fixed paddle had not been made nearly big enough to impart the steering required, so a larger one was made, giving the boat greater stability as well as more effective ruddering.

Oden found sailing with Lippe exhilarating and soon mastered the techniques of setting the sail to catch the wind and allowing it to spill when preparing to turn. The boy had one ambition that burned within him above all others: to one day sail to where the lake emptied into the Great Sea that he'd heard about from the travellers. (In time, this would be known as the Baltic). At fourteen summers, he already felt as much at home on water as on land. He was not a big lad. Shorter than his father but with even broader shoulders, the bloodline resemblance was seen only in his features and dark brown hair. His barrel chest, sturdy legs and bronzed body added further to the illusion of a young man who'd spent most of his youth tackling arduous work. He was both strong and courageous, but was also inclined to be both selfish and headstrong, turning his courage into recklessness.

It became more and more difficult for Lippe to meet Oden's constant demands to take the boat on to the lake. The property he'd inherited from Ottar, added to his own substantial holdings, gave him the largest estate in the burgeoning town and, although he undertook little of its maintenance himself, he always had to be on hand to supervise certain elements of the work. Taken together with the many calls on his time by the Council of Elders, there was little left over to spend with Fride and the boys. Some days, he hardly saw them at all. So it was that Oden successfully petitioned his father into letting him take the boat out along with Odils, one of his peers.

As time went by, it required less persuading to get Lippe to agree to his taking the boat and, on each outing, the boys ventured ever farther afield, remaining out on the lake as long as they dared without causing concern. It was incontestably obvious to Lippe, on the next occasion he went sailing with Oden, that the boy's ability in handling the vessel now outstripped his own.

It was about this time that two occurrences took place that hastened Oden's long-held wish. The first was gripping; the second, distressing.

Lippe had gone to the little harbour to meet a merchant whose reputation had preceded him. Oden was there too. Merchant Dubchev told of the gateway to the Great Sea and of the treasures in the eastern lands he'd travelled through. Oden's eyes widened as the merchant embellished his descriptions of some of the customs of these far-off lands with both personal and second-hand anecdotes. Lippe, too, was impressed. To the point that, there and then, he mentally assented to Oden's comment that 'we must go there some day.'

The swarthy trader, with almost black hair that fell to his shoulders, commanded their full attention whenever he spoke. A scar which ran across his left cheek to just below the eye testified to his adventurous life. Dubchev was from the land of Rus, from a society that, in many ways, had progressed far beyond that seen in Sverige.

Whilst they stood listening to the trader, two canoes beached nearby. Each was manned by a fisherman that Lippe knew well. But, while one canoe exhibited the sleek lines of Helgo's fishing vessels, the other was a more primitively hewn and smaller craft. In addition to the fishermen, the vessels contained two women. In truth, one woman and a girl, one in each canoe.

Hans, the man Lippe knew better of the two, spoke first, 'We were fishing far down the lake when we found these two. They were exhausted from paddling. They were fleeing from a small village because they have little food.'

Their emaciated condition suggested that their shortage of food had not been only recent.

Hans continued, 'There has been much trouble at their village and they stole this old canoe. They were very afraid when we approached them but, after a while, they spoke your name. The older one claims to be the sister of your woman. And the other is her child.'

Lippe stared at them, aghast. As a mixture of emotions coursed through him, he stepped towards the unkempt figure before him, his arms outstretched, 'You're Bodil?'

'Yes,' the woman replied, breaking into tears and burying her head in his chest.

'Dubchev, you must excuse us. We will talk with you later. Come! Oden, bring the girl. We must go to Fride at once.'

The reunion at Lippe's large lodge was emotionally supercharged. There was so much to say. So many questions to ask. But, in these first moments, little was said. Tears flowed freely as Fride comforted both her sister and the forlorn girl who clung to her mother's wrap.

Lippe, in his usual way, took command of the situation and summoned Kilde and Ottar.

The Svear elder spoke urgently to his sons: 'Kilde! Fetch some milk. Ottar! Run to Gustav's and bring some fresh fish. Oden! Build up the fire and warm the pots.'

Lippe himself returned to join Fride and their fugitive guests.

With a change of clothing and some food in their bellies, the women began to speak more freely of the traumatic events that led to their throwing themselves at the mercy of the lake. Old Ake had died in the winter before last and, since then, the little band had become less diligent in its regard for proper measures in securing and maintaining its ongoing supply of food. What could only be guessed at as some form of food poisoning had decimated the village, two of the women and Ilf dying within the first few days of its onset. Among the remnant, tempers became short as each looked to his or her own survival. It was at this low point of morale that Bodil made her decision. Her son of nine summers had already died and so she took her daughter, whom she'd named Kael and, during the night, stole away in one of the two canoes the band had owned. Her action was, possibly, a selfish one. But if she was to die it would not be amongst the bitterness that now enveloped the little village. If she was to have any hope at all it would come from the direction in which she'd seen Lippe and his comrades paddle their large canoes many summers ago when, with sadness, they'd visited Ake's village. The gods had been kind to her. Once more, Lippe's lodge extended its hospitality to a widow in time of need.

Two days had passed before Lippe and Dubchev were able to continue their conversation. Eventually, the merchant broached the subject of his return voyage to the river Luga and onwards into Rus. The picture he painted was a masterpiece in colour and he applied his brushstrokes with unbridled enthusiasm.

Lippe explained, 'I would dearly love to come with you, Dubchev, but my responsibilities here prevent me from leaving Helgo for such a long time. Also, as you know, Fride's sister and her daughter will now make their home with us and it would be unthinkable for me to ask Fride to excuse me at a time like this.'

'Yes,' Dubchev smiled, 'It would not be good for you to leave here. I know you are a man of great importance. But your boy, Oden. He seems to want to venture on the seas. Would you consider—'

'Oden? He's but a boy,' Lippe burst in to stall the merchant's flow, 'He couldn't possibly go with you.'

'Hah! Lippe, the great weight of your responsibilities makes you like an old man,' Dubchev countered, 'and you forget what you told me, eh? You were how many summers when you yourself came to Helgo?'

'I know, I know. But that was different,' replied Lippe defensively, 'That was a short canoe trip of around forty miles. You are talking about taking him to the Great Sea and on to Rus.'

'Yes. And bringing him back. Bringing him back a wise man. And, with respect, honourable Lippe, it would not be the first time that I have looked after a young man on my voyages.'

'One thing you forget, perhaps. He is my oldest boy and very dear to me. And you're asking me to allow him to depart for how long? Four moons maybe? And with a man that we have known so short a time?'

'Well, perhaps. But he and I have talked many hours these past days when you were not here. I like him. I think he's ready to look at a bigger life than you have here at Helgo. Honourable Lippe, you could not give him what I could give him on even one voyage.'

Lippe's gaze held that of the merchant, eye to eye, for some moments, then he said, 'Maybe so, Merchant Dubchev, but I must think about this. I will discuss it with Fride.'

'And with Oden?' the man from Rus suggested.

'And with Oden,' Lippe agreed, if somewhat reluctantly.

Bodil and Kael were asleep. For the time being, they

occupied the large sleeping room which normally housed the three boys, the latter having installed themselves in the lodge formerly belonging to Ottar and Gritte. As she looked upon her sister's deep slumber, one thing began to gnaw at Fride's mind. Having put Bodil very much out of mind for so long, she began to wonder anew at her sister's decision not to accompany Lippe when he had returned to Ake's band to find her. It was one of the first things she asked when Bodil awoke.

Without any sign of embarrassment, the younger woman replied, 'It was hard for me to see Lippe go. Fride, you will never know how hard it was then. But I was so afraid. Afraid of what Ilf might do. He was much younger when you knew him and was a good man. But after he took me to his lodge he became worse. Often he hurt me. It was because he believed Lippe stole you from him. And our two children were not born of love. Many times he forced me to lie with him and one night even pinned me down and tied a stake across my mouth then bound me to stakes in the ground before he took me like an animal. Often, I wanted to run away but I was so afraid. He was not a man like Lippe. I could tell you many things but I hope...' Her voice trailed off as she buried her face in her hands.

'How awful,' Fride gasped, unable to come to terms with a situation that was totally foreign to her. 'You must try to forget him, Bodil. As for me and Lippe, we think of you only as our own. Life here in Helgo is good. You will see.'

The matter was never again raised between them. Only to Lippe did Fride disclose the sad tale, and at that, only after some days had passed.

The three women were seated around the outdoor fire

pit when Lippe returned. He nodded to them and, with a smile directed at Kael, said, 'You look so much better already. I think the air here must agree with you.' Then, to his own woman, 'Fride, I must talk with you. It is a matter of some importance. Shall we walk for a few moments?'

Taken a little by surprise, Fride excused herself to follow her man as he turned away from the lodge.

'What can be so important? Is it something to do with Bodil?' she inquired.

'No. Not Bodil,' he replied. 'It's Oden.'

'Oden? He's not in some trouble?'

'Not exactly that. But we need to make some decisions about him. I'll tell you plainly. It's to do with Merchant Dubchev, the man who brought the special cloth and the new metals from Rus. He has offered to take Oden with him on his next voyage.'

'But – we hardly even know this fellow.'

'I know, I know.'

'Aha. Then you have already made the decision?' she asked sharply, folding her arms and standing aloof.

'Not so. Come now, Fride. It's a big decision. I wanted that we should discuss it. The two of us.'

Fride fell in alongside him once again and asked, 'And just how long would our son be gone with this man? All summer?'

'Well, almost,' Lippe replied, the tone of his voice betraying that he, himself, was not entirely against the proposal.

'And why would you, his father, even entertain such an idea? What if he never returns?'

'There are good reasons and also some things not so good, I agree. Maybe you should discuss it with Merchant

Dubchev yourself. As for me, I think he's a good man. He will take care of Oden and the boy will learn much from seeing other lands.'

'But he's not yet fifteen summers,' Fride defended.

'Exactly! He's almost a man! Oh, never mind. I'll tell the trader to forget it,' Lippe said, with what seemed like finality.

'No. I'm not saying that,' Fride continued. 'But I should like to know more about this Merchant Dubchev. As you say, I will talk with him myself.'

'If you wish.'

'Does Oden know of this?'

'No. At least, I don't believe so.'

The boy was at the lodge when they returned, so Fride took the opportunity to probe, 'Have you been with the traders again today?'

'Yes,' Oden replied, 'and Merchant Dubchev took me on to his boat again. It's wonderful. So much bigger than ours.'

'Mmm. That's good,' Fride responded, 'Did he offer to take you on the lake in it?'

'No. I would love to. But I fear he is much too busy for that.'

Satisfied that he seemed to be unaware of the proposition concerning his immediate future, Fride dropped the subject. But she would make a point of meeting this Dubchev at the earliest opportunity.

Dubchev was a trader. And a wealthy one. He was well practised in peddling his wares. So it was that he impressed Fride as much as he had her man. It was agreed. Oden would be aboard the boat when it left Helgo, not on the next day but the one after.

It was Lippe who broke the news. But not to Oden

alone. He called all three of his sons together to explain his decision. It made him reflect on his boys in a new way. Here was Oden, who loved the water and took every chance to be upon it, about to become the helper to a far-sailing trader. Then there was Kilde, little more than a summer younger, whose outlook on life was entirely different. A softly spoken youth with ruddy complexion and his mother's fair hair, he loved his animals and would spend all day with them were it not for the requirement to do his share of fetching firewood. He'd raised two lambs on his own when their mother had died shortly after the birthing. Finally, there was Ottar. A summer younger than Kilde, he was more like Oden in looks but had the temperament of his father. He was a compassionate boy, always looking after those who were younger or less able than himself. In all, this seemed to Lippe to represent a curious mixture to have come from the same mating. In time, he guessed, each would take a different part in the play of life as it moved through its acts.

There was no outward show of jealousy on the part of Kilde or Ottar when Lippe spelt out the proposition made by Merchant Dubchev. There was only joy. Joy for Oden and the privilege that would be his. And almost outright disbelief on Oden's part. He was beside himself in anticipation of the days ahead.

Fride and Bodil became close companions once again. It was as if the intervening years had been wiped away and they were once more the two laughing, chattering sisters who played fourstones in a little cove at the farthest reaches of the lake from where they now shared the daily tasks that typified life in this ever-growing Svear town. Kael, like her namesake of bygone days, showed a keen interest in growing and cultivating just about anything that she could find to grow and cultivate. She often spent time in the fields with Kilde. He told her all he knew about his animals; she reciprocated with her knowledge of plants. More and more, young Ottar became his father's shadow, sometimes pleading with him to be allowed into the Council of Elders to hear what the wise men of the town had to say. Normally it was forbidden but, as a concession to Lippe, the other men agreed that, when matters weren't of too serious a nature, the boy could sit with them. Although he could understand well enough what the town's sages were saying, Ottar could seldom fathom their ramifications. Together, Lippe's household looked forward to the day of Oden's homecoming. Almost four moons were to pass before they could rejoice in seeing their returning kin once more.

Dubchev had been right. Oden was the wiser for his experience and none the worse in any other way and was only sorry that the merchant had to cut short his stopover, lest the onset of winter prevent his little craft from completing the return to Rus before the storms began and the waters became icy. The adventure left Oden with many memories, but the one visible legacy was his outfit. Completely out of place among his Svear comrades, and often the subject of their jibes, his Rus clothes were a constant reminder to him of the good times he'd had with Dubchev. Lippe and Fride ignored his bravado and, after a time, he wore the strange garments less and less. Despite the bitterness of the cold and the wrath of the winds, that winter was one of the happiest Lippe's enlarged blood group could remember.

*

In each of the next two summers, Oden again travelled with Merchant Dubchev across the Great Sea. When he returned from his latest exploit however, he surprised the people of Helgo for, with him, when he alighted from Dubchev's boat, was a Rus beauty who had become his woman. None like her had been seen in Helgo before. Not that her natural radiance outshone that of the best of Helgo's women; it was that her lips, cheeks and eyes bore colours that enhanced their form and made her appear as some would imagine a goddess. Against the plain faces of the Svear women, she stood out like a butterfly on a cabbage leaf.

Perhaps prompted by her unusual appearance, the implications of Oden's choice became all too apparent. For the first time in the known history of the Svear people, a man had taken a woman who was not a Svear.

Her name was Katrin. She was taller than Oden, with high cheekbones and her hair was completely black. One woman who saw them pass remarked, 'It's a bad thing that Oden has done. What kind of offspring will they produce?'

At first, even Lippe and Fride were cautious, the more especially as they found it difficult to converse for, unlike Merchant Dubchev who had mastered the Svear language, this woman had not. Katrin had learned a little of the Svear tongue from Oden and he a little of hers, but her tiny vocabulary limited any detailed inquiry Lippe and Fride may have wished to have made. The days that followed were difficult, particularly as no separate shelter was available to house the newly arrived couple. Some rearrangement of the sleeping quarters at Ottar and Gritte's old lodge was made but it was, at best, makeshift.

Despite the difficulties Katrin had in communicating, her limitations didn't prevent her from making the most of every opportunity to try to befriend Fride, Bodil and Kael. She often lent a willing hand to many of the regular jobs she saw the women doing but, peculiarly, only in the mornings. Each afternoon, she adhered to her practice of donning her best garments and applying colour to her face, thereafter to sit herself down to create intricate patterns in a form of needlework. On some days she would walk with Oden to the little harbour or along the nearby shore.

Kael showed a keen interest in Katrin's box of face colours and in the way she applied these to emphasise her features.

'You try?' the Rus girl offered one day. 'I help you.'

Kael smiled and nodded apprehensively, whereupon Katrin gave her the little box. The miniature chest was, itself, a work of art. Made from a sweet-smelling wood that was pink in colour, it had two shiny metal fixings that allowed a top cover to swing open and closed, a further fastening retaining it when closed. Kael had seen nothing like it before. Inside were trimmed bird feathers of various lengths and thicknesses, together with small, hollowed wooden blocks that contained the different colours.

'This here,' explained Katrin, as she dipped the blunt end of a quill into a red pot and began to draw it carefully but firmly across Kael's lower lip. The girls giggled. Both lips completed, Katrin selected another feather and, with a dip into an almost black pot, held Kael's cheek as she began making a sweeping line above her left eye. Soon, the Svear girl was painted as expertly as her Rus friend. When Katrin took a piece of highly polished metal from inside a fur-lined bag and offered it to Kael, the reflection she saw startled her. Not only did the enhancement achieved by the colours make her look unreal, but it was the first time she had seen her reflection other than from pools of water. For a long time she said nothing, turning the plate this way and that to look at her image from different angles. What she saw pleased her.

'It's good. I look so...' She paused, searching for a suitable description.

'Beautiful,' Katrin said, completing the sentence for her.

'Do all the women in Rus do this?' Kael asked. Katrin's quizzical expression indicated that she didn't understand and it took a combination of sign language and simple words before Kael got her meaning across. Their conversations were often like this.

Conversations of a different kind took place between Lippe and Oden. The father, so glad to have his son's company, commandeered him at every spare moment to ask about his latest experiences in Rus.

'There are some very big lodges there,' Oden explained. 'I have seen some that are as high as four of the largest lodges here in Helgo, one on top of another. These are castles, all made with stones and with very thick walls.'

'Why would anyone want to build such a dwelling?' inquired Lippe.

'It is to make a safe place to go if barbarians come, attacking the people. In the castles there are many strong men, the soldiers, who are well trained in the use of spears, axes and other weapons.'

'That's a wise idea. For a long time we have discussed something like this in our council meetings here in Helgo. Soon after you left on this last voyage with Dubchev, we began exercises to be prepared for such an attack. We have been fortunate that no barbarians have ever attempted to raid the town, but maybe one day, who knows? The younger Frarad is teaching new skills with many types of weapons, but we don't build castles like you describe.'

'Maybe that's not so important when you are on an island. The best thing is to have lookouts at all times who can give warning of boats approaching, especially if they look to be filled with armed men.'

It was during one of these serious debates, on the day that Kael had been experimenting with Katrin's colours, that Bodil came rushing towards them, obviously displeased.

'Do you know what your woman has done to my daughter?' she bellowed at Oden, then rhetorically continued, 'She's made her look like a Rus barterbody.'

It was a strange description. A 'barterbody' was a prostitute and Bodil had certainly never seen a Rus one. But the slur was not lost on Oden; he quickly translated it to mean 'a girl of ill repute like your woman.' It took all of his self-control to prevent his tongue from giving full vent to the anger and indignation he felt. Instead, he countered with, 'You mean she's been transformed into a beauty like Katrin?'

'Huh! You can tell your Katrin that I don't want her to go near Kael again. The girl is pretty enough without all that stuff on her face. This is Helgo, not Rus.'

Lippe tried to rescue the situation. 'I think maybe that's going a bit too far, Bodil. I'm sure Katrin meant no harm. It's clear that in Rus they do things differently.'

'Maybe so,' replied Bodil, 'but we've been through enough, Kael and I, and I don't want this kind of influence on her.'

'Please don't spoil their friendship,' entreated Oden. 'I'll talk with Katrin when I get back.'

Bodil glared at him then stomped off, leaving the two men sheepishly looking after her as if she'd insulted them both personally.

'You see what I mean,' Oden said, picking up the conversation again, 'Rus is quite different from here.'

They returned to the topic of defence of the town and Oden sketched in words the various weapons in use in the land Dubchev had introduced to him. He spoke, too, of the way the Rus soldiers trained for battle and Lippe began to develop a new respect and admiration for this place that had so enthused his son.

For ten or so sunrises, Bodil had gone out of her way to ensure that Kael had little opportunity to spend time with Katrin. There were times, too, when the Rus girl wandered over to the fire pit where Fride and Bodil were sitting chatting as they worked at preparing food or were engaged in some other sedentary task. Although nothing was said directly, it was clear that Bodil had taken a dislike to Katrin. She excluded her from conversation, talking so fast in the Svear tongue that the foreigner could not possibly understand. When she offered to help, Bodil would get in ahead of Fride with some comment like: 'We Svear have a certain way of doing that,' or 'I don't think you'd do it this way in Rus.' It was very hurtful and Katrin became more and more aloof, her emotions confused and increasingly in turmoil. Although Fride had not openly turned against Katrin in the way her sister had, as the discriminatory rejection continued, so she, too, began to feel lacking in warmth towards her son's chosen woman.

Katrin shared nothing of her inner hurt with Oden. After all, these were his people and she, the stranger, would have to find some way of becoming accepted among them. The situation became unbearable, however, on the day that the town was having its Midsummer celebration. Kael had encouraged Katrin to take part in a race amongst the women in which a seabird's egg was to be carried on a wooden spoon by each of the runners. The winner would receive a basket of eggs that had been elaborately decorated in natural dyes; the runner who came last would be ceremoniously beaten by the spoons of the others, all the way back to the starting line. This was known among the Svear as 'taking the wooden spoon.'

One of the older women, Els, was to give the hand-clap that would start the race but, as the entrants milled around in readiness to line up for the signal, Bodil smiled at Katrin and took her spoon, holding it in front of her.

'Do you know what this is called?' she asked the Rus.

'Paddle?' replied Katrin innocently.

'No. It's a spoon. A special symbol here in Helgo. I'm sorry, but only the Svear women who know of its significance can take part.' She smiled again at Katrin and, confiscating the spoon, turned towards the line just in time to steady her gull's egg before Els banged her hands together, accompanied by a loud 'hei-ja.'

Oden had already positioned himself near the finish mark to cheer on his woman over the final stages. He couldn't see her in the ragged line of bobbing runners, now past the halfway point. Nor did he see her running from the excited, shouting crowd as she fled, in tears, back to the dwelling.

The next day, frustrated, Oden sought out Lippe. 'Father, you have not been to Rus so you can't begin to imagine what it is like and how people live there. Here, in Helgo, it is very hard for Katrin. She is not as other women here and the way of life is strange to her.'

'*The* way of life? You mean *our* way of life,' Lippe interrupted.

'That may be so,' Oden went on, 'but it is too different

from the way she knows. I fear we must leave when Dubchev returns. It will be easier for me in Rus than for her here.'

Lippe said nothing. He stood with his back to his son, staring off into the distance.

Sensing his father's anguish, Oden ventured, 'I'm sorry, father. But she is my woman. I must care for her.'

Lippe's thirty-four summers seemed like forty-four. Turning to face Oden, he asked, 'What will you do there? How will you live?'

'I haven't thought. But there are possibilities.'

'Hmmf, possibilities? It will take more than that to build a lodge and bring home food.'

'We will need no lodge. Katrin's father has a small castle with many rooms. Perhaps I will help him with his horses.'

'His what?'

'Horses. They're large animals. Like the elk, but with no horns. Men ride on them and use them to pull heavy loads. You wouldn't understand, father.'

It was becoming clear to Lippe that he was getting out of his depth in pursuing the matter. These trips to Rus had shown his son things that were from a different life. A life that Lippe wished he, too, could embrace. It would be like comparing Helgo with Kuelin's village. The new against the old. The progressive against the backward. He sensed that his only chance of maintaining any kind of relationship with this boy he loved so much would be to take a more positive attitude.

'Then perhaps you're right. A day will come when many of our people will travel to other lands. It is the way life must be. Already you have said that in Rus there are things we don't have here. Dubchev also says so. But, Oden, you must go there not only for yourself. From time to time, come back to Helgo and bring us some of the new ideas. That way, we will grow wiser, too.' In his heart, Lippe was not yet convinced that it was the best decision, but he seemed powerless to change the inevitability of the situation. Oden's actions spoke louder than any words he could have mustered just then. He embraced his father tightly and the two men stood on the fringe of the settlement clinging to one another for some moments before walking, slowly, back to the lodge. When they reached the smoke-blackened entrance to the large lodge, Lippe bade his son wait outside while he fetched something from inside. In a few moments he reappeared, clasping a small drinking horn which he thrust towards his son.

'Here! You must take it! It belonged to the old seer who first instructed me in the ways of the Asa. Always keep it with you, then the Asa will be your guide – just as they have always guided me.'

That winter was a mild one and, to Lippe and his folks, appeared to pass very quickly. Too quickly. Before they realised it, the lake shore was once again busy with both their own fishing boats and those of the itinerant traders. The weather, at least, was pleasant on the day that Oden and the unhappy Katrin boarded Dubchev's sturdy craft; the mood was not. Six days after its arrival, the vessel once more pulled away from the small harbour. As it distanced itself from the shore, those who waved to the departing couple felt a sadness at their kin's going. They had no Holy Bible to instruct them that 'A man will leave his father and mother and cleave to his wife, and the two will become one flesh, no longer two but one.' The cleaving they could accept unreservedly, for that was the way of the Svear, but the leaving they found hard to bear. Their sadness would have been replaced by an even deeper grieving had they foreknown that Oden would never again return to Helgo. Even the knowledge that he would become a successful and wealthy trader in the blossoming village of Nevagorod, close to the spot that would one day become a town renowned throughout the world, would have brought little consolation. In those days, the village that would become St Petersburg was at a trading crossroads between Europe and Byzantium. It was but two days travel from the little castle on the banks of the Luga.

Fifteen moons had passed since Oden and Katrin left Helgo. The springtime had passed, too, and there had been no customary visit from Merchant Dubchev. Consequently, there was no word from Helgo's first expatriate. By contrast, the young Ottar was becoming more and more Lippe's companion. Growing in both stature and wisdom, the youth showed an increasing interest in the politics of the town. On these warm, early summer evenings, he and Lippe sat around a small glowing fire set in the outside fire pit and talked of matters concerning the welfare of their fellow citizens. Lippe enjoyed that. One thing concerned him, however, about his serious-minded son, although he never mentioned it to the lad. It was that, caring and loving as he was, he appeared to show little romantic interest in members of the opposite sex. It could be, Lippe thought, that this was an area of Ottar's growing into manhood that was not yet mature. The same could not be said for his brother Kilde. He and Kael were almost inseparable and it was no surprise when, that summer, Kilde suggested to Lippe that he would like to build his own lodge.

'It's not that I'm unhappy sharing with Ottar,' the young man explained, 'but I feel that it is time for me to be on my own.'

'On your own?' Lippe teased, 'Why would you want to go off and live by yourself?'

'It's just that I need more space, father.'

'For what? Are you going to bring your animals into the lodge?'

Not as bright as his younger brother, it took some time – and several baited comments from Lippe – before Kilde abandoned his evasive line of argument and, in bashful admission of defeat said, 'Well, myself and Kael, we want to make a shelter for ourselves.'

Lippe beamed at the boy, the twinkle in his eyes betraying that he'd realised all along the real intentions in Kilde's mind. 'She's a good woman, Kilde. You and she, together, will be good for our blood group. It is wise that you take a woman close to our line. She is good with the earth and you with the animals. Together, you can be good for Helgo. Yes, I will help you to build your lodge. In the Council we will discuss a piece of land for you that will be better than in the bottoms where most of the free land is. Now we must also tell Fride.'

'Of course. And Bodil, too,' the relieved youth added.

Once Kilde's intentions had become known and a small, but good, piece of land decided upon, there was no shortage of helpers to carry the boulders needed to form the base walls of the shelter. In a matter of days the main structure was complete and it was Lippe, himself, who performed the finishing touches to the small, but adequate, new lodge. In keeping with the age-old custom of his people, Kilde took Kael to his lodge on three successive nights before it was announced that she was, rightfully, his woman.

To Bodil, the union brought a special joy. Since she had lived twenty-seven summers when Ilf died, she knew that it would be most unlikely that she, herself, would ever have a man again. This was the way amongst the Svear. All her dreams were for her daughter and, for Kael to have found a man like Kilde fulfilled the hope she'd harboured in her heart as she'd watched the two young people grow together since those first days after their arrival at Helgo.

*

Despite the ravages of another infectious epidemic, the population of Helgo had risen to more than six hundred souls in the twelve summers that had come and gone since Kilde took Kael to be his woman. They'd had two sons and two daughters of their own and lived no longer in the town but on the other side of the island. Here, land was more plentiful and, as Lippe had predicted, their combined skills had amply shown that 'they were good for each other.' In farming both crops and livestock, they'd been successful.

Kilde had changed little in all that time. He remained the quietly spoken, shy individual that he'd always been. Kael was the lively one. It was, without exception, she who invited neighbouring blood groups to join with them in their periodic feasts of thanksgiving for the harvesting of a crop; the safe arrival of lambs or kids; or, indeed, any other event that could, with the least stretch of imagination, be made the excuse for celebration. It was during just such a time, having feasted on roast hog accompanied by wild mushrooms, turnips and a brew of mixed herbs that the mood of the evening was devastated by ill tidings. Kael had just recounted the time her man had been cornered by a rampant he-goat and had fallen backwards into a thorn bush. As their laughter pealed across the fields, blown inland by one of Mälaren's gusty squalls, the raucous revellers were stunned to silence when a messenger arrived from the town and, almost breathless, gasped his news: 'It's Lippe. Lippe is...' Still panting, he scanned the semicircle of anxious faces, 'We fear he is dying. He fell at the entrance to his lodge. At first, Fride thought that he had slipped but he did not rise. They have put him on a sleeping pallet but he is not good. Still he breathes, very low, but he has not opened his eyes.'

In the few moments that followed, Kael organised and mobilised all but herself and Kilde, getting some to look after her children; others to see to the fire that still blazed in a fire pit enlarged for the occasion. In what seemed no time at all since the messenger arrived, Kilde and Kael hurried back with him towards Helgo, their hearts heavy but yet each refusing to accept that they would not see alive again the grey-haired old man they both loved so much. But their running was futile; their hope, in vain. Even before the messenger had reached Kilde and Kael's outlying farm, Lippe had died.

Fride was distraught. She, herself, had seen forty-three summers. This was a heavy blow to an old woman.

Although he was the younger son, it was Ottar who took charge of the burial arrangements. He was also one of the youngest of the Svear people at Helgo ever to sit on the Council of Elders. Never having taken a woman, his whole life became dedicated to the welfare of the community. He took the initiative to ensure that this last act of welfare towards his own father would also be to his design.

The procession comprised most of Helgo. Or so it

appeared, as the wailing lines of mourners followed the Holy Man who, like his predecessor, was called Ewulf. All day long men had toiled to prepare the ground and base for what would become Lippe's burial mound, for there was to be no common pit for this champion of the people. He was being accorded the honour due only to those held in highest esteem.

Ewulf called out in strange tongues and waved all manner of paraphernalia in the air as he called upon the gods to bear Lippe safely through the voyage to his afterlife. As the last turf was laid near the top of this artificial bump on the island's landscape, Fride threw herself against the side of the mound, crying in anguish. Before death would, finally, catch up with her too, she would bring to mind many memories – not all of them pleasant ones – of the times she and Lippe had known together. Their exile from Kuelin's band had been occasioned by the utmost brutality and violence. At Helgo they had found peace, prosperity and the love of many friends. They never did have the daughter they'd longed for, but were reunited with Bodil. Their sons: wealthy trader, farmer and statesman, had made their own lives. Tuma and Talna would have been proud.

Part Three
The Warriors

For Addy and Uller

Those who are victorious, no matter how they gain the victory, are never shamed by it before history...
                              Niccolo Machiavelli

It was clever. But it was cruel. And yet, summing it up, it was just nature's way. The hawk had made a wide circle and then, with the sun directly behind it, dropped like a stone until it seemed that it would bury itself in the peat. Running countless calculations through its tiny brain as it sped earthwards, narrowing the distance between itself and its unsuspecting prey, at a speed that was awesome it ascertained the precise moment at which to apply its air brakes. Bucking its tail-end downwards, spreading its pale brown wings at the right angle of tilt and stretching its talons in front of its plummeting body, the hawk swooped in near silence in its death strike. The rabbit spoke twice. First, it gave a piercing scream, not dissimilar to that of a human child experiencing an equally sharp pain. Its final utterance was hardly more than a pathetic yelp.

Still standing beside his horse, holding it tightly reined, Gustav Adolf watched the hawk fly low and parallel to the ground, its prey dangling beneath it like a plumb-bob. Coming to rest, at last, on top of a small rocky outcrop, the hawk began to devour its meal, alertly looking up between snatches at the limp body of the rabbit.

'Strike fast and come at them from where they'd least expect it.' These were the thoughts running through the young king's mind as he lingeringly reflected on the tragedy of nature he'd just witnessed. The 'them' that he had in mind were the Danes; the old enemy: and the Poles; still sore at the incursions led by his father, Karl. The year was 1611 and he'd been on the Swedish throne for only nine weeks. It was time to begin planning for an extension of the freedom that had been won by his grandfather, Gustav Vasa.

Continuing his dreamy surveillance of the meadow, he let his mind summarise events of the past that had been handed down to him.

From the earliest days of its growth towards emergence as a great nation, Sweden had looked to Lake Mälaren as the symbolic mother from whose womb would be born its centres of power, trade and administration. From the old Svear settlements on the western extremities of the lake men and women moved eastwards to establish Birka, the country's oldest town. But, as trade with the merchants of the Volga decreased, so even Birka disappeared. Sigtuna, on the northernmost fingers of the lake, became the next magnet for traders and indigenous manufactories. Then, in 1255, the township of Stockholm was established at the eastern end of the Lake. This town was destined to grow into a considerable metropolis, guarding entry to the lake from the Baltic Sea.

The Svear and Gotar peoples had intermingled to produce the 'Swedes' and the Sami, or Lapps, inhabited isolated pockets of the vast northern region. In the south, the counties or provinces of Skåne, Blekinge and Halland were occupied by the Danes.

Indeed, the powerful kings of Denmark had long been the scourge of their Swedish counterparts and, time and time again, Swedish uprisings against the Danes did little more than dent the supremacy of their strong and wealthy neighbour. Engelbrekt Engelbrektsson led a rebellion in 1434 following disputes over taxes levied by the Danes. In 1471, Sten Sture struck a major blow for Sweden by defeating King Christian at the Battle of Brunkeberg. The last straw of Danish malevolence was played out in 1520 when their king held a great feast in Stockholm for Sweden's leading citizens, lulling them into a false sense of well being and security for, after much eating and drinking, he signalled his troops to converge on the town's main square and massacre its occupants. Although most escaped, eighty-two met their death. Among those killed were the father, brother-in-law and two uncles of a young patriot who was exiled in Denmark. His name was Gustav Vasa, Adolf's grandfather. Escaping from Denmark, he returned to Sweden to raise a retaliatory force and became the country's king in 1523, leading the nation in a major reformation.

'Two generations later, here I am,' thought Gustav Adolf as he saddled up, 'and now it's up to me to set the matter straight, once and for always. We will not be subservient to other kings.'

Although king of the realm, Adolf was still a youth of eighteen years. A precocious and imaginative young man, his general bearing and appearance were impressive. As he turned his horse to head back across the heath, he looked so much the archetypal Cavalier who, within another thirty years, would wreak havoc in England's Civil War. With his ruddy cheeks, smouldering eyes and the beginnings of a shapely moustache, he already effused a mature charisma. His long, curled locks flowed from beneath a wide-brimmed hat set at a jaunty angle as he eased his horse to a trot.

Adolf heard, before he saw, the horse that drummed over the dry heathland towards him. As the galloping beast and its rider bobbed up and down, dipping into little hollows and then caroming over the low rises, Adolf reined in, raising a hand over his eyes to get a better contrast of view in the glaring sun. Only when the rider got within two hundred yards was his identity apparent beyond confusion. It was Ulrich, his mother's cousin. Originally from Leipzig, he now considered himself a fully fledged Swede.

Hardly seeming to drop pace as he raced towards the stationary king, the young man, just a year older than Adolf, raised an arm in greeting then brought up his horse sharply, almost alongside.

'Hei. What's all the fury?' Adolf asked, a smile breaking across his eyes and mouth simultaneously.

'We were worried, that's all. You said you were coming out here on a short ride, but you've been gone for hours.'

'Well,' he drawled, 'Sometimes a man needs space and time to think. And I've been doing a lot of thinking, Uller.' Adolf always used his second cousin's pet name when talking directly to him. And sometimes on other occasions.

Ulrich responded in like fashion, 'That's fine, Addy, but you might at least have said so before you raced off this morning. I don't think it's wise any longer for you to be out in the countryside alone.'

'Hah! Come, come, Uller, I've a good blade and a fast horse.' Then, taking his line in bravado a degree further, the king took off his hat with an exaggerated sweep and, standing high in his stirrups, yelled, 'Come and get me, you lurking Danes!'

Both men laughed and Ulrich shook his head, as much as to say, 'Sometimes, Addy, you're just too much for your own good.'

'Anyway,' the monarch continued, 'Who wants to know? And what's the hurry?'

'It's Axel. He wanted to discuss something. Didn't say what.'

Axel Oxenstierna was Adolf's adviser. He was also one of his closest friends. Inordinately good when it came to reckoning with figures, Axel was 'an old man in a young frame' but, in contrast with his king's often flamboyant behaviour, he brought a steadying influence to their relationship.

'Very well,' said Adolf in a tone of resignation. 'Now, let's see. Yonder tree, standing on its own to the left of the small copse; you see it?'

'The one that's leaning?'

'The very one. I'll race you. First one to touch it wins. Are you on?'

'You know me, Addy. Always ready for a challenge.'

'Right.' Replacing his large, floppy hat and fixing it hard down over his head, Adolf shouted, 'Ride!'

With almost mechanical synchronism, the two horses responded to the yelps, whoops and goads of their respective madcap riders and hammered their way back along the track that Ulrich had so recently travelled in the opposite direction. By no more than a horse-length, the king took the honours.

Adolf was not one to waltz at another's tempo. Exceptionally well educated, he showed a well-honed inquisitive interest in all manner of articles, events and circumstances around him. As he dismounted in the palace courtyard, the loud crack of a Snaphane musket on the other side of the wall swamped his attention and drew him like a fresh cow-pat draws flies.

Leaving his horse in the care of a stable hand, he bounded up a short flight of stone steps to the vantage point of a small portal which overlooked the external exercise field.

'What's the event?' he shouted to the cluster of men who gathered beneath the still hanging cloud of bluish smoke resulting from the weapon's discharge.

'We're having a musket match, Your Highness. Only two men left in. Tomas and Ulf.' This instant summary of the situation was given by the man who instructed the sharpshooters: Willem, the Dutchman.

'Don't let me disrupt you. I'll watch, but I won't wager,' the king shouted back.

Their target was a riksdaler – a Swedish dollar. The coin was held by a split stick pushed into the ground. At thirty paces, it made a tiny mark. So small that the sight-pin of the musket would have obliterated it completely had not the marksman used an 'under aim', meaning that he placed the sight under the target so that he looked along the barrel and sighted the riksdaler just on top of his sight-pin.

Tomas shot his piece first. Following the loud crack and the huge, wafting cloud of saltpetre smoke that lingered above the shooter, there was an audible groan as the two dozen or so onlookers saw the coin unmoved.

Ulf primed his piece and stepped forward to the line.

'Best be prepared to part with the "pot" this time, comrades,' he said, smiling confidently. The 'pot' was a riksdaler from each man who had started in the match.

Ulf was still enveloped in smoke when the cheer told him his boast had not been a hollow one. But only just. The lead ball had clipped the edge of the coin and sent it spinning high and sideways, completely clearing the buttressed wall to go clinking among the cobbles of the inner courtyard.

Adolf beamed. He always admired skill at arms, whether it be sword, dagger, lance or modern musket. Turning from the portal, he removed his soft leather gauntlets and made his way towards the chamber where, he knew, his chancellor would be awaiting his arrival.

'It's the Danes again, I'm afraid,' opened Axel, making

no comment with regard to the king's later-than-expected return. 'They're demanding a payment that amounts to no less than a new version of the "fire tax" of the Vikings. Otherwise, they'll raid our harbours yet again. It'll be another Kalmar disaster unless we can stall them.'

'Axel, today I have made a decision. We will no longer lie down to the Danes. Nor to the Poles. We will repel them. I'll have the troops assembled and ready to march in the morning. Where do our spies tell us they will focus their attack?'

'It's to be Alvsborg this time. Our only western port. Christian is trying to keep us guessing. Kalmar last time, now a switch to the west.' Christian the Fourth was proving to be as pugnacious as his predecessors.

'Mmm. Then we haven't much time. Send out orders for the men to assemble at the midnight hour on Västerdalen field.' For the first time in his short reign, Adolf was being forced to adopt physical warfare in place of his preferred diplomacy. The threat was real. And pressing.

Despite young Adolf's assertion to dispel the threat of the wily Christian of Denmark, the practised astuteness of the Dane was to prove more than a match for the Swede's youthful enthusiasm. It was a woeful month. Not only was Alvsborg lost but, knowing its vital importance to Swedish trade, Christian held the country to ransom. The victorious Dane demanded one million riksdalers in exchange for withdrawing his occupying forces from the port. Axel had to exhaust the national coffers to meet this sum and, in an act of demonstrating his involvement rather than of necessity, Adolf directed his chancellor to donate some of the royal silverware to the cause.

The young king was in an abject mood. He sought solace, not from his adviser and friend Axel, but from a young lady whom he'd courted for some time in the past: Ebba Brahe.

The shafts of sunlight flickered through the leaves and cast wavering golden curtains across the glade as Adolf and Ebba walked shoulder to shoulder, so slowly that their progress along the twig-strewn pathway was hardly more than snail pace. 'You know you've always given me a special inspiration, Ebba. At a time like this, that's what I need most: some inspiration.'

'But what can I say? We used to be so close, you and I. But now we've moved apart. There isn't the same feeling any more.'

'Perhaps not from your side, but I don't believe we've moved as far apart as you think.'

They stopped. Turning to face Adolf, Ebba sighed and looked coquettishly at the man who was now her king. They both smiled.

'That's better,' said Adolf, squeezing her shoulder.

During their perambulatory passage of around three hours of intimate discussion, Ebba somehow managed to trawl from the depths of her bygone feelings for Adolf the revitalising chemistry that he had so wishfully sought from her. When he returned, late in the afternoon, to conduct a formal meeting of his senior army officers, he felt a lift in his spirit that would galvanise his actions in the coming weeks. Just to be with Ebba again had been good for him.

The legacy bestowed upon the civilised world by Martin Luther had launched a new theological movement: Lutheranism. The work of another Martin, thirty years before Gustav Adolf was born, had advanced the cause of the Lutheran Church with some vigour. Martin Chemnitz was largely responsible for writing the *Book of Concord* from which the new cause took its practical guidelines that, allied to the truths of the Bible, became its driving force. Adolf had found this vibrant new form of the Christian Faith appealing and its tenets refreshing. He avidly imbibed all that he could of the Lutheran doctrines and tempered his life with a piety that countered his more earthly responses to calls upon his time and judgement. Faithful and stalwart in his beliefs, Adolf called for prayers even in battle lines within sight of the foe. Thus, he drew inspiration from three sources: from Axel, when he needed practical guidance; from Ebba, when he required emotional strengthening; and from his Lutheran beliefs, when he needed assurance of his convictions in both moral and spiritual matters. In these first years of his reign, an inspiration akin to divine afflatus he sourced from these three repositories to equip him in the best possible way for his task of creating a nation that would upstage its Danish neighbour.

*

Many Dutch and Walloon merchants and artisans came to Sweden in these days. One man, Louis De Geer, became the founding father of what would become a great arms industry. He began by setting up a foundry and workshop near the town of Norrköping. One of the first of this new breed of Swedish gunsmiths to work for him there was Tomas Ulfsson. Over the next century, four more generations of Ulfssons would follow in his footsteps.

De Geer had brought with him a particular expertise that was to revolutionise gunsmithing. He introduced the local smiths, accustomed to building the smooth-bored Snaphane muskets, to an elementary form of rifling. In turn, Tomas explained it to one of his apprentices, Nils

Palme: 'The two grooves are cut all the way down the inside of the barrel. And they twist, slowly, as you can see here.' The master gunsmith lifted the tube to the boy's eye so that he could see for himself, peering down the thumb-sized hole to examine the effect of the spirals. 'For these first ones, Louis has suggested we make the twist to be one half turn over the length of a two cubit barrel. I will show you how we will do it on the rifling bench.'

The rifling bench was an incredible wooden frame that resembled a bed-base. Clamps held the piece of tube that was to become the barrel and various wheels, blocks, screws and other bits of mechanical paraphernalia made up the complement of parts needed to undertake this extraordinary task.

Young Nils let his eyes wander up, down and over the strange contraption for some moments before building up the courage to ask his master, 'And how are the grooves actually cut on the inside?'

'Ah, yes. I'm coming to that. But first of all, you need to see the cutting tool – that's this little piece here.' He drew a small, hardened metal cutter out of a greased ragbag and showed it to the boy.

'Uh-huh. And how long does it take to complete one piece?' the apprentice inquired.

'Well, lad, I've done four now, by myself, and I'd say I'm getting better at it. The last one took just on seven hours.'

'Seven hours?' the boy gasped.

'Ah, yes,' Tomas assured him, 'but it's well worth it. These guns are really accurate. Can knock a rabbit at a hundred paces.'

'Wow! I'd like to see what one of Willem's men could do with a piece like that!'

'Yeah. Might give us a chance of taking out some of

Christy's horsemen next time, before they get to do much harm to our boys.'

'You're right,' the apprentice concurred, 'Adolf's men need all the edge they can get. Else we'll all finish up as Danes.'

Through his parliament, the Riksdag, the pulpits of the clergy, and by any other means, Adolf was promoting his rallying cry: 'Sweden for the Swedes!'

'Now look, boy, I'll show you how it's done,' Tomas said, fixing the barrel in place on the bed of the rifling bench. 'We fix this cutter to the end of the long rod and tighten it fast. Then it's clamped into this index wheel. That's to make the grooves exactly opposite each other.'

The master smith carried on with his instruction, showing Nils how the rod was inserted into the barrel and slid to the farthest end.

'We make the cuts on the drawback and this second wheel moves in a spiral as we take a shaving off the metal inside the barrel. We have to do that many times until the groove is deep enough. See?'

'It's ingenious,' the apprentice beamed, itching to take over the job from his master. 'But I can see why it takes so long. Pity we can't hitch up a donkey to do the pulling.'

'Ach! Laziness, laziness. Besides, you have to watch it all the way each time or the cutter may bind.'

'Do you have a bigger cutter for the cannon barrels?'

'No. Not yet. One day, perhaps, but that will need a different technique to take account of the cannon's breech.'

To suggest that the younger man was impressed would be an understatement of his enthusiasm for the new idea. But it would be nothing when compared with the reaction from Willem the Dutchman when he experimented with shooting these first De Geer rifles.

Gustav Adolf was growing into kingship at an enforced rapid pace. In truth, he had little rest from either mental or physical exertion. No sooner had his accession to the throne been formalised when he'd been plunged into the Kalmar war with Denmark. The Catholic Imperialists were threatening from beyond the Vistula in Poland. There was serious infighting among the nobility at home and the peasant farmers were demanding representation in the Riksdag. Had this catalogue of events not been sufficient to spice the life of any monarch, there was the matter of rebolstering the national treasury following the huge ransom paid to Denmark; the Russians were now becoming more menacing, bringing a war threat to the very doorstep of Stockholm – and the king had somehow found time to follow in his father's footsteps and marry a high-born German, Maria Eleonora.

Having won a makeshift surrender from the Russians at Stolbova, Adolf concentrated his efforts on turning back the Catholics in Poland. He was gone for several weeks on a sortie that would serve to provide a valuable grounding for his main campaign.

Maria was turning out to be a poor choice of a wife for the king. Of hysterical disposition, she made his home life more burdensome than he could tolerate at times. It was fortunate, as it happened, that she became largely a war widow, due to his many absences on expeditions during which he insisted on leading his troops by example.

Axel, too, was kept exhaustingly busy. His sharp-witted ways of channelling finances made best use of the taxes and levies from the nobility and from the Baltic revenues which formed the backbone of the country's income. And he invested personally in the building of an exquisite castle home at Tido where his wife, Anna Baath, had inherited a sizeable estate. It would be years before the finishing touches would be applied to Tido Slott, but it was destined to become one of Sweden's most beautiful country houses, set amidst rolling parkland and copses of mature trees which lent a grace to the surroundings that set off the Slott in much the same way as a finely crafted setting does for a classic gemstone.

His office demanded much of him. And a new constitution had been put in place, too, at last allowing proper representation of the peasantry within the parliament. That was important, for it was largely from these farmers that Adolf recruited his soldiers. Together, the king and his chancellor formed as formidable a spearhead as had been known throughout the country's history. Their relationship was close. But it was formal.

With so many pressures upon him, Adolf often felt that the confluence of all these forces would bring him down. It seemed to him, almost daily, that whichever way he faced, another mountain confronted him. Just when it seemed impossible to eke out a temporary respite, the opportunity was most often presented to him by his second cousin, Ulrich.

'It's getting to you again, isn't it?' his peer would say. That was usually the platform for an excuse to engage in some distraction or other. Almost as wise as his king, in his own way, Ulrich would sometimes play a game of deception to fuel the bond between them.

'Listen, Addy, I need your help.'

'What've you got this time?' the king inquired.

'Oh, can't explain till you've seen it. Can you ride with me this afternoon?'

'All right, Uller. Just for you. But is there no one else who can help you?'

'No, Addy, only you.'

That settled it. Early in the afternoon Ulrich rode up to the royal stables and Adolf was already there, just taking over his horse from the old groom.

'Where are we going? Far?' Adolf asked, bringing his mount alongside Ulrich's.

'Not so far. But I can't do it without you,' the stockily built, straw-haired man replied, his pale blue eyes twinkling in a devilish laugh that matched the grin slowly settling across his lips. 'Let's ride! Follow close by!' he called to Adolf over his shoulder as he brought his horse up to a brisk walk before giving it free rein to take up a canter.

They rode at a reasonable rate for close on quarter of an hour before Ulrich signalled with his left arm and turned behind a row of willows, slowing to a trot.

'Over here! Over here!' he yelled back to Adolf who was, by now, growing quite suspicious of the whole episode.

Now down to walking pace, and ducking to avoid the tangle of branches, Adolf pulled up sharply as his horse broke into a small clearing at the edge of a dew pond. Ulrich stood in front of him, already dismounted and with his hand raised gesturing a stop.

'What's this all about, Uller?' the king asked.

'You'll see. Tether the horses here.'

They tied off the reins of their mounts to low branches and Adolf followed his secretive friend along a narrow track that was circuiting the pond. Suddenly, Ulrich spun around to face the oncoming sovereign: 'You see, Addy, I need your help. Some of the fish here are so big I just can't land them on my own.'

There was a pregnant silence before the full meaning sunk in. Then the King of Sweden, arms set akimbo, stared at his companion, his face wreathed in mock disbelief: 'Uller! You devious rogue! You mean you've brought me out here just to do some fishing?'

'And why not? Even kings have to enjoy life sometimes. See, I've hidden two rods and the other stuff here in the reeds.'

Adolf hadn't moved. At least not his body. But a broad smile was now superimposed on his previously incredulous face.

As on other occasions when Ulrich had successfully lured Adolf away from Axel, Maria and the demands of the Riksdag, it worked. The perch were neither overly large nor particularly engaging in the fight to land them.

'It's a perfect spot on an afternoon like this, hei?' Ulrich said, breaking the silence of the king's contemplative mood.

'It's all of that,' replied Adolf, his eyes fixed on the gently rippling surface of the pond.

'I often come here to paint,' Ulrich went on. 'If ever there was a place that showed the world the real Sweden, this is it, I think. It's so serene. And not many, it seems, know of it.'

'Yes, we're fortunate people to be living in a land like ours. God has blessed us with forests and lakes like I've seen nowhere else. This must be the most beautiful haven on earth. Pity is, we have so little time to enjoy its wonders.'

The few hours of relaxed fishing put them both in jovial mood as they ambled their mounts back to the palace.

'Thanks, Uller. Devious scoundrel you may be, but sometimes I think you know me better than I know myself. The fishing was by no means capital, but I'm the better fitted for the tasks before me because of it.' Their harmonious laughter signalled the end of the happy episode. But Adolf would admit that to no one else. Not even to Maria.

*

The start of the Thirty Years' War, in 1618, took Sweden's armies into a wide arena of conflict. King Sigismund of Poland became the first target for Adolf's forces. Through marriage of his mother into the Swedish royal family, making him part-Swedish, the strongly Catholic king tried to use this relationship to press for the spread of Catholicism throughout Sweden. The anger and outbursts resulting from this affront added the dimension of a Holy War to Adolf's purge of Sigismund's followers. When the two armies met at Mewe, it was the Lutheran element who claimed the victory. But, to get right at the root of the Catholic Imperialists, the Swedish forces drove on into Poland, crossing the Vistula and smashing their way towards Dirschau.

The pride of the Polish army was its cavalry. And they marshalled it to good effect at Dirschau. But not well enough to defeat Adolf's well-armed troops. The remnant of the badly beaten horsemen trailed from the field in retreat.

The successes in Poland strengthened Sweden's position, giving the hitherto second-rate country a strong presence in Europe. Triumphantly, Gustav Adolf returned to Sweden to be hailed as the new Warrior King. Some appended the cognomen *Lion of the North*.

Back at home, Maria was having a torrid time. She was pregnant and her period of gestation was not kind to her.

Coupled with her natural inclination to fret and throw tantrums, even without provocation, her ever-changing emotional moods heightened the whole experience and made life wearisome and worse for those around her.

Mercifully, she delivered a healthy child: a girl whom they named Kristina. She was to be the couple's only progeny.

The birth of Kristina had a sobering effect on the king. He loved his baby daughter dearly and made every effort to be near her. For the next four years, Adolf restricted his distant travels and, together with Axel, engaged in drawn-out diplomatic negotiations with the Danes in an effort to create a more peaceful and unified Scandinavia.

The royal family formed a strange triangle. A gulf was opening in the feelings between Adolf and Maria, but the king's bond with his daughter grew stronger as she grew older. She was his 'little companion' and he treated her like a son, encouraging the toddler to take an interest in simple scientific experiments. There were little pots of beans growing in dampened moss perched on the window sill of the nursery and rocking cantilever structures, designed both to instruct and amuse, cluttered the shelves. He often carried her on his horse into the woods and it was he who introduced her to the common flora and fauna of the region.

One day, returning home from a troop inspection, he found his four year old daughter dressed in an assortment of adult garments which included one of his old wide-brimmed hats and a braided, formal jacket. She was trailing an ornamental sword behind her and swinging her little arms in an emphatic and exaggerated manner.

'Kristina, my poppy, whatever are you doing?' her father asked.

'I'm a soldier. I'm guarding the flowers. No one shall be allowed to touch them,' the child replied precociously.

Smiling inwardly, but giving no hint of his mental chuckle to Kristina, he played along as if taking the whole matter seriously.

'Then you'd better watch out. I think I saw a flower thief hiding near the water butts.'

'Was he big or little? And did he have a hat?'

'Oh, he would be about your size, I'd say. But I don't think he was wearing a hat.'

'Goody. That means he won't have a hidden dagger.'

'Well, poppy, I don't think even a dagger would be a match for you and your sword, would it?'

'No. My sword is very, very, very sharp. See.'

Her attempts to unsheathe the long blade from its scabbard were so comical that Adolf was almost cross-legged in his attempts to keep a straight face and retain decorum. When he felt he could stand it no more he suggested, 'I think you'd better stand closer to the flower bed in case he sneaks up on you. I'll go and see if he's behind the stables.' With that, the king departed the scene and reduced himself to the level of all men in similar circumstances. He headed for the latrine.

Willem the Dutchman was ecstatic. He bounded back from the target butts towards the firing point at a rate of knots, wildly waving his practice target in the air. The target itself was a wooden shingle bearing a dark blue, almost black, 'X' mark on one side.

'Look at it, Tomas! Just look at it!' he squealed in delight.

'Let's see your efforts,' the gunsmith retorted.

In a close group just to the right and slightly lower than the centre of the cross were five neatly punched holes.

'It shoots well, eh? What a group! What a group!' Adolf's chief firearms instructor could hardly contain himself. At fifty paces he'd produced a better target than he was used to achieving at half that distance using his well-tuned Snaphane musket.

'Aye, that's fair shooting, Willem, but you're still pulling to the right. Even with these new wing-balls you still have to allow a little windage for the trigger pull.' The wing-balls were lead-cast bullets or balls with small spigots that fitted into the two rifled grooves in the barrel. The accuracy was astounding and, secretly, Tomas was more than happy with the results he'd seen from all the marksmen so far.

'One thing I've noticed, too,' the Dutchman went on: 'The barrel don't seem to foul up like the old 'un did neither. Must be the grooves takes all the soot in.'

'That's exactly what Louis told us to expect,' the smith informed him. 'Easier ramming and more shots before you have to douse 'er down.'

Willem turned to another onlooker who, until now, had said nothing. 'What do you think, Mister Oxenstierna?'

'I'm impressed, sir. That I am,' the chancellor replied. Even though he spoke the words, his facial expression remained blank and unreadable. His hands stayed in position, clasped behind his backside. Axel was not a man given to showing much emotion.

'I hear some of your sharpshooters have already given the rifles a pet name,' the smith said, a wry smile hinting from one corner of his mouth.

'So I've heard,' replied Willem. 'Loke's dart-gun isn't it?'

The reference was to an ancient myth. Loke was the old Asa religion's equivalent of the Devil and there was a tale about how he claimed his victims with a dart that never missed. When the hapless victim recovered, he found that he'd been transported to a kind of hell. The nickname seemed to both Tomas and Willem to be quite appropriate.

The hour or so that he spent casting an eye over the army's marksmen was more in the line of duty than idle leisure for Axel Oxenstierna. Soon he was back to his table and ledgers. Only two things in particular brought him pleasure these days, and some relief from the pressures of his actuarial duties: his almost finished Slott at Tido; and the little princess, Katrina. Drawing satisfaction from watching the culmination of the immense building project was one thing, but his delight in Katrina was almost the antithesis of his great acuity in administration. Her simple antics amused him as did few other things in life. He thought of himself as her uncle and, when Adolf was absent for a few days at a time, the child, in turn, looked to him as a kind of father figure. Although always welcomed in the royal household, Axel had never really come to terms with the high-toned Maria Eleonora. To him, she remained an enigma.

'I'll never understand that woman,' he said to one of his aides. 'Today, it's as if I were her closest friend. Yesterday, she berated me for taking the little princess down to the quayside to see the fish being landed.'

'I know what you mean. It's not really my place to say so, sir,' the aide commented in hushed tones, 'but I honestly don't know what the king saw in her. She's pretty, I'd agree. But, most of the time, she seems to me such a disagreeable woman. It must be hard to live with her under the same roof. But...' he sighed, 'at least they've produced one child so she must know what to do with what she's got or else—'

'Enough, Lars, enough! It should not be for us to judge. At least not to speak it out.'

'No, you're right,' the aide went on, seemingly determined to have the last word on the matter, 'Perhaps if they have a son next time she will transform herself into an angelic mother who dotes on the boy and persuades the king to declare a week long celebration to mark the little milksop's birthday.'

The sarcasm was not subtle and was, by far, too obvious to render the remarks worthy of any acknowledgement, but Axel could not let the topic end without showing his rank. *He* would have the last word. 'Enough!' the prudish chancellor reprimanded firmly and with a tone of finality.

*

Ulrich would have been about twenty, he thought, when Chancellor Oxenstierna had called him 'that layabout painter of no repute' and a number of other not very complimentary things, summed up in phrases that ought to have diminished his confidence at the very least, if not to have persuaded him to give up entirely. And perhaps he was right. But that was then. Almost seventeen years ago. Now, his artistic talents were being praised by the many in Stockholm who had a sound eye for what constituted a good painting. Just how Axel would react, Ulrich couldn't guess. But he would make bold to find out in the most facile manner: by confronting the chancellor himself.

'Axel,' he began, nervously, 'I have brought you something as a gift. I hope you will like it.'

There was no obvious way to disguise the 'gift' he had brought. Its size and shape readily betrayed what lay within the cloth that wrapped the picture. And the puzzled look on Axel's face could not have been there because he couldn't guess what Ulrich held under his arm. It could only have been in anticipation of whatever dismal doodling the artist was about to reveal as he folded back the covering cloth.

'It's... well... as you can see...' Ulrich stammered, showing uncharacteristic reserve. He stepped back two paces and cradled his work in his arms to let Axel take in its full glory.

Axel, always so circumspect in his judgement, was quite taken aback. 'Why, it's... it's beautiful,' the chancellor said, barely above a whisper. 'You have captured the very essence of the place. Its tranquillity and... and even majesty.'

Ulrich's painting of the Tido Slott was not large. But it had been masterfully executed. The pastel washes and overlaid colours bathed the whole scene in an ambience that evoked the mood of an early summer's morning breaking over the mansion. The Slott itself was a masterpiece of design, combining baroque and renaissance styles under its tile and copper-sheeted roofs. Dragon's head water spouts, made in Stockholm by Peter Mitter, complemented the highly ornate sandstone portals that had been sculpted by Heinrich Blume especially for the Oxenstiernas. With its forty-three marquetry-panelled doors inside, and its strikingly geometrical baroque gardens outside, it represented the unique expression of Axel and Anna's dreams.

'Thank you, Ulrich. I'll dearly treasure it, that I will,' the chancellor went on.

For the first time, Axel saw the architectural beauty of his magnificent home as it was viewed through the eyes of another human being. And he marvelled: firstly, at the talent revealed by a man whose ability he had long ago written off as whimsical; and secondly, at the startling interpretation Ulrich had wrought through his brush strokes.

For Ulrich, the mere words of approval and acceptance were enough. To have his workmanship affirmed by such as Axel Oxenstierna was, in itself, all the thanks he needed. As second cousin to the King of Sweden, he could have thought himself of greater privilege than the chancellor, but Ulrich knew that, in reality, the man who owned the Tido Slott was second in the land only to the king. And he valued Axel's turnaround of opinion almost as much as had it come from Gustav Adolf. But the chancellor had more to say.

'Ulrich, I can't find sufficiently adequate words to thank you. I can only say this: it will have a place of honour in the drawing room of the Slott. When I entertain my guests there on a winter's evening, your painting will remind us all of how wonderful the house and grounds look in summertime. That it will.'

As the artist made to take his leave, Axel said, 'You will, of course, join me there one day so that you, too, may appreciate your own splendid work in its true setting?'

'That I will,' replied Ulrich, unintentionally mimicking the chancellor.

By the nearest reckoning, it had been only six weeks since Adolf had encountered the imaginary flower thief. But now his mood was sombre. In the session of the Riksdag just ended, Adolf had confirmed that he would lead the army in another campaign. The greatest Swedish military force ever assembled was to start for Prussia and Pomerania within two weeks. And once more, the banners would be unfurled in the cause of a Holy War, for the King of Sweden was responding to the call of the Protestant Princes who were, yet again, under the cosh of the Catholic Imperialists.

Gustav Adolf's closing speech had been delivered with a

strange sense of foreboding, almost as if he'd had a premonition of some calamity. The omen seemed to affect his behaviour, too, for he spent every spare moment with young Kristina, often hugging her and feeling emotionally overcome without explanation. And, too, when the main body of troops was gathered prior to their departure for the south, Adolf called for not only his customary prayers, but invited his men to join in the singing of an old Lutheran hymn: 'Sustain us by Thy Mighty Word.'

On the day before the great parade, he spent some hours with Axel at the Tido Slott. As he walked in the gardens, he was looking up into the tree tops when he noticed a hawk fly over. Instantly, his mind flashed back to a time at the start of his reign when he watched a hawk kill a rabbit. The same thought that he'd had then came back into his mind: 'Strike fast and come at them from where they'd least expect it.' It worked for the hawk and it had worked for him. When combined with the 'crab formation' he'd devised, the tactic would form a major part of his strategy when his forces met the might of the Catholic Emperor. The strength of the Imperialists was their heavy horse cavalry. But, even before he left Swedish soil, Adolf was convinced that good management of logistics and the deployment of a fast, light horse brigade would be a match for anything the Imperialists could throw at him.

More than fifty thousand men set sail for Rügen and, after disembarking there, marched steadfastly towards the Elbe. As ever, Gustav Adolf mixed with the ranks and his cavalier-like charisma continually motivated his troops. Staunch Lutheran that he was, he commanded the respect of men at all levels. Even the most foul-mouthed reprobate would 'clean the air' when the king was within earshot. More importantly, he would die for him. And many would.

The forward scouts brought news of the movements of General Tilly's Catholic army. They were advancing on Breitenfeld and, as expected, were accompanied by the Imperial Cavalry.

Adolf handed his orders down the line. His famous crab formation was to take up position and keep its shape at all costs. The Imperialists, on the face of it, had the better of the ground. The flat, open approach would suit their heavy horse charges. But Adolf was not unduly dismayed. What seemed to them to be their greatest advantage, the Swede would use to bring about their downfall. But it could prove costly in Swedish lives. And did.

Once battle was engaged, the enemy's cavalry charged headlong into the main body of the Protestant forces. The front lines broke and raced back in supposed retreat. That ensured that the Imperial Cavalry did not slacken pace and on they came, pell-mell into a barrage of lances that the kneeling men raised to form an abatis, spiking men and horses alike. An horrendous carnage resulted from that first charge.

Lead and steel filled the air as the Swedes, reinforced by troops from other parts of Europe who'd joined them near the Elbe, beat back the horsemen. The foe regrouped and charged again. And again. And again.

Bodies were strewn on the field, lying in every imaginable contorted shape, some clearly dead, others bleeding profusely. Unearthly cries and banshee wails broke from the throats of men who'd been badly wounded. Some, terribly mutilated but somehow still living, ran aimlessly around screaming and some, their senses wrecked, babbled like babies. Many were cut down even though unarmed and with no capability for further contribution to the fray. Gun smoke hung in clouds above the heat of battle, fogging the view of horsemen and stinging the nostrils of their mounts.

For nearly six hours, Tilly's infantry hacked away, following in the wake of the charging horsemen. But, after the first two charges had been broken, Gustav Adolf's crab began to draw in its pincers. And during those same six hours, the crushing effects on Tilly's flanks rendered his heavy horse brigade impotent and badly mauled his infantry. As the day wore on, success for the northerners became more assured and, in a final surge when light was failing, the Imperialists broke in disarray.

Calling his officers around him, Gustav Adolf gave thanks to God for their victory. In triumph, he led his men onwards into Saxony, harrying the foe at every opportunity until finally cornering him near Leipzig. He then sought to form an alliance with the Protestant Princes for, together, they would endeavour to lead Europe into a peaceful future. But the Princes dallied and no firm commitment was made.

The strange presage that had prefaced Adolf's departure from Sweden had not wholly gone from him. From time to time it resurfaced and, for days, would weigh heavy on his mind. He grew homesick and often withdrew into a lonely, personal world that few could share. One man who did was an infantry officer who led a detachment of Protestant Freemen, Martin de Montfort.

'What ails you, sir?' the big captain inquired. 'Is victory not enough?'

'It's not the victory, it's the gaining of it. Both armies claim to love the same God, but in our ways of worship we can't agree. Will never agree. Not while they put their Pope in place of Christ.'

'Ah, so it's religion that worries you so?'

'Not only that. I have a daughter whom I cherish. And I fear for her. Oh, that this war was over so that all of us might return to a proper living.'

'You're homesick, sir?'

'Yes, de Montfort, I'm sick for home. Very sick. But we have General Wallenstein's army in our sights. We must finish the job.'

'Do you think to be home before Christmas, sir?' asked de Montfort.

'Christmas? That's two more months,' the king responded, poking at an ember as he crouched over the small fire. 'Perhaps. But I no longer think in terms of time, only in terms of our objectives. So far, we have failed to unite our forces in the common cause other than for single battles. Once we break Wallenstein, as we did Tilly, then we can discuss going home. Not before.'

'Aye, sir, but Wallenstein's no Tilly,' de Montfort went on, 'I've heard he's a smart one. A real strategist. Not blinkered to the straight charge nor wasteful of his men.'

'A strategist, maybe. But can he fight? He's invaded Saxony, sure enough, but with what resistance? No one can judge a general who runs down some farmhands and women. We did the same in Skåne, twenty years ago, during the Kalmar War. It was pathetic. One of the regrets of my life.'

'Regrets? You mean you wouldn't do it again, faced with the same situation? Enemies are enemies,' de Montfort continued, 'Even your so-called farmhands would scupper you soon's your back's turned.'

There was no opportunity to further that particular line of discussion, for the two were joined by Adolf's chaplain, a man known as Fabricus. The chaplain was an all-right sort of fellow, but his appearance made him seem a simpleton.

He was on the short side, rather rotund, and sported a Julius Caesar hairstyle that, when he'd removed his hat, set him apart from other men. Why he chose, and persisted with, this hairstyle he never admitted. But it served well in deceiving those who knew him only by sight, for he was a man of letters. Widely read, widely travelled; and with a heart of compassion. He was also tough and had no small stock of courage.

'Evening Your Highness. Evening sir,' he said, on joining them. 'As cold as Sweden, I'd say, but much damper, hei?'

'Aye, winter's well on its way now,' responded de Montfort, 'so we can't expect much better.'

'You're right,' Fabricus went on, 'First of November tomorrow but who's counting, eh?'

Even Adolf smiled at the jovial mood his chaplain had introduced as they stood warming themselves, the last few branches having stirred up a decent flame.

'Adolf, Your Highness. I came over to talk with you to some purpose,' said Fabricus. Then, quickly, as if to prevent offence, he turned to the captain, 'But you may stay and join us. I didn't mean to interrupt your conversation.'

'Hah. Little consequence. We were just passing the time of evening. I felt that the sire needed cheering, that's all. I'll leave you to your purpose. I must return to my men.' Flapping his arm in a casual au revoir, de Montfort left them.

'Can't be long now,' Fabricus began. 'Scouts say they've been mustering for days.'

'How d'you hear what our spies have reported?' the king asked.

'Oh, doesn't take much. When you get close to the men

on a spiritual level, lots of little titbits are given away. Why? You worried?'

'Not worried for Sweden. Wallenstein's no pushover, I know, but our God will uphold the Righteous. No, I'm not afraid of Wallenstein. But I have this recurring feeling that dark times lie ahead. Can't say exactly what. It's just a bad feeling.'

'You mean like Jesus in the Garden of Gethsemane?'

'Something like that. And I don't think this cross can be taken away either.'

As Adolf squatted to take another poke at the fire, Fabricus put a hand on his shoulder. 'Take courage, brother. No one has forsaken *you*. The men are with you.'

'I know, I know,' the king replied. 'I couldn't wish for better. Their loyalty is beyond question. But I'll be happy to take them back to their homes. Unhappily, I know there are some who will never see Sweden again.'

There was a deeper truth in the words he'd spoken. A prophetic truth that Fabricus would recall in a week's time.

On the morning of 6th November 1632, the dampness brought a further dispiriting to the already chilled soldiers of both sides as they prepared for a great battle. The morning was a particularly dismal one, for the whole area around Lützen swam in a sea of mist. The ear was very much the scout of the eye, for movements could be detected well ahead of the sight that confirmed their source. But battles, unlike public festivals, cannot be postponed until a more convenient time. Wallenstein was at the ready. And so was Gustav Adolf.

The two huge armies stood waiting, each in precision-ordered formation. The light wind swirled the mist across them, between them and, sometimes, raised it like a canopy above them so that their sight of each other's might became apparent. But the unpredictable wind and the dense mist badly hampered communications and the battle commenced raggedly. Of the three combatants – the forces of Adolf and Wallenstein, and the swirling wind – the latter was to be of greater influence than either of the other two.

The Battle of Lützen was, in the parlance of the day, a 'close' battle, meaning that it was fought with much hand-to-hand combat rather than the charges and skirmishes of other fields. For 'close' read 'blood and guts'. That's how it was. And worse. Sometimes men cut down their comrades, so poor was the visibility.

The distinct formations, so prim and orderly before the action, became a disjointed, confused nonsense for most of the fray. When clear space appeared in front of a rifleman or musketeer, he deemed it safe to discharge his piece in the direction of the enemy. But most of the time, the battle surged to and fro in isolated tangles. Adolf and Wallenstein, both respected strategists and tacticians, could employ none of their well-planned schemes. It was a 'fight of might' – and the might lay on the side of the Imperial forces. For most of the day, they pressed home their numerical advantage and the hopes of Sweden and the Protestant north could so easily have ended when a bullet struck the king.

Adolf was badly shaken by the shoulder wound he'd sustained, but fought manfully to encourage his troops. Then a second bullet caught him, slowing his efforts and reducing his voice to a rasping staccato. The third ball, smashing into his chest, took his life. The king's grim premonition had not been without foundation.

Because of the closeness of the fighting and the ever-present mist, few realised for some time that Gustav Adolf was dead. Slowly at first, then with gathering momentum, the dire news spread. The forces of the former king began to crumble as they were forced back to the brink of defeat. Ironically, the forcing back caused them to bunch, and it was then that Fabricus, the chaplain, was inspired to bellow out the lines of the hymn they'd sung together with Adolf before leaving Sweden: 'Sustain us by Thy Mighty Word.'

In vengeance, the kingless company fought like tormented wildcats. Firearms were transformed into clubs and swords became short-range spears. Martin de Montfort, using his French-style sword, drove it clean through the neck of one man and on into the chest of one behind. But he found it impossible to withdraw the blade for further use. With flailing fists he windmilled forward, kicking a foe in the stomach and wrenching his sword out of his hand.

The great rush forward by the bunched mass resembled an elephant crashing through tropical plains and levelling all in its path.

De Montfort's brigade fared well in the fighting. Finding themselves on the extreme right flank of the main battlefield, they swung on the enemy in a vicious assault that caught their victims unawares. The concoction of dense mist and gunpowder smoke swept before them to reveal, first of all, their own position and subsequently that of the strung-out left flank of Wallenstein's men. Before the Imperial flank could take up any sort of defensive stand, de Montfort's men charged at them relentlessly. Most of those on the fringe of the line were run through or cut down before any resistance was established.

In the centre of the main fray, Fabricus bellowed on. Few guns were fired now. There was neither time nor opportunity to re-load the single-shot weapons. Losses to both sides were dreadful as the close-quarters fighting drew to its conclusion. The Protestant army surged on like men deranged, trampling over bodies to get at others, all the time yelling in a fiendish, high-pitched wail like thousands of tormented banshees. The raging Swedes stormed forward. Stabbing, cutting, hacking, clubbing. All along the front line they sensed victory.

The inspiration that stemmed from Fabricus carried the day.

When Adolf had harried his foe and destroyed his principal strongholds as he drove through Prussia and Pomerania, the treasures his men looted from the Emperor's castles, mansions and country retreats were returned to Sweden to furnish galleries and centres of culture in Stockholm and in the new city the king had chartered at the former Alvsborg, now called Göteborg. In the aftermath of Lützen, the treasures of Europe were sucked back to Sweden in huge numbers by the vengeful forces of the dead king, swelling the treasure store of what had now become one of the most powerful countries in Europe. Gustav Adolf, the military genius, had advanced the work begun by his grandfather, Vasa, yet his death, at thirty-eight, was most untimely. For he had sired no son to become his successor.

★

Kristina was barely six years old when Adolf was killed. But her father, the great warrior, had not left his country without the thread of continuity. It was unquestionably agreed that, until Kristina turned eighteen, a regency government would exist under Axel Oxenstierna. For so long the king's deputy, the new Regent understood well enough the ways of government. But it was from his experience as chancellor that he deduced the great financial problem now facing the country: the cost of the wars. With continuing unrest on several frontiers, the already badly diminished treasury had to cover the cost of supporting the army at an even higher level than previously. Axel had to find a long-term solution to financing the defence of the realm.

Caught between two pressing needs: to achieve something quickly; and to ensure that, whatever he did, it would be effective for years to come, the Regent resorted to selling estates back to the Nobility who, in turn, taxed their tenants to meet the levies required as a consequence of owning these large estates. Restoration of land ownership to the Nobles raised funds. But it also raised the profile of this hated strata of Swedish society once more. In seeking to deal with unrest at its borders, the regency government had created a growing social unrest inside the country. The freeborn farmers could foresee themselves becoming bondsmen.

Sweden's military greatness, attained over the last three generations of rulers, began to look vulnerable once more.

As she emerged from childhood to become a young woman, Kristina continued along the lines her father had laid down for her. It was said that 'Science is to Kristina what needle and cotton are to other women.' She was widely read, artistic, and was developing a great interest in philosophy. Around the age of sixteen, she also became intensely interested in the matters of the council led by Oxenstierna. Bit by bit, she found herself on opposite sides of the debate from her Regent and, when she became queen in 1644, there was frequent disagreement between them.

The Baroque court over which Queen Kristina presided was frequented by philosophers, scientists, inventors and other keen and learned minds of the time. Rene Descartes was one, and one of those for whom she had a great deal of respect.

But there was another side to Kristina. One that she'd retained from her childhood: her love of dressing up, pretty things and ceremonies. She sat on a silver throne and was surrounded by silver adornments. Her clothes and accessories, too, were extravagant. She imposed ceremony on others, but enjoyed the pomp and show immensely herself. This trait in her character eventually drew her towards the symbolism of the Catholic Church and she began to adopt its beliefs. Ultimately, she converted to the Catholic Faith and felt that she had no alternative but to abdicate.

Kristina's reign had lasted ten years. Ten years during which Sweden seemed to have lost its way. Ironically, it also lost many of the treasures that Gustav Adolf had plundered from the Catholic Imperialists. Kristina took them with her to Rome.

Before formally turning her back on both her religion and country, the queen arranged with her cousin, Karl, that he should be her successor.

History would, in time, reflect that she was a 'rose between two thorns'. An intellectual queen between two great warrior kings. In her own memoirs, *Memories and Aphorisms*, she paid particular respect to her former Chancellor, Axel Oxenstierna. Of him she wrote:

> Axel Oxenstierna was a learned man who had studied widely in his youth; and he continued

his studies even when he was dealing with the most important business. He possessed great abilities and a profound knowledge of the world. He knew the strengths and weaknesses of all the countries of Europe. He was distinguished by his wisdom, his great foresight, his many talents and his great generosity. He was indefatigable, a man of unexampled diligence and energy. Work occupied his whole time and was his only pleasure; even his leisure was spent in useful occupations. He was moderate in eating and drinking, and he slept well: he used to say that only two events had disturbed his rest, the news of the death of Adolf and the news of the defeat at Nordlingen. He has often told me that when he went to bed at night he stripped off his cares along with his clothes, forgetting about them until the following morning. For the rest he was ambitious, but loyal; incorruptible, but somewhat slow and phlegmatic. He became Chancellor in the reign of Karl at the age of twenty – a thing without example in Sweden. He served four monarchs in that office, and died six months after my abdication, which affected him so strongly that, at his advanced age, he was unable to survive the blow. (Axel died in 1654).

Not *all* of Queen Kristina's reign had been devoted to furthering the arts and seeking to find a solution to the country's social problems. The Treaty of Westphalia had been signed, ending the Thirty Years' War and extending Sweden's influence along the southern shores of the Baltic. Elsewhere, much of life went on as normal.

In the armoury at Norrköping, the legacy of Louis De Geer's ingenuity was still very much alive, in the hands of the Ulfsson family.

'Another load of iron from Bergslagen is due to arrive today,' Mats Ulfsson announced as he strolled across to the workshop where old Nils was filing the finial on a trigger-guard into the required shape. Nils, now fifty-eight years old, knew that his days were numbered. Not that he was sick. But his failing sight made fine, close work a great strain.

Last year, Per-Erik had had to give up. He was the son of Nils' original master, Tomas Ulfsson and he'd taken over the business from his father. Although only fifty-one, Per-Erik suffered a stroke and was left incapacitated. Now Mats represented a third generation of Ulfssons working in the business.

'For your cannons?' Nils replied, pausing from his filing as he looked up.

'Yeah, enough for four more once it's all got here. Only two cartloads due today, though, but it'll be enough to get us started.'

'Aye, but there's no big push right now, Mats, so why don't you spend a bit more time with Ulrika.'

'Oh, she's all right. We see lots of each other, don't you worry. She understands that what we're doing is important. Once we get things going in the foundry, I can leave the men to it, but getting the fire up is always a bit special. I don't like to miss it.'

'Please yourself. I just thought that – well, she hasn't

seen much of you these past three weeks. Eleven or twelve days you were gone to Bergslagen wasn't it? And since you've been back you seem to have been hanging around here 'most every day. It's not for me to ask, normally, but there's no problem is there?'

'Hei, no. Nothing like that. But when you've been chasing materials all over the place, the least you can do is stick around to make sure what you get is what you ordered. That's the only reason.'

The old smith smiled. 'I'll say no more, then. Just that I wouldn't want to see her fret. She's a good woman.'

It often struck Mats as funny, the way old Nils treated him like a son; always concerned, but sometimes inclined to mollycoddle. Perhaps it was because he and Anna had had three daughters. Maybe he felt he missed out on some part of fatherhood by not having a son. To Mats it seemed, in a way, to make up for not having his father around. Per-Erik was paralysed down his left side and could command very little speech. It made it hard to communicate anything that he might have felt. So Mats didn't mind too much the father-like care old Nils showed towards him.

At twenty-seven years of age, Mats had been a bit of a slow starter as far as women were concerned. He married Ulrika just over a year ago. The petite, striking blonde had come south from Sigtuna and was working in Norrköping, making leather goods, when Mats met her. Six years his junior, she had been a rather reserved and retiring girl who had moved to Norrköping with her brother.

With the growing number of incursions into foreign territory by the Swedish army, the demand for arms had grown. In lands such as Poland, there seemed to be a propensity for the construction of extremely stout forts.

Often, the invading army encountered strongholds with walls of between three and four feet thick. The only way siege troops could reduce these castles and citadels was by the use of heavy cannon. Producing these fearsome pieces of ordnance became of special interest to Mats Ulfsson and, although his armourer's shop and foundry were not large, they made a valuable contribution to Sweden's aspirations to extend her boundaries around the Baltic.

The day the shipments began to arrive from Bergslagen, Mats kept his men working until close on midnight unloading and stacking the pigs of iron.

'If the generals ever take the army back to Pomerania or Poland, some of the stuff we've moved tonight will be going with them,' Mats announced to no one in particular.

'An' I wouldn't mind being there to stoke up one of these beasts,' Anders the foundryman put in.

'Aye, 'twould be a sight to see the mess these big 'uns make of these castles along the Vistula they tell us about. But the way things are going we might be turning this next lot out for ornaments. I'm even surprised they've given us the seal of approval to go ahead with more cannon,' said Mats, rubbing his chin ruefully, after which he stretched in a wide yawn that declared: 'Enough for one day.'

'Yeah, time to douse the lights, eh?' Anders suggested. 'Tomorrow's another day.'

When Mats tiptoed through the doorway of the large, sprawling house that night he was surprised to see that lamps still burned in the bedroom. Ulrika was not only awake, but still fully dressed. She sat by a small table, head in hands. A weak smile crossed her lips and her normally bright blue eyes were dark with the tell-tale signs of recent tears.

'This night, of all nights, you had to be so late,' she complained.

'I'm sorry, my love. We just had...

'Don't apologise. I needed you here.'

'Why tonight. What's happened?'

'Oh Mats, come here.' A tear began to well up in the corner of Ulrika's eye once more. 'Matilde was here. She has confirmed that I am expecting a child. Our child.'

Warmly, Mats clung to her, burying his head into her neck.

'Oh, my love, my love. That's wonderful. I'm so, so sorry that I wasn't here when you learned the news. Is everything all right? I mean, with the baby?' Tenderly, Mats patted his wife's midriff.

Ulrika nodded and kissed him gently on the forehead. 'Yes. It's well. Matilde says that I'm almost three months.'

Excitedly discussing their happy prospect, they went, at last, to bed.

'You know Anders, our foundryman? He always says: "Tomorrow is another day."'

Their 'tomorrow' was not *just* another day. It was the day of Queen Kristina's abdication. It wasn't the enforced replacement of their monarch that so embittered so many Swedes, but her betrayal of the Lutheran Faith her father had so devoutly followed and taught her as a child. Practically overnight, the queen lost all respect of her former subjects. Few cared for her highbrow ways nor anymore attributed any good that had been achieved as being on her account. The people were angry. And rumours were rife. Who would succeed her? Would the Danes or the Russians seize the opportunity to invade Sweden?

Over the following months, Nils Palme looked on as four more mighty cannon were prepared at the Ulfsson armoury. And a new king sat on the Swedish throne: Karl Gustav. Although neither Nils nor the new king realised it then, both king and cannon would combine, in due course, to further spread Sweden's growing reputation as a nation of fearsome and merciless warriors.

Ulrika, now half way through her pregnancy, was a picture of loveliness. She'd just given up working with her brother Goran in his leather goods workshop and, on most days, spent time walking with her big sheepdog in the woodland not far from the house. With her honey-blonde hair tied back, and wearing a dark blue woollen coat, she strode through the woods as if to some purpose beyond sheer enjoyment of nature's wonders. The dog flushed out birds and the occasional rabbit and, to Ulrika, each of these ordinary occurrences thrilled her as if she was experiencing the sensation for the first time in her life. Consciously aware of her own reactions, she put them down to her impending motherhood.

A messenger called at the armoury, asking for Mats. He told Nils that he'd brought important information from Tre Kronor, the Royal Palace. And, indeed, he had. Not only important, but surprising. When Mats arrived, the man was seated in the workshop with Nils, the two drawing on long-stemmed clay pipes of tobacco. The pleasing aroma filled the air and, in the warmth of the smith's shop, created a sophisticated ambience that was welcoming to any who entered or walked even close by.

'For your consideration, sir. From the king's armourer,' the messenger said, after briefly introducing himself. Mats unfolded the paper and gave a low whistle as he read its contents. The new king was wasting no time. It was clear he wanted to build up armaments. And fast.

'We'd be happy to oblige, sir. Of course, I'll give you my written answer to take with you,' Mats told him.

'That's good. I know he was counting on you, as he is on many other small armouries around the country.'

'And do you know why?'

'No clues. Not yet, anyway. Just a general preparation. He's recruiting more men, too.'

After the messenger left, bearing confirmation that the Ulfsson shop would accept the order for what was, to them, a large-scale production, Nils began to reflect, 'I hope this Karl's not a hothead. We've had enough of an upset with her ladyship taking off to Rome and turning all Papal on us.'

'No, I don't think so. Not from what I've heard. But he does have a good pedigree for leadership of the army. I won't be surprised if he turns out to be another warrior like Adolf. You'd remember him, eh?'

'Oh aye. *The Lion of the North* we used to call him. Great man. Great leader, too. Pity he died so young. Only thirty-eight, I think. Great loss that was.'

'Well, for our new king, only time will tell.'

When Karl Gustav gained the throne of Sweden, unexpectedly and by an unlikely turn of events, his sudden rise to sovereignty brought with it a compulsion to find a queen. Not that he entertained any fanciful notions of passion or even romance: his sole aim was to procreate and, hopefully, produce a son who would, in the fullness of time, propagate his line in a lengthy monopoly of the monarchy. In this, at least, he would surpass the celebrated Gustav Adolf whose failure in the matter had ultimately paved the way for this present circumstance.

Without any foreplay of long-winded deliberation, Karl

chose the eighteen year old Princess of Holstein-Gottorp, Hedvig Eleonora. But, like others before her, she was very quickly destined to become a war widow. Hardly had the marriage been consummated and the curtains thrown wide to declare the end of their honeymoon than Karl was assembling an army to begin an invasion of Poland.

The Thirty Years' War had brought Sweden into contention among the leading nations of Europe. But it had also been very costly. With the country almost bankrupted and a huge redundant army at his disposal, Karl wasted no time in finding an excuse to deploy the resource on foreign fields. By targeting Poland he hoped to plunder many treasures from the rich Catholic churches and monasteries and, arguably more importantly, secure not only the Baltic coastline of Poland but a large piece of the hinterland.

'It should not be a difficult task,' he told Abel Van Der Post, one of his aides. 'They have no leadership; are poorly organised; and are, even as we speak, totally distracted by the door-knocks of the Lithuanians, Transylvanians and Brandenburgers, to say nothing of the encroachment of the eastern powers.'

'Poor Poland,' responded Van Der Post, 'She has become the "trampling ground of Europe" and it seems to me her king, Jan Kazimir, is almost content to pace back and forth while his country burns.'

'That's true, Abel. But we can't delay to press our own case there. Soon, I believe, there will have to be a partitioning and we must push to get the northernmost part for ourselves. What happens elsewhere I don't care. Poles, I've discovered, are both stubborn and stupid. Did I show you the letter from that man Radziwill of Lithuania?'

'No, sir, I don't believe you did.'

'Hah! He's practically begging us to come down there

and his whole family is behind him. They want to free Lithuania to independence and the Radziwills don't appear to have much love for Kazimir. I've already sent him a reply to the effect that he can expect us within the month.'

'So,' Van Der Post grinned, 'we're about to make Sweden a little bit larger, eh?'

'And richer, too. God knows, we could do with boosting our coffers right now.'

Just after Midsummer's Day, Swedish troops began making their way towards the south. What was to follow in the next three months could best be termed a 'lightning blitz' for the deluge that was about to be unleashed on the lethargic Poles would begin a holocaust of destruction that would reduce the country's population by a third within the next few years.

Around the middle of July, 1655, Karl Gustav's forces lurched into Poland. The initial resistance was crushed before the Swedish onslaught and the Radziwills surrendered Lithuania, pledging allegiance to Karl. Rumours were rife, to the effect that Jan Kazimir had abdicated and Karl Gustav was now king. He may as well have been, for, by the beginning of September, most of Poland had been overrun. Warsaw was taken on September 8th, then Krakow fell while Kazimir fled to Silesia. One after another, the provinces paid homage to the Swedish king. But Karl was single-minded in the agenda he'd set. Procuring wealth had been a bigger inducement for the invasion than had been a plea from a Lithuanian vice-chancellor. He gave his troops licence to pillage and plunder. And they did so with a vehemence that was unparalleled, including in the comparison the ravages of Ghengis Khan in an earlier century.

Whole villages were wiped out. Churches were

ransacked, then razed to the ground. Private dwellings and public buildings alike were plundered and destroyed. Men, women, children and animals were butchered without distinction. Never was such violent fury visited upon any nation as that meted out by the Swedes in 1655 on the Polish people.

Scavenging parties purposely and methodically combed the towns and villages for carts and wagons before setting the place to the torch. These they hitched to confiscated horses and stacked them with all manner of chattels. Books, even whole libraries; works of art; weapons; sacred adornments; ledgers and public records; furniture and practically anything of value that was removable was packed into the transports for return to Sweden.

The huge cannon that trundled along with the rampaging army were effective in reducing to rubble many castles, breaching the walls to allow the troops free access to whoever and whatever lay inside. Even the magnificent Krzyztopor Castle was assaulted.

During the 1630s, the wealthy Ossolinski family had had Krzyztopor Castle built to a grand design. The main structure surmounted a natural mound around which stout stone walls had been built so that the natural earth embankment formed a backfill to these outer palisades. The main gate formed a tunnel through the mound to the inner courtyard and few castles seemed more secure than the Ossolinski's masterpiece. So grand was it, that the main dining hall is reputed to have had a glass ceiling that formed the transparent floor of a massive fish tank. No expense had been spared on the decor or artefacts which were deemed suitable to its setting. It was a true treasure trove, housing much that represented the best of Polish highbrow culture.

When Karl's assault forces made little headway in their

siege of the castle, he simply called a halt to the proceedings and relayed a message requesting several of the large cannon to be brought into position. Once the bombardment began, it became obvious to both attackers and defenders that only a matter of time stayed the execution.

'Don't spread the shots,' the cannon-master advised his gun-layers, 'but just to put the fear of the Devil in them, put one high every now and then to take out a piece of their fancy towers.'

With no great haste, but with a steady and unrelenting monotony, the iron dragons breathed their untameable death gasp. Stonework and stout timbers splintered. Some balls ricocheted off already embedded ones to spread the damage even farther.

'Take heed that they don't escape from the south rampart,' Karl himself chastened. He was enjoying this. It was slow, grinding progress. But it was progress. And the prize would be worth the waiting. All day the cannon laboured. And all the next day. Then, after almost three days of intense bombardment, several breaches began to appear, like snow melted by a stream of hot water poured from a kettle.

'Load for one more volley,' the cannon-master yelled to his gun-layers through the hanging curtain of powder smoke.

'Musketeers and pikemen to positiooooooon,' came the bellowed command. It wasn't a call the foot soldiers liked for it took them well in front of the muzzles of the huge guns and was painful on the ears. But they scurried to form up in rough squares ready for the charge.

'Fire in the hole!' came the obligatory warning that had been bawled out countless times in the past three days.

The guns crashed simultaneously, spewing flame and shuddering the earth.

'Enough!' shouted Karl Gustav: 'Take them in!'

The cannon ceased their onslaught and, like ants raiding a newly found foodstore, the infantry poured towards and then through the gaps, leaping over fallen boulders and shrieking like devils. Once inside the walls, the leading group of musketeers stopped, primed and fired their pieces, standing stiffly to attention whilst the pikemen rushed past them to disperse among the chambers.

Here and there, individual defenders attempted a sporadic resistance but were overwhelmed. In the main kitchens, servants and women bunched together. The walls reverberated with screams of fear and panic. One woman, obviously of higher standing and bedecked in beautiful robes, stood with arms and legs outstretched as if by doing so she could somehow cast a veil of protection between the frantic huddle and the ravenous attackers. She was swept into the mass with two lances driving deep into her body. Soon the kitchens were awash with blood as the defenceless servants were shown no mercy. No one escaped the sack of Krzyztopor and, once more, the booty was loaded and sent back to the north under guard.

On October 22nd, Janusz Radziwill formally signed over Lithuania to Sweden, in part fulfilling the original desire to unleash it from Poland. A few pockets of resistance remained in various parts of Poland but, by and large, most of the people accepted the overwhelming defeat and were prepared to accept Karl Gustav as their king. But he had not come to gather more subjects. The material wealth and the northern coast had been his goal. Nothing else mattered.

'Don't leave one of them to cause future trouble,' Karl

exhorted his generals, directing them to mop up the worst of the remaining areas of defiance.

The Marian Shrine of Czestochowa Monastery was besieged by the Swedes for forty days, but the prior, Augustine Kordecki, his monks and a few soldiers who defended it held out until Christmas day. They managed even to make some sorties of their own, spiking the attackers' guns and killing a number of men. Disheartened and war-weary, the Swedes withdrew.

The vaults of the monastery housed the anointed picture of the Dark Madonna and, after their 'victory', the monks paraded the famous painting throughout the surrounding area, reinstilling religious fervour and a measure of respect in the communities.

Coincident with Augustine's rallying cry, Jan Kazimir also rose from the ashes of defeat to revitalise his people in many parts of the country and, eventually, with the help of Dutch and Danish forces, was able to drive the remaining parts of Karl's army from Polish soil. But it was not until 1660 that a formal peace was signed.

After the first main thrust of his attacks into Poland, the King of Sweden returned home for a few weeks. It was long enough, it seems, to fulfil another of his prime ambitions. Hedvig Eleonora became pregnant and, in due time, was delivered of the son that Karl so much wanted to ensure continuation of his family line on the throne. The boy was named Karl, after his father.

*

When the old Viking town of Hedeby was destroyed, a new town, Slesvig, grew up nearby. Slesvig was home to a man called Jens Tilderkvist who lived with his wife Ebba in a small farmhouse. Jens was a Dane. He was as Danish as any Dane could be, except for one thing. It was said, and he had no reason to doubt it, that his ancestors were from Sweden. They'd come from a town called Birka, somewhere near Stockholm. But that was centuries ago. Now, he was a Dane. His wife was Danish. So were his horses and his two dogs. His family name was reputed to be 'old Scandinavian' but that could mean anything. Across the waters of the Øresund lay other provinces of Denmark but, somewhere to the north of there was Sweden.

It had all gone through his mind once again as he contemplated the invitation from his old friend Claus Forsberg over in Skåne. The Forsberg family had originated from Småland, although one branch was known to have gone to the island of Bornholm. But Claus had spent most of his early years in Slesvig. Throughout their youth, he had been Jens' closest friend and, despite the passing of years, had not entirely lost contact.

The offer sounded good. A chance to farm alongside his old friend, trying his hand at some new crops. And the land sounded good, too, with high yields and very workable soil. There was just that one phrase that bothered him. He didn't know why. 'Of course, we're not far from Sweden,' the letter read.

'But Jens,' Ebba rationalised, 'we're not far from Sweden even here. And besides, most of the old scores are settled now. The Swedes make their warring in Pomerania these days.'

'You're for this idea, then?' the stocky farmer probed.

'You know what I always say. I'll go where you go. I've no cause to suppose that your friend Claus is lying to us. If we arrive at his farm he'd be in poor position to tell you then it was all a fantasy.'

'You're right. We should go. We Tilderkvists have always had that kind of spirit. Always willing to try new things. Will you help me compose a reply to his letter?'

'Ha! You mean, will I write the letter and you put your signature on it?'

He smiled. His usual, meek smile. 'Something like that.'

Having settled affairs in Slesvig, almost seven weeks had passed before the Tilderkvists' little wagon creaked to within sight of the Forsberg farm. As they made their way along the well-worn track that served as the main road leading to the farmstead, Jens suddenly stopped the horses and jumped down.

'Hei! What's happened? Is it the axle again?' Ebba inquired.

'No, the wagon's fine. I just want to look at the soil.'

Jens took a few paces into the field, brushing his sandy hair out of his eyes with the back of his hand. He bent down and grabbed a handful of earth, crumbling it in his fingers and letting it trickle back into the hole from which he'd so unceremoniously plucked it. Twice more he repeated his actions in different spots then returned to his waiting wife, his ruddy complexion adding to the glow in his eyes. He rubbed his hands across his thighs and looked up at Ebba.

'Well, he wasn't lying. I reckon you could poke an axe handle into that soil and it'd grow.'

'That good, huh?'

'That good.' He took up the reins once more and continued towards the house and its outbuildings. Even from half a mile away, it was clear that the Forsbergs' farmstead was laid out in the traditional pattern, the main dwelling being breasted by its two principal outbuildings to form three sides of a square, making a sheltered courtyard in their midst. Even in 1656 the Scandinavian farmers applied sufficient forethought to this pattern to ensure that, should one of the buildings catch fire, the conflagration would not spread to the others. A considerable gap was left between them. Ten years later, the people of London could, perhaps, have benefited from the same foresight. It may have saved much of that famous city from the Great Fire that engulfed it.

Over the last few hundred yards, Jens' excitement heightened. It had been close on ten years since he'd seen Claus. Both men had married in that time. And had been the recipient of differing fortunes. For the Tilderkvists, life on the outskirts of Slesvig had been a mere notch above a struggle. It was obvious to Jens and Ebba already that the Forsbergs were prospering.

As the wagon hove into view of the courtyard, four large white geese became aware of its approach. They seemed to be leaning as far forward as they could without toppling, their long necks thrust out like a line of advancing lancers and their combined voices deafening as their almost hand-sized webbed feet slapped against the hard-packed earth to carry them towards the wagon. These 'farmyard watchdogs' had succeeded in their role. The Forsbergs were alerted to the intrusion of strangers on their land. Claus, the tall Dane, fair of hair and complexion, emerged from the doorway and shielded his eyes with cupped hand to take in the approaching wagon.

'They're here!' he called over his shoulder to Kristina. Then, without waiting for her to join him, he bounded forward, waving in greeting.

'Hei! It's great to see you. Welcome to Skåne,' he beamed at his shorter, stockier friend of old.

'Rikard! Our guests have come. Would you water their horses,' he shouted across the yard, whereupon a youth of around seventeen appeared, ambling towards them.

'Come in! Come in! The lad'll take care of the animals,' Claus said excitedly. Jumping down from the riding board, Jens fell into Claus's outstretched arms and the two grown men embraced like children at a birthday celebration. Kristina had come to join them and the men introduced their respective partners. Claus was filled with emotion, his eyes watering and his mouth wearing a constant smile.

'How I've looked forward to this day, Jens. Kristina will tell you, I jumped clean off the ground the day we received your despatch. This is good land, Jens. God's second Garden of Eden. You'll like it here.'

'We do already,' Jens answered, laughing out the words in his sing-song way that, to Claus, instantly evoked memories of the many times they'd talked and laughed together as young men growing up in Slesvig.

'You must be hungry,' Kristina suggested. 'Come right inside. I've a bean soup just made this morning. We'll soon warm it up.'

So often, a journey or adventure looked forward to ends in anticlimax. Not so with the Tilderkvists. Their arrival at the Forsberg farm was, in some ways, a relief after the sea crossing and long wagon journey. But it was also a new beginning. It had to be. There was nothing to go back to in Slesvig. They had, figuratively speaking, 'burned their boats' in true Viking style. Weary though he was, Jens had the urge to go exploring the farm. Everything was so different from what they'd left behind. The sky was bigger, the grass greener. Even the air seemed fresher than the salt-laden atmosphere they'd known. There was a certain aura of well being that surrounded this place. This would be a new chapter in Jens and Ebba's life. They could hardly wait for its pages to unfold.

'How far does your land extend?' Jens asked, as he and Claus stood behind the house, looking across the fields.

'Almost as far as you can see. That's why we suggested you come over and join us. It's really more than we can manage effectively.'

'As I told you before, we really appreciate your offer. Can't wait to get started. But we must sort out our financial arrangement.'

'No hurry for that,' replied Claus. 'The first thing is to agree on a site for your buildings. In the meantime, of course, we'd planned that you stay with us.'

Together, the Forsbergs and Tilderkvists would make a good alliance.

*

On March 30th 1655, Ulrika Ulfsson gave birth to her first child, delivered by the midwife Matilde. Mats, the hardworking armourer, had already suggested that, should they be blessed with a son, they should name him Erik. Ulrika agreed.

The morning Erik Ulfsson chose to enter the world as a lively and very vocal bundle of life was fine and sunny. It could well have been the harbinger of summer's warmth. Squinting through his pink, screwed-up little face, baby Ulfsson brought a feeling of accomplishment to Mats and a joy to both Ulrika and Matilde. But, although nature declared the day bright, sunny and joyful, it was just one of many 'dark days' for the people of Norrköping.

The obdurate Lutherans, so intolerant of those who

thought or worshipped in any other way but theirs, were 'purifying the kingdom for God' by seeking out those whom, they believed, were agents of the Devil. It had been a growing trend over the past year or so, this idea that the Devil and his angels were personified by witches in the guise of otherwise normal human beings. It was not just in Norrköping, but throughout the country. Lutheran clergy everywhere were exhorting their congregations to become aware of 'the Spirits of Darkness manifest in human form' and to report anything they regarded as suspicious in their villages so that these evils might be exorcised.

What may have begun as a holy intention had become, perhaps through misinterpretation or misrepresentation, nothing less than a witch-hunt. Some zealots believed they had been anointed with a 'spiritual gift of discernment' and became quite belligerent in their flushing out of suspected witches. During these times the whole female population in the villages lived uneasily. Witchcraft was certainly being practised by some, but by no means was it as widespread as these Lutheran zealots believed. Innocent women were being detained by the dozen and many tortured and executed in this attempt to purge the evil from the land.

Erik Ulfsson was barely two days old and was being nursed by his mother when frantic blows rained on the door. Outside, a woman's high-pitched voice implored the occupants to give her entry.

'Mats!' called out Ulrika, 'There's someone at the door!'

Interrupting his ablutions, he rushed to unbar the door. Almost bowling him over, Anna Hedlund, wife of the foundryman, burst into the room.

'They've got Matilde! They've taken her away!' she sobbed in great distress and panic, flapping her arms up and down uncontrollably.

'Who? What? What's going on?' Mats asked brusquely, taken aback by her boisterous entrance. 'Sit here and calm down,' he urged her, grabbing her shoulders and almost forcing her to sit down.

'The witch hunters. Not ten minutes ago,' she gasped, out of breath. 'I heard her screaming and ran out. But they just dragged her off.'

'Dragged her off?' Ulrika repeated, incredulous.

'Ooooh Mats,' Anna bawled, burying her face in her hands, 'What can we do. She's no witch. She's one of us. She's never been a witch.'

'You wait here with Ulrika. I'll catch up with them and see what can be done,' said Mats, quickly donning his coat. It took quarter of an hour to find the men who were marching Matilde towards the town square. By the time Mats caught up with them, the group had detained two other women. None of the three were any longer persisting in their struggling. But the face of each one was tear-stained and filled with fear.

'Hei!' yelled Mats as he ran towards the ringleader: 'There must be some mistake. This woman here is a friend. She's the local midwife. I can vouch for her.'

'There's no mistake,' the spindly, sharp-featured man declared. 'We've been watching her for some time. Living alone. Coming and going at all sorts of hours, sometimes even in the middle of the night. No, there's no mistake, my friend. She's one of them all right. An agent of sinful darkness.'

'But... you're wrong. I can explain all that. You see, she's a midwife. She has to come and go at the times she knows she'll be most needed at birthings. It's nothing to do—'

'Save your pleas,' the man returned, 'for we have our own ways of getting at the truth of her behaviour.' With that, the women were hustled into a building adjacent to the square. For the time being, at least, Mats could achieve nothing. Frustrated and disheartened, he returned home.

'This is a terrible thing,' Anna was saying, almost as if she was in a trance, 'a dreadful, terrible thing.'

Ulrika had put the baby to sleep in the deep cot Mats had built for him. 'What are we going to do, Mats?' she implored her husband. 'Surely there can be no truth in their accusation. These people are just going crazy.'

'I know. Martin Luther must be turning in his grave. They call themselves Christians, but they're worse than the reprobates who rape and kill. But I have an idea. Only I don't know if it'll work.'

Catching the slight change of tone that accented the positive, the two women immediately looked directly at Mats.

'What idea?' asked Ulrika.

'May God forgive me if I'm a sinner in this, but I believe the innocent shouldn't suffer. Perhaps it's best if I don't tell either of you what I intend to do. But pray God it'll work.'

After Anna had gone home, Ulrika asked Mats to confide in her and explain his plan. But he said it would be best if he kept it to himself.

'There are things I need to do, of course, and it would be greatly to my advantage and, hopefully, to Matilde's, if you'd just turn a blind eye to things tonight.'

'Please, Mats. Do be careful,' she pleaded.

'I will. Promise.'

Despite having had little sleep, Mats rose early next morning and called on his foundryman, Anders.

'You can guess why I'm here, I suppose,' Mats began.

'Matilde?'

'Hmm. Didn't think you'd need a second guess. We

must get down there early and confront these fanatics with the truth.'

'You know the truth?'

'Believe so. That's to say, I can't imagine our midwife's a witch, can you?'

'No, I can't either. Maybe a case of mistaken identity. Or just some rogue using the guise of religion to do some mischief. One moment and I'll be right with you.'

As the two made their way briskly towards the square, Mats explained to his foreman exactly what he'd done. The religious leaders were already underway with their inquisition of a sorely distressed woman when the two men from the armoury arrived.

'We'd like to say something on behalf of Matilde the midwife,' Mats told the man who opened the door to them.

'There's nothing to say. We'll be dealing with her case this morning. Then she'll be sentenced.'

'I see,' Mats went on, 'so you've already decided that she's guilty. How, then, can the hearing be righteous and just in God's eyes? You call yourself a Christian but you're prepared to exact punishment on one of your own flock, eh?'

'One of our own? What do you mean? The woman's an evil witch.'

'You're sure of that?' put in Anders. 'Have none of your womenfolk been delivered of their young by Matilde? And do you realise she worships our one true God?'

'Go on,' the elder prodded.

Mats took up the defence. 'We've known her for many years. She's a devout woman. Of course her work pattern doesn't often allow for attending many assemblies, but when I called for her to attend my wife, she was reading the Holy Bible at home,' he lied.

'That's right,' Anders added, supportively, 'Have you searched her house for any sign of witchcraft?'

'We didn't think it necessary to—'

The elder's comment was cut short by Mats, raising his voice in anger: 'You *what*? You'd consider an innocent woman guilty without any firm evidence? Just on some busybody's say-so? Come! And bring another with you! We'll go together to her house to see what elements of witchcraft are strewn about as you imagine.'

The forceful looks put on by the two armourers and their bludgeoning words shook the man's previous bigoted stance and he meekly obeyed them, calling for a colleague to join them. They found the door of Matilde's home closed, but unlatched, the way it had been left when she was so brutally abducted.

'Now, where are all the signs of witchcraft? Look! Where?' Mats appealed to them.

As the Lutheran elder and his assistant stood looking around the simple dwelling, half-heartedly lifting homely objects as if hoping they concealed some blatant evidence of sorcery, Anders pointed to the underside of Matilde's bed-pallet and shrieked: 'Look! What's this?' Going down on one knee, he pulled out a Bible and a copy of Concord, the Lutheran doctrinal summary.

'There you are!' Mats said with a smile, 'We told you she was a devout woman. And one of your own. Satisfied now?'

'Mmm,' the elder replied sheepishly, 'It seems perhaps we were misinformed on this one.' Then, raising his eyebrows as he turned to his accomplice, said, 'This one we'll let go.' And then, to Mats and Anders, 'But she'll have to be careful in future. When a woman is out and about at strange times on her own there's no telling what work the Devil may find for her. Best she stays home and doesn't invite the Powers of Darkness to tempt her.' It was too much to hope for any kind of apology. But, at least, Matilde was released without further harm.

They took her back to Ulrika and explained what had happened.

Matilde was overjoyed to have escaped the terror she'd thought awaited her. 'God have mercy on you, Mats Ulfsson. You lying, deceitful rogue.' She took two paces forward and planted a kiss squarely on his cheek.

*

When later generations look back on the reign of Karl Gustav, Charles the Tenth of Sweden, they might wonder if any monarch, in so short a reign, had ever been so sorely pressed. As if matters in Poland had not taken enough of a toll upon him, the Danes chose this moment to declare war on Sweden. Frederik the Third, King of Denmark, decided that the time was right to make a concerted effort to regain some of the territories his country had lost to its neighbour during the Thirty Years' War.

When the news was relayed to Karl, then still in the throes of extricating his army from the punishing raids of the marauding Polish guerrillas, the king quickly beat a retreat through Holstein-Gottorp, the lands of his father-in-law, and began to infiltrate the main Danish land mass of Jutland. The Danes withdrew to Frederiksodde, a partly built stronghold that was being constructed to form a defensive hub to guard the southern entry to the country. It must be credited to Karl that he somehow remotivated his war-weary veterans in the assault on Frederiksodde Fortress for, after only a short siege, the Danes capitulated. Nearly four thousand of Denmark's *Army of the West* surrendered to the Swedish king. The remaining Danish forces withdrew to the comparative safety of the eastern islands.

But, as the winter of 1657 approached, the temperature plummeted dramatically. And for more than three months it remained so far below freezing point that the sea froze over to a significant depth. As in prehistoric times, the islands of Zealand and Fyn were once more joined to Jutland at sea level. Ever the eager tactician, Karl saw this as a 'Divinely appointed opportunity'.

In January 1658, with the bitterly cold weather persisting, Karl engaged in an experiment.

'Abel, we need to test the strength of the ice. Take a squad of cavalry and fifty foot soldiers and march out on to the Little Belt. If there's any sound of cracking, beat a retreat at once. Otherwise, turn the men around after half a mile and return.'

'Certainly, sir,' Van Der Post answered. The king's aide assembled the required detachment and carried out his orders. Gingerly, at first, they made their way on to the ice at a slow march. Deliberately, he'd formed up both infantry and cavalry in close order. The little Dutchman quickened the pace and led them the full distance before halting and returning as commanded.

'No give in it?' Karl inquired.

'Solid as bedrock sir,' Van Der Post replied.

'Good. Captain Andersson, prepare your cavalry to ride. The rest of the men will march in broken step, we're taking the short route to Fyn.'

Across the frozen Little Belt towards Denmark's central island of Fyn marched the Swedish army. Nearly fifteen hundred horsemen and four thousand foot soldiers. But, unlike Abel Van Der Post's experimental attempt, they spread out and marched in broken step, not taking any chances that the ice may not be consistently thick. And neither was it. Twice, in the course of the journey, frantic yells spread alarm as first one, then a second cavalry squad disappeared into the sea below.

'Keep marching! Eyes ahead!' bellowed the squad leaders of the various units who, hearing the distressed yells of their comrades and the whinnying of the stricken animals, instinctively made to go to their assistance. Too much was at stake and they'd already progressed on to the ice too far to consider a retreat unless they were faced with a watery gulf. The march continued. On and on they trudged, at last making good the shore of Fyn.

Once on the island, skirmishing parties were organised and, within two days, the island had been completely overrun.

Encouraged by their traverse of the Little Belt, Karl's officers pushed the men onwards on to the Great Belt towards Zealand. And again, a successful crossing was achieved. The daredevil tactics had taken an almost intact Swedish army to the very doorstep of the Danish capital of Copenhagen. In an attempt to effect a feint, Frederik took his beleaguered army north to Roskilde and, when further resistance seemed futile, the Danes surrendered and agreed to discuss terms.

For Sweden, the Treaty of Roskilde was to change not only its history but also its geography. Denmark ceded the provinces of Skåne, Halland and Blekinge as well as the coastal region of Bohuslan. When Karl had persuaded his father-in-law, the Duke of Holstein-Gottorp, to allow his men passage through his lands, he promised him sovereignty of his region once the Danes had been subdued. This promise he kept at Roskilde, making the southern province independent of Denmark. And the whole of the Swedish peninsula was now, at last, under the rule of the King of Sweden. The annexation of Skåne, in particular, was considered a major triumph. Separating the agriculturally rich province from Denmark also gave the Swedes the important port of Malmö.

In August, Karl took his troops back to Zealand once more, this time by a more conventional route, and laid siege to Copenhagen. The assault went on for months, but the burghers remained resolute and the city was never taken. Just as in Poland, it was the influence of the Dutch naval forces that came to the aid of the oppressed, turning back the Swedes – but not regaining the valuable southern provinces Sweden had acquired at Roskilde.

*

It was certainly a strange irony by which Jens and Ebba Tilderkvist became Swedes, along with most of the other inhabitants of Skåne. Only the Snaphanar partisans, conducting their own guerrilla resistance, still refused to accept that Karl Gustav was now king of Skåne as well as the rest of Sweden.

'I'm a Dane and will remain Danish as long as I live,' asserted Jens.

'Does it matter that much?' Claus asked him. 'We're people. We're farmers. Most of all, we're enjoying life. We come into this world in a certain little room of a certain little house that stands on a certain little bit of soil. Who in heaven cares what we're called, Jens? It's time all this patriotism was done away with and these artificial boundaries forgotten. Just think of it. You and I are closer than a man and wife sometimes are, yet we could so easily have been born yards apart but on either side of a border line. Would that really have made any difference to how we feel towards each other?'

'Maybe. Maybe not. It just seems all wrong that when we came here we were Danes; now they tell us we're Swedes. We have to give our allegiance to Karl and not to Frederik.'

'Ach. You've never shaken Frederik by the hand and I daresay you'll never discuss the matter with Karl Gustav either.'

'True, but that's not the point.'

'Hei, my friend, the world'll be a better place if we just get on with putting into life and taking out what makes us happy,' Claus opined.

'Are you two still arguing?' Ebba asked, with a shake of her head as she and Kristina walked across the yard towards their two men.

'No,' declared Claus, 'we've just decided that we're neither Danish nor Swedish. We're Peoplish and that's that.'

Cackles of laughter burst from the women and Ebba put an arm around her husband's neck and pecked him on the cheek. 'You're mine and I'm proud of you, that's what I know.'

'At any rate, how are the beets?' Kristina inquired, returning the whole conversation to a more relevant topic.

'They've been doing well,' Claus answered. 'We're just on our way to have a look at them now.'

'I should think so, too. They're more important to us than national politics or what you modern-day gods think the nationality of our children should be.'

Both Ebba and Kristina were pregnant and, as far as they could tell, their birthing days would fall due at almost the same time. But that was still almost six months away.

It was a beautiful morning. From a small copse of unruly woodland on the north side of the field, a woodpecker betrayed its presence with two staccato bursts at a long-dead tree. Brrrrr. Brrrrr. The chirrups emanating from a host of small birds provided the chorus to the woodpecker's short verse and as the two men walked jauntily along the grassy path that bordered the field, the woodpecker hammered away once more.

'Ah, Jens, you don't get land like this in Jutland,' Claus said, spreading his arms expansively.

'Hei! Now don't you start again. But I have to agree with you, it's as fine a spot as I've ever seen. And, Swedes or no Swedes, Ebba and I will be forever grateful to you.'

'Think nothing of it, as I've told you a dozen times. Since you came here, we've already achieved far more than we could ever have done on our own. Rikard's a good lad, but he's only a labourer. Doesn't have a farmer's brain like you.'

'Whatever you say, Claus. I'm sure you're right, though. With our continued hard work and a bit more help soon, we'll have the finest farm in Skåne.'

'Aye. We could do with another Rikard. I was thinking of making a trip to Lund next week. See if we can find another good worker. You want to come with me?'

'Mmm. Count me in.'

The sugar beet was, indeed, growing well. The bulky white roots were thickening up and the whole crop looked to be in good shape, with no yellow tops. Soon they would need all the help they could get to top, dig, cart, clean and pulverise it in readiness for processing into the sweet syrup that people loved.

The visit to Lund should have been little more than a carefree jaunt. After the dreadful winter of 1657–58, the weather had been much kinder. But, in 1659, there was more to be aware of than just the weather. As the two beet farmers nosed their mounts through a pass at the top of a long incline and between low, rolling hills, they were brought to an abrupt halt by a line of rough-looking men who confronted them. There were eight, Jens counted, each armed with a musket and with sheathed knives bound to their waists by woven sashes. From only the knowledge of their widespread reputation, there was no mistaking these menacing bandits. They were Skånian partisans of the Snaphanar guerrilla movement. No word of command to halt was needed. The awesome sight of one whom they supposed was the leader, standing in the middle of the road with his hand raised, palm towards them, was all the order Jens and Claus required.

'So!' opened the leader, 'You are the forward scouts for Andersson's men, hah?'

The two farmers looked at one another in bewilderment. 'Scouts? No, no. We're farmers, on our way to Lund,' Claus answered.

'Ach, don't give me farm shit. We've been watching you for the last hour, scouring the area for sign of us. And we know Andersson and his troops are not far behind you. Our own scouts have already told us. Get down!'

Without hesitation, the two men dismounted, automatically raising their hands above their heads. 'See! We have no weapons. Like we say, we are farmers paying a visit to Lund.'

'Search them!' the leader ordered two of the men to his right, waving them forward with a sweep of his musket. 'Then where have you come from?' he continued, his malevolent look showing his distrust.

Claus assumed responsibility for the reply: 'We're from Peterlöv. Our farm is—'

'Enough! Which way are Andersson's men headed?'

Claus shrugged his shoulders: 'Don't know any Andersson. Why won't you believe us?'

'Hah! Believe you? We know enough of these tricks. Come with us.' Unceremoniously, the farmers were bundled towards a small copse, their horses being led behind them. Deep into the small, dense wood they were marched, prodded on by the muzzles of the Snaphanars' muskets. In a tiny clearing, eight horses were tethered.

'We wait here for Svend,' the leader announced. 'Bind them. We will decide later what to do with them.' Claus and Jens were tied to saplings, their hands bound behind them. No sooner was this done than the sound of hoofbeats proclaimed the arrival of another rider, galloping strongly. Slowing as he neared the copse, the rider bore on in among the trees, ducking beneath sweeping branches while his mount snorted in response to the reining in his rider exerted. Coming to a stop, the man slid to the ground in one fluid movement.

'They're within twenty minutes of us,' the new arrival disclosed. 'Two brigades I'd say.'

'And Andersson's leading them, I suppose?' the leader suggested.

'Yeah, as far as I could tell. But who are these two?' The last remark directed at the farmers.

'Spies. Andersson's scouts. They more or less walked right into us.'

'What're you gonna do wi' them?'

'Reckon we'll slit the throat of one and use him as a decoy. We'll leave him propped up beside the road. That'll stop them long enough for us to pick off as many as we can. The other one we'll use as a shield. Give us a chance to get away.'

The veins stood out on Jens' temples and both men began to sweat. It seemed their protests of innocence had fallen on deaf ears. For no particular reason, it was decided that Claus would be the one to be gagged and kept as a shield. It mattered no longer whether Jens considered himself Dane or Swede. Within minutes he would be neither.

Peder, the lookout, threaded his way back through the trees to the clearing. 'Their forward scouts are in sight. And they're a good way ahead of the rest.'

'Scouts?' the leader blurted. 'More scouts? Damn them. That'll wreck our plan. We'll have to jump them. How many?'

'Two.'

'But Knud, I thought these two here were their scouts?' The insinuation of doubt was cast by Svend, the Snaphanars' own scout.

'Yeah, that's what we thought, but we don't have time for that now. Leave 'em tied and gag both of 'em. Svend, take Peder and get down there. We need both of those scouts. Do it quietly but, remember, we'll need one of 'em back up here. And I mean alive. Understand?'

Whether it was by some telepathic miracle, or intuition or some other inexplicable phenomenon, not even the men concerned would ever know. But Andersson's two scouts suddenly stopped, for no apparent reason, and rode back to join the main body of advancing cavalry. It can only be assumed they must have thought the way ahead was clear of guerrillas, for the brigades picked up pace and came on towards the intended ambush point in some haste. Their plans once more thwarted, Svend and Peder found themselves stranded behind the rocky outcrop that was to be their lair from which to spring on the unsuspecting scouts. Crouching low, they began to make their way back towards the copse but were spotted by an eagle-eyed cavalryman. Instantly, Captain Andersson summed up the situation and sent a detachment in pursuit. Shots rang out and whipsawed through the leafy branches. The partisans, completely stunned by the sudden turn of events, leapt on their mounts and made a speedy getaway, leaving the two farmers bound and gagged beside the clearing. They could hear the cavalry horses thundering around one side of the copse but could do nothing to attract attention.

'Flush them out men!' the captain bellowed as he led the remainder of his brigades up to the copse. 'Johansson, take your men in on foot. Lundberg, circle around the left side.'

So it was that Johansson's men came across the petrified prisoners and set them free. Their horses were still hobbled nearby. After a brief inquisition, their ordeal was over.

For some time, nothing was said. Claus and Jens, the closest of friends, rode side by side in silence. It was Jens who was first to break it, on the outskirts of Lund.

'You know, Claus, if that's the way our own countrymen treat us, maybe we'd be better off as Swedes.'

It was like taking the lid off a boiling pot. All the pent-up adrenaline suddenly exploded in peals of laughter.

'I only hope it's all been worth it. If we return home without finding a new helper we'd have been as well to have stayed in the woods.' However, Providence saw that fair justice was meted out to the two intrepid travellers. Within an hour, they found a young man who was eager to come back north with them and help with the beet harvest. His name was Jacob. A sixteen year old orphan, Jacob didn't even own a horse. But he was strong and good-natured and Claus felt he would make a good worker. Jens acquiesced. The lad took his bundle – all he possessed in the world – and mounted up behind Jens for the first few miles of the journey. The trip back to Peterlöv was concluded without incident.

*

Life had surely dealt an unkind blow to Karl Gustav's queen, the pretty, twenty-three year old Hedvig Eleonora. She seldom saw her husband and felt trapped in the continual round of formalities at the Royal Palace. Little Karl was four years old, but was proving to be a difficult child, prone to throwing tantrums and suffering from such frequent mood swings that Hedvig could never hold his attention for very long. During the day, the Queen resorted to delegating responsibility for the child to his several nannies. In the abundance of leisure time she had at her disposal, she taught herself innumerable card games until, at times, these became an obsession to her, often consuming a whole evening without respite. Even when Karl returned for a few weeks, so ingrained had the habit become that she encouraged his interest and taught him, among other things, several versions of Patience.

Time meant nothing to Karl. Only achievements mattered. So, when the New Year welcomed a new decade, he hardly noticed. Issues were being drawn to a conclusion in Poland and, soon, he would begin a new campaign – this time to Norway. But, probably guided more by feelings of duty than inclination, he did make time for his diffident wife and unpredictable son when he was at the palace.

'There's still a fair covering of ice on the ponds,' he announced to Hedvig one morning. 'Let's take the boy to see the ducks and grey geese. We'll take along some scraps and he can feed them.'

'It's rather cold, don't you think?' Hedvig returned.

'Then we'll have to wrap ourselves well. The fresh air will do us more good than harm.'

'Very well then. I'll arrange for Karl to be suitably dressed. Shall I ask Oscar to prepare a carriage?'

'Good heavens no! It's only a short way. We'll walk.' He looked at Hedvig and shook his head, pursing his lips in a gesture that questioned the robustness of his wife's constitution. 'We'll *all* walk, Karl included. You know, Hedvig, in years to come that boy will be king. He won't learn any younger what it is to face up to a few discomforts. I've had to put up with a goodly share in *my* time.'

The Royal threesome strolled around the palace ponds, Karl the Elder taking time to explain certain aspects of bird behaviour to the younger Karl. Even though the Tre Kronor Palace was but a stone's throw from Lake Mälaren itself, the ponds were a favourite gathering place for both wild and ornamental waterfowl. The groundsmen had faithfully, each morning, broken the ice at the edges of the ponds to allow the birds access to water and, here and there, drakes engaged in their early-season courting antics of head-bobbing. Hedvig looked on approvingly and all three took turns at tossing bread scraps to the noisy, squabbling ducks.

To Hedvig, one day was much like another when her husband was off warring. When he was home, her routine was altered, but there was still a certain boredom about her daily existence. Apart from the small portion of time she devoted to her son and the embroidery she picked at on occasion, there was little else she enjoyed beyond her endless hours of solitary card games.

For Karl Gustav, these times with his son were rare opportunities to be both enjoyed and exploited. The king put aside his regal status to return to childhood, enthusiastically joining in with the boy's simple war games and in playing hide-and-seek around the palace. It was a welcome relief from the pressures of politics and war that had so entangled his life over the past six years. Even so, he found it difficult to withdraw himself completely from the uncertain world that enveloped Scandinavia in this milestone year of 1660.

'You're growing into a fine lad,' the king told young Karl as they walked through the grove of finely manicured bushes that led back to the palace. 'By the time I return from Norway, you'll be up to here,' he said, holding his hand level with his abdomen. 'By then, it will be time to ask Oscar to put you on a pony and start your riding lessons.'

'Don't want a pony,' the precocious boy answered, 'I want a big, big horse like you have.'

The king laughed and ruffled the lad's hair. 'Have I ever told you about the horses we saw in Poland?' It was a rhetorical question, for the king went on, 'Big, big horses with their coats shaved in patterns like wall hangings. And dyed in different colours. It's a peculiarity of the Poles, this dyeing of their horses. I once saw one that was almost all bright red, but his mane was yellow and his tail blue. He looked a fearsome sight.'

'But was he fast, like our Swedish horses?' young Karl asked.

'Fast? He was swift as a hare. And the men who ride

these coloured horses have feathered wings on their backs, like eagles. They're the pride of the Polish cavalry. But you know something?'

'What?' The boy stood looking up at his father, his eyes wide in expectation of the answer.

'Our Swedish army beat them. Sent them running all the way back to their stables.' Karl Gustav chuckled at his own description of the repulse of the famous Winged Cavalry but the boy, too young to appreciate the significance of his father's disclosure, merely grinned.

Putting his hand on his son's shoulders, Karl said, 'Well, it's getting quite cold, so let's go indoors. I might just have a little something for you.' The king winked at his wife and the three made their way back to the relative warmth of their chambers.

'What is it father?' the boy asked, several times, before they'd made good their return to the haven of the palace. Unable to contain himself any longer nor create further means of distracting his son, the king produced a red-painted wooden horse that stood about knee high. 'He doesn't have a Polish cavalryman to ride on him, I'm afraid, but he's just like the dyed ones we saw.'

'It's a beautiful little horse,' Hedvig remarked when her husband placed it on the floor. 'Where did you get it?'

'Oh, he was made by a fine woodcarver in a little village near Mora, just for Karl.' The boy showed his delight by holding the little horse's nose by one hand and his father's left leg with his other. In future years, many a child would treasure such little red horses and, in another two hundred or so years when mass production techniques enabled similar specimens to be churned out by their thousands, countless adults, too, would collect these Dalarna souvenirs.

That evening, the king and his queen played host to a small party of guests. If nothing more, it brought an infusion of fresh conversation to the dining room. And, for the king, created a diversion from yet another evening of playing Patience with Hedvig.

Had Karl Gustav been given any presage of the night's events, he would hardly have begrudged a few hours spent in the company of his wife indulging in her favourite pastime. For he was stricken with a stroke. A stroke that was to leave him with the ultimate disability. It took his life.

The short, six year reign of Sweden's third great warrior king was over. After the earlier accomplishments of Vasa and Adolf, he had successfully separated the southern provinces from Denmark and his name would be logged in the annals as the warrior king who established the foundation of the Swedish nation that was to take shape in the centuries ahead. His marriage to Hedvig Eleonora had brought him little pleasure but he would have termed it a successful union on two counts: it had produced a son who would inherit the monarchy; and had given him the family links with the Duke of Holstein-Gottorp who provided the corridor by which he was able to execute his greatest triumph.

The young Karl was still only four years old when his father died. So, once more, Sweden was thrust under the jurisdiction of a regency government to shepherd the country until the young king came of age.

*

It was the first day of February and a heavy frost made the ground rock hard everywhere, but on the farm at Peterlöv there was a special celebration. In the space of six hours,

Kristina Forsberg and Ebba Tilderkvist gave birth to their first offspring. At almost exactly six in the morning, as closely as could be determined, Kristina produced a daughter. Then, just before midday, in the house they'd built two fields away from the main farmstead, Jens and Ebba welcomed a son to their humble surroundings. There were frequent communications between the two birthplaces and both Rikard and Jacob were kept busy doing jobs that were normally considered beyond the scope of their regular working day. It was not until evening that the two proud fathers found opportunity to congratulate one another personally.

'Yes, we have our little Maria Kristina,' Claus announced with a grin that appeared to stretch from one ear lobe to the other. 'We've named her for Kristina's mother, just as we promised.'

'Ja, she looks to be a fine girl,' Jens commented.

'And your son looks a noble boy, too. Have you named him?'

'Yes. We decided to call him Ake.'

'Uh-huh, a good *Swedish* name,' Claus teased.

'It's not for being Swedish or Danish. It's just a good name. Like the mighty oak. At the moment he's but an acorn, but he's got good Danish roots.' The banter continued as the Dane and the Swede scored verbal points from each other with their quick-witted remarks. Determined to get the last word, Claus claimed: 'At least he was born on Swedish soil, that makes him a true Swede.'

Although his verbal response was little more than a grunt, Jens reflected that, after centuries of absence, this branch of the Tilderkvists truly had, it seemed, returned to its roots.

Before long, it would be roots of another kind that

would concern the two farmers. Beet farming was almost a year round occupation and, having wound up the work on last year's crop three weeks before Christmas, new fields were being readied to take the planting of the next seed in two months' time.

Rikard and Jacob drove cartloads of manure to the fresh fields and all four of the men busied themselves in spreading and ploughing it in. The arrangement Claus had made with his neighbour, Tomas Lund, was a sound one. In exchange for the beet tops and remains of the pulverised roots that Tomas fed to his cattle and hogs, the Forsberg farm was always assured of a goodly supply of manure. And Claus was a good crop manager, too. Few of his beets had shown any sign of forking or bifurcation of the roots and, as in previous years, he was now ensuring that this year's crop would not be sown in the fields used last year.

The foresight, hard work and sound common sense of the Forsberg–Tilderkvist partnership was to ensure a growing prosperity for the two families and as sure a foundation as their offspring could hope for in establishing a long-term association with the small hamlet of Peterlöv.

Three other children were born to the Forsbergs. In time, Ake Tilderkvist shared his home life with a sister. But, at a time yet some way in the future, it would be the boy and girl who shared a birthday who would marry and see their own progeny establish a venture that would bring greater recognition to the Tilderkvist line.

★

Lounging on a couch in the drawing room of the spacious country house that was now his home, the sixty-nine year old artist, Ulrich, was neither indolent nor indifferent. It was just that his outlook on life in recent years had given him a more serene composure. He no longer strove to prove a point. His work was good; many had acknowledged that. And one of his paintings hung in the Tido Slott, possibly the most elegant of castle-mansions in the land. But, lately, he'd had little reason or motivation to pick up his palette and brushes. By and large, he was enjoying life here in the heart of Dalarna and saw no purpose in any longer attending the regular artists' gatherings in Stockholm.

With his thinning white hair and neatly trimmed goatee beard, Ulrich looked every inch a refined gentleman easing into the twilight years of his life. But there was just something deep within him that reawakened his innate talent following the death of Karl Gustav just over a year ago. It could have been that same something that, following the death of the previous king, had led him to sign all his work with the name Adolf had always used to address him: Uller. Without a doubt, the loss of his king, peer and close friend 'Addy' at the Battle of Lützen had left a chasm in his life. But in later years, following his own death, the painter's action would create a confusion in the art world that would split even the acknowledged experts of the day. 'Uller,' they would say, 'was most probably a German artist of little repute'. That he was of German birth was true; that a famous Swedish chancellor and regent had once labelled him as 'of no repute' was also true; but that he was Ulrich, a second cousin to Gustav Adolf, King of Sweden, few would recognise. The confusion was to be further compounded by his next, and last, great painting.

Alone now, but for her young son, Hedvig looked

forward to the occasional visits that Ulrich made to the Tre Kronor Palace, particularly now that winter was descending.

'You'll have some French wine, of course?' she offered her guest.

'Thank you, I'd be delighted,' the artist replied, taking his place in the high-backed chair that he customarily occupied during these visits with the attractive widow. The butler arrived with the wine and a silver platter of fancy cakes.

'You were saying that you'll be leaving Dalarna for a few weeks?' Hedvig posed, lifting the wineglass to her lips, her raised eyebrows emphasising the query in her voice.

'Two to three weeks, I should think. I intend going to Denmark.'

'Is that wise? Especially at this time of year?'

'Oh, I'll be all right, one of the groomsmen and a house servant will be travelling with me.'

'I see,' Hedvig said, haltingly, before taking another sip of wine. 'And am I allowed to ask the purpose of this journey?'

'Certainly you may ask,' he grinned, 'but that's not to say I'll give you an honest answer on that. Let's just say it's a secret mission. But, of course, not one that will endanger either myself or the future of our country.' He gave her a wistful glance and his hand hovered over the assortment of cakes before eventually descending on one that looked appealing. 'I dearly wish that you could accompany us,' Ulrich continued, 'but, when I return, I should hope to demonstrate that your remaining at home would better suit my purposes.'

Hedvig flushed slightly, feeling a real warmth for the much older man. 'I would never presume to force myself upon you. It's just that, of course, I'm concerned for your safety. I enjoy our times together and our card games. I would be distraught should some ill befall you.'

It was now Ulrich's turn to feel enamoured by *her* attentions. 'I appreciate your concerns,' he smiled, 'but I think I'll be in good hands.'

'When do you intend to leave?' Hedvig asked.

'Day after tomorrow,' he replied. 'We will make our final preparations tomorrow, and on Saturday morning we begin our travels.'

The afternoon passed pleasantly and the unlikely duo, royal widow and ageing artist, played out several games of cards before Ulrich deemed it time to begin his return journey by way of Uppsala, where he would spend the night. In the well-honed, charming manner that had become one of his hallmarks, he took Hedvig's hand, raised it to his lips and gently kissed it, then took his leave.

It was not easy to paint when the weather was so cold. As he sat on the low bluff overlooking Fyn's coastline, encumbered by his own thick winter clothes and with additional woollen blankets thrown around his shoulders, Ulrich stared out over the water and gave his imagination a loose rein to spread out, first on his own mental canvas, the picture he was about to paint. The resulting picture would comprise the confluence of what he now saw with what his mind's eye would suggest to him. Capturing the real, actual, factual view before him would not be difficult, even though he would have to use a little licence when it came to those parts of the Little Belt he would allow to be exposed in the final view. Overlaying his own interpretation of something that he held only in his mind would be more difficult; the more so because the mental picture he'd built up had been constructed around the reports of others. And these reports had not always been wholly consistent. In the four years since the event took place, minds had grown dim with regard to how it had really been. Some were genuinely forgetful. Others exaggerated. He knew only too well that the truth lay somewhere between. That's how he'd paint it.

Bivouac-living is a compromise at the best of times. It can even be quite enjoyable. But when night temperatures drop below freezing and a stiff breeze blows in from the sea, it's not the lifestyle of choice. It was certainly a far cry from Ulrich's gracious country home in Dalarna. But it was necessary. For three nights, man and beast endured the arduous conditions whilst Ulrich captured the views he'd come for. On the last evening, Ulrich's aides made no secret of their gladness that, next day, their journey home would begin.

Groomsman: 'I'm sure it's been much colder, but it doesn't seem so.'

Servant: 'I can't stop shivering. It seems impossible to get warm, even hanging over the fire.'

Groomsman: 'Ja, it must be bad when even the horses complain.'

Ulrich: 'You've no complaint. I'm the one who's had to try to hold a firm line with the brush.'

Servant: 'If I'd been doing it, I'd have done it in summer.'

Ulrich: 'It was just an idea to get close to reality. But I think you're right. I'll be glad to get home.'

Groomsman: 'Life in these conditions must be more easily accommodated when the enemy is hot on your heels. The brisk activity and the sense of fear would keep you warm.'

Ulrich: 'Well, thank God there's no enemy chasing us tonight. What food have we for the morning?'

Servant: 'We've eaten more than we'd planned, I'm afraid, but we'll have enough for the return if we limit ourselves a bit. There's cornbread and we still have some smoked fish.'

Ulrich: 'Bah! Be glad to get home to civilised ways again.'

The nodding heads showed a common accord with the sentiments Ulrich had voiced. But, between themselves, Ulrich's two underlings considered him mad to undertake such a journey, in wintertime, for so little material evidence of gain.

'Have you seen his efforts?' the groomsman asked the servant.

'Only at a distance,' the man replied.

'Hah! You'd see no improvement with your nose against it. Just some wishy-washy hills and what is supposed to be the Belt. He's mad.'

'Yeah, and it's all since he started visiting her ladyship. He's got worse than a teenager in love.'

'Can't see why she encourages him. But I wouldn't mind giving her one myself.'

'Aye, she's still a fine woman. Needs someone to show her a good time again. Someone a bit younger than old arrow-beard there.'

Ulrich's return to the shelter killed the conversation. At least on that subject.

Once back in Dalarna, twelve days after the three men had set out, Ulrich began the real work of turning his basic views into the masterpiece he'd envisaged.

Over the next ten days he dabbed and scraped at the emerging picture, standing back every so often to take it in from greater distance and at different angles. Finally, he sat back on his stool, his bottom lip pushed up under his top and his few remaining teeth tight clenched to produce an expression that signified his satisfaction. His triumph. It was an achievement of which he was justly proud. And, in future years, many would gaze on the masterpiece in wonderment and adulation. But they would find it hard to trace its creator. Running across the bottom right-hand corner at an oblique angle, he'd signed in red: *A Daring Raid*. Then, underneath, there was simply the letter 'U'.

'Aha, the intrepid adventurer returns,' were Hedvig Eleonora's words of welcome when Ulrich arrived at the palace.

'May I show you the fruits of my labours?' the artist beamed, his chest swelling in pride, anticipating the royal widow's reaction once he'd unveiled the piece.

'Bring it to the drawing room, we have at least one empty easel there. It's probably just waiting for your picture. Come.'

Carefully, Ulrich placed his work across the wooden pegs and pulled away the loose cover that had protected it. And there, in the full glory of its rightful surroundings, if not its final position, was his dynamic portrayal of the first crossing of the ice by Karl Gustav's men prior to their eventual success at Roskilde. He had painted it to show the landing on Fyn Island, with the Swedish army advancing towards him. It was all there. The sense of expectation and determined inevitability written on the faces of the infantry. The majestic awesomeness of the cavalry horses. He had the foot soldiers marching in broken step. The first group to have reached the shore exuded an elation that made you feel, as you looked at them, that you'd want to have been on their side and woe betide the enemy.

In Amsterdam, a few months earlier, Rembrandt had completed his own masterpiece. He'd entitled it *The Syndics of the Cloth Guild*. Ulrich's painting was no Rembrandt, but it won a place in the heart of Hedvig Eleonora. And a place on the walls of the Royal Palace.

Hedvig remained a widow during the remaining fifty-three years of her life. But, even when Ulrich himself passed on, his picture of the raid on Denmark, her husband's greatest triumph, evoked many memories of the happy times she'd spent with the charming artist.

Part Four
The Artisan

For Tomas and Sten

Our sweetest songs are those that tell of saddest thought.

Percy Bysshe Shelley

It may have been prophetic. Predestined by fate. More likely, it was simply coincidental. On January 16th, 1705, exactly one hundred years to the day since Tomas Ulfsson was born, his great-great-grandson entered the world. His parents named him Leif and, by the time he'd passed his middle teen years, he followed in the footsteps of four previous generations of Ulfssons and became a gunsmith. His great-great-grandfather had been privileged to work with the famed Louis De Geer, the father of the Swedish firearms industry and so, it seemed, the influence was set to continue for another generation.

In later years, Leif Ulfsson ran his business from a well-equipped workshop in Kristianstad where his links with the Bergengren family of silversmiths was of mutual benefit. He would never consider himself an expert engraver and, when such finesse was required to satisfy the desires of a demanding purchaser of one of his fine sporting guns or matched pairs of duelling pistols, he contracted the work to his neighbour. In payment, Leif provided beautifully carved plinths for many of the silversmith's display pieces.

No longer did the Ulfsson Armoury produce cannons or guns of war, for the Sweden of the early seventeen hundreds was a relatively peaceful country in the midst of a relatively peaceful Europe. In England, Queen Anne saw out the last of the Stuart Monarchy. In Russia, Peter the Great, having defeated the Swedes at Poltava, founded his capital city of St Petersburg near the site of the former township of Nevagorod. The Danes were insularly contained within their much reduced kingdom and France had some years to go before its citizens revolted. Leif's business was geared more to the supply of custom guns for the gentry and landowners. Some of his customers were very wealthy, others were local farmers who wanted a quality gun that would double for sport and self defence if the need arose.

When the tall, wiry-haired craftsman answered the knock on his workshop door around noon on a March day in 1740, he was surprised to find a strapping youth of around fifteen or sixteen years standing there, a coarse sack slung over one shoulder.

'Are you Mr Ulfsson?' the lad asked, flicking a few strands of sandy hair from his deep blue eyes.

'I am he,' the smith replied.

'My father sent me. He told me to ask—'

'Just a moment. Who's your father? Do I know him?'

'Jan Tilderkvist. In Peterlöv. He has visited you several times and, last year, you made a flintgun for him.'

'Ah, yes. The beet farmer. I remember. He told me about you. You're the one who does the wood carvings, yes?'

'Yes sir.'

'I'm afraid I can't recall your name, but I'm sure Jan told me before.'

'It's Tomas, sir.'

'Well, Tomas, come in boy, come in.' The smith wiped his hands across the front of his dark blue apron and pulled a stool from under a bench, indicating that the lad sit down. 'And what brings you here, not trouble with the gun I hope?'

'No sir. I've come to ask if you'd consider taking me as your apprentice. I've brought some examples of some of my carvings. Father said you may wish to see them.' Still uncertain of the reaction he might expect from his proposal, the mouth of the sack remained clenched in his fist.

'Apprentice? Well, I'm not sure—' He stopped mid-sentence, then changed tack to ask the boy to show him the contents of his sack.

'These are just a few of the ones father suggested I bring to show you.'

It was the moment of truth Tomas had been dreading as he'd ridden towards Kristianstad. The little carvings looked so good when he'd stood them in a row on the farmhouse table back in Peterlöv but, as his eyes wandered around the part-finished gunstocks and display plinths that stood around the workshop, his confidence began to vaporise. His was the whittling work of a keen youth. There was nothing of the fine chequering or sweeping, cultured fleur-de-lis scrollwork that was in evidence before his eyes. The work of a master.

'Mmm. How have you done these? Only with a knife?'

'With several different knives and some small scrapers, sir,' Tomas answered shyly, his eyes now fixed only on the small ornaments that had consumed so many hours of his time in the making.

'No need to be ashamed, boy. They're good. Very good. You've a fine eye for balance and symmetry. This candle holder, for example. Don't know as I could do much better myself.' The master craftsman was being gracious in his compliment. 'How old are you, boy?'

'Almost sixteen years, sir.'

'Sixteen years, eh. And when did you start carving?'

'Dunno sir. Maybe when I was six or seven.' Tomas hadn't yet warmed to the occasion. He still felt bashful under the scrutiny of the legendary carver and gunsmith.

'Then your father is a wise man.' Tomas wasn't certain, but there seemed to be a misting coming into the older man's eyes. 'I'd always longed for a son who could be like you. But, alas, it seems not to be. I can see why your father's so proud of you. I suppose that's why he sent you here. No interest in farming then?' He smiled at the boy, as if almost willing him to answer in the negative.

'No sir. I like being in the woods. And most of all I like carving when I can find a good piece to work on.'

'Yes, I can see.' Leif screwed up his eyes and pressed the butts of his hands into them, rocking back on his stool. 'All right. I will,' he said, still covering his eyes. Then, removing his hands and stretching his brows as if to get his eyes to line up with the holes once more, repeated: 'I'll do it. I'll take you on as my apprentice. I have no other at the moment.' Then, almost as an afterthought, and to cool the lad's elation, added, 'There's a lot to learn, mind. You'll have to start at the beginning.'

'That's fine, sir. Honest. That's just fine, sir.'

'All right Tomas,' the smith began. It was the first time Tomas had been aware that Leif had addressed him by his proper name. 'We'll have to find you some place to bed down. I'll have to talk nicely to Mrs Ulfsson so, in the meantime, give my regards to your father and come back in one week's time. Then I'll get you started.'

'Thank you, sir. I'm most obliged. Really I am, sir.'

'And one more thing before you go,' the master craftsman added, 'You can be done with the "sir" – "Mr Ulfsson" will do just fine. Now you'd better be going. Are you on foot?'

'No sir, I mean Mr Ulfsson, my horse is tethered to the big tree outside.'

After making fast his sack of carvings, Tomas leapt on to

his horse. He felt as if he could have leapt completely over the horse. This was a great day.

The road into the Tilderkvists' farm was sorely in need of repair. The previous winter's ice had left it potholed and uneven. A knee-high wayside stone bore the name *Peterlöv* and, just beyond it, a red-painted sign indicated the entrance to *Tilderkvist Farm*. It was the most northerly habitation of the small hamlet whose one main street ran to the almost square Lutheran church at its southern end, before the road bent westwards to join the main highway that led to Lund.

Tomas spurred his horse on into the yard that was formed into a hollow square by the three main buildings of the farmstead. He swung out of the saddle, almost leaving his left foot still in the stirrup, he was so much in a hurry.

'I got it! I got it!' he squealed as he ran into the house. Jan and Berthe, seated around a big heavy wooden table, simultaneously rose to their feet as he entered.

'He's agreed to take me!' the excited youth blurted out, eyes wide and face flooded by a broad grin.

Once the initial euphoria had subsided, Jan began to probe a little more deeply into his son's intended move to Kristianstad. 'You'll be living with the Ulfssons? Is that what you're saying?' Jan asked.

'I'm not really sure exactly. Mr Ulfsson said he would see to it before next week.'

'Uh-huh. And what did he say about money? How much is he going to be paying you?'

'Don't know. We didn't discuss it,' answered Tomas, shifting uneasily in his seat as he began to realise the implications behind his father's question. Getting a proper apprenticeship was one thing, but how was he going to live?

'You mean you didn't even ask?' said Jan, putting on a

good act at being incredulous. He appreciated only too well that it would most likely have been the last thing on the boy's mind when he'd made him go alone to seek out Leif Ulfsson. But doing things by himself was important. He would learn, in time, to think for himself and become his own man. 'Just as well the Ulfssons are honest as churchmen. Leif'll treat you straight, I've no doubt. But you should have made it clear before you agreed.'

'Me? Agreed? I wasn't the one doing the choosing, pa, I was just so glad that Mr Ulfsson liked my carvings.'

Jan smiled at the boy, then walked across to him and extended his hand, formal fashion. 'Son, I'm proud of you.'

A week later, Tomas Tilderkvist became indentured to Leif Ulfsson, with the added privileges of lodgings provided in a small annexe room and his meals cooked for him by Mrs Ulfsson. Every two weeks he was given a trifling sum towards the upkeep of his clothing. But Mr Ulfsson had promised him that, once he began to contribute in a real way towards something that might be profitably sold, he would receive a proportion for himself.

It was a bit of a wrench having to leave his parents and the woods at Peterlöv but, all in all, Tomas was a very happy youth.

*

The Lutheran Faith had become established as the principal Protestant denomination in central and southern Sweden. And the Ulfssons were staunch supporters of both its doctrines and its practices. Each Sunday was set aside as 'the Lord's Day' and no effort was expended unless vital to life's existence. Even then, most of the preparation of food was done on the previous evening. Potatoes were cleaned, turnips peeled and chopped, pulses washed and all were steeped in water-filled pots in readiness for cooking next day.

On the nearby farm of the Nilssons, Sabbath day life was sung from a different hymn sheet. The ordering of the routines of livestock does not accord with that of their human owners at the best of times. Sabbath day or not, they still expect to be fed, cleaned and tended in their normal way. And they were.

Not overly religious himself, Tomas Tilderkvist conceded in part in that he attended the Sunday morning assembly with the Ulfssons but, during the remainder of the day, he deciphered 'day of rest' to mean that he was free to wander in the woods and do anything he pleased that did not constitute servile work or disturbance of the peace. So he explored the surrounding countryside. That was how he'd come across the Nilssons' farm. And their not unattractive daughter, Ulla.

Tomas had been in Kristianstad for six months. It was the beginning of September and harvesting of the grain was underway when he saw the lass stacking stooks in the field. He ambled towards her, his swinging gait suggesting that he, too, was more of country stock than city-bound government office courier. She'd liked that. She liked his open face and confident manner, too. And his muscular build and those piercing blue eyes. Taken together, his physical assets impressed the girl and she was more than happy to accept the offer of assistance he'd made to her.

It was in the summer of the following year that the truth came out. Leif had never suspected that his novice craftsman had stolen off after church on all these Sundays to visit the Nilssons' daughter. Nor did it ever cross his mind that, from time to time, the lad had been putting in his share of work on the Sabbath day on the Nilsson farm. But, when Tomas confessed, he took it all in his usual congenial manner and, like the fatherly figure he was, just gave a little chuckle. That was the thing about Leif Ulfsson that made him most endearing. He was now just past thirty-six years old, but could have been sixty-six. Benevolent to a fault; slow to anger; wise beyond his years and all of it wrapped in a frame with characteristics summarised by his face. Pale complexioned and with early-greying hair, his face was wreathed in a huge, unruly beard equally greying and his lips and eyes often combined to produce an effect that was disarming. When he looked at you that way, he could have placed his arms firmly behind his back and yet you'd still feel that he was hugging you. That was the way he looked at Tomas now as the youth's tale unfolded.

'So, you've fallen for this girl?' Leif asked, his eyes mischievously a-twinkle.

'Getting to seem that way,' Tomas answered, his cheeks reddening. 'She's a nice girl and we get on well.'

'I don't know the Nilssons too well,' Leif continued, 'What's this Ulla like? She pretty?'

'Well, I think so,' the apprentice resumed, blushing profusely. 'She's... well, she's sort of average build; about my height; fair hair and lovely eyes and... and she wrinkles her nose in a cute way. I really do like her a lot, Mr Ulfsson.'

'A man needs a good woman, son. But she'll have to wait awhile. Point of fact, you'll both have to wait awhile before you can think about settling down to a future together. You're young. Things may change. But, even if you still feel the same way in a year or two, it'll be nearly four more years until you're a craftsman in your own right.'

'I know. She knows, too. We've talked about that.'

'You've talked about it? Goodness, the love bug must've stung you bad, huh?'

But things didn't change. And Ulla waited. On the day Leif called his apprentice into the kitchen of his home to give him the papers he'd written to formalise his graduation from apprenticeship, Tomas hurried around to the Nilsson farm and asked Ulla's father if he would countenance the fully fledged craftsman's betrothal to his daughter.

Kristianstad's Lutheran church was more than half filled with well-wishers on the day that Tomas took Ulla to be his wife and the newly wed Tilderkvists began their life together in a room of the Nilsson farmhouse.

Leif had taught his neophyte well. From the good, but elementary, wood carvings the boy of fifteen had created in Peterlöv, the mature craftsman was now gaining his own reputation for both his fine woodworking and, particularly, as a maker of handsome guns. He excelled in the working of metal and wood and, when he combined the two, it was easy to see why he'd gained so much recognition before even his time of indenture had been completed. When laying in a barrel to its hardwood stock, it was almost impossible to slide a thin sheet of paper between the wood and the metal, so intimately were they fitted together. It was sad, but of no surprise to Leif, when Tomas told him one day that he was returning to Peterlöv to set up his own workshop next to one of the barns on his father's farm. He would purchase the raw, unfinished gun barrels from Leif, but the other facets of the manufacture he would undertake himself. So, after nearly six years of living in Kristianstad, Tomas took Ulla with him to set up home in Peterlöv.

Jan Tilderkvist had been brought up at the farm and, just after the turn of the century, had inherited it. He and Berthe had had two children during the first five years of their marriage, a boy and a girl, but both had died before the age of two. Tomas was born to them after a barren fifteen years and he was their only surviving child, the more precious to them because of his birth so late in their lives. The elder Tilderkvists were both sixty-three years of age when Tomas and Ulla moved to the farm. It had been hard work for them these last few years since the boy had gone to Kristianstad. One of their two helpers had recently left them and the remaining one, Lennart Lund, was twenty-five years old, chronologically, but perhaps a little over half of that mentally. He was strong, by and large obedient, and always willing to run errands or turn his hand to almost any simple labouring job they asked of him. But when Ulla arrived at Peterlöv, her new in-laws were thankful that their son had chosen a good farming lass to be his wife. With her background and experience, she would more than make up for the loss of Karl, the young man who'd gone to seek work farther south.

The farm grew corn and beets and a small barn, formerly used as a storage shed, had been converted into the home of Berthe's small herd of hogs. The main buildings were in good repair, but some of the smaller outbuildings were in need of major fixing. Jan was sure that Tomas would see to that.

In one very busy month, a lot had been achieved. The lean-to workshop had been built, roofed and windowed. Tomas had dragged back from Hälsingborg a rough looking but workable wood-burning stove that now sat in the centre of his 'shop', its flue snaking under the eaves and upwards. Again, not architecturally pretty, but sufficiently effective to give a good draw to the burning chamber. The overall appearance of the shop was one of homespun simplicity. But the same could not be said of Tomas's workbench. On this, he had expended the greatest of both effort and fastidious care. The tools he'd accumulated during his time with Leif were neatly arrayed. Two vice-clamps were built into the bench itself and a boring rig, to be used for making ramrod channels, took up one end. Before even a shard of metal had been chipped off or a flake of wood scraped, the place held an aura of creative expectancy. It was like a cauldron of spells awaiting the swish of the wizard's wand to release their magical powers.

Where he could, Jan had done his bit to help with the construction. From time to time, Lennart the labourer also lent a hand. Meanwhile, Berthe and Ulla had bonded like mother and daughter. Despite her many years on her father's farm, this was Ulla's first encounter with hogs and she had soon found them to be the loveable creatures Berthe had boasted them to be. Except for their peculiar smell. It wasn't distasteful, but proved devilishly hard to remove from her hands after she'd been petting the beasts. It was as if some kind of 'smell bugs' had crawled right into the pores of her skin. But she was happy. Happy to be on the farm; happy that things were working out between her and her mother-in-law; and happy most of all to see that Tomas rose each morning full of eagerness to get his own business under way.

The following week a visitor arrived, announced by the creaking of cart and harnesses and the rattle of cartwheel rims across the cobbled yard. It was none other than Leif Ulfsson himself.

'Hei! Thought I'd drop down to see how you were getting fixed up. And brought you a few bits 'n' pieces you might find useful. Oh yes, and a goodly pile of lead. You'll need that, come the time.'

'Thank you Leif, I'll never be able to repay you,' Tomas said, unaware that he'd now fallen into addressing his former master by his first name and not as 'Mr Ulfsson.'

'Just seeing your workmanship is sufficient thanks. It credits us both, but you most of all. You've a way with these flintguns that outdoes me, Tomas. And to prove it, I've brought you some work.'

'Some work? What kind of work?'

'The kind best suited to you. From Ulf Stromberg; you'll remember him. Been to see us a time or two. He wants you to build him a two cubit flintlock rifle in sycamore wood with sliding patchbox cover. Interested?'

'Interested?' Tomas gulped, 'I'll say I'm interested, but why haven't you taken it on yourself?'

'Oh, I've enough to do right now and I figured you could do with a good start. Ulf's not a hard man to deal with. Keen on getting the best quality workmanship but not fussy over small decorative details. I've taken the liberty of sizing him for the drop of the butt and I've a template in the cart there that you can use.'

Templates were important in the building of a custom gun for an individual. Not like military contracts, where all gunstocks were made to a uniform pattern and the men who used them just had to get used to the size and shape of the butt. A man with a longer-than-usual neck was liable to get a badly bruised cheek from the recoil, but the army cared nothing for that. When a private civilian was forking out his own hard-earned money for a gun that he would treasure, such compromises didn't enter his thinking. The gun's balance and fit had to be right to suit his build and thus afford him the greatest comfort, making it a pleasure to shoot with. And, whereas the army required mostly smooth-bored barrels to reduce cost, speed production and, most importantly, to allow much faster loading in the field, the vastly improved accuracy that came with a rifled barrel was appreciated by the gentry who frequented Leif's own workshop.

'Come in and have a look at what we've done so far. See what you think. Then I'll give you a hand to unload the cart,' suggested Tomas.

'This looks good,' Leif enthused. 'Plenty of natural light and enough space in the right places, too.'

'Ja, you taught me well. I can't wait to get started. Word'll soon get round. You know how it is. My father, Jan, has already been telling all and sundry that I'm setting up here in Peterlöv.'

'I wish you well, Tomas. Like I've already told you, I was sorry to see you go but I know it'll be for the best. Let's get these things stowed and I'll head back to Kristianstad.'

In a matter of days, Tomas began work on the piece for Ulf Stromberg. With practised eye, he carefully selected the piece of sycamore from which he would create the gunstock, its long straight grain crossed by alternating light and dark tiger bars that were characteristic of wood of the maple family. Along the bench he laid out the pieces of ironwork that would go into the making of this rifle: the buttplate, trigger guard, ramrod pipes, muzzle cap and barrel pins. He chose a long-ranged, two cubit barrel, trigger mechanism and, finally, a lock that he'd made whilst in Kristianstad. The ramrod tip and iron sights he'd fashion when the time came. He marked up the wood with a fine scriber and began the process of removing wood from what would become the bed into which he would lay the barrel, tight and snug as if fused to the wood itself.

Jan kept a watchful eye over the whole proceedings, spellbound by the way Tomas handled his tools in shaping the hard wood to fit the finished article he held in his mind's eye. Every scrape, gouge, rasp and draw-file was executed with precision and care as the lump of sycamore tree yielded to his skill and was transformed into a thing of beauty.

'I think it was the wisest thing I ever did, sending you off that day to look up Leif Ulfsson with your little bag of carvings. Now I can see you really are a master craftsman. With skills like that, you'll go far, my boy.' Jan, the rough-and-ready farmer, remained enraptured as he sat on the high stool at one end of Tomas's bench and continued to observe his son's mastery of the myriad skills that are required to be performed in equal harmony to produce a slender but strong, and beautiful but practical long-gun.

Over the four weeks that it took Tomas to create the rifle, Jan had watched, full of pride, as his son wrought the individual parts and fitted them together so that they blended to give a paradoxically strange gracefulness to what was, in reality, a weapon capable of destruction. Four weeks was a short time; it would have taken another two had he been forced to produce the barrel and lock mechanism from scratch.

'I'll have to take it to Ulf tomorrow so that he can decide on the best finish and whether any adjustments are needed,' Tomas informed his father.

'Ooh, I hope it doesn't mean changing anything. I don't know how you have the heart to undo what you've done,' Jan said.

'Shouldn't come to that. It matches to the template that Leif made up from measuring him. Maybe just a small thing here or there,' Tomas replied with confidence in his own interpretation of the man's requirements. He took from a small pouch a knapped gunflint and, wrapping its blunt end in a small leather patch, aligned it in the jaws of the cock and tightened it securely. It was a good flint, too. Not the white-flecked grey that was so prevalent amongst the local stocks, but a uniform black one imported from Grimes Graves south of the Wash District in eastern England, an area that was prolific in producing the best flint. That, too, had been amongst the treasures Leif Ulfsson had brought to give the new craftsman a sound beginning.

When Ulf Stromberg first saw the fruits of Tomas's labours, the gun was still 'in the white': no form of staining had yet been applied to the close-grained wood. It looked stark and its appearance belied the sturdy, accurate weapon that would prove to be its ultimate destiny. Painstakingly, Tomas had slid off the woollen coverslip and held his almost completed masterpiece at arms length for Ulf to take it from him. On the lockplate was deeply engraved the mark that Tomas would forever afterwards use as his maker's symbol or logo. It resembled the Greek letter *pi*, formed from the initials of his name thus: TT. Behind it was inscribed, in subscript, the numeral '1', denoting the first of his own-built guns. Ulf took the piece and hefted it to his shoulder. It came up easily, following the fluid movement of his arms, and settled quite naturally into his shoulder, its protruding cheekpiece snuggling comfortably against his face.

'Perfect! Just perfect!' the Kristianstad lawyer exclaimed with firm satisfaction. 'Almost as if you'd poured it into position. Leif told me you'd make a perfect job of it and he was right.' He eased back the cock and tipped the frizzen down on to the pan, then pulled the cock all the way back until the full sear took up with no roughness or loud click – just a smooth engagement.

'Would it harm if I were to snap it?' the lawyer asked.

'Not at all. It's a new flint and that's what it's meant for.'

Ulf took aim at some imaginary target on the other side of the room and squeezed the trigger. The sizzling shower of sparks spilled into the air, the tiny shards lingering alight for a moment before disappearing.

'Perfect,' said Ulf resoundingly once more, after he'd checked to see that the light featherspring had returned the frizzen or anvil to its wide-open position again. He held the beautiful piece at arm's length, scanning it up and down and admiring its graceful lines, turning it end to end and finally swinging it so that he could look into the muzzle at the tell-tale beginnings of the eight grooves that were its accuracy-giving rifling.

'And the finish?' Tomas inquired. 'Would you like the wood stained dark?'

'A rich dark brown will set it off perfectly.'

Ulf gave the gunsmith an advance payment and Tomas returned to Peterlöv to complete his commission, satisfied that now, at last, he had made the grade in his own right: Tomas Tilderkvist, maker of fine guns.

In the two years that followed, Tomas's business blossomed. Now and then, he turned his hand to producing specially commissioned pieces of furniture but, in the main, it was his creation of these fine custom-designed guns that won him admirers and a respected clientele. He was crouched over his bench in accustomed pose, filing into shape the mainspring for a lock, when Ulla drifted to his side, undetected. His concentration consumed by his task, Tomas was startled by his wife's voice, no more than two feet from his left ear.

'Hello father,' she said, barely above a whisper.

'Wh-what? What's that?' he said, turning sharply and wobbling precariously on his high stool.

'I said "Hello, father." We're going to become parents,' Ulla confided. 'I didn't want to say until I was certain. But now I know. We're going to have a baby,' she beamed, pushing out her stomach to add more visual conviction to her words.

'Hee-ja!' the father-to-be yipped, a broad smile engulfing his face. 'Aren't you the clever one, eh?'

'You too. It took two,' she beamed back at him.

Letting his small file slip through his fingers on to the wooden bench top, he swung off the stool and clasped his wife to him. 'I love you, Ulla,' he said, unashamedly kissing her full on the lips in a long, passionate kiss. 'Hope it's a boy,' he murmured.

'A girl!' she teased back.

'A boy!' Tomas quipped, enjoying the fun.

'Well, I'll settle for either, just so long as it's strong and healthy,' summarised Ulla.

It was a boy. And Jan and Berthe were overjoyed. As the hard work of running the farm and the passage of time itself took greater toll of their well being, they'd both begun to despair of having the pleasure of a grandchild. Now there was little Sten, nearly eight pounds of bubbling new life to brighten theirs.

'Looks a real Tilderkvist,' Berthe enthused. 'And your mother and father are coming tomorrow to see him,' she said to Ulla.

'Yes, and they'll probably say he looks a Nilsson,' the proud mother laughed back.

'Whatever, he's a real bundle of joy. Jan and I have longed for this day,' she added, wiping aside happy tears with one corner of her apron. 'Was beginning to think I'd have to make do with my piglets!'

The farmhouse was a good size, but by no means immense, and makeshift arrangements had to be put in place to accommodate the Nilssons during the three days they'd stayed with Jan and Berthe. The quartet of grandparents enthused, celebrated and, generally, enjoyed one another's company during the visit. For them, it was all over much too soon.

Tomas took everything in his stride. Amidst all that was going on around him, it became impossible to concentrate on work and, after the first day of intermittent endeavour he succumbed to the new demands of parenthood. For now, business would have to take second place to his much-acclaimed baby son. So, too, would Berthe's hogs.

For one person on the Tilderkvist farm, Sten's birth was no great cause for celebration. Particularly over the three days that the Nilsson folks were there, the normal routine of daily tasks – and more – fell to Lennart Lund. The simpleton labourer was irked by the attention given to the newborn child and resented the extra burden he carried, albeit temporarily, as a result. Lennart was a few inches above six feet and seemed to carry not an ounce of fat on his lean frame. Out of his hearing, Jan and Berthe sometimes referred to him as 'Lennart the Long.' He was an insular character, perhaps even secretive, and kept to himself whenever possible. Pleasant enough on the surface, when he had to be, he was otherwise a rather scruffy man whose mid-brown hair was more often than not a matted thatch, sorely in need of thorough washing. His hair was long and it was his preoccupation with frequently running his none-too-clean fingers through it that gave it its web-like appearance. And there was something quite odd and inconsistent about Lennart's behaviour. He looked after the hogs well enough when required and had cared for the farm dog before it died, just prior to the arrival of Tomas and Ulla at Peterlöv, but he displayed a spiteful streak. Once, Jan had gone looking for him in the woods that bordered the farm and had followed the sound of frantic squeals. He came across Lennart crouched by the edge of a clearing. He'd trapped a rabbit and was cruelly torturing it. The little furry body was bloodied from countless lacerations and Jan had snatched the knife from his labourer before pushing him aside and cutting the rabbit's throat himself to end its misery. Although Lennart vehemently denied it, Jan had good reason to believe it had not been the first time that he'd engaged in the nauseating practice. Once both men had returned to the farm, however, it was never mentioned between them. It may have been partly this inbred rancorous nature and partly a childish jealousy that sparked the resentment in Lennart when Sten was born, but he never made so much as a fleeting call on the house to see the child. He just kept well away and busied himself in his round of farm jobs. Tomas remarked on this observation to his father at the time, but the old farmer had just shrugged it off with a throwaway comment.

'He's a solitary one, that's for sure, but he does his share and that's all that matters.'

To Tomas, it seemed uncanny, looking back on it. For, four years later, when Ulla gave birth to their second son, whom they named Bo, the dimwitted labourer took the same stance, distancing himself from the newborn child and from the round of celebrations that accompanied his birth.

In the past six years, Tomas had become renowned for his fine flintlock guns and rifles. Not only were the externals beautifully crafted to produce these fine works of art, but he paid no less attention to the parts that mattered most when the gun's eventual owner would one day have a deer or other game in his sights and be hoping for a sure shot. The secret lay in the firing mechanism behind the lockplate. Tomas was fastidious in his setting up of tumbler and sear so that only a light trigger squeeze was needed to send the cocked flint arcing down on to the frizzen to create a sure-fire shower of sparks. He'd developed his own way with the touch-hole, too, and would crown-bore the tiny hole, like a countersink, to bring the full charge of black powder that had been rammed down the muzzle and into the chamber very close to the fine priming in the lock's pan. Once sparks from the frizzen spilled towards the priming powder, ignition was almost instantaneous. In an incalculably short moment, spark ignited primer; primer flashed through the touch-hole; main charge ignited and the grease-patched ball flew down the barrel. Unlike the large-bore military muskets of the day, with their inevitably slow clunk, fssst, boom, a Tilderkvist gun would answer the shooter's trigger movement with almost immediate response to ensure that the six-tenths of an inch lead ball would go where directed and not fly wildly from an unsteady muzzle caused by delayed ignition and harsh firing action. It was this close attention to fine detail that drew many of Skåne's elite gentry to the little workshop in Peterlöv. Tomas lavished care on each gun as if it was to be his own and his output was not high; eight or nine in a year, at best. But his customers paid him well.

The latest order Tomas received would be challenging to fulfil. The Bergengren family in Kristianstad had asked him to produce six identical flintlock rifles in a calibre suitable for moose hunting. It was the kind of challenge he would rise to. And the famous silversmiths would pay him well. He'd spare no effort whatsoever on the Bergengren guns. They would be built without compromise and modelled after the sturdy, highly practical German 'Jaeger' hunting rifles. He'd even give them a special notation. On the lockplates, following his customary 'TT' sign, he'd denote their origin by the first six letters of the Greek alphabet – the letters he'd discovered on the frontispiece of an old Greek-text Bible: alpha, beta, gamma, delta, epsilon and zeta.

The spring of 1753 was one of the warmest Sweden had known in recent years. The new thermometer in Tomas's workshop showed eighteen degrees. The device had been invented by a young scientist, Anders Celsius, whom death had called when he was in the prime of life – a mere forty-three years old. The legacy of his thermometer had been the kind of scientific landmark that touched the general public. Everyone wealthy enough to own a Celsius thermometer had one. And Tomas was making use of his at this moment.

'Whee! Hottest day of the year, so far,' he announced. 'Just right for a visit to Kristianstad. I've all but finished the Bergengren guns so I'll take one with me to show Johan. We can discuss how he wants them cased. Oh, and I'll drop in on Leif, he'd like to see it too, I'm sure.'

'Are you going on Vasa?' Ulla asked.

'No. His hoof is still tender. In any case, I was thinking to take Sten with me. Old Leif'll enjoy seeing the lad, so I'll take the cart and he can ride on the buckboard with me.'

'Oh, do be careful, Tomas, he's only five years old,' said Ulla, showing concern.

'Ach! Before you know it he'll be riding himself.'

Sten jumped around like he had a whole colony of ants

down the back of his breeches. He couldn't wait to get on the buckboard and climbed up to take his place long before Tomas had finished hitching up the horse. Ulla held the year old Bo in her arms and waved his tiny hand in a goodbye gesture as her other two 'boys' pulled out of the farmyard. It would be a long day for Ulla. Tomas would not be back until nightfall and, with Jan and Berthe down at the market, she would be on her own for most of the day.

'At least *you* haven't gone and deserted me,' she told Bo, rubbing her nose on his and gently pinching his cheek. 'But I think you can have a sleep while I do some baking. What do you say to that, young man? Mmm?'

The gurgled answer could have been interpreted in a thousand ways.

Tomas could have gone no more than two miles with Sten snuggled close to his side when he became conscious of the lad's suddenly tightening grip on his arm.

'What's the matter? You all right?' Tomas asked him.

The boy began to whimper. 'Gonna be sick,' he replied, clutching at his stomach.

Tomas brought the buggy to an abrupt halt, swung down from the seat and lifted Sten to the ground. Barely had the boy's feet touched bottom when he spewed on to the grass and retched several times. Tomas reached into the back of the cart and drew out a cloth that he used for wiping down his gunstocks.

'Here! Let me clean you up a bit,' he said, dabbing at his son's mouth with the cloth. 'You gonna be all right now or shall I take you back?'

'It's the bumping. It makes my tummy feel funny,' the lad answered, still looking miserable and feeling a mite sorry for himself.

'Well, let's just tether up here for a bit and we'll see how you feel.'

Meanwhile, Ulla had succeeded in getting Bo to sleep. He was in a side room and she'd gone back to the kitchen to begin baking some scones. She hummed an old melody as she laid out her utensils and ingredients and must have been dreaming of another place, another time. Certainly, she was oblivious to the presence of anyone else in the kitchen. She'd heard no footstep, no breathing, no rustle of clothing. Ulla froze rigid as the hand that clasped around her mouth almost stifled her breathing. The tiny nerves around her neck and scalp tingled as she fought against the strong arm thrown around her waist, its hand scrabbling at her clothing in a rough, uncouth, animalistic way. Struggle as she might, she couldn't loosen herself from her assailant's grip. Her head felt as if it would explode and she sweated profusely. She was now in a corner of the kitchen and her head banged off a wall as she heaved and tossed vigorously in a vain attempt to free herself. She twisted to get a glimpse of her attacker and dug her fingernails into his wrist but he overpowered her. One hand still covered her mouth, the other fought to invade her decency. And succeeded. There was a ripping of cloth and one of Ulla's breasts hung free. The brute forced her to the floor and grabbed roughly at her nipple. Frantic with fear, the sturdy woman's arms thrashed the air then both sets of fingernails bit into flesh. She was now forced to kneel in the corner of the kitchen and could no longer move her legs to any great effect. Suddenly, her assailant transferred his hand from her mouth to the back of her head, grasping a handful of hair close to the roots and jamming her head forwards towards the floor. He bucked hard behind her until she was curled in the corner, her neck feeling as if it would break, when he thrust a hand between her legs, tugging aside her underclothing and burying deep into her crotch. She couldn't catch enough breath to scream and the combined noise of rapist and victim resembled that of two dogs in a mad fight. Ulla could feel a sharp aching in her neck and pain seared across the back of her head where the man screwed her hair in his fist. She was beaten. It was useless to fight on. Her attempts to push his hand from under her were futile and, in an instant, she just let go and fought no more. She hardly cared anymore as the evil brute raped her from behind, lifting her hips high to complete his violation of her privacy. She collapsed in a sobbing heap.

The temperature had continued to rise throughout the morning and Tomas reckoned that it must now be somewhere around twenty or twenty-one degrees. For twenty minutes or so he'd wandered among the trees, their branches full of young buds. The carefree birdsong reminded him of the many springtimes past when he'd wandered freely through the woods in communion with nature's realm.

'So, how do you feel now?' he asked Sten. The boy had returned to a more normal colour but his early morning's enthusiasm had vaporised.

'Want to go back to Mummy,' he said, looking forlorn.

'Mmm. Might be the best thing. Road's even more bumpy from here on.' Tomas picked up a small rock and hurled it into the undergrowth. 'Come on, then. Let's go back.' He lifted the boy back on to the buckboard, unleashed the reins and swung himself up beside his son. At a gentle pace, so as not to provoke another bout of nausea, Tomas retraced his route back towards Peterlöv.

Father and son would have been barely a half mile from the farmhouse when the sound of a shot reverberated across the fields.

'What the hell!' Tomas's head jerked up and, with eyes wide and his heckles raised, he stood full height and lashed the big chestnut to speed towards the farm.

'Hang on real tight son! Could be someone's in trouble!' He goaded the horse to full tilt, forgetting entirely his young son's previous weakness or the fact that the five year old had little to restrain himself beyond his own feeble grip. On any other occasion, this would have been a recklessness well out of character for the careful gunsmith. The cart spun into the yard and hadn't fully halted when Tomas leapt off, hitting the cobbles mid-stride as he bounded towards the house.

'Ulla! Ulla! What's happened?' he yelled, bounding clear through the kitchen where his wife lay, unnoticed, slumped in the corner. Bo was awake and crying for attention. Seeing that Ulla was not with him sent Tomas into a frenzy and he shot back through the kitchen towards the door once again. Ulla's cry stalled him just as he was about to burst back into the outside yard.

'You all right?' he yelled at her in panic. 'What's happened?' he stormed. Then, taking in her shred clothing, disarrayed hair and deeply tear-stained face, he knelt beside her and asked in a softer tone: 'What the hell's been going on? Who was doing the shooting?'

'I don't know,' she answered, then flung herself into his arms and broke into unrestrained, loud sobbing; her shoulders throbbing up and down like millwheel camshafts. 'I don't know,' she repeated, through the sobs, 'I've been raped. I heard the shot but it was somewhere outside.'

'Right! Stay here!' he exhorted her and made to leave. She fought to keep hold of him, sobbing: 'No! No! He's mad! He's mad!'

Tomas wrenched his hands free, instantly remembering that Sten was still outside. 'Stay! I'll be back!' he shouted. His anger was fierce and he practically spat the words out, rising and turning to stride towards the door where he stopped; noticed Sten still in the cart; glanced quickly left and right then bounded towards his workshop. The air still smelled of black powder fumes and there, lying just inside the doorway of the workshop, were answers to the two questions uppermost in Tomas's mind. The body of Lennart Lund lay in a grotesque, buckled shape. The top of his head had been blown away and a mess of blood, tissue and brain matter was spattered across the door jamb and the ceiling. Beside him lay one of the recently completed Bergengren guns. Ashen-faced, Tomas bent down and picked up the suicide weapon. He shook his head in disbelief and, through misting eyes, saw the lockplate gleaming back at him. It was 'pi delta' – the fourth of the six Bergengren hunting rifles. Almost mechanically, Tomas stood the rifle against the wall, turned and, engulfed in bitterness, kicked the senseless, wrecked life that cluttered his threshold and stepped back outside into the brilliant sunshine. Head hung low, he made his way towards the cart, threw an arm around Sten and swung him to the ground. Taking the boy by the hand, he walked slowly back to the kitchen to comfort his distraught wife. It had been a tragic day for the Tilderkvists. And a tragic day for Peterlöv.

Ulla forgot about making scones. And Tomas forgot about making a visit to the Bergengrens. The genial artisan remained indoors with his wife and sons throughout the afternoon until Jan and Berthe returned. Sadly, he reiterated the day's events to the elderly couple.

'We must give God the thanks that no greater harm was done,' Jan said, trying to restore some semblance of balance and dignity to the situation.

'You're right, of course,' Tomas acquiesced, 'but I don't know that Ulla will quite see it that way. Not yet a while.'

'No, guess not,' the old man replied.

'What I can't get out of my mind,' Tomas went on, 'is that it was him. You know, someone right here on the farm. I know he was always a strange sort, but who would have thought...'

'Ja, it's a bad affair,' Jan cut in. 'But what have you done with the body?'

'Huh! It's lying where it fell. I haven't even thought about that.'

'Mmm. We'll have to take care of it, despite what he's done. And we'll have to inform the Lunds, too. Would you prefer if I—'

'No, no. This is my business. I'll take care of it.'

'Yes, son, but he was my labourer. I have a duty towards him. And to the Lunds. Besides, you've had enough trauma for one day.'

'All right, we'll do it together. What do you suggest?'

'Berthe has some old bedcovers. We'll wrap him in those and put him on the cart. First thing in the morning, we'd best take him over to the Lunds. It's almost a two hour ride, so it's too late now to be setting out.'

'Ja,' Tomas sighed, 'best get it over with.'

'And what will you do with the gun?' Jan asked.

'It'll go to the bottom of the dew pond. I never want to see it again. I'll have to tell Johan there's been some problem with it and I'll just have to make another one. The other five he can have, but he'll just have to wait for the missing one.'

'Seems a great shame. It's a beautiful piece. But I can imagine how you feel.'

Tomas felt almost as if his own hands were being indelibly soiled when he helped Jan roll the corpse on to the bedcover. The old man had wound scraps of linen around his former labourer's shattered skull and, together, they folded two sets of old bedcovers around the body before lifting it on to the cart. It felt strange. Quite eerie. Knowing that, as you slept, the dead rapist lay in his own, deeper sleep, not thirty yards away.

The next morning, hardly a word passed between father and son on the journey to the Lunds. Perhaps each wondered, silently, how they might be received. Or indeed, how they would break the awfulness of his deeds to the man's folks.

In the event, their stay at the Lunds was brief. Full of apology, mixed with their own grief, the Lunds made it known, without directly saying so, that they wished to be left alone with the remains of their simple son. The body was laid on a weather-beaten old table behind the Lund's cottage and the Tilderkvists began their journey home.

For the best part of a week, Tomas kept away from his workshop. He had no inclination to carry on with his work and, instead, spent many tender moments with Ulla and the boys.

'I love you, Ulla. I'll always love you. Whatever happens,' he told his wife.

'I know,' she answered him. 'But one thing we might have to face up to.'

With a puzzled look on his face, Tomas turned to her: 'What's that?'

'It may not happen, of course, and God forbid it doesn't, but what if I'm to have his child?'

The craftsman was stunned. His look of disbelief disclosed that he'd given the possibility no thought. 'Oh no! No, Ulla! You can't! We couldn't bring up a... a...' He searched for a suitable word. 'It would be impossible! Someone else's bastard!'

'Shhh, now, don't upset yourself. It's only the very faintest possibility. And there are ways of... of getting rid of it.'

'How would we know? How soon?' It was as if Tomas's normally controlled manner deserted him. He was speaking out without thinking and the anger and bitterness he'd felt on that morning almost a week ago returned to bite at the frayed ends of his emotions.

'We'll wait and see. If there's nothing between us and after three months my blood still comes, then we'll know it's not to be. But, if I do become pregnant, it's not the end of the matter. Like I told you, there are ways to deal with it.'

'Ja. Bad ways. Ways that will put your own life at risk. No Ulla, I know what we must do. We must go to see the Ulfssons. They're very devout folk. They'll pray for you in the special way they do. You know: they put oil on your head and lay their hands on you when they pray. I've watched them do it for some very sick folk. And they got well. That's what we'll do, Ulla.'

'As you wish,' she replied. 'If that's what you think is best.' Then she leant across and kissed him. It was the first time she'd shown any initiative towards him in this way since she'd been so brutally violated by Lennart. The significance was not lost on Tomas and he drew her close to him and held her in a lingering embrace.

It was while Tomas and Ulla were passing the time together that Jan sneaked into the artisan's workshop and took the suicide weapon. It had remained standing against the wall where Tomas had left it when he'd found Lennart the Long lying dead. It was certainly a beautiful piece of craftsmanship, Jan thought as he lifted it. Once his son's anger had subsided, he reasoned, he'd perhaps regret having thrown it into the silt and weeds of the pond. Jan had another idea. He cleaned the gun and wrapped it well, then took his hand axe and a length of rope and stole out of the farmyard. Climbing the slight slope towards the farm's topmost fields, he headed towards a copse in which there was an oak tree that had somehow grown in a deformed way, its trunk hollowed out but with only a narrow slit betraying the emptiness of the inner. When he reached the tree, he pushed the package into the hollow; used his hand axe to notch the base of a good-sized branch that grew out just below the start of the hollow part, and bent the bough back towards the slit, almost totally sealing it. It would make a sound cache, he reasoned. He looped the rope around both trunk and the bent bough and cut a stick from a sapling to use as a lever through the looped rope, twisting it until the bent bough was tightly wedged into the slit. He cut off the excess length of rope, then the old farmer shinned his way up the tree and tied off the top of the bough to prevent it springing back again. He slithered to the ground once more to survey his handiwork. Satisfied, he gave a wistful grin and walked jauntily back down the side of the field to the farm. He'd tell Tomas that he'd disposed of the gun himself then, one day, he'd surprise his son. When the time was right and his mood was receptive. At least that was the plan.

'We'd like to go to Kristianstad tomorrow,' Tomas announced. 'Just Ulla and myself.' He fidgeted with his fingers and looked unusually nervous. 'Mother, would you mind taking care of the boys whilst we're gone? If we leave early, we'll be back by nightfall.'

'Hei, go and enjoy yourselves,' Berthe responded. 'I'm sure the boys'll be just fine with me.'

'We'd appreciate that. I still have to go to the Bergengrens and we'd like to drop in on the Ulfssons.'

'Of course. It'll do both of you some good to get off the farm for a day. See some different places and different faces. Don't worry about a thing.'

Tomas scuttled around in the early morning light and loaded the cart once more with the five hunting rifles he'd built for the Bergengrens, together with a number of small items for Leif Ulfsson and some foodstuff. It was not yet six o'clock when he and Ulla drove out of the courtyard, sitting side by side on the buckboard, snuggled under thick woollen winter coats to combat the cold and damp of a typical Skånian morning. The time soon passed, or so it seemed, as the couple chattered throughout the ride. By the time the Ulfsson's white picket fence studded the horizon, both Tomas and Ulla felt they'd entered another world. As they slowed to a respectable pace, the buildings of the western part of the town became more visible. It was a busy town, cutting quite a contrast with the remote isolation of the small hamlet they'd left three hours earlier.

'Don't you think it's still too early to be calling on the Ulfssons?' Ulla queried.

'Not at all. If I know Leif, he was probably up and working shortly after we left Peterlöv. They'll be surprised, sure enough, but they always make folks welcome. You remember what it was like when I lived with them: they were parents to me then. Strangely enough, though, I never knew Mrs Ulfsson as anything other than Mrs Ulfsson. I don't recall ever hearing Leif call her anything different either. Must be some kind of old-fashioned Lutheran custom. Or maybe it's just a tradition in the Ulfsson family.'

The cart drew up outside the smart wooden-boarded house and Tomas leapt to the ground. 'Just hold on to the reins whilst I announce our arrival. Hee-hee, they're really gonna be surprised to see us.'

In all respects, Tomas had prophesied correctly. Leif and his wife were truly surprised to see them, and pleasantly so; they did, indeed, make the Tilderkvists most welcome; Leif had been in the workshop for two hours already... and, sure enough, he called his wife 'Mrs Ulfsson.'

'We thought we might have the pleasure of your calling on us one of these days,' Leif enthused. 'What a pity you couldn't have brought the boys. We'd have loved to have seen them.'

At length, the story of the tragedy concerning Lennart the Long came out and Tomas showed his old master one of the Bergengren guns.

'You've made a beautiful job of this, Tomas,' Leif drooled as he looked over the rifle, examining the detail of the sliding patchbox, the finely filed finial on the trigger guard and the elegantly carved cheekpiece with its enclosed vent-pick for use in clearing any fouling of the touch-hole.

'Yes sir, you taught me well.'

'Now, now, there's no need for this "sir" business. I told you before.'

Both men burst into childish laughter as the comment

evoked memories of those first conversations when Tomas took his little collection of carvings for the great master to appraise.

'Now listen, Leif. While I've got you on my own, there's something I wanted to ask you.'

Leif put on a quizzical look and nodded. 'Well?'

'It's concerning Ulla. She's worried.'

'Worried?'

'Ja, it's not easy to say but... well, when she was... when the labourer raped her, you know?'

'What are you trying to say, Tomas. You think her scarred emotions won't heal, is that it?'

'No, it's not that. She's afraid in case she may become pregnant with his child.'

'Aha. It's possible, of course, but most unlikely.'

'I know that, too. But you and Mrs Ulfsson; you're both very... you know... powerful in your faith. I've known you pray over people in a special way and they become well again. And we really came to ask if you would do this for Ulla. She was talking about going to see one of those women who can get rid of the child from her womb but I persuaded her that you could do it without risk to her own life.'

'Just a moment, Tomas. How can you know for sure that she's pregnant? There hasn't been enough time for that. You said it was only two weeks ago.'

'True. But I thought that if you and Mrs Ulfsson were to pray for her, she wouldn't have to worry about it. Have I misunderstood something?'

'Not at all,' the older man smiled, 'It's just that it seems to me you have as much faith as we do. Maybe even more. Certainly we'll pray over her. Let's go in right away and explain to Mrs Ulfsson.'

Once the request had been shared and Ulla agreed to go ahead with it, Leif produced a small bottle of vegetable oil, daubed some of it on Ulla's scalp and forehead and suggested she bare her midriff. Without pausing even to consider any embarrassment, Ulla complied and Leif daubed some oil on her belly. Having completed the anointing, both he and Mrs Ulfsson laid their hands on the young woman and Leif prayed aloud and at some length in a strong, sonorous voice. The remainder of the brief visit was conducted in a more sombre atmosphere than had prevailed when the Tilderkvists first arrived. The Ulfssons bade them au revoir with promises that they would continue to pray for Ulla's deliverance from both the memory and any physical aftermath of her awful experience.

By contrast, the visit to the Bergengrens was both brisk and formal. Without any forewarning of the Tilderkvists' arrival, it was purely by chance that Johan was at home. He accepted the five hunting rifles and paid Tomas as they'd previously agreed, the heavy bulging bag of riksdalers appearing somehow obscene in exchange for the beautiful pieces of craftsmanship delivered by the artisan from Peterlöv. Despite the payment he received 'on the spot', Tomas was crestfallen when Johan declined the offer to have them individually cased. He was further taken aback when the silversmith also turned down the replacement of the sixth piece at a later date.

'One was for father,' Johan explained, 'but he seems to have lost his enthusiasm for hunting. These five will fulfil our needs entirely. They're excellent examples of their genre; I've never seen better; but, in this family, they have to be "working guns" so I'll have fleece-lined leather field slips made for them so that we can ride with them in front of our saddles.'

Tomas could only accept that the man's sentiments were very different from his own. It had become his practice to follow up all his orders for guns with an invitation to produce an individually designed and fully fitted case to hold the gun and its various accoutrements. Each man to his own, he thought, as he picked up his small, but weighty, sack of riksdalers and returned to the cart where Ulla had remained patiently throughout the forty or so minutes that he spent with Johan.

'I suppose we got most of what we came for,' he said with a shrug of his shoulders. 'The Bergengrens have paid for the five guns I actually delivered. They no longer want the sixth one. And, best of all, we can trust that you won't be having any baby. Not by the Lund man, at least.'

Ulla wrinkled her nose and gave one of her cheeky smiles, leaning hard into her man and squeezing him around the waist.

It was only half past two in the afternoon. Their visit had been shorter than they'd envisaged it might be.

'Never mind, the boys'll be glad to see us back early, huh?'

'I'm sure they'll have missed us. I just hope they haven't been too hard on your mother.'

'Ja, she's a dear old soul. Really loves those boys of ours. I imagine she'll be the one who'd rather we'd stayed away a little longer.'

Giggling and laughing like two teenagers who'd just sampled their first ardent spirits, the Tilderkvists bounced out of Kristianstad and made their way along the country road at a steady trot. Old Berthe had been right. A day away from Peterlöv had brought a new lightness to their spirits. And they were enjoying it.

Whether by the effectual prayer of a righteous man and his wife or by the efficacy of nature's own arrangement, Ulla did not become pregnant by Lennart Lund.

'What can I do with this farm?' Jan sighed. 'You are so busy with your own work, Tomas, and I have no other help now that the Long has gone.' Jan no longer referred to Lennart Lund by either of his proper names. When, by dint of circumstance in a conversation, he found it necessary to mention his former labourer, he would always call him 'the Long.'

'You can't possibly manage on your own, father. You're what – sixty-eight years old?'

'Seventy,' Jan corrected him.

'We could ask Ulla's folks for help with this year's harvest, perhaps, but you'll really have to consider taking on more labourers.'

'Maybe so,' the old man replied, then fell silent as if thinking through the situation one more time.

'Would you like me to have a talk with the Nilssons?' Tomas suggested. 'See if they could help get in at least some of the harvest?'

Still the silence dragged on.

'Father?' Tomas pressed, 'Have you other ideas?'

'No. I just...' He shook his head, eyes closed and eyebrows raised in a gesture of exasperation. 'I just think maybe it's time I gave up farming. We have a little money saved, your mother and I, and we could probably sell most of the better tools and implements. Maybe that's enough. Berthe could keep her hogs. We'd make out all right.'

'And what about this year's crops? Wouldn't you—'

'Let 'em go! Let 'em go!' Jan cut in, waving his arm in a

throwaway manner. 'I'm tired of it all. Don't have the stomach for it anymore.'

Tomas furrowed his brows as he stole a quick glance across at his father then looked away. He was perplexed by his normally stalwart father's attitude. Sure, he admitted to seventy years of age, but this wasn't the mischievous, tough little farmer who, until now, always leapt life's hurdles with a bound of energy and who faced each new situation with a pragmatic approach that generally produced a practical and workable solution. Here was a defeated man. A fine man, Tomas thought, who'd succumbed to the wearing down of limb and spirit that attends the twilight years of a life whose flame had all but sputtered out in the draught of endless heavy labour since boyhood.

'That's how you feel now,' Tomas said, 'but with a bit of help, and once the crops start coming in, you'll see it all in a different light again.'

The old man smiled weakly, 'No, Tomas, it's not that simple. I can't really explain it, but somehow these last weeks have sapped any enthusiasm I had for it. Now I just want to see you and Ulla make the most of *your* lives. The farm will be yours one day, of course, but already I can see that *you* won't want to carry it on. Ulla, perhaps. But the world's changing, Tomas. Skåne's changing. The future's not in farming. Men like you, who can use their hands to build mechanical contrivances; men like you will turn the world upside down one day.'

'You think so?' Tomas replied, a bemused look crossing his face.

'For sure. Just look at the mechanical developments that have taken place in the past few years. Someday, men will—'

'Exactly!' beamed Tomas. 'Just look at them! Most have

been in farming. The farms of the next generation will have so many mechanised implements that a holding the size of ours could be worked by one man. And in less time than it takes now, even with one or two labourers.'

'Maybe so,' Jan said, philosophically, 'but everything on a farm is specialised. That's not where the big gains will be made. Like I was saying before, someday, someone will find a way to make interchangeable parts. Then, great machines will turn out tools and other things by the hundred. But someone has to design and build that kind of machine. It'll be men like you, Tomas, who'll change the future. Not farmers.'

'Come now, father, we'll always need to eat! With farming, you already have a mass production facility. Only, in time, it'll all be done more easily.'

Father and son debated the subject for the better part of an hour. Towards the end, despite Tomas's attempts to infuse some measure of optimism, Jan lapsed once more into a morose state.

That night, Tomas shared the deep concern he felt for his father with Ulla.

'It's as if something has suddenly just snapped in his spirit. He's lost the will to do the thing that's been his life. You know what he's like, Ulla, everything has revolved around the farm.'

'Yes, I know. I wonder how much of it has to do with Lennart.'

'I've been wondering the same. He doesn't like to talk about him and the change has been so sudden.'

'Whatever the cause, maybe it's time he began to take things a little easier. I'm sure we could help them out a bit. After all, your business is growing now.'

'Yes, but money's not the problem. It's the way he feels

about things. Seems to think the world's going to suddenly change because of all the new mechanical ideas and it somehow seems to overwhelm him.'

'We must talk with your mother. There must be something we can do to restore his self-esteem.'

Their concern was justified. Within a matter of weeks, Jan shrunk to a shadow of his former self. He became withdrawn and lost weight; his face becoming gaunt and his old vitality a distant memory. He sloped around the house like a half-shut pocket knife, showing little interest in anything, not even the meals Berthe prepared for him. But, on the last day of August, for some inexplicable reason, he perked up a little. As the day drew towards its close, Jan drew Berthe's attention to the beautiful sunset. It was the last one he'd ever see. For on September's first morning, he didn't awake. He never did get around to surprising Tomas with the hidden Bergengren rifle. His intended surprise died with him.

*

After the death of King Karl the Twelfth in 1718, Sweden declined as a military force in Europe. Since a new constitution had been put in place in the year following the king's demise, the country had been ruled by its parliament, the Riksdag. The monarch was reduced to no more than a 'rubber-stamper' of the Riksdag's decisions as, for all practical purposes, the true regent was the President of the sixteen-member council. The parliament was made up from four houses, or Estates: the Nobles, the Burghers, the Clergy and the Peasants. Each of these Estates met in its own chambers and there was only intermittent cross-fertilisation from the transactions of each of them.

However, majority voting decreed that the assent of three of the Estates was required in order to pass any resolution. In time, other politicians sought a more direct form of deliberation and two separate parties were formed, known as the Caps and the Hats. The former supported provincial policies while the latter majored on industrial issues.

Although higher-level education had been made available for many years – Lund University was established in 1666 – there was, by 1755, only sparse provision for elementary schooling. Most of those who attended the universities were the individually tutored sons and daughters of the rich and upper middle classes. The Caps, in particular, pushed for a widening of education, but their periods in power were few and, as a result, these proposals gained little momentum. But in Perstorp, not far from Peterlöv, there was a school.

Gunnar Persson was thirty years old when he moved to Perstorp to commission the building of the schoolhouse. It was a small, two-storeyed affair; the top floor served as Gunnar's meagre home and he taught his classes in the one-roomed lower floor. It was large enough to seat around twenty-five children, at a push, but his class of 1756–57 numbered only nineteen, and those showed a spread of ages from eight to fourteen years old. Nine year old Sten Tilderkvist was one of them.

It was Ulla herself who urged Mr Persson to take the boy. Tomas had agreed to try to provide whatever funds would be required to give the lad a formal education. Both he and Ulla had learned to write and to figure, but had never had the benefit of a proper teaching. For Sten to have the opportunity, just a few miles from home, was a chance that could not be passed up.

In the three years since his grandfather had 'gone to be

with the angels' young Sten had become his father's shadow. It seemed that, wherever Tomas went, there would be Sten. Almost surreptitiously, he would materialise as if from nowhere whether Tomas was in the workshop, hog barn, stables or around the house. And he was so inquisitive; always asking questions. Tomas often smiled to himself as he saw another question being framed, for the precursory pattern was always the same: a quick finger-combing of the tousled light brown locks that fell centrally on to the boy's brow, followed by a licking of the lips and then the slow, drawled: 'Faaather?' It was comical, thought Tomas, but in a cute sort of way. It was just something the boy had developed, almost as if he had to do it to pluck up the courage to ask his question. At the schoolhouse he went through the same rigmarole, but now it was 'Mr Persson, sir' instead of 'faaather.'

'You have a very bright boy, Mrs Tilderkvist,' Gunnar told Ulla one day. 'I can't wait to get him reading some "good books" once his ability develops a little more.' By 'good books', Gunnar meant some of the translated early English classics. The four years the teacher had spent in England had afforded him the opportunity to evaluate some of the best literature of the time, but so little of it had been translated into Swedish. He had, himself, translated *The Lonely Pigeon* as a primer and Sten was already reading the simple story with fluency and confidence.

'He takes from his father,' Ulla replied. 'My husband taught himself to read, write and figure. He is slow, of course, but persistently tries to improve. We both so much want our boys to learn the correct ways. When our younger son is old enough we hope to be able to get him to schooling, too.'

'That's wise. I believe all children should have schooling

in the basics. One day, perhaps, it will be so. But for now, I do my best to give them something.'

Gunnar Persson was unmarried. Not that he held any ideals against women. So far, romance just hadn't happened in his life. He thirsted for knowledge with an untameable passion and, perhaps, it was his obsession with words and figures that drove away many would-be sweethearts. He was no Adonis, but neither was he any slouch. Of average build; blond and blue-eyed; he displayed an engaging manner. In these attributes he was typical of many in Skåne's rural areas. Only in his choice of conversation topics did he stand out. He knew nothing of farming; little of nature; he would, instead, hold the floor on any aspect of politics, literature, art or mathematics and had a reasonable grasp of the major sciences. He also spoke fluently in English and German as well as other Scandinavian languages. In that way, he was completely out of place in Perstorp. His single status may have advantaged his charges for he taught them unreservedly and with single-minded devotion. Few people, even parents of his pupils, ever referred to him as anything other than 'Mr Persson.'

The evening mealtime in the Tilderkvist household was brightened each schoolday as Sten summarised his day's learning. It was Gunnar Persson's habit to include in each day's lessons a 'gem for today' where he gave the class a new word, phrase, witty saying or simple formula which he made them repeat ten times over. Tomas, Ulla and even Grandma Berthe would look forward each evening to the time when, at the conclusion of the meal, Sten would be invited to share with them the latest gem. The most popular were the proverbs or witty sayings and, most agreed, their favourite was: 'He who would have the fruit must first climb the tree.' A close second was: 'The only man who makes no errors is one who makes no effort.' Sten was always happy to be the conveyor of Mr Persson's 'gems' to the family and they were happy to benefit from this second-hand education.

Life in Peterlöv had changed in many ways since old Jan passed away. The fields which had borne crops and provided the family's livelihood over past decades now lay fallow and unproductive. Ulla grew a small mixture of produce in a sheltered patch and had taken over the looking-after of Berthe's hogs. These were the only semblances remaining of the former farming lifestyle. Almost entirely, the family was dependent upon Tomas to find a continual stream of customers for his guns, carvings, small-piece furniture and items of metalwork. But his reputation ensured that he could work neither quick enough nor long enough to satisfy the demands of all those who sought his workmanship.

In the January of 1760, Bo joined Mr Persson's school class. The 'pre-schooling' he'd had around the evening meal table would ensure that he would begin to grasp his learning quickly. In February, Berthe celebrated her seventy-seventh birthday. Only in this past winter had her aching joints kept her from her daily visits to the barn to help Ulla feed the hogs. Her eyesight was still good, but her mouth was now almost bereft of teeth. Those that remained resembled a row of condemned city houses when she smiled. She smiled often, and complained seldom.

'Still no signs of a thaw,' Tomas proclaimed, stamping the snow from his brogans. 'It'll soon be March, so it should start to warm up before long.'

'Yes, I hope so,' Berthe replied. 'I've never been over-fond of winter. In the old days it made travel a little easier, of course. We used the rivers and the lakes when they were frozen. But it's always hard on the animals. No, for me, I'll be glad when summer's here. You feel the cold more as you get older.'

'I imagine so,' Tomas chipped in. 'I'm not yet half your age and I feel that way already. It's been a devil of a winter, though, and the thermometer's still not showing so I guess it'll be cold for a bit yet. At least we have plenty of logwood cut, so we won't freeze. Not yet awhile.'

'No, I can't bring myself to go far from the fire these days,' Berthe sighed. 'I'm glad Ulla has taken to seeing the hogs are well cared for. Guess *they'll* be glad when the weather turns warmer. I'll get out to see them then. I sure miss the little squeakers.'

But Berthe never did get to see her little squeakers again. She died three weeks later, just as the thaw began. A fishbone stuck in her throat and, despite Ulla's best efforts to dislodge it, Berthe collapsed at the kitchen table and her life gave out. She was buried next to Jan in the graveyard near the Lutheran Church.

*

With Berthe now a recent memory and her two boys at school, the days in the Tilderkvist home seemed drawn out for Ulla. That, and her growing fondness for Gunnar Persson combined to encourage her into the role of matchmaker that summer. She and Tomas had invited the schoolteacher to their home on several occasions and they enjoyed his company. After a couple of shots of Tomas's aquavit, he'd regaled them with tales of his travels in England and Germany. His little bachelor ways amused them. He was so neat; so tidy; and almost automatically assumed the housewife's part in clearing away after the meal and in helping Ulla in the kitchen. It was after his fourth visit that it occurred to Ulla the man needed a wife with whom he could share more regularly the interesting anecdotes and experiences he'd garnered through his thirty-five years.

'Despite his funny little ways, he'd be a good catch,' Ulla told her husband. 'It must be lonely for him, living in that little cabin above the schoolhouse all by himself.'

'Hah! He's an independent, that one. Wouldn't know what to do with a woman around. You've seen how he is. Self-sufficient in everything. He's his own man.'

'I don't think so,' Ulla retaliated. 'I think he's just made his own little world as a kind of defence. Probably never had much time for women before – with all his travel and studying and that. But I'm not so sure that he doesn't just need a bit of pushing in the right direction.'

'So, you think you're the one to do the pushing, eh?'

'I'm not saying that. It's just that...'

'What? What are you cooking up?'

'Nothing. I was just thinking... well... you know Liesl in the village?'

'The Bechler woman?'

'That's right. Liesl Bechler. I reckon she and Gunnar might just get along together. Perhaps if we...'

'Oooh, I don't know about that. She's been in Peterlöv around ten years and never set a foot beyond the village more than a few times. I doubt she'd have much interest for him.'

'But, before that, she'd been to a few places, seen a few things. I don't think you really know her. I've often talked with her at the church market. She's no dumbskull. And her Swedish is almost perfect now.'

'Yeah, that's one thing. At least they could talk to each

other in German if they felt like it.' Tomas's comment bordered on sarcasm. For some reason he'd grown to distrust Germans. And Liesl was a German. Born in a small village on the Elbe, she'd grown up in Bremen, then lived in Denmark for a time before drifting into Sweden some ten years ago. She'd arrived in Malmö and was making her way north towards Göteborg when she stumbled on this small village and, somehow, became one of its residents.

'I'm going to have a talk with her,' Ulla enthused. 'Who knows? They may not even like each other. On the other hand, getting them together might do them both a good turn.'

Tomas gave a quiet chuckle. He'd watched his wife become fonder of the blond schoolteacher but had never harboured any feelings of jealousy. He and Ulla were probably closer to one another now than they were even in their courting days on the Nilssons' farm. He was bemused by the role his wife was adopting.

'I'll say this, Ulla: if there's one person around here who knows how to get people to socialise, it must be you. But just be careful. Remember, the future of our boys lies in his hands.'

'Typical of a man,' Ulla said, hands on hips, 'Always the practical, never the romantic.'

'Just be careful. That's all I'm saying.' For once, Tomas had the final say.

Liesl was taken by surprise when Ulla called on her next day.

'May I come in? There's something I wanted to discuss with you.'

'Please,' the German woman responded, throwing the door wide open and standing aside to allow Ulla to step into the small wooden-sided cottage. 'Sit down,' the host offered, waving loosely towards one of the four chairs in the room. 'I was just going to have some cheese. You'd like some?'

'Mmm-hmm, thank you,' Ulla answered as she took stock of the object of her intended matchmaking with a more careful appraisal than she'd afforded the woman on any of the many times they'd passed the time of day at the market. She saw Liesl in a new light and was instantly happy with what she saw, apart from her clothes. Not pretty, but solid and with a pleasant manner. With her short-cropped blonde hair and fair complexion, she'd pass for a Swede if one didn't already know of her background. But those clothes! They did nothing to enhance her femininity in any way. They were more appropriate to a farmboy. She'd need some advice on that, Ulla thought.

'How is your husband now?' Liesl asked. 'I was sorry that his mother died so tragically. He must miss her.'

'We both do. She was a fine old lady. Beginning to fail physically, but as bright as silver in her mind. We'll get over it in time, of course.'

Their conversation strolled down the broad avenues of small talk for a time as Ulla tried to find a loophole that she could exploit to develop the real reason for her visit. But it became unnecessary. Liesl may have looked every inch a Swede, but her German pedigree, with its characteristic bluntness, remained ingrained within her.

'So! You had something to discuss with me.' Her tone presented it as a statement, rather than a question, expecting her visitor to launch directly into the purpose of her visit.

'Yes. It's... well... how should I begin?' Ulla fumbled. 'You may not know, but our two boys attend schooling classes in Perstorp. A Mr Persson teaches them reading, writing and figuring.'

Liesl sat with hands steepled under her chin and brows slightly furrowed in a quizzical look as she hung on every word to catch the significance.

Ulla still searched her mind for some diplomatic entry to the proposals she had mentally formulated. She continued, 'He speaks very good German, this Mr Persson, and English too. He has visited us several times and he's a fine man. He always makes us laugh with his stories, but the school is his life. He lives above the schoolhouse and loves his work. He visited us again yesterday and we thought of you then.'

'But I'm no teacher. I don't see how I could help,' Liesl chipped in, wrongly anticipating the direction of Ulla's drift.

'Well, it wasn't as a teacher we were thinking,' Ulla recommenced, giving a nervous little cough as she did so. 'The fact is: he's a fine man; you're a fine woman. And you're both on your own. So...'

'Mrs Tilderkvist! Whatever are you suggesting?' the German woman exploded.

'Don't you think... well... wouldn't you even care to meet him? I don't know all of your circumstances, of course, but...'

'How old is this man?' Liesl put in, laughing.

'He's thirty-five, we think. Or maybe thirty-four.'

'Aha, one year behind me. Well, at least he's not fifty! Tell me a little more about him.'

Ulla expanded all she knew about Gunnar Persson. For more than an hour the two women traded blows on the pros and cons of the two meeting but, in time, Liesl warmed to the idea and agreed to join the Tilderkvists in a meal at which Gunnar would be present, if they could arrange it, two weeks hence.

'That's a one-sided duel,' Tomas observed when Ulla recounted her visit to Liesl Bechler. 'I suppose you expect me to even the score by approaching Mr Persson?'

'No, it doesn't have to be like that. Gunnar can just come along as normal. We'll explain when he gets here that I'd been telling Liesl about his visits to Germany and that he spoke her language very well. She was interested to meet him. That's all.'

'Ulla, my love, you're a real conniver.'

'Of course,' she smiled, 'How do you think I got you?'

In the event, there was no embarrassment on either side. The meal was conducted in near silence but, afterwards, when Liesl began to speak in her native tongue, Gunnar rose to the bait and began gabbling away. Not being able to make much sense of their exchanges, it was all the excuse the Tilderkvists needed to withdraw to 'attend to a few little chores' while their guests became more self-assured in one another's company.

'Seems to be going well, eh?' Ulla whispered to Tomas as they began cleaning the plates in the far corner of the kitchen. He said nothing by way of reply. Merely threw back his head and raised his eyebrows, with a look that said: 'You little schemer.' When they rejoined the would-be couple, the conversation switched back to Swedish and, for the remainder of the evening, centred around no topic in particular. Ulla was happy. She felt her debut as matchmaker had started well. But the biggest surprise was yet to come for, when the evening began to draw to a conclusion, Gunnar turned to Liesl and asked: 'Your home is not so far?'

'No. It's in the village.'

'Then may I see you safely to your door?'

'Thank you. I'd be happy for your company.'

Then, turning to Tomas, the schoolteacher suggested, 'I shouldn't be too long. Do you mind if I return for the horse later?'

'Not at all. You know where he's stabled. Help yourself. Most likely we'll be asleep.'

It was all too much for Ulla. She was elated. No sooner had the door closed behind the departing pair when she turned to Tomas and prodded him firmly on the breastbone: 'See! I told you! I told you! Hee-heeeee!'

The vacuum in Ulla's life, bequeathed by the loss of her mother-in-law, was soon amply filled. Not only had she acted as Liesl's matchmaker; she now became her confidante. At least twice a week over the following months, the radiant German spent the afternoon with Ulla. With astute guidance, her dress sense improved. She was always full of questions. And full of life. It seemed she and Gunnar shared more than just linguistic interests. Liesl, too, had a good knowledge of the arts. And, from time to time, she'd helped in the preparation of Gunnar's lessons.

'So. You think you'll make a good schoolteacher's wife?' Ulla ventured.

'Sshh. Don't tempt the Fates. Just give us time. We're still getting to know each other. But, yes; I like him. I hope... well, who knows? Like you told me in the beginning, he's such good company. Even if things don't work out in any permanent way, I'll always feel beholden to you for your courage in coming to see me that first day.'

'A woman's intuition, that's all.'

Four months later, Mr and Mrs Persson emerged from the arched doorway of the little Lutheran Church to the cheers of the villagers, a group of friends from Perstorp and, without exception, the whole of Gunnar's class which now numbered twenty-four.

'They'll have to knock down the small schoolhouse and build a bigger one,' Tomas suggested.

'No need,' Ulla replied as they stood clapping the newlyweds, 'It's all taken care of. For now, they'll live in Liesl's cottage, right here in Peterlöv. In time, the top floor of the schoolhouse will be made into another classroom. Liesl will teach the younger ones there.'

For one more time, Tomas had the final say: 'Why! You little schemer!'

*

In the spring of 1761, four new arrivals appeared on the Tilderkvist farm and a highly excited Ulla called her husband from his workshop.

'Aren't they darlings?' Ulla enthused. 'I got them from Bengt Hallstrom. Couldn't resist them.'

'Huh! More little squeakers,' Tomas said, showing none of his wife's admiration for the wriggling piglets.

'Hei, you big softy. You love them really. Don't you?'

'Hogs is hogs to me,' he replied. Then, softening his expression into an expanding smile, he threw an arm around his wife's shoulder and agreed. 'Of course I do. It's just that I never have the time to get over here. They're your babies. You have to have something to lavish your love on, I suppose. But, with three handsome men to look after I'd have thought you had enough.' Untwining his arm from around her, he gave her a friendly pat on the buttocks and, still smiling, made his way back to his workshop. He seemed to be very busy these days. Overly busy. For the past week he'd risen early and only the fall of darkness had summoned him to the evening meal table.

'Whatever are you doing out there?' Ulla asked in a tone

of exasperation. 'I wasn't aware that you had so many requests to fulfil.'

'No, it's just something I have to get done. You'll see. Two more days.'

'Aha. So it's some kind of surprise.'

'Well, it would be no surprise if I told you, would it?' Tomas answered, giving nothing away. His reply seemed to suffice for the time being for no more was said of his lengthy working hours.

Ulla seldom ventured into her husband's workspace for she knew that he liked to concentrate on whatever he was doing – a state that had much improved for him since Bo, too, had been attending lessons at the schoolhouse. For her part, Ulla was besotted with her newly acquired piglets and made countless rounds to the barn to watch their antics.

True to his prediction, Tomas wandered into the kitchen at an earlier than usual hour two days later to pronounce his project complete.

'Like to come and see it?'

Puzzled, Ulla followed him around to the lean-to workshop.

'What is it?' she inquired.

'It's here. Look!' he invited.

There, taking centre stage on the floor of his shop stood a most beautiful small table. Square, ornately carved and with a small drawer on each of its four sides. The highly figured grain glinted through the dark, deep red dye and polish that Tomas had so carefully applied.

'It's beautiful. An absolute masterpiece,' Ulla exulted.

'Yes. It's to be our gift to the Perssons for the new house they're building. They're the kind of people who'd appreciate it. I've been doing a little bit each day when my customers' work was at a convenient stopping point.'

'Oh, Tomas. Why didn't you say? I was beginning to think you'd taken some kind of umbrage because of my piglets.'

'Ha! I started work on this long before your piglets arrived. These last few days have been just coincidental. I wanted to get it finished before next week. That way we can take it to them before I have to visit Norrholm with the hunting rifle for Kari Ruuska, the Finnish timber merchant. Since I'll be gone three or four days it was best to get it done now.'

'Oooh, they'll fall in love with it, I'm sure,' sighed Ulla. 'Shall we invite them here?'

'No. Let's take it down to the cottage tomorrow as it's not a lessons-day. They're sure to be home. Besides, I'd like to ask Gunnar if Sten can be excused from classes for a few days so that he can come with me to Norrholm. We don't get the chance to spend much time together these days. It'll be good for both of us.'

Next day, Saturday, at around ten o'clock in the morning, Tomas and Ulla loaded the table on to the smaller of their two carts ready for the five hundred yard journey to its destination at the Perssons. They'd looked forward to surprising the recently-marrieds but the sting was taken out of their hopes when it appeared the couple were not at home.

'What shall we do, Tomas? Take it home and come back later?' Ulla asked, trying to be constructive in her obvious disappointment.

'Might be the best—' Tomas didn't finish for, as he looked up, the door was at last opened. And there stood Liesl in some disarray. It was patently obvious that the Tilderkvists had chosen to call at a most inopportune time. Nonetheless, seeing who her interrupting visitors were,

Liesl begged them to wait and, moments later, invited them in. The embarrassed laughter all round accurately summarised the situation.

'Isn't it time you two had some water on the stove?' Ulla remarked, breaking the discomposure of the moment. 'We've brought you something for your new home.' With that, Tomas carefully lifted down the table and carried it into the room, setting it down in a space near the spot where Ulla had sat, seemingly only yesterday, when she'd first told Liesl about the schoolteacher.

'My goodness! That's for us?' Gunnar exclaimed, disbelievingly. 'What a treasure!'

Spontaneously, Liesl threw her arms around Tomas, kissing him on both cheeks. 'How can we possibly thank you? What a wonderful gift.'

Once the initial overwhelming had subsided, Tomas took the opportunity to ask Gunnar if he would excuse Sten from classes for the next few days and, not surprisingly, the teacher agreed.

'You know, he's one of the brightest we have,' he told the Tilderkvists. 'A short absence will not impair his progress one little bit. I'm not saying that just because he's your son. He really is a fine young man and assimilates new ideas so quickly for a thirteen year old.'

'You have to go all the way to Norrholm again?' Liesl questioned.

'Yes. I'll be delivering a very special hunting rifle to a man there who runs a large timber business. He's a Finn and you know what some of these Finns are like. Always within arm's length of the aquavit and always letting you know they're the ones paying the money.'

'Well, when you get back, you must come and share some of *our* aquavit,' Gunnar invited.

'We will,' Ulla confirmed. And the Tilderkvists left the couple to what recently-marrieds do best.

Neither Tomas nor Ulla had mentioned to Sten the possibility of his accompanying his father on the trip to Norrholm. When they did so, the boy was overjoyed. Nine year old Bo wanted to join them, of course, but was told that he was too young for such a long buggy ride with promises made to repair his omission when he was older.

This would be Tomas's third visit to the thickly forested area in a little over as many months. Kari Ruuska was a difficult man to deal with. He'd heard of Tomas by reputation and sent a message to him requesting the gunsmith to visit the sawmill. He dearly wanted Tomas to build a very special hunting rifle but insisted always that the gunsmith make the round trip to Norrholm – a round trip of three days in the best of weather. But he was willing to pay well. Very well. Since he began his business near Tampere in his home country, Kari had become a wealthy man. Once he moved to Sweden to supply the growing shipbuilding industry at Göteborg, he'd become obscenely rich. But he was both bullish and arrogant, insisting that Tomas visit him to discuss the specifications and make stock templates to get a perfect fit to his shoulder, then re-visit when the gun was part-completed so that he could make any changes he deemed desirable. Now that the rifle was finished, Tomas had to undertake the journey once again.

Ulla consoled young Bo by suggesting he would be the 'man of the house' whilst his father and brother were absent, and told him that he would be in charge of the piglets. She would, of course, be his helper. He accepted the accolade and ceased complaining.

Thin, wispy clouds bedecked the otherwise bright blue

sky on the Sunday morning as father and son prepared to leave Peterlöv. The climbing sun promised a bright and warm day. Tomas wrapped the long, highly polished gunbox in two layers of woollen blankets and stowed it on the cart. Alongside, he placed the two baskets of food that Ulla had prepared for 'her boys'. It was no later than eight o'clock when the cart clattered its way out of the yard and on to the dusty road that headed towards Perstorp. Passing close to the old schoolhouse, soon to be demolished to be replaced by a bigger version near the Lutheran Church in Peterlöv, Tomas was once again reminded of the great strides his son had made in learning since attending Gunnar Persson's classes.

'Have you had any more ideas on how you're going to use all this learning Mr Persson's been giving you?' Tomas asked his son.

'Oh, I have some ideas,' Sten replied, suddenly jolted from his spellbinding daydream that had been fuelled by the panorama of nature that enclosed the road on either side.

'Such as?' Tomas asked, provoking the boy to be more forthcoming.

'Well, someday I'd like to travel to some of the far places Mr Persson has told us about.'

'Huh! He's put the wanderlust in you, eh? That's all very well and good, but it costs, you know. What will you do for money?'

'I'll earn as I go,' the quick-witted youngster replied. 'If I get the chance, I may join a ship,' he added with some conviction.

'A sailor, eh?'

'No. A navigator,' he corrected.

'What's that?'

'The most important man on a ship,' the boy replied, 'excepting, perhaps, the captain. He's the one who calculates the course the ship must take, bearing in mind the wind and the currents.'

'But you don't know of such things. How can you...'

'I can learn!' Sten said with a tone of indignation.

So their conversation continued. Father and son discussing 'deep' matters. It was what Tomas had hoped for. The chance to spend uninterrupted quality time with his boy, getting close to him once more and sharing in his life's aspirations.

For Ulla and Bo, time seemed to fly past at twice the speed of its normal passing. The piglets were growing fast but still exuded a cuteness that stamped a peculiar character on each one. Unlike the 'sacks of flour with a leg at each corner' that they were, they took on almost human attributes when individually named and spoken to as if fully conversant with the Swedish tongue. Their spoken replies, limited to snorts, squeals and grunts, were nonetheless interpreted in perfect grammar to have real meaning. Mentally, Bo assumed gigantic proportions as he made out to be 'pig farmer supreme' in the freedom that Ulla allowed him around the barn. Sunday night was upon them before they knew it.

By contrast with the preceding day, Monday seemed to drag. Bo was once again back at his classes and Ulla was left to her own devices. There was not even the briefest of highlights to her day that would have been occasioned by a visit from Liesl. Mrs Persson was fast becoming a fully fledged teacher of elementary lessons and spent her days with her husband at the schoolhouse. Ulla busied herself with baking some cakes and, donning her yard-clothes, moved several large piles of straw to the front of the barn in readiness for replacing the hogs' bedding. To the Tilderkvists, there had only ever been two designations in the life cycle of a pig. When it was very small, it was a piglet. It then became a hog. They never delineated between barrow, boar, sow, gilt or shoat. They were just hogs. When Bo returned home, Ulla had decided, they would marshal their efforts into renewing the straw bedding. Until then, she would ensure that the old farmhouse looked neat and tidy. Gunnar Persson, at least, would have approved of her methodical orderliness.

Tomas and Sten spent their first night away from home at a wayside inn just south of Falkenberg. It was one Tomas had used before and, most likely, they would stop there on the second night also as they returned south. Tomas knew the innkeeper only as Arne. He couldn't recall ever having heard the man's family name. It had been a long and tiring drive and both father and son felt stiff and aching from the unaccustomed length of time they'd spent on the seat of the cart.

'You gonna let the lad have a taste of ale?' Arne asked as they settled into deep, high-backed chairs in the ale room. 'It'll make 'im sleep real good.'

'Oh, I don't think either of us will need encouragement to sleep. Even so, I'll have an ale and you can pour a small one for the lad. Best he doesn't develop too great a taste for the stuff.'

Arne guffawed in his usual loud, coarse manner and set about serving the measures of ale. The best parts of the day had been warm, but the atmosphere within the confines of the inn was warmer still. It was all that Sten could do to keep his eyes open. He sipped at the ale and screwed up his face as its bitterness bit his palate. Manfully and courageously he fought down the small measure. Within an hour and a half of their arrival at the inn, both Tomas and Sten were fast asleep in their beds.

The visit to Kari Ruuska's mill took somewhat longer than Tomas had imagined. The big Finn kept the gunsmith waiting for some time before he extricated himself from giving instructions to his foreman and work crews. Then, when he did finally appear, the bumptious man hummed and hawed about pernickety little details, then haggled with Tomas regarding the price. For a man so rich, his behaviour seemed miserly. Suddenly, almost as if some other being had taken over his mind, he changed tack completely and asked his clerk to pay Tomas a sum that was greater than the artisan had asked in the first place.

'The little extra is for goodwill,' the Finn explained. 'I'm a busy man, Mr Tilderkvist, and I thank you for your trouble in making your visits here. I can't just leave the mill, you understand, even though my foreman is a good man. No, not even for a fine gun like this. It's a masterpiece, my friend, and I'll be proud to carry it on the hunts. And now, I must return to business. Time is money where milling timber is concerned. I'll bid you good day.'

'What a strange man,' Sten observed as they prepared to drive off. 'He seemed not to notice I was even there with you and he was very rude. He treated you like dirt to begin with.'

'True, but we don't choose our customers, boy; they choose us. And they pay. That's why we have to accept all their rudeness and say nothing. It's the way of the world. In time you'll see.'

On their second night at Arne's inn, they were much less tired, but equally stiff and sore. This time Sten refused the offered ale. They met up with another traveller who claimed he was a naturalist. He was heading north to study various plants. Father, son and the interesting man spent a leisurely evening together, discussing many aspects of nature and woodland craft.

In Peterlöv, it had not been so leisurely. In fact it had been disastrous. And worse.

As planned, Ulla and Bo set about making both the new piglets and the older hogs more comfortable. Together, they tackled the hogs first, goading them into a side pen while they removed the disgusting mess that had covered the floor of their sleeping area. Ulla's earlier efforts in redistributing the piles of straw to the front side of the barn made it easy to get the job done. It was only because young Bo was helping her that she tried it this way. And it seemed to be working well for, in good time, the hogs were able to return to their proper pen. Next, it was the turn of the piglets.

'Hold the gate open while I chase them through,' Ulla instructed. She stood behind them, waving her arms and shouting as her 'little squeakers' moved into the side pen without showing any great obstinacy. It was when Bo jumped down from the fence rail to close the gate that the trouble started. The last of the piglets to go through the gate, suddenly alarmed, somehow squirmed under the fence and went rampaging towards the main store of straw at the back of the barn.

'Quick! Cut him off!' yelled Bo.

'I can't, he's too fast!' Ulla bawled back, lunging through the outer gate to chase the runaway across the barn. 'He's gone behind the straw. Make sure the others are secure. We'll have to try to corner him.'

'Shall I bring some sticks?' asked Bo.

'No, we'll try to grab him. But I don't know where he's disappeared to now.'

They poked among the straw and tried to work from both ends, forcing the piglet into one corner. There was no movement to betray his whereabouts. Somewhere, in the deep recesses of the straw pile, he was catching his breath. They continued prodding at the piles.

'It's too dark in here to see properly,' Ulla said. 'Keep guard while I get a lamp.' She returned in a few moments, having used a strike-a-light and a sure-fire taper to get an oil lamp alight. Its golden beam lit up the rear of the barn and, almost at once, they saw the tell-tale movement among the straw. Then it bolted. Like a flash it shot between them and headed for the pile of straw at the front of the barn.

'He's got the devil in him, that one!' Ulla shrieked, whirling after the disappearing animal. Twice more he crossed the barn, evading the clutches of his pursuers. Once again he made ground to the front, turned, and charged directly at the converging mother and son. Ulla spun wildly, letting the lamp fall behind her and Bo sprawled his full length in a vain dive to grab at a pumping leg. Regaining her footing, Ulla continued her momentum towards the backside straw piles. She lunged headlong into the straw, catching hold of one of the piglet's back legs.

'Pin him down! Pin him down! I can't hold on!' she yelled. And Bo thrashed among the straw to get his arms around the squirming beast. Exhausted, they lay panting, holding the piglet fast. It was only then, in that moment of relaxation, that Ulla heard the crackling behind her. The discarded lamp had set fire to the front side straw and the blaze was already taking hold. Rolling tongues of flame licked their way across the front of the barn and smoke billowed up to the rafters and outwards, even through the smallest openings.

'Bo!' screamed Ulla, letting go of the piglet. 'We're

trapped! The whole lot's going to go! Quick! Let me try to get you up and through the back window.'

The small aperture was not really a window at all. It had been intended as an air vent and was high up on the wall. Frantically, Ulla and her boy piled the tied bundles of straw so far untouched by the fire against the wall directly under the opening. Twice, Ulla stood on the piled straw and twice concluded that it was not yet high enough for her to push Bo up to the opening. All the time they dragged the piles and built their ladder, the fire spread further, penetrating to one of the backside corners and along the boarded sides. Panic-stricken, Ulla decided to give it one more try.

'Come on, Bo! You're going to have to get help as fast as you can. Quick! Get up on my shoulders.' She stooped down, swaying unsteadily on the compacted straw. Bo climbed on to her back, put his hands flat against the wall and then wedged one foot on each of his mother's shoulders as she straightened up to get him as close to the escape hole as possible. Sweat covered both their bodies; their eyes and nostrils began to sting.

'Push, mother! Push!' the boy yelled, his fingers scrabbling to get a hold on the rough wood that framed the vent. Ulla grabbed his ankles and thrust him upwards with all the strength she could muster. In one instant she felt both Bo taking a firmer hold on the frame above, his feet thrashing free and banging the wooden barn siding, and her own feet pushing deeper into the straw, throwing her off-balance. She plunged sideways towards the inferno and the searing heat and smoke engulfed her. Through the blackening swirl, she could hear Bo screaming as she fought to regain the unburnt straw at the back of the barn. As she peered upwards, she could see his little legs thrashing around as he tried to lever himself those last inches through the hatch. Was he stuck? She couldn't tell. Her vision of him came and went, came and went. Then came no more.

Just outside Halmstad, Tomas and Sten pulled their cart beneath some shady trees in a little grove. It was early afternoon and the spot made a fine stopping place to stretch their legs, rub down those parts that ached most, and finish their remaining morsels of food. A few more hours and they'd be home, looking forward to the hearty meal that Ulla would prepare for them.

'We live in a beautiful country, don't we?' Sten remarked.

'We sure do, son. And to think all you want to do is hop on a ship and leave it all.'

'I didn't say that,' the boy protested. 'I just said I'd like to see some of the far-off places Mr Persson's been telling us about. Then, I'll come back. I would always come back to Sweden.'

'Ja, it's a fine place. And to think all these areas around here once belonged to Denmark.'

'That was over a hundred years ago, father. It's all part of Sweden now.'

They walked through the sunny glades, soaking in the beauty and tranquillity until Tomas felt that man and beast alike had had sufficient rest and replenishment.

Once they'd got south of Perstorp and within easy distance of home, Tomas burst into song. The road was a principal travel route, but no one else was within earshot, so he bellowed out an old melody without inhibition. Father and son had enjoyed their trip but were glad to be nearing Peterlöv once again. As their cart trundled off the thoroughfare and on to the little track that led to the farm they could make out the figure of a man running towards them.

'Hei, looks like Gunnar's the first here to welcome us home.'

Sten stood up part way, his knees bent to maintain his balance, and waved exuberantly at his approaching teacher.

'Stop! Stop!' they heard Gunnar shouting. Tomas reined in as the panting teacher stopped running and stood with one arm raised, signalling them to pull up. It became immediately apparent that all was not well. The teacher was ashen-faced; his eyes seemed lifeless and lost somewhere at the back of his skull.

'There's been a terrible accident,' the distraught man blurted out. In staccato gasps he summarised the tragedy: 'The hog barn caught fire last night. It burned completely. Ulla and Bo...' He sprang forward, clasping Tomas by the biceps and lowering his head so that he faced the ground. Tears began to soak his cheeks.

Tomas shook him. 'What's happened to Ulla and Bo?' His voice trembled. 'Where are they? Are they all right?'

Gunnar looked directly at him, his mouth pressed tight shut so that his top lip bulged forward. Slowly, he shook his head.

'Oh no! No!' Tomas wailed, forgetting the horse, cart, Sten and Gunnar Persson. He ran pell-mell towards the farmstead and could now see for himself that the barn was no longer silhouetted against the skyline. Eight or nine villagers milled around where the barn had been and looked up as he charged towards them.

'Where's Ulla? Where's my Ulla?' he yelled like a madman. Two of the men caught him and tried to calm him down.

'It's no use,' one man said, 'it's all over.'

Gunnar and Sten came running up behind Tomas. The two Tilderkvists shed no tears. They were in a state of shock. It was two hours later, in the Persson's small cottage, that Tomas and Sten learned the truth. A villager had heard Bo's screams and saw the smoke. He raised the alarm in the village and ran to help the boy who seemed to be stuck in an opening high up on the barn wall. At length, the man found a ladder and was able to pull the boy through, but the lower half of his body was already badly burnt. Bo lived only long enough to outline what happened. Ulla had been cremated where she'd fallen. The hogs and piglets had been roasted, unceremoniously. Both father and son were overcome with grief and Liesl made each drink a strong draught of a herbal mixture she'd prepared. The hour was already late, but no one felt like sleeping.

Two days later, after Bo and the charred lump that had been the boy's mother were buried, Tomas felt the full weight of bitterness. He told Gunnar: 'This place will never be my home again. I'm quitting Peterlöv. And taking Sten with me. There are too many sad memories here. You and Liesl are just beginning. You'll need things for the big new house so take whatever you want from our furnishings. Sten and me, we won't be taking much. We'll travel light.'

'But Tomas, where will you go? What will you do? Your workshop is here. All your tools.'

'I know, Gunnar. But my bad memories are here, too. At this moment, they outweigh everything else. I've heard they're to build many large ships over at Karlskrona. That's where we'll go.'

'But Tomas, why don't you—'

'No! No, Gunnar, don't even try to persuade me otherwise. My mind's made up. You and Liesl have been good friends. We'll miss you. And Sten will miss your teaching. But we'll do the best we can. Only don't expect to see us back in Peterlöv.'

Turning to Sten, Gunnar pleaded with the boy, 'You will write, won't you? Let us know where you are and how you're faring?'

'I will, Mr Persson, sir.'

In a matter of hours, their cart reloaded, the Tilderkvists prepared to leave.

'Here! Take these two baskets of food. They'll fill your bellies for today, at least,' Liesl said, holding out two well-stuffed market baskets. With Liesl's food, some tools, a few personal belongings and the money from Kari Ruuska, Tomas and Sten left Peterlöv for Karlskrona, the burgeoning naval port almost due east of Peterlöv.

For miles they travelled in silence. Suddenly, Tomas spoke, as if released from some other-worldly spell. 'I want to forget Peterlöv. I want to forget the farm. Me and you, Sten, we need to start a new life. The newest life we can. I never want anybody to know about what's happened. From now on, I'll no longer be "Tilderkvist". I'll take a different name.'

'What name would you choose? Persson?'

'No, we need to take a new name.' Unconsciously, Tomas used the plural pronoun, including Sten in the decision he was making. The boy raised no objection. 'Maybe just shortening it to "Tillkvist" is enough. There won't be any distant relations popping up who'll recognise that name.'

'Sten Tillkvist. It doesn't seem such a big change but it sounds quite different. I think I could grow used to it.'

'Me too. It'll do. We'll have to keep saying it to each other so that we do get used to it. Remember, whenever we meet people, we're "Tillkvists" and we've always been so. If anyone wants to know, we'll tell 'em we're from Norrholm. It's far enough away and is so small hardly anyone will know of it. Apart from Ruuska's mill people there aren't too many others there anyhow.'

The boy who, overnight, had become a man, shrugged his shoulders. 'Fine by me.' And they began carrying on a conversation about some imaginary topics, using their new names as often as possible. It helped pass the time. And helped develop their new personae.

Under normal circumstances, the route to Karlskrona would have taken them through Kristianstad. And under normal circumstances they would have called on Leif Ulfsson and at the Nilsson farm. But these were not normal circumstances. Leif might well have connections with the naval armoury at Karlskrona; the Nilssons would want chapter and verse on their daughter's death. Neither would in any way help the Tillkvists establish the new start in life they needed. Both would drag them into past remembrances. There would come a time to reminisce; it would be in later years, not while the bitterness and grief still stabbed at their souls. So they bypassed Kristianstad, following an old road that skirted the lakes and brought them back to the main thoroughfare some miles to the east of the town.

'It's best we camp out tonight,' Tomas informed his son. 'We'll break out some food at supper time and we can sleep under the cart. I've brought some blankets.'

'I suppose we'll be safe enough. Mr Persson told us that Skånian Snaphanar bandits used to roam around here. But that was many years ago.'

Tomas took hold of Sten's wrist, firmly but not harshly. 'Listen son, I know the Perssons were our close friends. The best, dammit. But I don't want to hear Mr Persson this and Mr Persson that. It's hard on both of us, but we must try to forget them for a while. Understand?'

'Why, father? I promised to write to Mr Persson. Are you telling...'

'I know, I know. You can write sometime, but don't say exactly where we are. And just sign it "Tomas and Sten" or something vague. We want to try to break all our old links with the past.'

Sten secretly felt his father was taking this 'new life' idea too far, but he kept his thoughts to himself.

When Tomas and Sten swung into the broad streets that characterised Karlskrona, they were impressed by the rows of neat cottages and the contrasting fine buildings. They made their way towards the docks and pulled in before a livery stable where they could leave their means of transport in good hands while they tried to find work. They walked towards a substantial stone building, its front elevation studded with windows. The two felt out of place in such austere surroundings and entered cautiously through a large oak door. They were greeted by a young man in naval uniform and told him they were seeking work. He directed them to the office of a Mr Ehrlich. The Tillkvists' real introduction to Karlskrona was through the enigmatic German immigrant, Jurgen Ehrlich. He had come to Sweden to work in the Kosta glassworks, several miles to the north of Karlskrona. The factory was run largely by a team of Bohemian glassblowers and, after a few months, Jurgen could stand no more of their clannish ways and walked out. Now he was in charge of dock labour at the naval port.

'What kind of work is it you wish to find, Mr...?'

'Tillkvist. Tomas Tillkvist. I'm an artisan trained in gunmaking. I can work wood and metal; build furniture; do fine joinery or even rough carpentry, come to that.'

'If you're so good, why are you looking for work?' the labour boss challenged.

'I'm from Norrholm, just south of Göteborg. Work there is short but we heard...'

'The young man? He's also a gunsmith?'

'No. This is Sten. He's my son. He can read, write and figure. Speaks some German, too.' Tomas threw in the last, hoping that it might help gain some added favour.

Turning to Sten, the man sought to verify the qualification. 'Sprechen Sie Deutsch?'

'Ja, ein wenig,' the boy replied, 'aber hoffentlich, mit der zeit, es wirt besser sein.'

'Schön.' Then to Tomas, 'You have papers?'

'Certainly.' Tomas reached into his coat and took out the papers Leif Ulfsson had drawn up for him. He held them out, suddenly realising that they were written for his old name. He hoped the labour man wouldn't spot the discrepancy. And good fortune was with him.

'Fine,' Jurgen said abruptly. 'But I don't know that we have any work for a gunsmith at present. Go directly down to the yard and ask for Johan Tornstrom. Tell him I sent you. Now, as for you, boy. Maybe I can find something for you here. I could do with an assistant.'

Tomas thanked Jurgen Ehrlich, left Sten in the man's charge and found his way to the yard where he located Johan Tornstrom. Introducing himself, he reiterated his credentials.

'Well, I suppose if you're a gunsmith you can carve accurately, yes?'

'What kind of carving did you have in mind?' Tomas asked.

'Figureheads. More like sculpting in wood, but they need a good eye and careful control.'

'Just give me the chance. I'll show you what I can do. I've been carving wood since I was a boy. I reckon I can close on make it talk.'

Johan laughed, thrust out his arm and shook hands vigorously with his new starter. Tomas had never seen a ship's figurehead, but he was confident that, whatever it was, if it was formed from wood he could do it. Johan Tornstrom was a likeable man. Of average height but broad in the shoulder, his skin was swarthy and his grey-blue eyes smouldered under a thatch of long mid-brown hair that he wore tied back. He took Tomas into the workshop where two figureheads were partly completed. One was of an extremely voluptuous woman with long flowing hair, her arms stretched straight behind her as if she was being thrust forward by some incredible force that drove at her spine. The other depicted a handsome male clothed only in a loin cloth but sporting a helmet surmounted by small wings on either side.

'These are typical of what is required. Perhaps now you can see for yourself the kind of carving it takes. A little different from your gunstocks I think, eh?'

'Hmph. Quite a different art. Everything is on a larger scale. But I'd like to try it. I've always enjoyed the challenge of something new. Now, tell me, why are you carving two side by side?'

'Two reasons. One practical, one personal. First, the practical: it's not my choice to have male or female on the bow, so I do one of each. Sometimes I'm told specifically what is required, like a god or a nymph. Second, the personal: for some strange reason that I can't explain, I'm more creative when I work on the one for a time and think about the other. It's like making a fresh start each time and the ideas for the facial expressions or small adornments come better when I do it that way.' Johan spoke in a quiet, slow way and his manner indicated that he worked in the same way, holding that life had no deadlines.

Sten's working career got off to an entirely different start. No sooner had Mr Ehrlich whisked the lad into the big office than he sat him down at a desk on which a large ledger lay open. With only a bare outline as guidance, the German had him tallying columns of figures. Jurgen Ehrlich was a human whirlwind. It seemed to Sten that his new boss could juggle three, four or more different tasks at any one time and succeed in completing all of them.

The Tillkvists had begun their new life. Once they'd settled on some accommodation, father and son would blend transparently into Karlskrona's growing cosmopolitan populace.

*

Coincident with the job-seeking wanderings of the Tillkvists, a wanderer of a different ilk but with the same mission arrived in Norrholm at the sawmill of Kari Ruuska. He was easily distinguishable by his clothing. His colourful homespun jacket, leather trousers, heavy shoes and, most of all, his flamboyant conical cap, denoted that he was one of the Lapp or Sami people from the north of Sweden. In his physical appearance, Anta Utsi was typical of many Lapp men: around five feet in height with broad shoulders and short legs, dark straight hair and egg-shaped face, his complexion olive and his cheekbones high. His eyes were dark and straight and showed no inclination towards the epicanthic folds commonly found in the more easterly of the northern peoples.

Unlike the relatively short sojourn of the Tillkvists,

Anta's journey had begun many months before, several hundred miles north. The Riksdag's encouragement to the migration of 'southerners' into the northern wilds over the past few years had squeezed Anta from his own land where, for more than four hundred years, his forebears had herded reindeer. He travelled south, first by sled, then at varying times by horse and foot, stopping off wherever he thought it possible to eke out some kind of living. Eventually, he made his way to the west of Lake Vanern and now found himself in the small mill community of Norrholm. Kari Ruuska was at first reluctant to employ the Lapp on account of his small stature but, as the northerner appeared to show a healthy appetite for hard work, the big Finn relented and allowed him to join one of the work crews on the log-handling and debarking machines.

The fact that Anta Utsi was one of the Sami, with a mother tongue of Lappish and an ability to speak Swedish only passably, had not been major factors in the mill owner's judgement. He was in a not too dissimilar position himself, speaking Swedish as a second language. Kari believed the Lapps to be resourceful and tenacious, but also very independent. However likeable this 'wanderer from the north' appeared, the real question was: how well would he fit into the small team at the mill? Kari's second concern had been in respect of the Lapp's ability to sustain long periods of working on relatively mundane activities. There would be no outlet for a Lapp's artistic appreciation; strong sense of design; or the consideration of colour and craft that were, generally, the hallmarks of these people. Certainly, the normally inherent characteristics of orderliness and a systematic approach to almost every facet of life would be benefits that, alloyed to a well-motivated work ethic, could help improve the quality and output of the Norrholm mill.

'If only it doesn't mean he'll be gone in a month,' Kari muttered to himself, 'the little man could become a real asset.'

There was one aspect of Lapp culture that the big timberman had overlooked, ignored or was unaware of: their inordinate self-reliance. For a Lapp to ask for help would be considered by many to be an ignominy. Any self-respecting Lapp had learned to fend for himself and, although not an ungenerous people disinclined to offer hospitality, they did, nonetheless, tend to adopt a 'man mind thyself' attitude.

The Norrholm sawmill benefited from Kari Ruuska's experiences in Tampere, where he'd first become involved in the timber business. Times had changed. Mostly for the better. Huge circular saws now cut the wood into planking. The five foot diameter steel blades were driven by leather belts slung around pulleys, their prime movement being initiated by water wheels that drove the pulley-geared shafts. The whole process was an infinite improvement on the hand-drawn saws that had been worked over a pit in former times. The old saw pits had been condemned to history – a history that sawmillers held in contempt, for it had been a hot, dirty, sweaty labour to produce planks in that way. A top-man and a pit-man had drawn the long, broad saws up and down to sever the trunks into planks, the pit-man having to suffer the fall of sawdust into his hair and eyes. The Norrholm mill was the epitome of the modernisation that now spurred timber production to meet a demand that was fuelling an unprecedented growth in the industry.

Anta Utsi was fortunate to find, in Lars Petri the foreman, a man who was fair, just and, above all, impartial to the colour, creed or kinship of those who worked for him. The same could not be said of the other mill workers. They extended no warm greeting to Anta as he joined them in securing the heavy chains around the trunks to be dragged to the debarker. The churning knurled discs of the debarker would chew off the outer layers of each tree before the exposed white wood was fed to the first of the saws that would remove the irregular wood to leave a rectangular cross-section that would, ultimately, produce planking of various thicknesses. None of the men addressed Anta by his proper name. Nor did they refer to him as Lapp or Sami. Almost as if by some unanimous prior agreement out of his hearing, they called him 'Lappi.'

'Never worked in a mill, have you Lappi?' one of the crew called to him. 'Big difference from herding reindeer. You'll see.'

Anta refused to rise to any of their taunts. He gave no verbal response to their inaccurate summaries of a Sami's lifestyle, but raised the corners of his mouth in a half smile.

Despite Lars Petri's many attempts to ensure that all his workers carried a fair share of the load on each crew, it seemed that Anta Utsi always wound up with the dirtiest work. Or the most difficult. When the foreman took his occasional rest days, Anta suffered most. But he did so without complaint. It was not only because he was a Lapp that the men excluded him from their jokes and, usually filthy, stories. Nor was it because the little man spoke their language so imperfectly. They were irked by his incessant questions. Sometimes he asked his fellow workers about the whys, wherefores and what-ifs of sawmill practice. Most often, he asked Lars Petri. And that was what annoyed them. He seemed to be currying some kind of favour. Building some kind of inside track with the boss. He was, like them, just a worker. There was no need for him to know any more than they did, the men opined.

'How you keep sharp the saw?' 'Why we not cut with bark on?' 'What best tree for timber?' Anta's questions went on. And his fellow workers became more discriminatory.

'One day we'll teach that smart Lappi bastard a lesson,' one man said.

'Ja. Ever since Ruuska gave him a cottage like the rest of us, Lappi thinks he's some kinda god. Be better off in his pole-tent again. That'd bring 'im back to earth.'

Almost every day some comment was made to the hard-working Lapp about his suitability for reindeer-herding; his inability to speak properly; his strange clothes or some other aspect of his culture. He became even more of a provocation to his fellow workers for two reasons: he never tried to retaliate; and he worked indefatigably at whatever task he was set.

Anta was meticulous in his attention to cleanliness. Each day he brought his work clothes to the mill in a draw-neck hide bag, changing before and after each day's work. One day, at the end of his labours, he prepared to change back to his street clothes. As was his custom, he removed his soiled work clothes in the ablutions area – a small rectangular cabin that was formed by rough stakes stood in the earth and the same to support the sod-covered roof – and proceeded to sluice his face, hands and body with cold water from the bucket provided. He reached into his hide bag to find the piece of cloth he used as a towel but, in the dark recesses of the bag, his fingers trawled through a gummy, sticky treacle that fused thumb and forefinger together and the three remaining fingers became as one. His clothes had been removed and the bag part filled with pine resin. Withdrawing his hand, Anta looked at the mess that covered his skin. He could force the digits apart but had no means of removing the viscid substance. Nor could he find his clothes but, even had they been to hand, he would not have been able to touch them without transferring the gluey mess. He was in exactly the predicament his conspirators had plotted and the scheming workmen hid some way away, but within sight of the hut, so that they could witness the Lapp's utter embarrassment when he was forced to expose himself, hopefully completely naked, to seek help. But Anta gave them no such pleasure. Using only his uncontaminated hand, he wiped himself down with his hat; snaked his way back into his work clothes; plunged his hand into the mud to nullify the gluing effects of the resin; then picked up the bag, burying his hand underneath it, and jauntily swung his way out of the ablutions hut, whistling as he went, and crossed the yard as if nothing untoward had occurred. He walked home in his work clothes, rather than give satisfaction to those who despised him.

Next day, when the work crews broke from their labours to take a well-earned brew, the roles were reversed. It was Anta Utsi who was absent, spying on his comrades through a chink between layers of cut timber. The men noted his absence and took leave to make some innuendo directed at the Lapp. But it was Anta who, on this occasion, would have the last laugh. His plan worked better than he could have envisaged for, in celebration of the joke they'd just made at the missing Lapp's expense, they raised their tin mugs in mock salute. 'Skål!' the voices echoed. And a second later those same voices framed other words as the five men yelped and leapt about when the hot liquid cascaded on to their chests. Anta had carefully bored a tiny hole in the side of each tin mug a little more than half an inch from the top. It was undetectable until the mug was tipped. Then, as each drinker raised his cup of brew to his lips, a needle-like spout of hot liquid jetted down the neck of each cup-holder, causing each man great alarm. And providing a great deal of amusement to Anta Utsi. Somehow controlling and constraining his facial muscles in order to keep from smiling, he walked nonchalantly towards the group, 'Sorry to be late. You have some left?'

That afternoon, as if spirited there by some unseen discarnate, Anta's street clothes reappeared. These two days represented a kind of high water mark in the uneasy relationship that had existed between Anta Utsi and his work mates at Norrholm for, following the two confrontational incidents, the men held the little Lapp in greater esteem. Their insinuations and suggestive comments fell away and all but ceased. Only a mild ripple of undercurrent flowed and ebbed between discriminatory misunderstanding and mild contempt. Anta Utsi was making his mark.

*

As the weeks mutated interminably into months, the Tillkvists' reshaped lives became an accepted norm for Tomas and his son. Imperceptibly, the months became two years. During this time each, in his own way, contributed to the fabric of life in Karlskrona as if no melancholy had ever attended the past. Tomas worked harmoniously with Johan Tornstrom to fashion a stream of unique and fancy figureheads and Sten had become a great favourite with Jurgen Uhlrich.

'So, young man,' Jurgen said to Sten one day, 'You were

telling me that you'd like to sail on one of these ships in due time.'

'Yes sir, I would. I really would,' Sten replied, laying down his quill and swivelling in his seat to face the man who had taught him so much since his arrival at the dockyard. 'I'd like to be a navigator.'

'A navigator! Why, that's almost like being a captain. Indeed, most captains I know do their own navigating.'

'Maybe so, sir, but that won't deter me. Someday, I'll chart the way to someplace that no one has ever discovered.'

'Mmm. That'd be a fine thing, Sten, but I don't know as there's anywheres left to discover. Not now the New World's been found and men are settling it all over. North, South, East and West, I hear. Soon they'll have people living in all four corners of it. I've heard tell that the British took over Quebec some time back and have pressed on through Canada, opening up the north. Some of our folks might even venture there one day.'

'That's all as maybe so, sir, but I'll wager there are still some faraway places no one has yet discovered.'

'Anyhow, it takes a great deal of study to know all about the oceans, the winds, the stars. All the things a navigator has to know. But, if you really want to find out what it takes to sail a ship all over the oceans and bring her back to port safely, I'll take you down to meet some of the men for whom it's all in a day's work. Would you—'

'Mr Ehrlich! That would be wonderful! For months I'd hoped that such an opportunity would arise. I was too scared to ask you in case you thought me impertinent.'

The sandy-haired German laughed, his ruddy cheeks pulsing in and out and his eyes, firmly fixed on the young man before him, twinkled impishly. 'I'll take you down to meet Flemming Hansson. He is captain of the *Tacitus Rex* and has just brought her back to Karlskrona from Canton, almost halfway around the world. In one month he will take on a new ship, because the old *Tacitus Rex* is to be stripped out and refitted as a battle frigate.'

'Will I be able to go aboard?' Sten asked exploratively.

'Oh, I should think so. They'll have just finished unloading her and Captain Hansson will have a great deal still to do before he relinquishes his cabin to begin his shore leave.'

For Sten Tillkvist, now sixteen years old, the past two years or so had been a curious mixture. In those first months at the dockyard, trying to become used to his new situation and swapping stories with his father in the evenings, it had all been quite exciting. Then, during that first harsh winter, his thoughts had turned back to Ulla and Bo. And to the Perssons. He pictured Gunnar still at the little schoolhouse in Perstorp but, had he returned at that time, he would have found that it had been pulled down, with the new, larger version, already operating in Peterlöv. Under Jurgen Ehrlich's firm but down-to-earth guidance, Sten had advanced his knowledge at a faster pace than even Gunnar Persson could have envisaged. The dock office offered no formal teaching, of course, but the mentor–apprentice relationship that had been forged between Sten and his overseer often took the boy's mind beyond its daily necessity of concentrating singularly on the columns of figures that represented the costs for the myriad materials to fit and refit the various ships that, practically, provided Karlskrona's lifeblood. Jurgen Ehrlich, himself an unstoppable fireball of energy, infused the same enthusiasm into Sten Tillkvist – a voracious hunger for learning, always stretching the mind and developing a preparedness to tackle virtually any task that presented itself. In Sten, Jurgen had found a ready convert. The lad was bright, alert, quick to learn and with solid powers of retention. He needed telling only once. And with practical matters, his performance was even more impressive. He had a photographic memory: the ability to observe even peripheral details and to store away all that he saw in brain cells that could be tapped at some later date to divulge, in perfect replica, the information originally scanned by his never-miss-a-thing eyes. Always eager to keep on the right side of his master, Sten had never ventured to mention his aspirations to the ebullient German. Now that he had done so, he was ready to grasp at whatever this new opportunity might offer. The University of Life was about to confer a further degree on one of its most promising graduates.

The ship was much smaller than Sten had imagined. From the end of the gangplank there was little space to turn into the walkway that led along the deck towards the captain's quarters. He followed in file behind Jurgen as the dockmaster led the way.

'Captain Hansson, good morning. I have a young man here who would like to ask you some questions. He has it in mind to chart the way to regions unknown and seeks your advice.'

Sten shuddered. It was not the way he would have phrased his own introduction. Mr Ehrlich was throwing him in at the deep end of a pond he'd never swum.

'Aha. And who am I addressing?' The captain rose from a small table at which he was writing entries in a large book. He removed his monocle and peered at Sten.

'Beg your pardon, sir?'

'Your name? I didn't catch your name, young man?'

'Sten, sir. Sten Tillkvist.'

Before either could explore the situation further, Jurgen Ehrlich embarked on a lengthy monologue that extolled the lad's virtues and summarised his own observations of Sten's work and character over the past two years. The lad flushed in embarrassment.

'Hmm. Quite a promising young man,' Flemming Hansson concluded. 'Leave him here with me. I'll see that he is returned to your office in an hour or so.'

The 'hour or so' edged close to two hours. Two hours during which Captain Hansson opened Sten's eyes to a whole new world. He talked of ports in lands Sten had never heard of. He showed the lad how a course was plotted and demonstrated the use of compass and sextant; made a tour of the ship and explained the setting of the sails. Flemming Hansson was forty-seven years old. He'd been at sea since he was Sten's age and had operated under both naval and merchant flags. He was a hard-bitten driver of men and suffered no fools. But, in Sten, he found a young man that was all the dockmaster had boasted. And more.

'How can I best begin to learn to become a navigator?' the lad asked at length.

'Oh, you can study for many years,' the captain replied. 'From books written by learned men you can find out about the stars, the winds, the oceans. It's all very interesting. In time, you could become a professor in all these things. But there's only one way to learn navigation. You need to be on the sea. Sail with a man who has learned to steer his ship to safety when his life depended on it. That way, you'll become a true navigator. For now, forget your dreams of finding new lands. Sail the well-charted waters and, one day, when your little vessel is alone in the midst of a mighty ocean and the winds and waves are about to overwhelm you, God will put a new dream in your mind. Do you believe in God?'

'I certainly do, sir.'

'That's good. Even the meanest buccaneer believes in God sometimes. Especially when he thinks he's about to die. But I sense you believe a little more than that. Would you like to go to sea?'

'I would, sir. I truly would.'

'Hmm. Don't be fooled, lad. It's not all excitement, you know. The sea's hard on a man. Changes a man. I've seen the worst of them become like children in a storm. That's when they all believe in God. Other times they curse Him. You think you've got the belly for it?'

'I believe so, sir.'

'Then I'll see what I can do. First, I must speak a little more with Mr Ehrlich.'

That night, Sten had so much to tell his father that the two sat talking until close on midnight. By the time he went to bed, Sten's mind was a stadium filled with a thousand voices – some jubilant, some despairing, but all shouting for a different champion. He tossed, turned and wriggled. It was hours before he drifted into a deep sleep.

Barely a month later, Jurgen Ehrlich walked briskly into his office and came to an abrupt halt before the desk at which Sten tallied the endless bills, transferring the subtotals to the ledger and cross-checking all the entries he made. 'Put down your pen and listen to what I have to say,' the labour boss said in a matter-of-fact tone. 'Captain Hansson is to take over a new ship, *The Draken*, and he has asked whether you might be considered as Cabin Attendant. I've told him that I will be quite willing to release you from your duties here. You have until noontime

Thursday to make your decision. As it's only Tuesday morning now, that gives you two clear days.'

'Incredible! I don't need—'

'Wait!' Jurgen burst in. 'Remember all our conversations. And the things you discussed with the captain. Talk it over with your father. It's a big decision and you have the chance to think about it. Don't rush into anything as important as this. Your whole life may be turned upside down if your choice is ill-founded.'

On the Thursday afternoon, Sten thanked Jurgen for giving him the position in the dock office and for all the seeds of wisdom the energetic man had sown into his life. On Friday morning at eight o'clock sharp, Sten Tillkvist reported to Captain Flemming Hansson aboard *The Draken*.

*

If it's true that anyone who wants to climb the ladder of success needs a role model, a mentor or just someone to provide that spark of inspiration that sets the sights on a higher goal, Anta Utsi had found his. At first it had been Lars Petri, the foreman. Latterly, he took his many questions directly to Kari Ruuska. The man seemed to know everything there was to know about the native trees, their management, the behaviour of the wood when cut and about sawmilling in general. On the subject of the business around which he had based his life and created his fortune, he was a walking encyclopaedia.

'How you choose which trees to be chop?' Anta asked him.

'You mean "felled",' Kari corrected. The busy mill owner always made time for the inquisitive Lapp and threw back at him some questions of his own. He was often astounded by the insights the little man had developed concerning the wider aspects of producing, marketing and using timber.

'We calculate the yield of the tree in the forest, before it's felled. It's what we call the English Measure, after an Englishman who found it to be the best way of estimating the volume of usable wood. First, we measure the girth of the tree in inches, about this high from the ground.' Kari held out his arm to a height that was around Anta's chin. 'And we take a quarter of that to be the side of a square. This square gives us the area in square inches. Next, we estimate the height in feet and multiply this by the area. Finally, we must divide by one hundred and forty-four to convert our square inches of girth to square feet. The answer gives us the volume of wood we can expect.'

'It's good. Now I know it.' The little Lapp scurried off, carrying his latest piece of knowledge in his head until he was able to write it down. On another occasion he asked Mr Ruuska, 'How you choose big saw or little saw for cut?'

Again, the big Finn exercised great patience in explaining the reasoning. 'The deepest cut you can make is from the centre of the saw to its edge. We call that the "radius". But you have to allow a little for the log to pass clear, so we take off a "knuckler" – that's the distance across your knuckles or about two inches.' As always, Anta thanked Mr Ruuska profusely. Then he found a solitary spot where he would write in his little notebook the latest addition to his learning. Each night, when he returned to his Spartan mill cottage, Anta would read through the notes he'd made. His appreciation of the many facets of the industry was steadily growing, though he never flaunted his knowledge nor mentioned to his fellow workers the things he'd been learning from Kari Ruuska. Although he was still 'Lappi' to all the men except Lars Petri, he was generally accepted as one of the crew. But the old animosities, which had been buried for the past three years, suddenly flared again one afternoon when one of the men crossed the yard to find a convenient spot behind some trees to relieve his bladder. He spotted Anta scribbling in his notebook and rushed over to the little Lapp.

'What're you doin' here? What's that you're writin' down?' The labourer snatched at the notebook and a scuffle broke out between the two men. Anta was knocked to the ground and the heavier man sprawled on top of him. The pair thrashed around on the needle-strewn forest floor, not a hundred yards from where Lars Petri directed the alignment of a large log. With a lung-bursting lunge, Anta thrust his left hand towards the notebook as his assailant crushed it in his fist. The swift, upward thrust and Anta's scrabbling fingers tore the book from the labourer's grip and the Lapp kicked himself free, somersaulting into a stride that carried him clear of the trees and back towards the debarking machinery. The disgruntled labourer picked himself up; carried out his original intention; then made his way back to join his crew. But, as the men ceased work that evening, three of them cornered Anta as he changed his clothes and demanded that he hand over the notebook for their scrutiny.

'Is only for me to read, not you,' the little Lapp defended.

'Lying bastard! He's been making notes about us. Bet that's what he shows to Ruuska when he goes up there.'

'Not for Ruuska! For me!' Anta retorted once more.

'Let us see, then. C'mon! Give's it!'

Having anticipated the possibility of just such a

confrontation following the earlier episode, Anta had secreted the notebook in a pile of logs.

'Is not here,' he parried, holding out his arms with his hands palms up.

'Then we'll find it. Let's get the sneaky bastard.' The three men pinned Anta to the ground and ransacked his clothing. Exasperated by their failure to turn up the notebook, they bullied him remorselessly, leaving him bruised, cut and bleeding. As they turned to go, the man who had first discovered the suspected spying swung his foot hard at the prostrate figure, catching the downed man on the temple and knocking him unconscious.

By the time Anta came to, the men had gone and he was shivering. Dragging himself to a sitting position, he shook his head violently several times then staggered to his feet. When, at last, he was able to piece together what had happened to him, he stumbled across to the log pile where he'd hidden his book and retrieved it.

That night, Anta Utsi left Norrholm. Wrapping his meagre possessions into a bundle that he strapped to his back, and with the savings he'd accumulated from his wages and kept hidden beneath the floor of the mill cottage, he stole through the darkness towards the main highway that led towards Falkenberg. Once more, he'd become a wanderer.

In making his initial start in a southerly direction, Anta Utsi unconsciously assented to the pursuit of his future in Southern Sweden. In that same instant, he had turned his back forever on Jokkmokk and his former life there. His future in the south must surely be more assured than it was in Jokkmokk, or indeed throughout Swedish Lappland, he reasoned. There would be no overbearing tax to single him out as a Lapp. His relatives still suffered as a result of the imposition of 'Lapp land tax' whereby they now had to pay for the rights to fish or graze lands that were formerly open to them. And their old communal system was under threat, too, since only the establishment of a fixed dwelling was deemed to confer ownership. Thus, the Lapps could only lease the land of their birth and heritage – they couldn't own it. Only by betraying their natural lifestyle, following the ways of the southerners and building permanent dwellings, could they ever hope to reach a par with the settlers who were trampling down more and more of the best lands in their region with each passing year. Anta Utsi would never return to Lappland, he affirmed in his mind. At least not to settle or live there.

It was in early August 1765, five months after he'd fled Norrholm, that the wandering Lapp found himself in Nybro, a few miles west of the old port of Kalmar and not far from the glassworks at Kosta. During his meanderings through southern Sweden, Anta had found both hospitality and casual work with such frequent sufficiency as to satisfy his temporal needs and supplement his hoarded savings. The wily, astute Lapp could not have timed his arrival better had he spent a lifetime planning it.

At the small roadside inn on the outskirts of Nybro, he engaged in conversation with a greying, weather-beaten man in his early sixties. Jacob Jacobsson, known to the locals as 'Ya-Ya' on account of his alliterative name, had run the nearby sawmill for over thirty years and he became keenly interested in Anta's experiences in Norrholm when the subject arose during the first minutes of their acquaintance.

'How can you know so much about sawmilling?' the older man asked. 'You're the first Sami I've ever met who knows about anything other than reindeer.'

'I start at bottom. Chain-hauling logs and debarking them. Then I move to flitch-saws, push-saws and finishing. But I spend some time among growing stands, too, selecting best trees and calculating yields,' Anta lied. Most of what he told Ya-Ya was not entirely true, for although he had watched others in these tasks, his own knowledge was limited to his copious notes. So thoroughly had he committed to memory the accumulation of notes in his little book that, in his own mind, he'd actually done all of the things he spoke about.

'It's like a miracle!' Ya-Ya exclaimed. 'I was on the point of putting my mill up for sale and now, today, I meet someone who might breathe new life into the place. It's hard finding good mill men around here now; the big draw is Karlskrona, with all the shipbuilding and repairing going on down there.' He quaffed his ale then, turning to Anta, asked, 'You wouldn't consider taking on the running of my mill, would you? I'd pay you a small wage and share any profits you could make.'

'But I haven't seen your mill. What kind equipment you have? How many labourers?'

Ya-Ya launched into a positive description of the rundown sawmill, painting a rosier picture than was justified by reality. But Anta Utsi was no fool. That afternoon, he accompanied Ya-Ya to the mill and saw for himself its true state. Disappointed but not discouraged, Anta put his own proposition to the older man.

'I will accept offer,' Anta began, 'but must make changes.'

'Changes?'

'Yes. I do all work, you sell timber. After three year, you sell me mill. We agree price now.'

'Good gracious! Here am I, offering you a job, and you counter with an offer to buy me out.'

'You like to think about it?'

'Yes. No. I mean, it's something I hadn't considered. What price did you have in mind?'

'We discuss tomorrow. I take a good look around, eh?'

'Sure. I'll show you what we've got and how it's working today.'

The following day, Ya-Ya listened to Anta's proposals and some of the plans he had to improve the mill. The price Anta offered was not much less than Ya-Ya felt he could have realised from an outright sale so, after very little haggling with the Lapp, he agreed.

'We'll go to see a lawyer and have the papers drawn up,' the old mill owner suggested. Within three days, the deal was legalised.

*

Tomas Tillkvist was lonely. His son's absence from the tidy but tiny carpenter's cottage had left a vacuum that Tomas found hard to fill. Since the catastrophe at Peterlöv, he had vowed never to re-marry but he longed for the kind of homely company that a wife provided. Supping ale with the other dockworkers in the local tavern made a poor substitute, he found.

By contrast, life aboard *The Draken* revealed new wonders every day to the captain's Cabin Attendant. Often there was time that, if not profitably redeemed, could allow shipboard life to introduce its own boredom. But these were the times Sten put to developing his writing ability. After the first two days at sea, he asked Captain Hansson if he could have some writing materials and the skipper had willingly obliged, equipping the lad with quills, ink, blotters and a large notebook. Armed with these necessary tools, Sten brought to bear his own battery of skills as he began writing a diary, not only of current occurrences but of as much of his own life as he could remember. The highlights of his days at Peterlöv and in the schoolhouse at Perstorp consumed the greater part of his entries. But always, he was careful to refer to his family as 'Tillkvist' and never as 'Tilderkvist'.

Flemming Hansson was a strict disciplinarian and stood no nonsense from his crew. But when a seaman showed particular initiative, he was generally supportive and often provoked his men into assuming roles or tackling tasks that they may have considered beyond their station or ability. And Sten Tillkvist, the young Cabin Attendant, showed a lot of initiative. In Captain Hansson the young man saw not the strict, hard-bitten overseer that the captain surely was, but a man with a well-ordered and hugely embracing knowledge of life who could provide him with a seemingly endless source of learning. And, likewise, the captain appreciated the youth's probing questions, well-reasoned conclusions and thoughtful responses. With the right advice and a bit of good fortune in his future relationships, the lad could make it to the top of the tree, the captain figured. Flemming Hansson determined that he would do what he could to give this bright young man every chance to reach that tree top. When the ship returned to Karlskrona four months later, the captain began engineering one of Sten's future relationships. He paid a visit to Kalmar to call on a man he'd known for many years, Olaus Berg. As always, the two men enjoyed a good meal, admirably concluded with some of the best quality aquavit. They swapped stories of their relative fortunes since last they'd met. Then Flemming switched the conversation to another matter.

'Tell me, my friend, your daughter Birgitta, is she seeing a young man at present?'

'Huh, Birgitta? She has many who call for her, but none that she finds pull severely on her heartstrings. Could be, of course, her mother has something to do with that.'

'Louisa? Why? Is she jealous?' The men laughed, in the way that men do when discussing women.

'Nei. It's just that she's our only one. I don't think Louisa can bear to think of the day when she won't be here to help in the kitchen, the garden, taking an interest in her dressmaking and so on.'

'It's just that... well... I know a young man who might well make a stronger pull on her heartstrings than most. Name's Sten Tillkvist, originally from up-country. He's my Cabin Attendant, but he'll go far, that lad. Very bright. Most amiable, too. And prudent.'

'Hei, Flemming, what's got into you? Matchmaking's women's work. Is the sea getting to you?' Again they laughed. The same thin, hollow laughter.

The jocular slight caused no alteration in the course the captain had set: 'He's eighteen years old. Still a bit of a beard to grow, but he'll need a good woman one day and I just thought...'

'Bring him along next time you call. I'm sure Birgitta won't need our aiding if he's of the right stamp.'

It was another four months before Flemming Hansson took Sten to Kalmar to join him at dinner with the Bergs. And Birgitta was there, prompted by her father that 'a very fine young man' was coming to visit. She was arrayed in her best attire and looked positively stunning. Small-featured, with a crystal-clear complexion that glowed from within the framing effect of her long silk-blonde hair. Sten Tillkvist, cutting a handsome dash himself, could not fail to be impressed by the Berg's daughter.

The dinner-table conversation was conservative and polite, but nonetheless allowed Sten just sufficient latitude to assert himself. The effect was not lost on Birgitta. She took an increasing liking to the uniformed young man. After the meal, whilst Louisa tended to the kitchen and the men retired to enjoy their aquavit, Sten and Birgitta walked together in the extensive grounds that surrounded the Berg's substantial house. On that mild autumn evening, the seeds of their courtship were fertilised. Neither knew it then, but the gestation period would approach two years.

During the months Sten was at sea, Birgitta kept herself busy. She saw less and less of the tag-along young men who vied for her affections. She shared Sten's dreams and had set her heart on becoming the wife of a man who would one day, she was certain, become captain of his own ship. In the June of 1769, the first ever Mr and Mrs Tillkvist emerged from the high-arching doorway of the Lutheran Church in Kalmar.

Not far away, in Nybro, a week later, Anta Utsi became the legal owner of a prospering sawmill.

*

For fifty-three years, Sweden had revelled in what was popularly called the 'Age of Freedom' when arts, science and other forms of culture flourished. The Riksdag ruled, first through its Estates and then through its two parties that represented the widest spectrum of the country's social scale: the high and noble Hats; and the common man's Caps. But in 1771 it all changed.

When the twenty-four year old Gustav the Third came to the throne, he was already a charismatic leader who strode through life with a precociousness and sense of ambition that readily drew others to him. Furthermore, he rejoiced in the knowledge that he was the first Swedish-born monarch of his country since the 'Age of Freedom' began. This he interpreted as some kind of omen that he should end the Riksdag's free rein and take on a more dictatorial role himself, assuming full power to govern as had the pre-Parliament kings. In the year following his accession, Gustav carried out a bloodless coup: reducing the power of the Council; limiting the influence of the Riksdag; disbanding the Hats and Caps parties and dissolving the Secret Committee. The move made the new king very popular throughout the country, and many paid tribute to him in poem and song. Carl Michael Bellman, a famous troubadour, wrote and sang songs and ditties in the king's honour. Other minstrels did likewise and the country was awash with verse and song to the king. Many of these were little more than limericks celebrating the 'first citizen among a free people'. A typical rhyme ran thus:

> *We honour Gustav,*
> *Finest king in all this northern land.*
> *We toast the freedom*
> *he has granted by his royal hand.*
> *We praise the wisdom*
> *of our king, protector, seer and scholar.*
> *We pledge allegiance*
> *to the one whose head's on our riksdaler.*

Gustav's tremendous popularity united the common

people. He reformed the coinage, with its history of so many denominations: dirhems, marks, ore, shillings, pennies, carolins, ducats and dollars, to name but a few. The new silver riksdaler became the principal coin. And Gustav raised the tempo of life in Karlskrona, too. He instigated an accelerated naval preparation programme to include the building, repairing and arming of a large number of vessels to provide a tighter curtain of defence of the Baltic.

Tomas Tillkvist was happy to be in Karlskrona under the reign of the new king. The upsurge in investment in the Navy extended Tomas's horizons – and, he could see, could become the vehicle to launch him back into gunmaking. Besides, Johan Tornstrom was encouraging his own son, Emanuel, to join him in sculpting and carving the ships' figureheads that were still very much in demand. The one aspect of Tomas Tillkvist's life that was not satisfactory was his continuing lack of homely company. But, by spurious chance, he solved that matter, too.

In August 1772, when *The Draken* docked once more in the safe haven of Karlskrona, three events took place, each of which would play a significant role in the future of the Tillkvists:

Firstly – Sten discovered that he had become a father. Three days before his ship docked, Birgitta had given birth to a beautiful daughter. Mother and baby were being cared for by Louisa in the Berg's large home at Kalmar. Sten and Birgitta named their daughter Kristina Louisa.

Secondly – Captain Hansson formally filed his recommendations that Sten Tillkvist, Senior Deck Officer, be promoted with immediate effect to the position of Second Mate.

Thirdly – When Sten visited his father in the small carpenter's cottage, a surprise awaited him. For Tomas no longer lived alone.

'This is Hans,' Tomas informed his son, introducing a boy who claimed twelve years but carried the air of self-assuredness more appropriate to a fifteen year old. Sten greeted the youth openly but, within himself, felt a measure of resentment. 'For now, I'm giving him a home. His parents and brother were taken with the consumption. Jurgen Ehrlich brought him to me.'

Later, when he and his father were alone, Sten asked: 'This orphan, Hans. Can you trust him?'

'Trust him? Why? I have no option. The boy needs a roof over his head and I miss having a son. It's been a lonely life here since you left.' Then, quickly, he added, 'Not that I begrudge your seeking adventure on the sea, you understand. It's just that sometimes a man needs another being to converse with. Someone near at hand to care for and be responsible for.'

'But you don't know him. You don't know anything about him. He might be some devious scallywag who'll run off with anything he fancies one day.'

'Maybe so, maybe so.'

'And what do you do with him during the day when you're at the docks?'

'He works there, too. Runs errands for Jurgen. And you should know, more than most, that Jurgen's not such a poor judge of those who work for him.'

'That's true. I hope he's not made a mistake this time, on your account.'

No more was said about the orphan. Sten regained a more positive composure and informed Tomas that he was to be congratulated on becoming a grandfather, giving as complete a picture of baby Kristina as he was able. He had climbed. Now he was about to enjoy.

'And you might congratulate me, too. Captain Hansson has appointed me Second Mate.'

It was like old times. Father and son who, together, had walked fiery coals, were once again drawn into intimate sharing of their experiences.

'I don't have any promotion to boast about,' Tomas disclosed, 'but at least I have the chance to get back to gunmaking. In two weeks I'll be leaving Jurgen's side of things to work for the Navy. They're setting up a new ordnance works here and I'll be joining them. Pistols and short-barrelled carbines mostly. But it's a step in the right direction.' The two men talked without respite. It was as if they were peers, the difference in their ages transparent.

Just as Sten made to leave, Hans returned. The entrance of the gangling youth reduced the free-flowing conversation to a more stilted exchange. Sten wished his father well, but harboured some doubts about his new-found lodger. The Second Mate of *The Draken* returned to Kalmar with mixed feelings.

During the next five years, the sun shone warmly, figuratively speaking, on the Tillkvist family. Jurgen Ehrlich's judgement of the orphan Hans proved sound and the boy became like a third son to Tomas. Surprisingly, he turned out to be quite a remarkable cook and brought a sense of culinary adventure into Tomas's life.

Sten and Birgitta's daughter Kristina was a delight to her parents and the couple had two more children, Lars and Per, born at more or less two-yearly intervals. The far-sighted reforms of King Gustav had made provision for a vastly more widespread schooling and Sten wasted no time in enrolling his daughter to take advantage of the provision.

Tomas had risen to a position of high regard in the ordnance works at Karlskrona and he and Hans had relinquished the little carpenter's cottage to build for themselves a larger house that afforded a panorama view of the bay. In other ways, too, Tomas had made his mark. Quite literally. For at the base of every figurehead he'd fashioned and on some inconspicuous part of every gun he'd built, he had left his mark. It resembled the Greek letter *pi*.

Under the expert tutelage of Flemming Hansson, Sten had studied hard and progressed well. In the spring of the 'year of three sevens' he was rewarded with the captaincy of his own vessel. And on the day that *Peleus* manoeuvred from its moorings at Karlskrona to point its bow towards the open Baltic, a cheering, waving line stretched from bollard to bollard on the dockside: Tomas and Hans; Olaus and Louisa Berg; Birgitta and Kristina, Lars and little Per; Captain Hansson and Jurgen Ehrlich; Johan and Emanuel Tornstrom. They made a formidable send-off party for Captain Tillkvist and his crew.

As he stood on deck, returning the enthusiastic waves of his family and friends, a tear glistened on Sten's cheek and into his mind flashed one of Gunnar Persson's 'daily gems': 'He who would have the fruit must first climb the tree.'

He had climbed. Now he was about to enjoy the fruit.

Part Five
The Emigrants

For Bjorn and Millie

'Tis best to weigh the enemy more weighty than he seems...

William Shakespeare

'Good riddance tae ye, Auld Reekie, ye've been a scunner tae us.' Andrew Bryce pronounced his judgement on Glasgow, specifically, but on Scotland as a whole, as he hung over the rail of the ship that would carry him and the remnant of his family to a new life in the New World. The burly, red-headed Scot, with his wife Mary and their ten year old daughter Martha, was turning his back on the country of his birth, disgusted by the way he'd been treated by the high-and-mighty landowners who had made life a misery for him and his kin these past ten years. The Bryces had six children: Stephen, James, Carrie, Tom, Ella and Martha. The first four had all married and were widely dispersed around Scotland. Ella had left home two years previously and was 'in service' at the mansion of a wealthy businessman in Edinburgh and only Martha had shared these last two dismal years in their little cottage in the Ayrshire village of Kilmaurs. Squeezed out of the farming mould in which he'd been cast, Andra – even Mary called him that – had turned to cobbling shoes to eke out a living. It was never enough and he was tired of the make-do existence he'd been forced to adopt. When the chance came to seek out a better life, he'd seized it.

'We'll maybe miss the sun settin' over Arran. That, and oor bairns left behind. But that's aboot a' we'll miss o' this place,' he continued.

Mary had needed no persuading. She'd come from a long line of Crawfords who'd always prided themselves in being front runners whenever there had been the least hint of a new venture that might hold promise of a good return.

The Crawford family had spread from its roots in Argyllshire down to Dumfries and figured among the small group of country folk who'd made the transition into modern industrial life with more than a modicum of success. And, despite the many hardships she'd borne in raising her offspring, Mary held tremendous reserves of mental strength that had constantly buoyed up Andra when times had been at their hardest. She was of the right stock to take on the unfathomed challenges of the New World. And challenges there would undoubtedly be, for the Bryces knew not a soul in America. They would be 'going it alone'.

That had been eight years ago. Eight years that had changed the fortunes of the Bryce family in a way that even they could never have foreseen. When they embarked from Glasgow that April day in 1850, a soft, drizzling rain enshrouding their passage to the mouth of the River Clyde, none of them had heard of the Schuylkill, let alone known how to pronounce it. Now, their flourishing farm in Reading, Pennsylvania, stood out as one of the neatest and best ordered in the area. With the help of Ethan Whitney's local knowledge, Andra Bryce had 'made it good' in the New World. Ethan had known where to find the best dairy stock; had some ingenious ideas about how to drain the land to produce good pasture; and had formed a network of connections with the most reliable tradesmen from as far away as Harrisburg. To the Bryces, just finding their bearings in this new land, finding Ethan Whitney had been a God send.

For Martha, childhood memories of Kilmaurs and her summer days on the pleasant sands at Troon had all but vanished. She'd found the schooling to be quite a different kettle of fish from the puritanical Scottish regime practised with Presbyterian strictness at the little school she'd attended on the outskirts of Kilmarnock. Not only were the '3 Rs' – reading, riting and rithmetic – taught with their practical usefulness always in mind, but Martha had been introduced to a new subject: social studies. The mix of history, geography, politics and economics roused a curiosity in the lass that put a new dimension on her horizons. Here in Pennsylvania, she reasoned, we have all these things but, out west, they have next to nothing. Out there, it's only just beginning. The things she'd heard in the lessons about Lewis and Clark's expedition and the Louisiana Purchase had fired her imagination in a way that the ritual singing of 'The Lord's My Shepherd' never had. Always something of a tomboy with a passion for the outdoor life, Martha had coalesced all these facets into her being, distilling them into a lifestyle that would become synonymous with the 'All-American Woman'. One day, she hoped, she would get to see 'the west'.

Now a buxom eighteen year old with long, red-gold hair and green eyes, Martha distinguished herself as a head-turning figure of beauty whenever she visited the men-strewn streets of Lancaster. Even Ethan, fifteen years her senior, wished he could have been 'in the running' as one of the contenders for her favours. It was in Lancaster that Martha first discovered the pleasure and risky fun of casual romantic liaison. But she was destined to find true love elsewhere.

'Ethan! Whaur hae ye pit the wee broon harness?' Andra asked his right-hand man.

'The harness? Oh, the little brown one? It's still hanging under the maple tree behind the kitchen. One moment and I'll fetch it.'

It was a curious thing that had happened to Andra. For no logical or explicable reason, he'd become exaggeratedly more Scottish than he'd been even when he left Kilmaurs. His accent had artificially thickened; he'd developed a longing for the porridge that had years ago been his staple; he'd sing the old Scottish melodies as he worked around the farm; and, when he and Mary visited friends in the evening, he'd taken to wearing the kilt. Why he did this, not even Mary could fathom. His parochial mode of speech was often indecipherable by people around Reading, particularly those of other European extraction. Even to some of the other Scots immigrants it was baffling. But Ethan Whitney had taken it in his stride, accommodating the eccentricity without comment even though, sometimes, he had to openly translate Andra's words into American-English before he could form a reply.

The Reading farm was a prosperous venture. Mary Bryce had worked as hard as her husband to put the family on its feet and, together with the ingenuity and sound judgement contributed by Ethan, the Bryces' fortunes had so dramatically changed within the eight years of their settling in Pennsylvania that, perhaps, Andra felt he merited the opportunity to masquerade as a Scottish Laird. That was the irony of it. He was modelling his behaviour on that of the very people he'd despised eight years before. The people who'd so pressed him – so disgusted him – that he'd fled from all the things he now ennobled. It concerned Mary little. She smiled at her man's eccentric ways yet showed him the love and concern that she truly felt for him. One evening, they were about to leave the farmhouse to visit the Provans, a family who'd come to Reading from Lanark in central Scotland two years before. As Andra, bedecked in his Highland regalia, swirled across the veranda, Mary called to him, 'Andra! For goodness sake come here. You can't go around to the Provans like that.'

'Whit's wrang, wumman?' he queried, showing some annoyance.

'Your stocking-tops are turned over on the squint and your sporran's not hanging straight. Let me get you sorted.'

Despite his 'Laird of the Manor' ways he turned around, in childlike fashion, and she corrected his state of dress.

'Thanks hen, that'll dae fine.' He seldom called her by her own name. Most times it was 'hen', sometimes 'ma dearie'.

Andra's ultra-patriotic behaviour was an embarrassment to Martha. In the eight years she'd spent in Pennsylvania she'd lost all notion of being 'a wee Scots lass'. She spoke like an American. She dressed like an American. She felt American. And she felt, too, that at the first opportunity she would like to get away from Reading and all her father's 'Scottishness' that harped back to a past she'd rather forget.

*

The Gustavian reforms of the late eighteenth century in Sweden had bequeathed an unfortunate and ironic postscript. With better medical treatments, increased production of a wide range of more wholesome food, and fewer major conflicts to inflict severe losses of life, the country's population was rising dramatically and, rising with it, discontent. Two consecutive years of serious famine heightened the growing discontent and a movement began that was to nullify much of the good that Gustav had achieved: the exodus.

The growth of commercial shipping and the opening up of America's west accidentally conspired to instigate mass emigration on a grand scale. The more aggressive of the shipping companies appointed their own agents to fuel the cause by pre-arranging passages to fill the available berths so that each voyage would carry its full complement of passengers. By 1850 there was a groundswell of one-way traffic across the Atlantic.

As if the general conditions in the country had not been enough of a driving force to suggest to Per-Erik and Anna Lundberg that a better future might be afforded them in North America, they suffered a further blow. Per-Erik's mother Kristina, herself the daughter of a once great mariner, Sten Tillkvist, passed away. She was seventy-eight years old and had survived her husband Steffen by seventeen years. To the Lundbergs, it was the last straw. They approached Per Dahlin, agent for EAL – the Europa America Line – and asked him to arrange passage to New York for themselves and their two children, Joel and Louisa. Once the ball began rolling in this direction, it became an unstoppable avalanche. As the day of their departure drew closer, the Lundbergs grew in excitement and took no account of any possibility of mishap nor of the potential hardships their journey might entail. In the event, their hardships amounted to little more than two days of dispiriting sea sickness for Anna and the two children. Louisa was twelve and still very much a little girl, but Joel, at fifteen, resented being classed as a child. He was a young man. And an able young man; as he demonstrated when he carried both his own and Louisa's sack of belongings from the baggage compound at the New York docks.

'We're here!' Joel yelled enthusiastically, dumping both sacks on the ground and stamping his feet on the dry earth. 'This is America!'

'It smells so different,' Anna declared, sniffing the air in an exaggerated way.

'Yes, it's certainly quite different from Växjö,' Per-Erik added. 'And look! Just look at that!' Eyes wide, he pointed towards a horse-train making its way up from the dockfront. A 'team of six' was pulling three laden carriages, hitched one behind the other. It was something they'd never seen before and it augmented the many stories they'd already heard about America's bigness, and spaciousness, and differentness. As they watched the horse-train vanish among the dockside warehouses, a twangy-pitched voice arrested their thoughts.

'You folks jess arrived from Sweden?' The speaker was a shortish man with a neatly trimmed moustache, cloth cap on his head and wearing a smart tweed jacket.

'Yes,' replied Per-Erik, eyeing the man up and down.

The stranger thrust out his hand. 'Name's Issac Conrad. Jess call me Zac. You folks have a place to go?'

'Yes. We've been allocated to the Staten Rooming House, you know it?'

'The Staten? Sure, I know it. You have much baggage?'

'All this lot,' Per-Erik replied, waving his arm in the general direction of their mound of bags, sacks and two large trunks.

'No problem. I'll fix you with a transfer. What money do you have? Swedish? American?'

'American. We changed all our money to dollars on the ship.'

'Jess fine. Give me five dollars and I'll fix everything up.'

'Five dollars? That much?'

'It's a long way, mister, and with this lot, you and the missus there and your brood here, you'll need a whole cart to yourselves.'

'If you say so,' muttered Per-Erik, delving his hand into

a leather drawstring pouch in which he kept half of the family's money. Prudently, he'd divided their meagre monetary assets between himself and Anna. 'Five dollars, you say?'

'That's right.'

Per-Erik counted the money into the man's hand and the dapper stranger nonchalantly dropped the coins into a pocket of his jacket.

'Wait here. I know jess the man. Jess don' move from this spot an' I'll be right back with a good cart.'

For nearly half an hour the Lundbergs stood in a huddle until the dock was practically empty of new arrivals scurrying to their temporary residences. There was no sign of Zac Conrad nor the cart he'd gone to fetch. At length, a porter approached them.

'Say, you folks takin' root?'

Per-Erik furrowed his brows. 'Sorry, I don't understand. Can you repeat it.'

'I'm sorry. I mean: are you waiting for someone?'

'Yes, we're waiting for a Mr Zac Conrad. He's gone to fetch a cart for our baggage.'

'Mmm, plenty of carts around. What does this Zac Conrad look like?'

Per-Erik described the man, more or less accurately.

'And he had a waistcoat with a gold chain,' Anna added to the description.

'You give him money?'

'Five dollars.'

'Oh my God, not again,' the porter sighed. 'It was Zac Conrad today, was it? No, ma'am, that's Billy Turner. As big a rogue as you're likely to come across. Here, let me help you.'

Staten Rooming House was no more than three hundred yards from the docks. Joel had been right: this is America.

There would be many evenings around the supper table when the Lundbergs would look back on that day they arrived in New York and see it in a different light. They laughed, with hindsight, at their naivety, but their embarrassing experience had taught them a lesson that would better equip them for life in America: always be in another man's debt; never part with money until you have the goods and are satisfied with them. During those early years, as they'd made their way to Ohio, they'd had to face similar situations many times. But now, working alongside the many other immigrant Swedes who'd been drawn to that State, life had become almost an extension of the one they'd known in Växjö. But there was a difference. It was, somehow, more purposeful. And more prosperous. In just four years they'd been able to purchase eighty acres of good land. In another four years they'd made that land fruitful. That was the difference.

Had the Lundbergs settled in New York, New Jersey, Connecticut or Delaware – somewhere not too distant from their port of entry into the country – Joel and Louisa may have looked on things differently. As it was, the long overland journey to Ohio had been an eye-opener to the youngsters. The saw new things; gained new experiences; began to develop for the first time some conception of how big their newly adopted land really was... and sowed within their souls the first seeds of yearning to see more of this wonderful new land. Seeds that would emerge very slowly from an almost dormant state to erupt one day into a maturity that would carry brother and sister far from home.

Back in those early days, Per-Erik had found work on a farm and the family lived in one of the small cabins the owner provided for his workers. Joel took great delight in exploring the copses and small areas of woodland that stood within a mile of the farm and it was not long before he hankered for a rifle to shoot the small game that was plentiful there. His persistent pestering eventually led Per-Erik to buy for the lad a much-used but workmanlike squirrel rifle. It was fitted with a percussion lock but was only .36 calibre – just big enough for turkeys, rabbits and the like if hit fair and square. The boy learned how to cast balls from soft lead. They were no bigger than shelled peas. He cut patches, about three-quarters of an inch in diameter, from some 'four-by-two' cotton that Anna spared him. The patches he lubricated with melted-down pork fat and soon became adept at loading the little rifle even from a crouching position. Day after day he shot at both real game and artificial marks until he became a proficient marksman. Many were the meals when, after thanking the Lord, the Lundbergs also thanked their son for providing the meat.

It was during this time that Joel began to imagine what it must have been like a hundred years before. 'How I would have loved to have lived then,' he thought. 'I'd have been a "Long Hunter" and gone trapping, shooting and exploring with men like Daniel Boone and Simon Kenton. Then I'd really have travelled the land and seen its wonders. If only I could do that now.' The seed that was sown during those first weeks of crossing the country from New York were just beginning to awaken. But even now, eight years on, he was no closer to satisfying his dreams.

*

Three weeks before her nineteenth birthday, Martha Bryce swapped the stark whiteness of the farmhouse in Reading for the equally stark whiteness of the hospital in Harper's Ferry, Virginia, to begin her training as a nurse. Few would have thought of Harper's Ferry as 'out west' but Martha had chosen it because it seemed, to her, to be a move in the right direction.

The little town of Harper's Ferry, wedged into the apex formed by the confluence of the Potomac and Shenandoah rivers, was a quiet backwater. Quiet until, uninvited, an egotistical slavery abolitionist from Connecticut, John Brown, and his gang of ruffians had stormed into the town and forted themselves in one of its buildings, defying the government troops that swarmed after them. The repercussions of that day in Harper's Ferry would reverberate throughout the whole of the Eastern States. And from this unlikeliest of sources, the Bryce and Lundberg families would become incontrovertibly entwined.

Despite her sometimes fiery temperament and tomboyish ways, Martha was a compassionate and caring young woman. Her years in Pennsylvania had brought her caring ways to the surface, firstly with her many pets and even her father's cows, but latterly with people. Her clement ways had first emerged when she tamed a young raccoon that Ethan had found by the edge of the stream that ran through a small copse of woodland behind the farmhouse.

'Why, he's so cute, he looks like a highwayman,' she cooed when Ethan had brought the bewildered creature into the kitchen.

'Careful now, these critturs can deal you a fair bite, even a young 'un,' Ethan had warned.

'Then we'll just have to teach him not to bite,' Martha said, matter-of-factly. 'I'll look after him. It is a "him" isn't it?'

'Yep, he's that all right.'

'I'm going to call him Turpin,' Martha advised, 'after the famous highway robber.'

'Then just watch he don't rob you when he's on a bit. These critturs are mighty cunning. Have hands like humans, too.'

Martha pushed a finger into one of the animal's front paws and gasped in delight as its thumb-opposed grip closed firmly on her extended digit. She spent an inordinate amount of time with Turpin over the next few weeks and had him so tamed that she could walk across the yard with the raccoon snuggled around her neck.

When Ethan Whitney had slithered down a steep bank and twisted his ankle, it had been Martha who had cared for him and nursed the painfully swollen joint. Ethan had made the most of his recuperation at the hands of such a pretty nursemaid and his many complimentary comments may have gone some way to laying the foundation of the thought process that led the girl into believing that this was what God had created her to do.

Ethan had one irritating fault: he was nearly always right. And the warning he'd given to Martha three months earlier proved the point.

Apart from their cute appearance and amazing agility, raccoons are exceedingly strong. They are also exceedingly persistent and, once they set their minds to removing an obstacle or breaking down a barrier, they'll keep at it until they succeed. So it was with Turpin. The crate in which Martha kept him in Andra's tool shed had seemed eminently suitable when Ethan first brought him home. Now, it was totally inadequate.

Turpin had shown no signs of aggression or unusual behaviour when Martha had put his bowl of food into the crate and pegged it shut. But sometime during the night, Turpin applied his brute strength and natural cunning to the device which kept him captive. Soon he was rampaging around the tool shed, knocking over small boxes of screws, nails and other parts that Andra and Ethan had carefully tidied. Turnscrews, chisels and scrapers he pulled from their orderly slots at the rear of the bench and discarded them in every which direction. Off cuts of wood he pulled to the floor and a pot of casein glue went tumbling over a sawhorse where it came open, smearing its contents over the sawhorse, the floor and on to some of the strewn hand tools.

Next morning, as Martha surveyed the chaos, Turpin was nowhere to be seen. The lid of the crate had fallen closed although the peg that normally held it shut was missing.

'Turpin's gone!' she shrieked. 'Someone's taken Turpin!'

Ethan came running, stopping short at the door of the tool shed where he gasped loudly as he, too, came face to face with the disarray.

'No, no one's taken him. The little bugger's escaped from his crate. But he'll be around somewheres.' They didn't have far to look. There, on a rafter in one corner of the tool shed, was Turpin: peacefully asleep, with his black-barred tail hanging limply down.

Joel Lundberg had admirably fulfilled his role as his father's 'right-hand man' but had grown discontented with the insular life that he considered farming to be. In February, 1859, he joined the Army.

'This is a big country, mother,' he told Anna, 'and I mean to see some of it. What better way than on a soldier's pay.'

'And what about the savages? You've heard what they can do to people,' she remarked fearfully.

'Oh mother, the Army does a lot more than chase Indians. Most likely I'd hardly get to see an Indian. Besides, most of what you hear is scaremongering to keep people off the sacred tribal hunting grounds.'

'You know best,' she conceded resignedly, 'You're well nigh twenty-four and have a mind of your own.'

Per-Erik was less accommodating. He berated his son for turning his back on the 'golden opportunity' that, to him, the flourishing farm represented. Resorting almost to mental blackmail, he pleaded with his son to change his mind, citing a catalogue of dangers he would probably face, with exaggerated concentration on the thieving, torturing and double-dealing ways of the many Indians he was likely to encounter. Seeing that he was making no impression, he tried the 'Louisa route', reminding Joel that his younger sister was now 'spoken for' and would most likely be married within the year. Both of them leaving home in the same year might be asking a lot of Anna to bear, he argued. But Joel's rolling stone still harboured enough moss to cushion him from his father's tirade. Two weeks later, Private Lundberg was receiving his training at Pittsburgh, Pennsylvania.

There were thirty-two recruits at the training camp, ranging in age from eighteen to twenty-five. They'd reported to Captain Guthrie, a veteran of the Mexican War who'd suffered a number of injuries and had been 'pensioned off' to devise and supervise the basic training given to novices in what the Army had denoted Central Northern Region. The nomenclature sounded strange to the civilian ear, for they also had an East Northern and West Northern Region, but that was typical Army semantics. Everything, it seemed, was back to front; like 'knapsack brown' or 'leggings leather medium'.

For the most part, Guthrie was as straight as a ramrod. But in one area he showed a leaning towards a meanness that, sometimes, bordered on cynicism: he singled out one particular recruit and, during the whole of the man's time at Pittsburgh, he would become the butt of Guthrie's jokes and schoolboyish humour. This time around, he picked on a nineteen year old from Missouri. His name was John Purpose and he pronounced his home state 'Mizzoura.' He was tall, thin, and had a habit of standing with his fists by his side, level with the top of his gut so that his elbows stuck out behind him. The bony joints seemed to come to a sharp point and he reminded Guthrie of a grasshopper. That, in itself, gave rise to a host of taunts about the lad's appearance. Guthrie grew fond of shouting at him: 'Hop to it, boy! Like a grasshopper! Hop to it!' Then, one day, when the whole squad stood to attention while Guthrie inspected their dress, he stopped in front of Purpose. 'Purpose! I hope to God you never make it to the top, boy, cos then we'd have a General Purpose. Ha ha ha ha ha.' A few of the others smirked at the line the boy had probably heard many times before in his life. But never in front of his adult peers at a formal parade. That night, Private Purpose disappeared and was never seen again.

If John Purpose had stood out because of his bony

appearance and play-on-words name, Joel Lundberg drew attention for other reasons. It wasn't only the remaining undertones of his mother tongue in the way he spoke that made Joel stand out among the other recruits at Pittsburgh. It was more likely his physique. Standing an even six feet tall without boots, he was broad-framed and well muscled from an abundance of field work at the Lower Sandusky farm. As if that was not enough, his piercing blue eyes and sun-bleached blond hair, set off against his deeply tanned skin, gave him the look of a veteran of the Plains. And his fine marksmanship may have counted for something, too. It quickly became evident to Sergeant O'Malley, the harsh Irishman who drilled the novices and put them through their paces in most facets of their training, that Joel was in a league of his own. True, the Swede was a year or two older than most of the other recruits and, because he was so self-assured, O'Malley had picked on him during some of the exercises, pushing him to a point well beyond the norm expected. Only when asked to accomplish the near-impossible did Joel falter. In fairness, the sergeant stated his high regard for Private Lundberg in his *Recruit Training Summary Report* to Captain Guthrie.

In some ways, Joel was lucky to be undertaking his training at Pittsburgh. Even though Sergeant O'Malley was tough, sometimes brutal, the grub was edible and the recruits were introduced to the newest equipment, particularly the weapons. Their General Issue kit included the new English-made Enfield rifles – single-shot and .577 calibre, firing a hollow-based Minie bullet that carried true up to two hundred yards and beyond on a man-sized target. They had the new Colt six-shot revolvers, too, in a nominal .45 calibre. And each man was given a leather-sheathed knife, its blade stamped with *Sheffield Steel*. Joel wondered why it was that, close on eighty-five years after the country had declared its independence, his rifle and knife came from England, but he felt it wise not to raise the subject with Brendan O'Malley. The ginger-haired Irishman used strong language even when his charges were making the grade on the gruelling exercises he set for them; any mention of England might just light the fuse to what Joel had heard the local the miners call 'an uncontrolled explosion'. So he bit his tongue – and kept on wondering.

It was following a close-combat exercise where the sergeant was instructing on the use of the knife that Joel pushed his luck too far. O'Malley had set up a cross-cut of a log on a trestle and called the men around him.

'Doin' what we've bin doin', yer sculpin' knife's only good ta ye if ye kin git in close. Sometimes ye canna afford ta let the booger that near. Here, now, watch!'

He drew his knife and, in one fluid movement, flicked it effortlessly towards the cross-cut. It struck barely an inch from centre and quivered, its point buried deep in the grain of the wood.

'That's what ye'll be learnin' next,' O'Malley told them, looking around the recruits with the put on, mean-eyed expression he used when he wanted to emphasise a point.

'Can you do it with an axe, sir?' Joel piped up.

'An axe? Na, son, ah never carry a bloody axe so ah've no need to throw one. Am ah ta take it ye can do it yerself like?'

'Sure, sir. I'll show you.' Joel fetched a hand-axe while the sergeant retrieved his knife and the other recruits pulled faces at one another, smiling at the gamesmanship the Swede had introduced. Joel returned and, at about seven paces from the wood block, hurled the axe. It flew through the air, making one complete turn, and thwacked into the block.

'Verra good, Lundberg,' O'Malley remarked, 'Could ye do it again?'

'I can, sir,' he answered, brimming with confidence at his one-upmanship over the sergeant. Again, the axe left Joel's hand on its way to the cross-cut. All the time, Brendan O'Malley had been standing on a level with Joel, but some way to one side. As the blade came out of its turn to thwack into the block once more, O'Malley's knife was already there, sticking at an oblique angle that deflected the arriving axe-blade to send the chopper looping off on to the ground.

'Too slow, son; too slow. If ah'd a bin the block ah'd a ducked, but ye canna beat a knife.' Once again, O'Malley retrieved his deadly missile, turned towards the still gawping squad and gave a pronounced wink as he re-sheathed the weapon and walked away. It had been a tense moment for Private Lundberg. The sergeant had brought him back to what he really was: a rookie with a lot still to learn.

At the final Passing Out parade, the captain congratulated Joel and commended him highly. Taking him aside after the parade, Captain Guthrie confided: 'Maybe it's time the Army took a view on recruiting more fellows like you. Fellows who've been around a bit and can take some stick. I get sick and tired of some of the "wet behind the ears" bunch that come through here. You'll do well, Lundberg.'

Their basic training over, those of the recruits who'd been pronounced acceptable had to remain at Pittsburgh a further two days to find out what post they'd been assigned.

Two days of relaxation before they found out what the United States Army was really like.

★

It was a rare event when mail arrived at any small-town home. The event itself was worthy of almost as much celebration as the subject piece of communication. When a letter arrived for the Lundbergs, its receipt triggered an effervescent mood that rose exponentially to a crescendo as Per-Erik first deciphered that it was from his cousin Ingvar Tillkvist and, secondly, that he was coming to America. Ingvar was ten years younger than Per-Erik and had been working in an iron works at Bergslagen the last time they'd heard. He had traced the Lundbergs through Anna's sister Marianne.

'When does it say? When are they coming?' Anna bubbled over, pulling the neatly scribed sheet towards her and almost tearing it out of her husband's hands so that she could see the words for herself.

'They'll be here in a month or so,' Per-Erik read.

'A month? Just four weeks?' Anna let go of the letter and threw her arms around Louisa, the two of them jigging around in a pique of excitement.

'How I wish Marianne could come, too,' she said, dizzily plopping herself on to one of the wooden benches that sat alongside the stout kitchen table.

'They'll have to squeeze into Joel's room,' Louisa suggested.

'Yes,' agreed Anna, 'and we'll have to give the place a good clean before they arrive.'

'It's four weeks, Anna. You'll have plenty of time for that,' Per-Erik reminded her, trying to inject some reality back into the exuberance that pervaded the farm kitchen.

With Joel off serving his adopted country's interests in a place called Front Royal and Louisa's courtship with Tomas Bergelin, a neighbouring farmer's son, beginning to wane, the impending arrival of their kin from the 'old country' became a new highlight on the calendar.

Back in Sweden, the drain on the population due to emigration was rising steeply. It was beginning to cause concern in high places because a new trend was evident: no longer were these adventurers drawn mostly from the dispossessed or down-on-luck working classes; some of the ablest men and women were taking leave to apply their skills to the vibrant challenges offered by North America. And Ingvar Tillkvist fell into this category. One of four children born to Lars and Marianne Tillkvist and the grandson of the famous sea captain who'd sailed his little ship *Peleus* practically around the world, Ingvar had studied geology at the university in Uppsala. He and Iri had gone through the not uncommon tragedy of losing a child shortly after the birth, but had been blessed with a fine son two years later. Bjorn was now fifteen years old and, like so many young Swedes at around this time, was set to accompany his parents to North America.

In the ten years since the Lundbergs had made the same journey, travel had become much more sophisticated. So, too, had the emigrants' first taste of America when they disembarked at New York. The whole operation was carried out smoothly, with almost military precision. The Swedes, Danes and Germans who made their way, mostly northwards and westwards, to begin a new life were swiftly despatched to their destinations by coaches or the new railway system. A decade before, the craftsmen brought their tools; now a more elite class brought their learning.

'Hei, welcome to Ohio!' Anna called out, not in Swedish but in heavily accented English, as the Tillkvists arrived at the farm.

'Hei! It's good to be here at last. And now you're speaking English, eh?' Ingvar remarked.

'English? No, no. We speak American. You will, too, before long,' Anna replied.

Lapsing back into their mother tongue, the two families jabbered away, bridging both the miles and the years, as they reminisced over past events and people they'd known in what became commonly referred to as 'the homeland'. It had been approaching three in the afternoon when Ingvar, Iri and Bjorn arrived but, by seven o'clock, they were settled into the Lundberg's ample homestead and were beginning to feel the weariness that had been brought on by the last stage of their journey. Involuntarily, Bjorn had already fallen asleep.

'I have a little something I'm sure you'll appreciate,' Ingvar announced as Louisa and the four oldsters settled into fireside chairs. 'Something perhaps you haven't enjoyed for some time.' The tall, angular geologist ran his fingers through the thinning strands of sandy hair that fell unevenly across his tanned forehead; propelled himself forward on to the balls of his feet and let the momentum carry him out of the chair and towards the room that had once been Joel's. Moments later he rejoined the company, cradling an oversized flask, his face beaming an earlobe-to-earlobe grin. 'Hei, hei. Genuine aquavit. The best of Swedish. From Skåne.'

There were three things in particular that Per-Erik and Ingvar had in common: both had married later in life than was normal for the average Swedish male; both had married women much younger than themselves; and both had a strong liking for aquavit. Especially Skånian aquavit.

'You'll join us, ladies?' Ingvar invited, holding up the flask.

'Of course they'll join us,' Per-Erik replied on their behalf, his firm response overruling any possibility of their declining, 'and Louisa, too, on this special occasion I should think?' The last part was a question, his raised eyebrows and querying look in Louisa's direction begging her affirmation.

'Mmm. Just a little, thank you,' she answered.

Anna had already made her way to a narrow wall cupboard and placed five small tumblers on the table. Ingvar unstoppered the flask, poured four full measures and half filled the fifth.

'Skål!' the voices united as they toasted their homeland.

'That's one thing that doesn't translate into American in the same way,' Per-Erik commented: 'Somehow "skål" sounds much better than "your good health" or any of the other salutations they use here. We might try to be American in most other ways, but we'll always be Swedish when we drink a toast.'

Later, as the Tillkvists prepared for bed, Iri asked her husband: 'D'you think we'll change like that? They're hardly Swedish anymore.'

'Well, it's not as if we can just go back to Sweden if we feel like it. We made our decision, my love, and this will become our country now. So, yes, I imagine that after we've been here ten years we'll be just as American as the Lundbergs.'

'I'm not sure that I ever want to be an American,' Iri said, as she pulled a brush through her long, almost black locks. Then, quietly, she began to sob; her ruddy complexion – so starkly contrasted with Ingvar's sallow, tanned skin – reddened ever more. She flopped on to the edge of the bed like a rag doll carelessly discarded by some thoughtless child. Ingvar, part undressed, gently lowered himself beside her and tenderly put an arm around her shoulders.

'What is it? What's wrong, my love?' For such a big man, his voice carried a mild compassion that was at once both soothing and indicative of a deep, heartfelt concern. In situations like this, where he sought only to bring comfort and understanding, his overflowing compassion sometimes served only to heighten the emotion and induce floods of tears. This was one of those occasions. Iri became practically bereft of all physical strength as she collapsed sideways against him, her crying almost silent but profuse in its deluge from her tear ducts.

'I just don't know, Ingvar. It all seemed such a big adventure when we left Göteborg, but now I...' She gulped twice, her breasts rising and falling in quick succession as the intake of air whistled past her almost perfect, slightly yellowed teeth. 'I just didn't think I'd miss Sweden so much.'

'Oh, it's only to be expected,' Ingvar began his consolation, 'Life here is quite different. Everything's different. We've seen that already. But we'll get used to it. Just look at Anna and Louisa.'

'That's what made me cry, I suppose. Exactly that. Even when they talk in Swedish, it's not like home anymore. It's like they're speaking a foreign language. How could they change so much? I don't want us to become like them. Life's not a game of masquerades: you can't be Swedish one day and American the next. I just want to be Swedish, even though we live in a new country.'

Ingvar bit his lip. This was an attitude, a depth of

feeling, that he hadn't bargained for. He began to feel undermined and disappointed. America held so much promise; he knew that. The Lundbergs could never have become so prosperous had they remained in Växjö. And he and Iri had so much more to offer. They were better equipped. Nothing he had seen so far had altered his opinion or vision that here they could make a good life for themselves. A good life that would give Bjorn perhaps an even better one in the future.

'I'm sure it'll work out the way we want. *You* know – we *both* know – life doesn't just happen; we have to make it happen. Even in Sweden that would be possible, but it's not easy. Here, we have to make an extra effort: to learn the language; learn the customs; fit into whatever community we end up in; and make friends with people other than just other Swedes. Then, I'm sure, we can really make things happen.'

'I know, Ingvar, I know. It's just been too much, too different, all in such a short time. And I'm tired out. We've talked and talked all night. Maybe tomorrow will be better.'

For one immigrant Swede, being an American wasn't a matter of objective choice – it was a way of life. Now that he was in Front Royal, Joel Lundberg looked forward to starting his life in the Army for real. Frustratingly, however, he was beginning to discover that Army life wasn't all action and adventure. He'd been at the Front Royal camp for more than two weeks and had cause to wonder when he was going to get the chance to use some of the training Brendan O'Malley had so gruellingly put him through. The year was dragging its heels through winter and life was a daily routine of boring inactivity, for the most part. The only light shining from the other end of this dead-end tunnel was the rumour that they would be posted to field action 'sometime soon'.

Joel was cleaning his mess kit in the ridge tent he shared with three other recruits when Private Samuel Watterson burst in to break the news.

'They're up! The postings are up on the board! And guess what?'

'Go on.'

'We're gonna stick together, you an' me. Stayin' right here in Furjinya.'

'Virginia? Right here?'

'Not quite. We've drawn a real cosy one. Guardin' a Federal arsenal a few miles from here. Seems fifteen folks got killt there when some anti-slavery gang stormed the place.'

'Right. That'll be Harper's Ferry. I heard they'd had a spot of trouble. Got the ringleader, though. Some religious headcase from Connecticut: John Brown, I think it was. Believe they hanged him.'

Sam Watterson was two years younger than Joel, born in South Carolina but had spent most of his life in Ohio. Right from the first moments after they'd met, they'd paired up like two old school chums. Both coming from Ohio helped, perhaps, and their respective senses of humour complemented one another so that their time together at Pittsburgh provided the bonding that dovetailed the two into close companionship. Over the next year and a half, the two became almost inseparable. To some, their close relationship may have raised doubts about the normality of their sexuality. If that had been the case, those doubts would have vaporised when the two attended a Gala Dance at Harper's hospital in the summer of 1860. For most of the evening, Joel danced with a red-haired nurse from Pennsylvania and Sam worked his charms on a lass from Roanoke.

'You sure don't sound like you come from Ohio,' the red-haired nurse remarked to Joel. 'Sometimes you pronounce things in a funny way.'

'I was born in Sweden. My parents are Swedish and, although we always speak American at home, sometimes we use Swedish words.'

'Ah, so that's it. All the way from Sweden.'

'But you say some funny things, too. Like when you slipped on the dance floor, you said you'd got a "skelf in your pinkie" or something like that. I've never heard that expression before.'

Martha Bryce threw back her head and laughed, her eyes twinkling in a way that totally captivated the dashing Swede. Then she teased him, 'That's because I was born in Scotland. My parents are Scottish and, even though we speak American at home, sometimes we use Scottish words. Look! This is a pinkie!' She wiggled the little finger of her right hand. 'And a skelf is a splinter of wood, like the one that stuck right there when I fell.' She held up her little finger, a few inches from his nose, as if by doing so Joel would be able to see the tiny hole from which she'd squeezed the offending sliver of floorboard at the end of the dance.

'There's no skelf in your pinkie now,' he said, countering her efforts at teasing. Then he pulled her hand towards his lips and kissed it.

'Thank you. That's really healed it for good.' And once again, Martha threw back her head in an unrestrained laugh.

On the other side of the room, Joel could see, Sam was

making equally good progress with his own slim, dark-haired nurse. That sultry Saturday night in mid-July marked the beginnings of courtship between Joel and Martha... and between Sam and Cynthia.

Since that disturbing day the previous year when John Brown and his followers had attempted to force their way into the armoury to steal enough weapons to arm a goodly number of slaves, the town had been mostly peaceful. There was little excitement or even activity to break the boredom for the detachment of troops that formed the armoury guard. There was more than ample free time and both officers and men filled it in the most imaginative ways they could dream up. After the first month or so, pitching a ball around failed to satisfy. Some of the men built rafts and held a race that narrowly escaped becoming a serious disaster. The less adventurous ones fished. Others built a skid-cart that was little more than a sled-like structure with wheels. The idea had been to ride it down the hill towards the river. And it worked. Once.

Joel and Sam had been two of those involved in building the cart and Sam had sat aboard the contraption with another private when they launched it from the top of the hill. The small wheels may have functioned close to perfection on a smooth and level surface, but the hill made quite a gradient and its surface was by no means smooth. As the machine gathered speed and its wheels bounced wildly over the cobbles, it became wholly unsteerable, much to the delight of those who'd taken up vantage points along the route. The two privates who attempted to keep it on some kind of course gripped both the baseboard and each other in a display of terror that was at first purely mock but became more real as the plummeting vehicle swerved out of control, careered off a wall then swung broadside across the street, spilling its occupants violently to send them tumbling a bruising ten or twelve yards downhill on the cobbles. The skid-cart was a crumpled wreck and was pitched, with due ceremony, into the river. The two privates were also wrecks, but were given a more forbearing treatment.

In the weeks and months following the Gala Dance, the off-duty spells were no longer tedious for either Joel or Sam. At least not on those occasions, which were often, when their free time coincided with the nurses' own off-duty times. Whenever possible, they made a foursome and always seemed to find somewhere to go that was new to them. Both sets of friendships were becoming serious and they began to talk of the future and how life could be if they managed to stick together as two married couples. That was, until the day a debate arose among them concerning the right to keep slaves and the place of 'niggers' in a white society. Martha sided with Joel on the anti-slavery stance while the other couple drew together on a pro vote.

'My folks have always considered niggers to be a kind of sub-species – and I think the same,' Sam asserted.

'You have to admit,' put in Cynthia, supporting him, 'they have a capacity to stick at heavy labouring tasks that any white would give up on after a while. It's not just their physique, in fact I think it's got more to do with their mental level. As Sam says, they're almost like a different species.'

'They're human beings, just like us!' Martha railed back. 'Just dark-skinned, that's all.'

'No, it's not just their skin,' Sam contended, 'Look at the shape of their heads. Not like us at all.'

'Anyway,' Joel defended, 'they deserve better than to be treated like trash. We don't have brow-beaten slaves in Sweden.'

'Nor in Scotland,' supported Martha.

'That's the trouble with you two. You're not real Americans like Cynth and me,' added Sam, provocatively. 'One day, every true American household will have nigger servants, you'll see. Down home in Charleston you can't survive without niggers to do the work in summertime. You've never been there, so you don't know. In Ohio you have horses; in the South we have niggers.'

Joel detected the subtle switch to 'you' and 'we' that divided their opinions. He summarised, 'Let's just say it depends on circumstances. But segregation is morally wrong. All men are created equal.'

'But some more equal than others,' Sam concluded.

Emotions ran high until Joel, as the oldest and perhaps wisest, called for a truce. No major rift between the couples surfaced in the days that followed, but the seeds of a more sinister division began to manifest themselves during April of the following year.

Tensions had been rising for some time between the north-eastern industrial states and their agricultural south-eastern counterparts. Sam Watterson's home state of South Carolina had already seceded from the Union, yet Union forces still occupied a strategic island fort offshore from Charleston. At four o'clock in the morning on 12th April, matters came to a head as South Carolinian troops began to bombard the fort. The Union troops who occupied Fort Sumter in Charleston harbour could be re-supplied only by ship and were in no shape to withstand the constant shelling from the shore. They surrendered within a day and a half, bringing to an end the first engagement of the Civil War or, as it's more correctly known, the *War Between the States*.

The engagement at Fort Sumter coincided with another engagement in the northern corner of Virginia for, on that same day, Joel and Martha formally announced their intention to marry. The wedding was set for August, with Sam Watterson to be the best man. Cynthia, Sam's girl from Roanoke, was to be one of the bridesmaids. As good wishes were exchanged and toasts drunk in honour of the engaged couple, little could they have imagined that, before August, Joel and Sam would be fighting under different flags... against each other.

*

Ingvar and Iri grew wearisome of kicking their heels at the Lundberg's farm and felt it was time to find their own place. The direction of their move was dictated by the job Ingvar had secured at the Mining & Minerals Corporation. Since he was to be based in the outskirts of Toledo, that's where they set up home. Bjorn looked forward to the move as it held the possibility of his meeting others of his own age. Life with the Lundberg's had been restricted in that respect and he felt caged in by the lack of peers on the farm. He would not be disappointed, his father assured him.

During their time at the farm, the Tillkvists had delved into only the most accessible of their personal belongings. The large trunks they'd brought from Sweden had remained intact and unopened and this aspect of moving into a home of their own had more of a settling effect on the family than they might have anticipated. Unpacking familiar ornaments, books and small items of furniture at once created an ambience that gave them a feeling of homeliness they'd missed. For Bjorn, in particular, rediscovering his squeezebox brought a great delight and, even before the unpacking was completed, he sat down on a three-legged stool that had been made by his uncle and began to play some old Dalarna folk melodies. Ingvar and Iri were content to leave him to provide an accompaniment to their toing and froing as they distributed items around their new residence, the debris of their careful packing three months ago now strewn around the stool on which Bjorn squatted like a pixie from some fairy tale amidst a regalia of discordant colour created by the discarded materials that, for the most part, had served their purpose.

Ingvar began his exploratory work at M&M, leaving Iri to turn the Spartan shell of a house into a home that would be welcoming both to himself when he returned each evening and to their many neighbours for whom the Tillkvist's home quickly established itself as a centre of hospitality. Iri no longer entertained her strong feelings of resentment at being forced to adapt to the American way of life. Nor were the expectations Ingvar had conveyed to his son unfulfilled: Bjorn very soon began to integrate into his age group, making friends of both sexes, astonishing them with his talent and dexterity on the button-squeezebox.

With the Tillkvists gone, life for the Lundbergs returned to its plateau of pedestrian equilibrium. For Louisa, that meant having more time to face up to her disintegrating courtship with Tomas Bergelin. She'd used the presence of their guests as an excuse to turn away her suitor's approaches over the past few weeks. As she contemplated her future, she became convinced that Tomas would not become a consideration in her long-term plans. She wrote him a letter, distilling on to three sheets the thoughts, arguments and feelings that, when summed, added up to a formal termination of their friendship.

'Why won't you even talk to him?' Anna admonished her. 'Just when your father and I thought you'd found a good husband, you throw away the chance. He's from a very fine Swedish family, too.'

'Yes, mother, *too* Swedish for my liking.'

'Whatever do you mean? How can anyone be *too* Swedish?'

'Quite simple, mother. He thinks like a Swede in Sweden, just like his parents. Tomas'll never get anywhere or achieve anything in America. He's a charming man, but he'd be quite content to stick around here for the rest of his life and I don't want that.'

'Oh, I see,' Anna said, contemplatively. 'And I suppose you mean to traipse around the country like Joel, so we'll never see you?'

'Well, I mean to see some of the country, yes. But that doesn't mean I'd never come back to see you and Papa.'

For the time being, the conversation fizzled out. Louisa delivered her letter to the Bergelins' farm and, as far as she was concerned, that was the end of the matter. But two weeks later, her life was turned upside down.

The Convention Hall in Lima became a magnet every two months for all those of the farming community who enjoyed a good hoedown. There was always good music, good dancing, good food and farming families often brought their friends and relatives so there would be lots of laughter and, right through until eleven o'clock on the Saturday night, a rowdy evening of simple, country-style fun. The eleven o'clock closedown was to allow folks ample time to return to their homes before the Sabbath. Louisa had been to these hoedowns on a number of occasions but none matched this latest one. The music, the food, the dancing were much the same as before. But before, there had been no Dan Catlin.

It was one of those flukes. The sort of coincidence that starts conversations along the lines of: 'If only you had...' or 'Any other time I would have...' and so on. Dan Catlin was a rancher from upstate New York and the only reason he was in Lima that Saturday night was because he'd been delivering two Hereford bulls to a man in Fort Wayne, Indiana, and had taken the opportunity to stop over with some friends not far from Lima. When Louisa Lundberg walked into the hall, the stocky twenty-six year old bachelor wasted no time in making enquiries as to who she was and if she was 'available'. Likewise, when Louisa first caught sight of Dan's tightly curled locks and craggy features, it was as if a lightning bolt had singled her out and blasted its way through the roof of the Convention Hall to strike at her heart – or whatever part of us is responsible for that indefinable chemistry that stirs our emotions when we fall in love. When Dan approached her to ask if she'd partner him in the first dance, Louisa fell for him. Deeply. Very deeply.

For his part, the big rancher immediately warmed to her and they danced together at every turn. Neither knew it then but, within a matter of ten weeks, they would become Mr and Mrs Catlin of Cayuga Flats, New York. Per-Erik was proud of his daughter and was happy that, after the disappointment she'd had with the Bergelins' son, she had found someone whom she both loved and respected. Anna was crestfallen to think that neither of her children had chosen to marry one of their own kind but was consoled to learn that Dan Catlin was not just 'some American cowboy' but was, in truth, a very wealthy young man. The ranch at

Cayuga Flats was fifteen times the size of their own spread. When Joel married Martha Bryce, just a month later, Anna became quite disoriented. It was as if, within the space of four weeks, a large part of her life had been severed, leaving her somehow emotionally naked.

During the remainder of the summer of 1861 nobody believed that the growing unrest between North and South would continue beyond the end of the year. 'It'll be over by Christmas,' was the opinion of not only the common man but also of the majority of those so far caught up in the confrontation. Some saw it as little more than an adventurous distraction. Sam Watterson was one.

'Now's our chance, Joel. No more lolling about on useless patrols; let's get some action. I've heard Victor Bembridge down in Lynchburg is raising his own Brigade and I aim to make my way down there to join them. You coming?'

'Old man Bembridge? He's for the Southern cause, isn't he?'

'Sure. But does it matter? He's equipping his men with some good stuff and there's sure to be some real action where Old Vic's involved.'

'No Sam, it's not for me. Shouldn't be for you either. You know that old cuss, he's a scoundrel. He's only got what he's got because of his extortions and blackmailing ways. That's why they drummed him out of West Point and just about everywhere else.'

'Like I say, does it matter? This thing'll blow over by Christmas so we've got to take our chances at the sharp end of things. Come on, Joel.'

'Nope! And I'll give you three good reasons why not: first – you know how I feel about the ways of the South;

second – I have Martha to consider; third – I'd never want anything to do with that blowhard.'

'Suit yourself. I'm leaving tomorrow. Throwing in this lot and heading for some real soldiering.'

'How does Cynthia feel about this? You talked to her?'

'She's coming, too. Should have no trouble picking up a nursing job down there.'

Joel and Martha were saddened by Sam's attitude. They were sorry to see the pair go, but the couple's mindset, so different from their own, created a gulf between them that, in an incongruous way, made the separation not only bearable but, in the end, preferable.

The high spirits that surrounded Sam and Cynthia's elopement to Lynchburg were to prove their undoing. Mixing with the unruly Confederate gang that constituted the greater part of Bembridge's brigade, Sam's attachment to his girl began to loosen. It was when the Brigade decamped to Chesterfield, just outside Richmond, that the real breakdown in their relationship occurred. As Sam had predicted, Cynthia had no trouble in finding a nursing post, but that only seemed to spur his independence and he allowed himself to be led astray by Pete McGanley, a roughhouse rebel that Sam looked upon as a role model of the fighting South. McGanley introduced him to some of Richmond's most notorious brothels and he became enamoured with a French Canadian girl who went by the name of Monique. She became his favourite and a drain on his meagre purse. He drank heavily, too, encouraged by McGanley. Cynthia soon became a nonentity in his life.

While the battles at Fort Pickens and Bull Run were hardly enough to suggest the beginnings of a protracted engagement between the sides, both North and South were building up their armaments. The Union forces were making the slower start, just beginning to get to grips with the situation, when Joel received notice of his impending transfer from Harper's Ferry. It would be as well, he thought, since there was growing unrest in the area. Not in battlefield conflict, but politically. The mountain folk were banding together and petitioning to form a breakaway State. The formation of West Virginia had been rumoured for some time and he was glad that he and Martha could escape the volatility of the ugly situation where neighbours had begun spying on neighbours and minor infractions were a daily occurrence. He was drafted to Annapolis and coincidentally promoted. Roaming the glades and valleys with a band of ruffians might have suited a Watterson, but a Lundberg would rise through the ranks in a more dignified manner. As a Swede, he'd been an immigrant and a 'New American'. But, as a soldier, he was Union through and through.

When Robert E. Lee turned down the chance to lead the Union forces against the emerging Confederate States of America, choosing instead to side with his home state of Virginia and, therefore, the cause of the CSA, it ensured that Abraham Lincoln's campaign to hold the old Union together would be a lengthy one. The charismatic and tactically brilliant General Lee was to prove a thorn in the flesh to his former President for much longer than either imagined. But, a year after the first shots had been fired in this War Between the States, it remained largely a local issue. Certainly, the lives of the vast majority of the population were untouched by its growing intensity. The Bryces and the Lundbergs on their farms in Reading and Lower Sandusky felt little of its effect on their daily lives. The Tillkvists, now pillars of their neighbourhood in lakeside Ohio, were similarly unaffected and the Catlins, in far-off Cayuga Flats, barely kept abreast of any of the developments that would ultimately plunder the nation's manhood to an unprecedented degree. But, for the two sidekicks from Central Northern Training Camp in Pittsburgh and the girls who'd become such firm friends at Harper's Ferry, the war had become very real. Sam Watterson languished in a field hospital, his left leg a gruesome testimony to the effects of canister shot. His former girl, Cynthia, slaved under abominable conditions in a makeshift ward in Richmond. Joel and Martha were still in Annapolis, although Joel, now a sergeant, had seen his wife only twice in four months and then, only briefly for a few days on each occasion. The pundits now lengthened their odds on a quick conclusion to the war; the most optimistic gave it until the onset of winter, others foresaw a triumph for the South around the middle of '63, but even those guesses were qualified by whether or not England or France would back the South. The industrialised North had not yet found a way of galvanising its strength to good effect and the more cavalier southerners were beginning to chalk up a series of meaningful victories. A state of mental depression, frustration and pessimism was beginning to permeate through the Northern population. That the Union and its Government still functioned was, in itself, a wonder. But function it did. And one of the most far-reaching pieces of legislation that it passed was the Homestead Act, encouraging a wholesale opening up of the West, with promises of large land grants to settlers who would 'move and improve'. Despite the widespread gloom that surrounded Washington at this time, it seemed to be indicative of at least the Government's feeling that an end to the conflict would not be stalled for long, since the Act was opening the door to westward emigration at a time when manpower availability in the East was of paramount importance.

Joel Lundberg was lucky. While gangrene and the onset of pneumonia first disabled then took the life of his erstwhile friend, Sam Watterson, he had managed to escape, so far, without so much as a scratch. By circumstantial chance he'd avoided all of the headline confrontations. Indeed, the closest he'd come to a major threat on his life had been at Wendel's Ford, when a Confederate night raid had caught his detachment off guard. It was his first experience of the feared, blood-curdling *Rebel Yell* that shrieked and wailed as a horde of grey ghosts swarmed through the trees flanking the ford to rend the night air with a fierce, but speculative, volley of rifle-fire. The stunned northerners broke from their bivouac in disarray but, under Joel's cool leadership, had regrouped into two skirmish lines that firstly held, then repulsed, the men in grey, forcing them back across the stream. The temporary respite diminished the gunfire, which was now sporadic, but did little for the jangling nerves of either side. The poor visibility heightened their nervousness as the sound of movements among the undergrowth left only to the imagination what was really happening. One of Joel's men began to pray, the words barely audible even in the stillness of uncertainty that seemed to hang over both sides of the ford.

'They're probably praying over there right now,' Joel thought. 'And to the same God, too. Strange that. Wonder how He makes up His mind which of us to favour this time. Maybe He just flips a cloud: if it comes down smooth side up, Billy Yank it is; if it lands bumpy side up, Johnny Reb gets the vote. Let's hope it's smooth.' He dismissed the thought and began passing a new command along the line.

Sergeant Lundberg led them forward in a charge, each man producing his own version of a scream that might rival the Rebel Yell. The Rebels didn't break cover immediately, keeping low in the underbrush just long enough to unleash a concerted volley at their blue-clad assailants. Small branches whipsawed and leaves fluttered in uncontrolled flight to the ground as the Minie bullets whined through the air. Joel yelped as a shot nicked his left arm, just above the elbow. He shook his arm vigorously and alternately clenched and stretched his fingers to assure himself that the damage was slight. He charged on, undeterred. The two skirmish lines formed an inverted 'V' that funnelled the attackers into a compacted mass at the top of the bank so that, even in the low light of a partial moon, they became an easy target for Joel's men.

It could hardly have counted as a victory, for losses were few, in absolute terms, and the ford was hardly of strategic importance. Joel castigated himself for his lack of attention to installing proper pickets in the first place, but salved his conscience with the end result.

In the aftermath of the Union's victories at Gettysburg and Vicksburg, Joel – now holding the rank of Captain – found the opportunity to secure an administrative post in Washington and, to all intents and purposes, his war was over. In truth, he had grown weary of the enforced separation from his young wife and longed for a more settled existence. Since almost everyone now believed that the Confederacy had reached its high water mark at Gettysburg, the tide had turned overwhelmingly in favour of a Union victory that surely couldn't be delayed by too many more months and it was time now to think of the future. As it happened, he saw a little more of Martha, but not much more. She had graduated into a new kind of nursing at the Weir Mitchell hospital in Philadelphia where a neurological department, the first of its kind, had been established to treat nervous disorders largely brought on by exposure to continual heavy gunfire.

As the war ground on, the outcome became inevitable. Almost fully four years after he had taken up the gauntlet on behalf of the Confederacy, Bobby Lee finally admitted that further pursuit of the cause was futile. He surrendered to General Grant on April 9th, 1865, at the small Virginian village of Appomattox Court House. There, in the private residence of a Mr McLean, he accepted the not ungenerous terms offered by his worthy opponent. Grant was both magnanimous and compassionate in victory, allowing the demoralised southerners to take their horses 'for the ploughing that'll need doing when they get home' and, save for a few more months of isolated resistance in the South, the Union had been saved. Within five more years, when Virginia would be formally readmitted, the Union would be restored to a more harmonious entity than it had known for more than thirty years.

Following his discharge, Captain Lundberg joined Martha in Philadelphia and became a 'kept man' for some weeks, until he found civilian employment in a downtown clothing store.

*

The mass exodus of its population, with its superimposed 'brain drain', had left Sweden reeling. In 1523, Gustav Vasa had begun the build up of the country into a major European military force. Throughout the 1600s his foundational efforts were continued by Gustav Adolf and

Karl Gustav. The nation fell from its position of power through the 1700s and took on, instead, the culture and enlightenment sparked by Gustav the Third. Now it was entering a new phase, fighting a different kind of war to build itself into an industrial, rather than military, force to be reckoned with. The textile industry was booming – employing men, women and even children in its six-days-a-week, twelve-hours-a-day drive towards improving the country's economy. Iron ore exports were at their highest level ever and timber was not far behind. The giant Utsi Forest Products Company dealt not only in basic wood exports, but was developing a pulp and paper business based on the production of chemically digested pulp. The corporation that had begun life many years before, in the hands of a displaced Sami woodsman, was now a mass employer and one of the foundation stones of Sweden's future. Railway systems were growing, too, and areas that were previously the province of small farms and even smaller villages or hamlets were now burgeoning communities and townships. Sweden was fighting back.

The past hundred years had been unkind to Peterlöv, the tiny village that had been home to a renowned artisan, an adventurous explorer and a far-sighted schoolteacher. No one lived there now. Low protrusions rose from the ground here and there to mark what had once been the homes that had hosted dreams, tragedies and everyday life. The largest ruin marked the last decaying struggles of the Lutheran Church. The building's few remaining edifices echoed the demise that was occurring in the more organic realms of the Faith as it buckled under the charismatic fervour of a more evangelistic reformation that was sweeping the country. Peterlöv had received its Last Rites and awaited only the finality of its execution with no promise or even hope of a merciful Grace that might award it some reprieve. Soon, there would barely remain any record of man's existence there but, at the edge of an overgrown field, there stood an old oak tree that held, cocooned within its bosom and unknown to a living soul, a masterpiece of craftsmanship that could testify, given the chance, that man had certainly been here.

Not far away, at Hässleholm, the opposite was true. Here, a vibrant community was springing up around the railway station that straddled the new line. Good land and a benevolent combination of natural elements that blessed the area with a tolerable climate co-operated to make it a focal point for the upwardly mobile as it cast a new aura of hope and promise for the development of a prosperous community. Elsewhere in Sweden, the story was the same: wherever the railway went, there new life was implanted. Hamlets and small villages that had existed for centuries now withered where they were isolated from the twin iron lifelines that threaded their way unrelentingly across the land.

A new, invisible power was about to unleash its potential, too. Early experimentation with steam-driven generators had brought electricity into being. The cost was high and the problems of its economic distribution not yet solved, but the new source of energy was sounding the forewarning of a death knell to many of the manually tasked areas of the new production industries. Once hydro-generation proved a viable alternative to the steam-raising plants, cost alone would not be the prohibitive factor in electrification of towns and industries. The upsurge of technological developments was changing the face of the country, burying forever the stagnation that Sweden had known during the first half of the nineteenth century.

Sweden was not only fighting back; it was beginning to win.

The emerging status of the New Sweden would have its greatest impact, in one sense, on the expatriate clans now living in various parts of North America for, in the closing years of the century, one in five would find their way back to the homeland their parents had forsaken.

In the still prosperous farm near Lower Sandusky, Anna was in good spirits. She was happy to learn that her son had come through the conflict without serious injury. But that had little to do with her happy mood. Today was the day the 'Cloth Man' was due to visit and his calling would have an added meaning on this occasion because she and Per-Erik had received a letter from Dan and Louisa saying that they'd be coming to visit in two weeks' time. Anna had risen early, along with her husband, and was churning some butter in a small hand churn.

Watching his wife making butter always amused Per-Erik. Even though he'd often kidded her about it, she couldn't help but continue to follow her natural inclinations. She did it now. Sitting astride a chair with the churn between her knees, she expended all her efforts on the task, her tongue poked out to one side of her mouth and her eyes a study in concentration as she grew red in the face from her efforts to turn the milk skimmings into a creamy-white emulsion.

'If you die before I do,' Per-Erik remarked, 'I'll see your ghost sat on that chair churning. Your shoulders will be shaking, your face like a beetroot and your tongue curling round the corner there like it was going to hook the butter out on to the table.'

'It's all right for you,' she retorted, 'but you're the one who enjoys it the most when I've made it. As if I didn't have enough to do already without keeping you supplied with butter.'

The Lundberg's house was now a grand affair, Per-Erik having gradually transformed it by various extensions and improvements into a replica of a Swedish mansion. It was more than enough to keep Anna busy maintaining it in homely order but, despite its size, it always looked a showpiece. Yet it was homely. The new wing Per-Erik had just completed had all of its principal windows facing south and sunlight flooded in to make it a haven of warmth and comfort, even on a day that was uninviting on the outside.

'What're you hoping Big Jim'll bring you today?' Per-Erik asked. 'Some more of that blue broadcloth?'

'No, not this time. I've ordered some fine yellow linen. I want to make a dress for Louisa. It'll make a fine surprise for her.'

'But we haven't seen her in months. How will you know her sizes?'

'Oh, she won't have changed that much. Besides, it'll be a pinafore dress so exact sizing isn't important.'

She might as well have told him the sea was blue because it wasn't red. Her answer meant nothing to him and added little to his scant knowledge of dressmaking. He merely shrugged his shoulders and smiled thinly.

The visit of the Cloth Man was a big event in the lives of the 'blue earth' farmers' wives. These travelling salesmen were treated like an extension of the family and, sometimes, a woman would gather several of her friends in one house to receive him. Big Jim always got a kick out of seeing these frontier women picking through his samples to find something that would fire their creative imagination.

'Elizabeth and Heidi will be here soon so I must finish churning and get ready.'

'Huh! You're as "got ready" as you'll ever need to be. This must be the tidiest homestead in the area.'

'No matter. I always like to have it just right when the other wives are coming over.'

Big Jim did a roaring trade. His visits to Kenton, Lower Sandusky and surrounding districts were as regular as clockwork. He always arrived in the area on a Wednesday; always at two-monthly intervals from March through September. Each of the four occasions was celebrated by the womenfolk like they would a daughter's birthday. Cakes were baked and the two hours that the salesman was in the house were always happy occasions. He was always smiling when he arrived. And smiling even more when he left, his little notebook filled with orders to be fulfilled on his next visit.

Anna got her linen. And ordered some more of the blue broadcloth that formed the staple of her sewing to provide the 'round home' clothing both she and Per-Erik customarily wore. That evening, she beavered away at the material, cutting it to shape in readiness for sewing into the dress that would, in all probability, be finished only just in time before the Catlins arrived from upstate New York.

The incongruity of Joel Lundberg's new occupation, to a man who was the brightest of his recruit intake at Pittsburgh, irked him. It was a 'make-do' job that gave him no sense of fulfilment and he was constantly on the lookout for a more fitting way to employ his many aptitudes. At least being able to share his feelings with Martha each night was some recompense. And being resident in Philly gave them both the opportunity to visit Martha's parents at Reading.

Their first visit to the Bryces in over three years was both a delight and a shock. As their two-in-hand rig rolled down the sweeping driveway towards the wide, shady, post-and-rail veranda, the skirl of bagpipes burst forth in a droning Scottish lilt. There stood Andra, resplendent in full Highland regalia, proudly exhibiting his new-found talent as a piper. Martha blushed.

'God help us, Joel, he's getting worse,' she murmured as they first took in the sight and sound that greeted them.

'Go easy, girl. Just try to humour him. It's just his way.'

'I'm beginning to feel sorry we came even before we get there.'

Mary rushed towards them as Joel brought the horses to a disciplined halt. Andra continued his droning.

'How good to see you both. So pleased you've come. It's been so long.' She threw her arms around Martha almost before her daughter's feet touched the ground, engulfing her in a smothering embrace. Andra continued his droning. He played on until the tune reached its musical conclusion then, wiping his mouth on the back of his hand, strode forward with outstretched hand to greet his son-in-law.

'Ach, noo, ye huvna changed a bit,' he bellowed as he swung his pipes under his left armpit and grasped Joel's hand, wringing it enthusiastically. Then he slung an arm around Martha's shoulder and marched her towards the door.

'Come in, bairns, come in.'

Affronted by her father's blatant exhibitionist antics, Martha said little. Joel was left to do most of the talking, bringing the Bryces up to date with their latest news and, in general, with happenings in Philly. His view of his in-laws was little coloured by what he termed their 'quaint ways' and he soon felt quite at ease in their company. Despite the resentment Martha harboured towards her father's peculiar conduct, she still felt close to her mother and enjoyed the renewed opportunity to talk with her on a woman-to-woman basis. It was like that now: they were no longer mother and daughter; they were equals, with similar ways of thinking. The first few hours of the Lundbergs' visit seemed to set the pattern for the eight days they spent with the Bryces: man-to-man and woman-to-woman. Nor did the situation change much when Ethan Whitney and his wife of two years, Charlotte, joined them on several occasions.

Fortunately, the weather remained fine throughout their stay and allowed for al fresco picnics and two day trips that the young couple would fondly remember, each in his and her own way. For Joel, the highlight of the time at Reading was a visit to nearby Baumstown where he was able to pay homage to his boyhood hero, Daniel Boone. The old frontiersman's birthplace home had been much altered, but there remained sufficient to provide Joel with a feeling of reverence as he stood by the old fish smokehouse near the entrance and looked over the acres where, he imagined, Daniel must have played and learned his first lessons in nature's lore.

For Martha, it was the trip to Ephrata that filled her memory with those same feelings of reverence and awe. In her case, it was no man-made structure that awakened her spiritual being. Sure, she appreciated the tranquil serenity of the old Protestant monastery of Ephrata Cloister, but it was a family of simple Amish folks who won her heart and everlasting respect. It was by chance that she met Ephraim and Rebecca Zooks at the Ephrata market. The couple ran a small stall that sold, amongst other things, rather plain-looking children's dolls. None of the dolls, Martha noticed, had a face. When she'd remarked on the fact to Rebecca, the Amish woman painstakingly explained the reason for their plainness.

'God's Word tells us: "Thou shalt not make to thyself any graven image, nor the likeness of anything that is in Heaven or in the earth beneath," but our children love them, just the same.'

The more Martha talked with the couple, the more she held them in high esteem. It seemed to her that their way of life made a stark contrast to her own father's flamboyant and pretentious ways. The simple lifestyle appealed to her and the sincerity with which the Zooks spoke of their beliefs moved her deeply.

Despite the fearful remarks Martha had made to Joel when they arrived on that first day, when the day of their departure drew close she felt the time had gone all too quickly.

'Promise you won't leave it so long before we see you again,' Mary pleaded as the couple prepared to leave.

'We won't. You can count on that,' Joel replied for both of them. 'We'll come over again before the fall.'

As the Lundberg's trap pulled away from the front of the sprawling farmhouse, there was no skirl of pipes. Andra and Mary stood side by side and waved until the couple were out of sight.

*

Being a 'new American' had been no drawback to Bjorn Tillkvist. Being an exceptionally good squeezebox-player with an appreciation of a wide range of musical styles had proved a definite advantage. The button-squeezebox was a popular instrument, but what marked Bjorn's performances was not just his speed or accuracy of playing; it was the way he interpreted the classics of some of the Old Masters, even though the pieces had been written for orchestra, pianoforte or violin. Throughout his teen years, Bjorn had never gone short of friends, his easy manner and his uninhibited willingness to play at any social gathering ensuring that he often took centre stage amongst his peers. At the very least, Ingvar and Iri justified their migration to Ohio on the grounds that Bjorn had been introduced to a lifestyle that he would never have known had they remained in Bergslagen. Consequently, they were unstilted in their support of any enterprise that involved their gifted son, even when it meant travelling some distance to allow him to take part in some musical extravaganza. Had they lived in the age of automobiles, the duty of ferrying their son around would have been an accepted part of the youth's growing up and now, at twenty, he'd have driven himself. But, in 1866, each trip was undertaken only after a great deal of consideration and thoughtful planning. Distances of travel were, of course, restricted to what they could achieve within any time that Ingvar could justify being away from his work at M&M. Their latest trip, to the south-west corner of the State, took the family away from Toledo for two whole weeks. Bjorn's reputation had spread, both within and beyond Ohio, and he'd been invited to play at a Festival of Music in Cincinnati.

On the second day of the festival, an unusual spectacle etched a deep impression on the Tillkvists. One of the solo performances was given by a greying old black man who played the fiddle. Such elevation of the blacks was still not commonplace and, in the ante-bellum period, even in remote Ohio, would never have been countenanced as appropriate or proper. The man's appearance on the platform was not the chief novelty: it was the way he handled his instrument. Almost casually – some would say disrespectfully – he tucked it under his armpit instead of between chin and shoulder. But irrespective of his position and hold, the man produced sounds that few had heard before or would ever have associated with the compass and timbre of the violin. He used the bow to great effect, twisting and turning it, sometimes bouncing it to produce a range of effects that he blended naturally into the colourful country tunes he wrought from the old instrument with great aplomb and obvious alacrity. Whenever he played, feet tapped to the lively rhythm and the music was so infectious that it would have been difficult for even those with little appreciation of it to have remained unmoved by its emotive vibes.

He was followed by four young men who sang in harmony, unaccompanied. They sang 'mountain songs' with long, drawn-out notes that allowed them to interweave the four parts to produce spine-tingling chords in which the combined voices rivalled a small orchestra.

When his turn came, Bjorn contributed admirably to the proceedings, delivering a selection of Baroque and Romantic pieces that included Corelli, Pachelbel, Beethoven and Schubert. He ended his performance with a short piece that no one recognised but many instantly enjoyed. As he prepared to dismount the plankwood podium to an enthusiastic applause, the Master of Ceremonies restrained him.

'Ladies and Gentlemen, I'm sure that your good selves, like I, would be happy to be favoured by an encore, yes?'

There was a resounding affirmative, accompanied by more applause. The MC spoke in an aside to Bjorn then announced, 'Mr Tillkvist has agreed to favour us with a further rendition of the final piece in his medley which, he assures me, is of his own composition.'

The piece was set in the key of G major, but Bjorn began playing it at a slower pace, extemporaneously transposing it into the relative key of E minor for the first few bars. The effect was to give the piece a more haunting aura at the beginning. As he slipped back into the major key and upped the tempo, the crowd listened appreciatively once more to the beautiful melody which, although intricate, became easily memorable.

That such a musically knowledgeable audience should gather in a place like Cincinnati amazed Ingvar and Iri. When their son rejoined them after his turn, Iri queried, 'I've never heard you play that piece before. Did you really compose it by yourself?'

'Yes, a few months ago. I've written others, too, but that one I think is my best.'

'It was excellent. Went down well with most folks, I'd say,' Ingvar put in. 'Does it have a name?'

Bjorn laughed. 'I call it "A Tale of Spring" because that's the mood in which I wrote it. A bit fanciful, perhaps, but I wouldn't dare be so pretentious as to give it some classical name.'

'When you can play like that, my boy, you can call it what you like,' beamed Ingvar.

The festival had been a showcase for many, very different musical acts. There were several singing groups of one type or another; banjo and guitar players; a man who played the mouth harp and a Welsh woman who played the Clarsach – a small version of the harp. When the final day rolled around, a competition was held at which each of those taking part had to play just one piece. Ingvar and Iri encouraged their son to do 'A Tale of Spring' once more.

'You've a good chance of winning the fifty dollars with that,' Ingvar enthused. 'Only Mr Marcus comes anywhere near, in my opinion.'

Mr Marcus was the black man. His name was Marcus but, since he claimed no family name, the MC had introduced him as 'Mr Marcus' and it had stuck.

'I agree with your father,' added Iri. 'Everyone liked it so much last time. I'm sure you'll get the vote.'

It was perhaps unfortunate that, when the names were drawn out of the hat, Bjorn was picked to go on first. He played his heart out and got a good reception.

Two more acts followed, then 'The Palmetto Four' came on, singing in their close-harmony style, as before, but this time with a very humorous song. They were outstanding.

Drawn last in the line-up was the amazing fiddler, Mr Marcus. Not only was his playing brilliant, but he was full of tricks. The fiddle was like a drum major's baton in his hands. He played behind his neck, between his legs and, as before, under one arm. The man was sensational and the audience leapt up and down in wild appreciation. Undoubtedly, he was the clear winner and the fifty dollars would have been a fortune to him.

When the judges gave their verdict, they placed 'The Palmetto Four' first, Bjorn second and a ladies' singing trio third. The decision was not entirely popular and a loud buzz went through the crowd. When the Tillkvists approached the MC saying: 'We thought Mr Marcus was the most popular by far.' They were told, curtly: 'Well, yes, very entertaining but quite unconventional. Wholly improper way to play a violin. He was disqualified.'

The Tillkvists were aghast. Ingvar became quite angry with the man. 'It was supposed to be a *music* festival, not a university examination of technique. He was clearly the winner. How can your so-called judges be so heartless?'

'Ah, Mr Tillkvist,' the MC replied, 'it's for the best. You know the niggers; the prize money would only go on hard liquor and he'd be in some jail by sundown. The judges made the right decision.'

Ingvar scowled at the pompous man and quickly shepherded his family away.

'In that case, Bjorn, I'm glad you didn't win it for I reckon you'd have to be handing over the prize money to the real winner.'

Unperturbed by the outcome, Marcus leant against a marquee pole, his face wreathed in a huge grin. Secretly, he knew, he'd been the best.

On the long journey back to Toledo, the family relived many moments from the festival but, after a time, the immediacy of the fine time they'd enjoyed began to fade and they lapsed into small talk.

'Ever think of going back to Sweden?' Iri asked her son, out of the blue.

'Perhaps one day. But not to stay. All my friends are here and it would be like starting all over again.'

'That's true. But your father and I had to start all over again when we came here and just look at the circle of friends we have now.'

'So you wouldn't go back to Sweden then?' Bjorn fired back at her, smiling cheekily.

'Like you, perhaps one day. And, like you, only to visit. It would be nice to see the old places again but I think I'd always want to come back to Ohio.'

Ingvar gave a loud guffaw. 'Now there speaks a woman who, six years ago, wanted to get back on the next ship to Göteborg.'

She had to admit it. She'd become an American.

Most people who played a squeezebox used the instrument to churn out simple, singalong tunes. As far as anyone knew, Bjorn Tillkvist was the only person in all of the north-east of America who had taken the instrument seriously and applied its potential to what Ingvar had always called 'proper music'. As a result, Bjorn was much in demand. By far, the majority of the concerts at which he played were in and around Toledo. The trip to Cincinnati had been a marathon journey, but one which, they all agreed, had been well worth while. Despite the distractions of the festival, the town of Cincinnati itself had made a big impression on Bjorn. An impression that was to last.

*

'Just as well your folks chose to live well to this side of the Mississippi and not over in Minnesota with all those other Swedes,' Dan remarked as he and Louisa prepared to leave Cayuga Flats for their journey to Ohio.

'Why? What's so special about this side?'

'Oh it ain't bein' so special that counts, it's bein' safe. According to *The Tribune*, dozens of farmers have been murdered by hostiles in south Minnesota.'

'Hostiles? You mean Indians?' queried Louisa. The idea of wild Indians that raided and killed wantonly was a foreign idea to her. Something she'd read about but couldn't really imagine. The only Indians she'd ever met were either friendly or drunk.

'Yep, it's the Santee Sioux again. Killin', scalpin', burnin', just like before.'

The uprisings had begun in 1862, when the War Between the States was at its height and had distracted the

Army's main resource to sheltering Washington and the Union.

'You think they'll cross the river?'

Dan rocked with laughter. 'Didn't you study *any* geography? The Mississippi's miles west of Lower Sandusky. It's the other side of the Great Lakes.'

'Oh, I see. But you said there's lots of Swedes there?'

'Lots went over that way, but I guess the hostiles...' Dan hung his head, as if searching for an ant on the ground, then whirled around: 'Look! Why don't we just forget about it. I'm sorry for those poor farmers and I'm sorry I brought up the subject. All right?'

They talked about it no more but the sudden outburst with which Dan had closed the conversation had sown seeds of discomfort in Louisa's mind as they contemplated their westward journey.

With full confidence in his Head Stockman, Dan left the care of his huge Hereford herd in safe hands and headed for Ohio with his just pregnant wife.

'You do feel up to this, don't you?' he asked.

'Sure. It's early days and I don't feel at all sick or anything like that. Papa and mother would be really disappointed if we didn't go now, after writing to them to say we're coming.'

Reassured, Dan left Cayuga Flats with an air of expectancy as he looked forward to seeing his Swedish in-laws again. It was still early and the low-hanging mist was the harbinger of yet another warm summer's day.

At the Lundberg's farm, Anna was putting the final touches to the yellow pinafore dress that was draped over the crucifix frame she used as a stand just for this purpose. Laid out on the table by her side was a neat row of buttons that she would sew into place to complete her creation.

'Looks fit to grace a princess,' commented Per-Erik as he stood back, reviewing her fine work.

'Louisa *is* a princess. She's *our* princess. Always will be,' Anna called back at him, her eyes never lifting from her sewing.

'She's all of that. But doesn't time fly? It seems like only yesterday since she was sitting on my knee begging me to tell her stories of the old Vikings.'

Anna smiled. 'Yes, life seems so short, sometimes. I never dreamt of a day when our daughter would be living miles and miles from home. I guess times are changing.'

'Ah, the world's becoming smaller every day and the new railroads are going to make it even smaller. But it's the life here, too, that makes folks that way. If we'd have stayed on in Växjö she'd most likely have married someone from the town and taken to living in the next street.'

'Yes,' Anna sighed, 'Sometimes I wish it was still like that.'

'Not me. I wouldn't swap what we've got here for what we might have had in Växjö. It'd be nice to make a short visit to the homeland, perhaps, but unless we have some very rich relative somewhere—'

'Oh, it wouldn't take that much. I hear the Tillkvist boy is talking about going back sometime.'

'That's as maybe, but I'll bet he'll be disappointed. Sweden's no place for a young man of his talents.'

'Don't be so sure. It's not only America that's changed with the times. I hear they have railroads in Sweden now, too.'

'Maybe so, maybe so.'

Anna had decided that Dan and Louisa would occupy the girl's former bedroom. Always keen to promote a little bit of melodrama, she moved her dress stand into the room with an impish twinkle in her eyes, standing the finished dress in one corner of the room. It looked a picture of prettiness and she could already imagine her daughter replacing the stand and more amply filling the contours of the yellow fabric.

The arrival of the Catlins was signalled by the barking of Per-Erik's dog and the Lundbergs rushed to greet them. Once the first flush of exchanges abated, Louisa made the announcement, 'Guess what? You're going to be grandparents!'

Dan stood beside his wife, an arm around her waist, beaming like he was sitting for a daguerreotype.

Anna's face shone back, 'Really and truly?'

'Really and truly.' Then, to her mother, Louisa confided, 'I've missed for two months now, so I think it's for sure.'

Anna suddenly thought of the yellow dress and drew her hand to her mouth as if to choke off her words.

'What's wrong mother?'

'Well it's... it's... no, I mustn't spoil things. I had a special surprise for you, but I didn't know about your news, of course.'

'A surprise? Whatever is it?'

'Come!'

The two women went indoors, leaving the menfolk to their cursory comments about farming.

'Oh, mother, it's delightful!' exclaimed Louisa as she stood in the doorway admiring her mother's handiwork. 'It's really delightful,' she repeated as she walked towards it to finger the soft material. As the wife of a well-to-do New York rancher, she could have bought a dress from the latest fashion lines in Rochester, but she appreciated at once the work of heart and soul that Anna had expended on the garment and thanked her mother profusely.

'It'll fit for now, I'm sure. Then I can put it aside for a while when I'm big in front and it'll be nice to get into once the little one is born.'

Soon, the young couple had unpacked their things and carted them to the room.

Per-Erik rummaged in a corner cupboard then said, 'It's time for a little ritual that says "welcome home to Lower Sandusky" so – will you take a little of our very own, home-made aquavit?'

The drinks were poured and Dan prompted to do the right thing. Then, as the four raised their glasses, their voices combined in a loud 'Skål!' Even though it had made him feel a little self-conscious, Dan fitted right in and downed the spirit in one gulp, sucking in his breath and smacking his lips in the aftermath of the fiery attack on his throat.

'Just like old times, eh?' summarised Per-Erik, returning his empty measure to the table. 'But I think we'll save another for after supper to celebrate your good news.'

'*Our* good news, too!' added Anna.

Once more, Dan's facial features embarked on their now familiar journey to form a wide grin.

During their time at the Lundberg's, Louisa insisted on dragging Dan off to visit some of the nearby places that had become her favourite haunts. On one day they went over to an accessible part of the Black Swamp that was a haven for wildfowl; on another day they travelled up to the Peninsula at Marblehead to see the old lighthouse that had stood there for almost fifty years. It was on the Black Swamp day, as they made their way back towards Lower Sandusky, that they chanced to meet up with Tomas Bergelin – Louisa's one-time boyfriend. He had, so far, never married and from the limited conversation they had, Louisa felt a little sorry for him, but was gratified to learn that her prediction had been correct: he was showing no signs of ever being any more than a farm worker. As they continued on their way, Louisa squeezed Dan's hand. She had made the right choice.

*

Bjorn Tillkvist helped repair boats along the waterfront of Toledo by day... and practised his squeezebox by night. The new instrument he'd been given for his twenty-first birthday was far superior to any he had played or even seen before. The bellows box was larger, making it less effort to sustain long notes and the compass was greater, giving him a wider range of notes. A new facility had been added, too, allowing the instrument to take on three different *voices* – treble, middle and bass. It was a joy to play and he loved to have it in his hands. He spent hours practising, but it would be wrong to suggest that his music had become something of an obsession. Millie Ryan saw to that.

When Bjorn first saw Millie, he'd just walked into a Baptist Church hall in downtown Toledo when she was partway through a violin recital. It was the church's Silver Jubilee celebration and the Organising Committee had pulled together a programme of music and song that was to be presented the same evening. Like others, Bjorn had gone along that Saturday afternoon to get the feel of the acoustics – and there was Millie, rehearsing one of the pieces she had chosen to include in her set. Slipping into a side seat, Bjorn watched as her nimble fingers darted up and down, unerringly picking out the fast, tripping notes of an Irish jig. Millie didn't just play; she *performed*. It was almost as if she played with her face as well as her hands: her eyes rolled and her eyebrows danced to the jig as, from time to time, she tossed her head to send a swaying wave through her long, chestnut tresses. Even her neat, tip-tilted nose joined in on the act when she hit the higher notes. Bjorn was captivated by both her carefree style of playing and her girlish charm. There were no more than six or seven people in the hall at the time but, when Millie finished her piece, Bjorn rose to his feet and applauded unashamedly. The petite lass nodded in his direction and, from where he stood, Bjorn could detect her lips forming a demure 'thank you' before she turned to dismount from the low dais.

'Where did you learn to play like that? You can almost make that fiddle talk.'

'Hardly that. But I've been playing for twelve years. Started when I was seven. I don't take it seriously though; it's just something I enjoy doing. Gives me some kind of outlet for my moods.'

'So, you're nineteen and you don't rate yourself?'

'Clever fellow. You can count. And no, I didn't say that. Not exactly. I know I play well but I just don't take it seriously, that's all. If I did, then, after twelve years I should perhaps be better than I am. Anyway, what do you play?' When he told her she giggled. 'And does a squeezebox-player make a good judge of the violin?'

'Music's music. I loved yours, I hope you'll like mine.'

It was after she'd heard Bjorn play that she began to take him seriously. To hear classical pieces expertly played on a squeezebox was something that didn't square with her preconceptions of the instrument's capabilities but, as the player had said: 'music was music' – and he certainly could play.

Bjorn had elected to include among his pieces a very old

and well-loved piece that was one of his favourites: the Canon by Pachelbel. With its repetitious, revolving chords, the music might be considered unexceptional, but his own rendition of it displayed a talent for transforming the written work into a much more expressive interpretation. As the austere opening sequence broke into an up-tempo staircase of individual notes, Bjorn swung his box in time and looked as if he and his instrument were part and parcel of each other. There was nothing 'wooden' about the way he played; it was the communion of grace and vitality, undergird by a sensitivity that brought to life even the dull, strict, measured sequence of chords that characterised the Canon.

When the piece ended, Millie Ryan returned his compliment. 'Bravo! Bravo!' she hollered from her seat; not in derision or sarcasm, but with a heartfelt honesty. Here was a kindred spirit. A man who loved his music and was not content to play even a classic 'as written' but, rather, to explore the avenues of each cadence and the cul-de-sacs of each coda to extract the utmost from the composer's work.

As Bjorn walked between the orderly rows of chairs to where Millie now rose to her feet, the vivacious girl smiled warmly at him.

'That was wonderful. I can't wait until this evening. I just know these Baptist folks'll love it.'

'You know them, then?'

'Oh, I've played here before. Twice. They're mostly older folks. Real God-fearing bunch, but they've got hearts of gold.'

'Good. Then I'll look forward to it, too. And to your own playing.'

Bjorn bade his fellow artiste farewell and made his way

back through Toledo's busy streets towards his home on the edge of town. As he walked, he passed many young women and thought, 'Mmm, pretty, but not like Millie.' In a matter of two very brief hours he'd become smitten by the charming violinist. He'd learned her name only from the mimeographed Silver Jubilee programme and knew nothing more of her than he had gleaned from their conversation at the hall as they watched the other performers rehearse. But she was stunning.

Millicent Veronica Ryan, whose parents emigrated from Ireland to Ohio two years before she was born, fostered the same kind of feelings. Unlike Bjorn, she couldn't contain them and burst through the door of the family's humble home near the waterfront to exclaim to her mother, 'I've just had the most amazing afternoon. Oh, mother, you must come along this evening, it'll be a treat. There's a fellow who does the most impossible things with a squeezebox and he's... well, he's... you'll really like him, I'm sure.'

Millie's mother looked at her knowingly and said, 'It sounds to me like it's you who likes him, if I'm not mistaken. Who is he?'

'His name's Bjorn Tillkvist and—'

'A foreigner! Trust our daughter to be chasing after the likes of a foreigner! How old is he?'

'I don't know, exactly. Not much older than me, I think. And he's not any more foreign than I am. Obviously his parents or grandparents must have come from somewhere in Europe with a name like that, but he's really good looking... and very charming... and he's a wonderful musician. Oh mother, please, please, come and meet him.'

'I'll talk it over with your father. We may have other

plans. But I hope you're not leading him on like you did with that Billy Connell. We don't want another episode like that one.'

'No, mother.'

At the evening concert, the Ryans accompanied their daughter and Millie took great delight in pointing out *her* Bjorn Tillkvist when she spotted him near the front of the hall. 'There he is! Doesn't he look a beau! Silk shirt, bow tie and all.' She left her parents in their seats, close to the end of a middle row, and scurried off to join the other platform participants.

The concert itself was a peculiar affair; an untidy mixture of wonderful talent and appalling singing, the latter only made bearable by an even more awful item that was an attempt at a synchronised tambourine display. The minister of the church then took up half an hour with a patronising preach from 1 Thessalonians, chapter five, based on his text of, 'Hold fast to that which is good.'

For the Ryans, the best part came at the end, when sandwiches, buns and cakes were provided. Millie introduced her new-found beau to her parents and the young couple found seats in a corner where they were able to consume their fare in relative solitude and get to know one another a little more than their first meeting had allowed.

That night, Bjorn confessed to Ingvar and Iri that he had fallen in love.

*

Even when he had his nose to the grindstone in the downtown clothing store, Joel Lundberg had kept his ears to the grapevine. He never gave up trying to find a way out of his dismal workaday existence and, when an opportunity presented itself, it came from a most unexpected quarter.

'There's a gentleman on the lower floor to see you,' the store manager Mr Goldstein informed Joel.

Briskly, Joel walked down to the lower sales floor and strode towards the silhouetted figure standing by the pay desk. When the man turned to face him, Joel's jaw fell open. Before him stood none other than his old drill sergeant, Brendan O'Malley.

'Captain Lundberg! How are you doing? I heard you'd left the Army and traced you to here. Joel, isn't it?'

'Yes sir.'

'Oh, you can forget the "sir" since I'm no longer in the Army either. Most folks call me Brad these days and I'd prefer if you did, too.'

Joel noticed that he spoke in a refined way; his Irish accent was much less pronounced and he was not at all like his blasphemous old self. He carried a little more weight but otherwise looked not a day older.

'Pity you left the uniform behind for I reckon you'd be up to Colonel, at least, by now.'

'I took myself a wife and couldn't see it as much of a life for a married man, so I came out after Appomattox.'

'I know. I heard.'

'And what brings you here. You living near Philly now?'

'No, I came over especially to see you with what you might call a proposition.'

'What kind of proposition?'

'Well, I always admired your confidence and you're the brightest recruit I ever had the pleasure to train so, when I heard of this thing coming up, I immediately thought of you and wondered how I'd find you. Are you free to talk?'

'Not really. Not here. But I have a short break just after noon hour; could we meet outside Vic's Bar?'

'Vic's Bar? Yes, I know it. Saw it on the way here. Sounds fine to me.'

They shook hands and Brad O'Malley strolled out of the store and on to the sidewalk. It was close on eleven o'clock and Joel could hardly wait until noon.

'Hello again,' Brad called out as Joel approached the small, circular table on the Saloon's veranda. The former sergeant ordered two bowls of chowder and got right to the nub of his mission.

'You were in Annapolis, right?'

'That I was.'

'How'd you like to go back to Maryland and get into uniform again?'

Joel gave a hollow laugh, shaking his head. 'No sir, not me.'

'I didn't say it would be a Union uniform.' Then O'Malley, too, began to laugh. 'And it wouldn't be in Annapolis either.'

'Then what?'

'Other side of the State. Near Hagerstown. Old outpost called Fort Frederick. Let me explain.' Annoyingly, the waiter arrived back at that moment with two steaming bowls of chowder, delaying Brad's explanation for some minutes while the two men downed the hot broth.

'I'm working for an outfit called THISTLE. Don't laugh; I'm on the level. The initials stand for "The Historical Interpretation Society's True Life Expositions" and that's a mouthful if I've ever heard one. But it's getting to be big business. What they do is this: they take over some genuine, former establishment of war and have people occupy it, dressed in the uniform or costume of some time past and give displays of how true life used to be. We have to talk about it, too, so we kind of build ourselves into a complete alternative persona so that it's just like living out the real thing.'

'Sounds crazy.'

'It may sound it, but it'll make you bigger bucks than I'll wager you're getting from old man Goldstein. And, besides, with the two of us working together, we could drum up a real surefire display: loading and firing old flintlock muskets, knife throwing and, in your case I seem to remember, axe hurling. Taking folks back in time to see how our heritage was built during the French and Indian War, right up to the Revolution. What d'you think?'

Joel was flabbergasted. He couldn't believe that people would pay good bucks to watch modern-day people make a pretence of the past.

'Who pays for all this? And, come to that, who'd be paying me?'

'THISTLE, of course. It's got sound financial backing and is run on strict business lines.'

'Sounds intriguing. But I'd have to talk it over with Martha, my wife. She's a nurse here in Philly.'

'Of course. I wouldn't expect less. But you're not averse to a move?'

'Not at all.'

They made arrangements to meet the following week and Joel went back to selling shirts with his head buzzing from the strange proposition.

Martha was more than just a nurse. She'd graduated to Sister and held a post of no small responsibility but, as luck would have it, there was a possibility of her transferring to the hospital at Hagerstown with no downgrade.

'You know me, Joel; always game for a new adventure. If

it means you can get away from Goldsteins and make more money into the bargain then I'm all for it.'

His wife's bold suggestion of support paved the way for Joel to give Brad O'Malley an unqualified affirmative when they met the following Tuesday. Three weeks later, the former Union Army Captain became plain Private Lundberg, reporting for duty as a Maryland soldier in the year 1758.

His first sight of the old fort took Joel aback. He was amazed at its huge expanse and equally amazed at the massive stone stockade that surrounded it. The fort had been named in honour of Maryland's Lord Proprietor, Frederick Calvert, and looked a formidable stronghold. There to greet them, as he and Martha entered the stout outer gate, was Brad O'Malley. Joel failed to recognise him at first sight, dressed as he was in full Redcoat outfit, topped off with a tricorn hat. Martha giggled and Joel had to restrain her, saying: 'You may well laugh, but tomorrow your own husband will be growing older by a hundred years and more.'

That evening, the Lundbergs were invited to dinner with Major Proudfoot, the brains and money behind the whole enterprise.

'You won't regret it, Mr and Mrs Lundberg. This whole thing's about to take off in various parts of the country. I'm only glad that THISTLE got into the act first. If our experience in Boston is in any way a guide, we'll be turning the clock back all over the north-east and folks will be flooding in to enjoy what we give them.'

Martha smiled at the irony of it. She'd so detested her father's exaggerated reversion to his Scottish ways and now here was her husband earning his wage in the employ of an enterprise that took its name from Scotland's emblem. But, as the weeks passed, she had to agree with Joel: his routine at Fort Frederick was better than selling shirts at Goldstein's store.

*

1867. The year began disastrously. Everywhere, newspapers carried the sad tidings of an atrocious event that took place just before Christmas. Out West, along the Bozeman Trail, a massed force of hostile Indians had completely wiped out a command of eighty men of the 18th Infantry led by Captain William Fetterman. There had been not one survivor and the disgustingly mutilated bodies had been frozen in their grotesquely misshapen state to be recovered next day. The awfulness of the tragedy was emphasised by the fact that the massacre had taken place within a gunshot's distance of one of the Army's main forts guarding the road used by settlers following the main route to Oregon. For the men and their families at the remote outpost, it had been catastrophic. By contrast, the year was not very old before happier times were to be enjoyed by the Swedish families who'd settled far to the east of these troubled territories.

On February 15th, Louisa Catlin was delivered of a baby girl. A month later, the gurgling little Naomi was the centre of attraction as the Catlins hosted a family get-together that, for the first time in eight years, would see the Lundbergs all together again under one roof. Per-Erik and Anna journeyed up from Ohio with the Tillkvists – who'd included Millie Ryan now as if she was part of the family. Joel and Martha travelled from Hagerstown to join them. Dan's folks made the short trip from Buffalo and, all told, the Catlin household had temporarily swelled to twelve adults plus the new arrival.

The large ranch house fairly buzzed with excitement and almost non-stop chatter as folks caught up with each other's latest news first-hand. Once Joel and Martha, the last to arrive, had made themselves comfortable, Per-Erik took charge of the proceedings, insisting that Louisa fetch some measures so that they might all partake of the aquavit he'd brought. Despite the splendour of their surroundings, the gathering resembled an old campfire meeting as the family stood in a full circle around the cradled Naomi and drank her well being with a hearty 'Skål!'

As that first evening wore on, Uncle Ingvar announced that Bjorn and Millie had brought their instruments and would favour the party with a duet.

'I'm afraid we don't know anything that might ever have been composed for Cayuga Flats, but we thought since Palmyra isn't so far away, the *Palmyra Schottische* would be close enough for "down-home" music.'

Bjorn sounded a note and Millie tuned to match it, then the pair began to play the well-known piece. No sooner had they finished, and with everyone clapping and shouting for more, than Ben Catlin, Dan's father, roared for them to play it again. Grabbing his wife Eliza by the wrist he pulled her to her feet and shouted: 'We can dance to that. C'mon, let's clear the floor.' After the first few bars, the four remaining couples all joined in and the drawing room had instantly become a dance hall.

'Swing your partner,' Ben called out, as the couples jostled for space to keep in step. Bjorn nodded to Millie and mouthed the word 'again' so that they repeated the whole tune to let the dancers have full value for their efforts. The

Palmyra was followed by the Cumberland Reel and a promenading dance that Ben explained to those who didn't know it. The promenade fitted well with the tune of Yankee Doodle Dandy. They danced on until some of the womenfolk were on the point of staggering.

'One thing about these Swedes,' Ben told his wife, 'Once you get them started, they sure know how to enjoy themselves.'

The party had certainly gone with a swing. Per-Erik's aquavit and Ben's enthusiasm had seen to that. And, in the corner of a neighbouring room, little Naomi slept soundly through it all.

The get-together was over all too soon. The two evenings the folks had spent together were quite different: the first, boisterous and noisy; the second, more subdued but equally enjoyable. Even at the weddings of their son and daughter, the elder Lundbergs could not recall having enjoyed themselves so much.

'Pity we can't do this more often,' remarked Ingvar as the second evening drew to a close.

'You're right,' agreed Anna. 'We'll have to wait for Joel and Martha to produce, then we'll have another good excuse.'

'What?' yelled Joel, in mock outburst. 'Bring up kids on an eighteenth century soldier's pay? Forget it. I'm too busy fighting the French.'

'It's all right having your fun and getting paid for it, but you watch out, my boy,' Anna lectured him, wagging a finger in his direction, 'for, one of these days you'll need to think about starting the next generation of Lundbergs.'

Joel curled up one corner of his mouth as he considered, 'I hadn't thought of it that way.'

After breakfast next morning, the various family members showered their last kisses on baby Naomi and drifted homewards. Joel and Martha, last to arrive, were also the last to leave.

For Bjorn and Millie, the jamboree at Cayuga Flats had been more than just a family get-together. From Millie's point of view, it had been the first time she'd been away from her parents, sleeping under someone else's roof. It had also given her an honest, unadorned insight into the life of the Tillkvist family – and its close offshoots, the Lundbergs and Catlins. She liked what she saw. In fact, she felt a part of it already. From Bjorn's side, it was almost the ultimate test: how would the others react to this young woman he loved so much; would she feel out of place among them? Millie, he felt, had come through with flying colours.

Two weeks later, Bjorn discussed the matter with the Ryans, after which he and Millie announced their intention to marry in the following spring.

The Ryans had been impressed with Bjorn. Not so much for the reputation he had built as a fine musician; they admired his business acumen and the way he'd developed his own boat repair service from the simple beginnings of his odd-job work along the waterfront. In that, he was a true Tillkvist: a young man of vision, honest craftsmanship and with a self-belief to carry it off. His current waterfront venture would never turn him into another John Jacob Astor but, the Ryans could see, he would use it as a stepping stone to bigger and more prosperous things.

Ingvar and Iri were happy, too. From those first times that Millie had begun coming round to their home, they'd taken her to their hearts. The two families – Tillkvists and Ryans – were like chalk and cheese, but Millie was an exceptional young woman.

'Your father and I have always wanted the best for you,' Iri told her son one day. 'We took a big risk when we left Bergslagen, but we always believed things would work out somehow, and that it would be the best for you. At the time, Sweden offered so little; America, so much. We're glad you've settled on a woman like Millie. She'll back you all the way in whatever you do, we're sure.'

The happy group who'd danced the night away up at the Catlins' ranch, back in March of the previous year, found just the excuse they needed to repeat their extravaganza – and it wasn't on Joel and Martha's account. The wedding of Bjorn and Millie took place in late April, 1868, at the Baptist Church in Toledo where they first met.

Unlike the evening of the Silver Jubilee celebration, the next-door hall was filled with a more rowdy gathering and a hearty meal substituted for the sandwiches, buns and cakes. The newly married couple were spared the task of providing the accompaniment to the evening's boisterous dancing. Seamus Ryan had organised a fine ensemble of Millie's friends to provide the music. This time, Bjorn and Millie took part in the dancing themselves.

'Just look at Ben and Eliza!' Millie gasped. 'They're really going at it!' And they were. The Buffalo Division of the Catlin Brigade were stepping it out with some gusto, augmented by Ben's frequent whoops and thigh-slaps.

'I don't think Ma and Papa have had such a good time in years,' she added, noticing her parents picking up the steps as they joined in wholeheartedly.

'Yep, it's a real good do,' confirmed Bjorn. 'I'm glad so many of our friends could make it.'

'Me too; but it's the oldies who're showing the way with the dancing. Hope we'll have as much energy when we're their age.'

Smiles seldom left the faces of the newlyweds as they toured the hall, stopping here and there to talk with folks and accept their good wishes. But, had they known what was in store, their joy would have topped out at new heights. In the event, they didn't have to wait long before it did.

Seamus Ryan took the floor; waved to the band to stop playing and held up his hands to command everyone's attention. 'Ladies and gentlemen,' he began, 'It seems appropriate that, for the next few days, the new Mr and Mrs Tillkvist will be spending time in Sin City. Sin-sin City, if you know what I mean.' (Bjorn was taking his wife to Cincinnati – the town that had made such an impression on him when he'd played at the festival there). 'But, tonight,' he went on, 'I would like to call upon our good friend Ingvar Tillkvist who has something rather special to announce.'

Ingvar took the floor, holding what appeared to be a scroll in one hand. 'Ladies and gentlemen, our good friends.' He paused, as if choosing his next words with care. 'As you know, Bjorn is our only child. Even now that he's a married man, Iri and I love him dearly. One of the great privileges of being a parent is to know the secrets of your son or daughter. In Bjorn's case, longings that he has cherished in his heart for some time but, due to the busyness of his life in recent years, has had to banish to some nether region of his mind.' There was polite laughter all around the hall. 'But now, his mother and I feel there could be no better time for us to help, in a little way, to make those dreams come true.' Then, turning to the couple, he beckoned them towards him. 'Bjorn and Millie, we would like to present you with passage tickets to enable you both to go to Sweden.' There were audible gasps from the guests, followed by unbridled applause, as Ingvar handed the rolled passage tickets to his son. He raised his hands to beg silence once more, then ended his speech: 'Not only to Sweden but, I'm sure you'll all be glad to know... back again, too!'

Bjorn responded in most uncharacteristic fashion. He did something that, as a grown man – and an undemonstrative Swede – he'd never done before: he threw his arms around his father and hugged him. Tears rolled down the groom's cheek as he broke his grip and rushed to where Iri stood to repeat his performance.

Seamus Ryan waved to the band once again and shouted: 'The night is still young! Let's have everybody up for the next dance.'

During their few days in Cincinnati, Bjorn told Millie the story of the old black fiddler, Marcus. Of how he'd won the competition at the festival but didn't get the prize. It was a sad reflection that stood out in stark contrast to their own good fortune and the wonderful trip they would embark upon in a matter of weeks.

'It reminds me of some things Papa told me about Ireland. They had real bad times there, too, in the old days,' Millie said.

'And in Sweden, also,' Bjorn echoed. 'But that was in the old days. It's not like that now. I can't wait to see our old home again. I still remember it, like I was there only yesterday.'

'Can you still speak Swedish?' Millie asked.

'Oh, enough, I reckon. But it's very rusty.'

'Rusty or not, you'll have to teach me some so that folks don't think me a mute.'

'Oh, you'll pick it up. We both will, I'm sure.'

Bjorn and Millie were made for each other. He told her so that night as they cuddled up in the bedroom of the inn where they were lodging. Their lovemaking was beginning to seem quite natural and was always warm and tender.

'It's just like when we play our duets,' Bjorn teased, 'You fiddle and I squeeze!'

Millie cuffed him playfully on the ear and they both fell back on to the bed, rocking the room with their laughter.

The weeks flew past and Bjorn was able to find a reliable local man to take care of his business while he was absent. That, in itself, had been no mean task for he now employed four craftsmen at the waterfront workshop and it needed someone with a good understanding of both business matters and the needs of Lake Erie's boatmen to fill the position. Bjorn was satisfied he'd found the right man but, nonetheless, asked Ingvar to look in from time to time to make sure everything continued to run as it should. Even so, he knew, he'd have to put in extra effort when he returned in the fall to keep the business on the up and up.

The overland journey to New York was a tedium. A mere obstacle that had to be overcome before the couple embarked on an enterprise of grander design. And Bjorn was relieved to have reached the docks without mishap or undue delay.

When they saw the great steamship, *The Esmeralda*, for the first time, it was as if their hearts skipped a beat. It seemed enormous. With towering funnels and no sails rigged, the vessel looked elegant and sleekly streamlined. Bjorn smiled to himself as through his mind flashed images he'd conjured from the tales Ingvar had told him of the old sea captain Sten Tillkvist who'd sailed his little vessel *Peleus* almost halfway around the world. And for Millie – born and raised on American soil – this was shaping up as the adventure of a lifetime. She felt like the President's wife as she walked briskly up the gangway on to the ship.

'Good afternoon. I'm Judd Clinton, Chief Steward. Welcome on board. May I see your cabin tickets? Very good. Just follow this way.'

Their cabin wasn't large. In fact, at first glance, it seemed tiny.

'My goodness!' Millie exclaimed when she stood in the doorway, 'Do you think we'll manage two all right in here?'

'Manage to what?' retorted Bjorn, giving her a nudge in the ribs. She blushed a bright pink and gave him the kind of look that said: 'Just you wait!'

They managed.

*

While the sun shone brightly for the Tillkvists, dark clouds gathered overhead for the Hagerstown Lundbergs. The venture at Fort Frederick was not going well. It had all started so promisingly with an initial flush of visitors that first summer but, in the two years that Major Proudfoot had been pumping money into the enterprise, visitor attendances had been dwindling.

'Can't imagine why it's not taking off here like it should,' the Major complained. 'Boston Harbour and Fort Monroe are going a treat. From the start of spring to late fall we have a constant stream of people through the gates. It seems there's an insatiable curiosity among the Eastern

Seaboard population to evoke memories of our nation's past glories. But not here.'

'Could be our location, d'you think?' suggested Brad O'Malley. 'The two you just mentioned are close to large towns. Here, we're out in the boondocks.'

'Could be. Yet it seemed to catch on in the beginning. Maybe our style of presentation needs changing. More variety; more blood-and-guts type of enactment, perhaps.'

'Is that what you give them in other places?'

'No. Not exactly. But then the themes are different. Boston is all Revolutionary stuff and Monroe is Civil War. We concentrate more on first-person talks given during a walkabout that looks at ordinary folks' living conditions at the time.'

Brad stroked his thick, well-chiselled beard, which he kept that way to add credibility to his persona then, wistfully, he suggested, 'Almost the same as we do here. It could be a problem of identity.'

'Identity?' The Major looked puzzled. 'In what way?'

'The French and Indian thing. It's well known that, at the time, Marylanders weren't too impressed with it all. They considered it as the British using Marylanders' blood to expand their own Empire. Could be today's Marylanders feel the same way.'

'Really? How do you know that?'

'Oh, from doing a bit of light reading. Let's just say that, since coming here, I've taken a real interest in the place and decided to conduct a little research into the characters we're all supposed to represent. But it's a fact, Major; I've read the same line of reasoning in more than one source.'

'I see. Very interesting, O'Malley. You wouldn't mind lending me a couple of those sources, would you? Perhaps I ought to talk this over with Spencer Hardy and the rest of the THISTLE committee.'

'Huh! Sounds like I might be cutting my own throat.'

Together, the two men walked across the parade ground towards the Sutler's Store and Major Proudfoot paused in front of the well-stocked store and shook his head.

'Sad, isn't it? We've put so much into this old fort. Can't just let it go on, though. We're losing our shirt on this place. Thanks for showing me around, O'Malley, and for your forthright comments. I'll do what I can to see that you won't lose out, whatever happens.'

When Major Proudfoot had gone, Brad sought out Joel to forewarn him that the future of THISTLE, as far as Fort Frederick was concerned, didn't appear to be too rosy. The old drill sergeant was unequivocal in spelling out his own prognosis. Like a chain reaction, Joel shared Brad's news with Martha that evening.

'Sounds like we'll have to be thinking of pastures new pretty soon, then,' she said.

'Kinda looks that way.'

'Well, there's something I'd like to do while we're still here.'

'What's that?'

'Ever since we've been here we've talked about going over to Harper's Ferry, but we've never gotten around to it. Why don't we plan on going over there next week. I'd love to see the old place again.'

'Sure. Let's do it.'

Harper's Ferry had changed hands many times during the war, but there was little that had changed about the town itself. As Joel and Martha walked along the riverside and climbed the hill that led away from 'John Brown's Fort' to afford them a view across the confluence of the two mighty rivers, Potomac and Shenandoah, many memories flooded back.

'I often wonder what happened to Sam and Cynthia,' Martha said, gazing out on the tranquil scene with a faraway look in her eyes.

'Me too,' returned Joel. 'And I wonder sometimes if only Sam had taken the Union side, whether we'd still be close friends.'

'Funny, isn't it, the way life works out. We were so close at one time and yet so far apart. I guess we'll never find out what happened to them. They could be big shots in Charleston or Savannah for all we know.'

Joel laughed at the idea and offered his own two cents' worth: 'More likely they're helping rebuild Atlanta.'

'Oh, Joel! That's unkind.'

They continued their walk to the top of the hill and turned, once more, to admire the view.

'You know, I wouldn't mind settling down in a place like this one day. It's so beautiful. So peaceful,' said Joel.

'I wouldn't mind,' Martha answered, 'but, right now, I think we'd best settle on moving back east. There's more chance you'd find some means of making a decent wage somewhere closer to a metropolis.'

'Unfortunately. But we'll cross that bridge when we have to. Old Proudfoot hasn't blown the whistle on us just yet, even though Brad isn't too hopeful that the Committee will come up with a rescue plan.'

Two weeks later, the whistle blew.

The Lundbergs made no instant decisions concerning their future. Neither harboured any bitterness or regret at the way things had worked out. Or hadn't worked out.

Martha continued to work at the hospital while Joel walked the streets of Hagerstown looking for work. He found nothing. At least, not directly.

It was when he called in at the Library that the seeds of a new direction for his life were sown. The head librarian was unable to offer him any gainful employment, but told him of the possibility of something that might just suit his experience – at the Smithsonian Institution in Washington. The helpful man told him all he knew of the opportunity. What he knew didn't amount to a great deal, but it was all Joel needed to know. Impulsively, he returned home; left a scribbled note for Martha; readied his horse, and headed directly for the Nation's capital.

In this seemingly most improbable way, Joel Lundberg was accepted for the post of Assistant in the Historical Record Verification Department at the Smithsonian. And, in doing so, he perpetuated an old adage: New house; new job; new arrival. For, three weeks after they moved to Washington, Martha realised that she was pregnant.

'Let's hope it's a boy,' Joel said to Martha when she told him the news, 'then mother will be happy that the American line of Lundbergs will continue for at least another generation.'

*

As *The Esmeralda* steamed its way across the Atlantic, Bjorn and Millie hung over the starboard rail and looked out on the endless plain of ocean that provided the azure backdrop to a multitude of twinkling stars as the sun caught the tops of the gently rolling waves.

'Right, let's hear how much Swedish you've remembered,' Bjorn suggested. 'Let's start with some basics. How about a simple "Good morning" to begin with.'

'God morgon,' she answered, keeping the *d* and *g* silent.

'Very good. How about "Do you speak English?" since it won't make much sense to anyone if you ask if they can speak American.'

'Talar ni engelska?' she replied.

'Excellent. And your accent's good, too. Now, what would you say if you didn't understand?'

'Jag förstår inte.'

'So, you can almost speak Swedish already. I must say, I'm impressed. Let's try a short conversation.'

Ultimately, their dialogue became stilted, but it was clear to Bjorn that his wife was no slouch at assimilating both the vocabulary and structure of the new language.

Throughout the voyage the weather remained pleasant and they suffered no storms so, each day, they spent most of the time on the open decks, practising Swedish and revelling in the sunshine and salt air. At night, when they retired to their cabin, it seemed somehow more spacious than it had at first appeared and, even with only its single, small porthole to admit natural light, gave rise to no feelings of claustrophobia. Millie thought it ingenious the way every little bit of space was used to good advantage. It was the first long voyage that she had experienced and, once a mild queasiness on the second day failed to materialise into anything more worrisome, she enjoyed the shipboard lifestyle immensely. Casual encounters with other passengers often produced good conversation and interesting anecdotes that helped pass the time and, on one evening, a concert was arranged. Since the Tillkvists hadn't brought their instruments, however, they were content to participate as members of the audience. Had some of the slapdash performers known that they were playing to such expert musicians, their mediocre performances may have become quite inhibited. As it was, Bjorn and Millie told no one of their accomplishments.

There had been many opportunities for Millie to practise and improve her language skills. Then, when the ship was estimated to be within two days of Göteborg, Millie asked her husband to explain to her once again just who they would meet and lodge with and what was their family connection.

'If everything goes according to the plan suggested by my father, we will make a kind of circular tour. From Göteborg, we will go directly south to Halmstad. There, we are to find my cousins Ulf and Annika. They're about our age and mother wrote to them to tell them we would be coming. If it's all right with them, we can stay there for perhaps a week or two. Then we will travel across to Kalmar to visit Grandmother, the oldest member of our family. She's ninety-four years old, so I guess that'll be quite a short visit. Should be interesting though. It's the town where my great-grandfather lived – the one who was the explorer.'

Bjorn scanned down the notes Ingvar had penned for him and outlined the highlights of the intended itinerary for Millie. They would, hopefully, meet the various branches of the Tillkvist family and also some of the Lundbergs, as well as taking in the sights and culture of the country in which Bjorn had spent his formative years.

The emerging railway system would ease their travel over the long distances they anticipated but, other than the growth of this new means of transportation, Bjorn had not envisaged that much else would have changed in his homeland. Even Ingvar could not have imagined the great strides Sweden had made in the past decade; changes that had revitalised the country and for which Bjorn was quite unprepared.

As *The Esmeralda* manoeuvred into the dock at its home port, the skyline seemed unrecognisable to Bjorn. Göteborg had grown enormously in the past ten years and, later that day as the couple journeyed south, there was ample evidence to demonstrate that times had changed. Sweden had changed. Everywhere were the unmistakable signs that the new industrial age had taken root and was becoming established as the fuel that fired the new Sweden. In that way, it wasn't so different from Toledo or Columbus back in Ohio. But it was markedly different from the images Bjorn had retained in his memory since he left the country as a wide-eyed teenager looking forward to the wildernesses of the New World where, he imagined, strange animals and even stranger people roamed the countryside.

Ulf and Annika had been married just over a year and were wonderfully welcoming to their 'cousins from America'. Their wooden-sided house in Halmstad was not large but, with some rearrangement of the furnishings, accommodated Bjorn and Millie comfortably.

'You don't have to apologise for it,' Bjorn told his cousins. 'After the cabin we had on the ship it's like a palace.'

In the end, the travellers spent nearly three weeks with Ulf and Annika, particularly enjoying the opportunity the young Swedes' many questions gave them to expound on the virtues of life in Ohio. But, as Bjorn had predicted, it was when they moved on to Kalmar that their visit took on a more intriguing perspective.

Old Grandma Tillkvist was a fund of knowledge and, even at ninety-four, was in full command of her faculties.

'I can't walk so far nowadays,' the elderly matriarch told them, 'but you're young; you can go. I'll tell you how to find the old house where Sten and Birgitta lived. Their daughter, Kristina, married Steffen Lundberg, you know. From the same family that now lives close to you in America.'

In an unsteady hand, she scribbled a rough map showing the route to the Captain's house.

'But, you know,' she went on, 'you really ought to go on down to Karlskrona. It's a lovely town, full of interesting buildings. It was there that Sten's father lived. He took to himself an adopted son, you know, and they lived there until Tomas died. The house they built themselves is still standing, I believe, though I haven't been there now for some years.'

'Tomas? He would have been my great-great-grandfather?' remarked Bjorn.

'That's right. An incredible man he was. Lost his wife in some accident. We never really knew what happened. Came down from somewhere near Falkenberg. I think it was called Norrholm. He used to make guns and it's said he carved figureheads for the old ships of war.'

'No one's ever told me about him. I've only ever heard the family history back as far as Sten.'

'No. It's sad when people forget. I think it's because he did himself no favours when he took the orphan boy to be his son. Sort of cut himself off from everyone.'

'And what became of the boy? Did he take the family name?'

'As far as I know, yes. But, when Tomas died, the boy inherited everything. Soon afterwards he disappeared from the area and no one heard from him again. It caused a lot of bitterness at the time, I was told.'

Bjorn and Millie found Sten's house and then did as the old lady had suggested. They went on to Karlskrona to try to find any record of Tomas and his adopted son. For more than a week they trawled the local tax and dockyard records but found nothing that would advance the scant knowledge Grandma Tillkvist had given them.

Millie suggested, 'Why don't we try to find this Norrholm place before we get back to Göteborg at the end of our stay.'

'Yes, I'd like to find out about him if I can. I think it's good to know about your own family.'

'Well, yours is interesting. I wouldn't go to the same trouble on account of the Ryans. I'd probably find they were a real bad lot in the old days.'

During the four months the couple spent in the country, they travelled a great deal and saw many parts of southern Sweden – looking its best in these summer months. Strangely, despite the enjoyment they experienced and the exhilarating sights they saw, the pair became homesick for Ohio and, as the time for their return drew near, they couldn't wait to be heading back across the Atlantic once more.

When they made the detour to Norrholm, they were once again disappointed that no one could throw any light on Bjorn's ancestors. The Utsi Forest Products Company owned the large sawmill in Norrholm and most of the surrounding houses and land. Had Bjorn known the story of Anta Utsi he would have marvelled at the wonder and irony of it. Once a wandering Sami, the man had built a wealthy timber empire and had bought out the Finnish-owned mill where he had once been humiliated and treated as an outcast.

Despite their being unable to track down any further

information about Tomas, they had, nonetheless, accumulated a thick wad of notes concerning the things they'd seen and the people they'd met. It had been, for them both, the experience of a lifetime.

In the second week of September, 1868, Bjorn and Millie boarded ship once more to begin their homeward voyage.

*

By 1876, the year that became most noted for the terrible catastrophe at Little Big Horn, where General George Armstrong Custer and all of his command were massacred by Indians, the two families of emigrant Swedes – Lundbergs and Tillkvists – had not only expanded their numbers but had become truly a part of the growing number of 'New Americans'. Joel and Martha now had two sons and a daughter. Bjorn and Millie had three sons, the youngest of whom were twins. From these, their parents hoped, would come future generations of Lundbergs and Tillkvists in America. Not to be outdone, Louisa had borne a son and three daughters by Dan Catlin.

Joel had risen to a position of some responsibility at the Smithsonian and Bjorn had expanded his boat repair business into boat building and, more recently, into the ferrying of freight across the lakes. His Great Lakes Transfer Company would, in less than a decade, make the Tillkvists of Toledo an even wealthier family than the Catlins of Cayuga Flats.

On those occasions when the enlarged family got together, Per-Erik and Anna, together with Ingvar and Iri, would recount their first days in this new land, shake their heads and laugh. The lessons they'd learned and the circumspect caution they'd exercised in those fragile first days as immigrants had served them well in teaching them never to underestimate the challenges that lay before them. Unlike so many of their countrymen, they had not rushed headlong after the glowing promises of the Homestead Act, but had remained entrenched well to the east of the Mississippi. Many of those hopeful west-bound settlers now enriched the soil of the land near where they had fallen, murdered by jealous neighbours, lawless renegades or hostile Indians. The Lundbergs and Tillkvists marched on to enrich the American culture in a different way. With their music, their folklore, their undaunted spirit and their appetite for hard work, they were contributing to the Manifest Destiny that would, one day, make their adopted land a great land. Some, disillusioned, would return to Sweden before the century ended but others, like the youth who once carried his sister's bags from the quayside, would forever assert: 'This is America!'

Part Six
The Inheritors

For Ulf and Annika

Progress... is not an accident, but a necessity...
                              Herbert Spencer

'It's no more than conjecture; someone's historical speculation. Since it was never accurately recorded, no one really knows.'

The speaker was Soren Branting, arguably the most distinguished of the debaters although he, personally, wouldn't argue on that point. He sat back, arms folded, his appearance giving the distinct impression of a Father Christmas lookalike. The whole debate had begun with four men; now more than a dozen congregated in this one corner of Leif Larsson's inn, four miles west of Ronneby and just off the main highway that connected with Karlshamn.

Arne Pahlsson tried to get the discussion back to the main issue: 'I can't see that it matters exactly when Jesus Christ was born, the problem concerns the real start of *any* century and not just the first one AD. So, whether you calculate on Christ's birth being 3 BC or AD 3 or some other time is immaterial. It just *sounds* ridiculous, that's all. Logically, He must have been born in Year One.'

'In a way, you're right,' Branting countered, 'but it's clearer to think of the first century beginning at Year Zero and not Year One as you said before.'

It was becoming clear that no out-and-out clear conclusion was going to be reached among the debaters. Those who believed the Twentieth Century would begin at midnight on December 31st, 1899 were in the majority, but Pahlsson and two others still clung to the notion that it would all happen exactly one year later.

'I'll say this, Arne,' Erik Edberg added, 'Me and my

folks'll be celebrating the new century fifteen days from now. If you and yours want to hold out for another whole year, that's your prerogative. From what's been said, I take it most of us here will be setting the party scene in two weeks' time.'

'So be it,' Arne Pahlsson replied. 'We'll have our own celebrations at the proper time – next year.' Then, as an afterthought, and to take any ill-feeling out of the gathering, he added: 'And we won't begrudge your joining us to welcome in the new century.'

'We'll forgive our friends their little aberration, won't we,' Soren Branting summarised. 'Leif! Drinks all round, if you please.' With that, the emotion of the debate was defused and the men drifted into small talk.

Fifteen days later, the midnight chimes heralded the dawn of the new century. At least for the majority.

By the year 1900, Sweden was riding on the crest of the Industrial Revolution's far-reaching waves. The currency of Kronor and Ore, introduced in 1872, was now in commonplace circulation; postage stamps had been in use for almost half a century; general and compulsory education was widespread; railways threaded their gleaming parallels throughout the country and new inventions appeared at frequent intervals. Lars Ericsson produced the desk telephone, revolutionising communications; Gustaf de Laval transformed the dairy industry with his cream separator; Alfred Nobel provided a spur to the mining industry with his nitro-glycerine dynamite and, everywhere, industries were intensifying their workforces and upping their outputs. Workers drawn to the big mines, sawmills, textile factories and papermills were often housed in multi-storey, barrack-room living quarters. In many instances, these developed into hovels that became breeding grounds for disease and heretofore uncommon illnesses. The work was often heavy, the hours long and the wages low. Yet, despite this concentration of effort to birth these industrial ventures, the impact was polarised and affected only one fifth of the country's workforce. Most of the huge remainder were still employed in some form of agriculture.

With what most saw as the exploitation of workers by the capitalist enterprises that provided the jobs, it was hardly surprising that worker-solidarity movements began to emerge. Formal Unions aligned themselves to the Social Democratic Party, and the LO or Landsorganisation swelled its membership to huge numbers to become the largest of the Unions.

For Ulf and Annika Tillkvist, life was neither so oppressive nor so volatile. Throughout their lives, they had been prudent as far as money was concerned and astute in their investments in property. The beautiful house they now owned, on the periphery of Halmstad, had served as home and haven during their son and daughter's last six years, affording a security and stability that Mats and Birgitta greatly appreciated. Mats had studied Law and now, at twenty-five, he was ready to enter his chosen profession. It was through his studies that he met, and fell in love with, Anna Hallstrom. She was a year older than he and their courtship had raised a few eyebrows and given rise to much teasing. They had announced their intention to marry in the spring of the next year.

Birgitta, on the other hand, was seen more and more these days in the company of a botanist, her senior by five years, from Oxford, England. His name was David Chettle and he was following up on some of the foundational work originated by Sweden's Carl von Linnaeus around the middle of the eighteenth century. David had met the effervescent young Birgitta during a field trip where she was assisting with sample collection. The spindly, black-haired Englishman, whose ruddy complexion brought a rouged glow to his cheeks, was instantly as taken with the tall, ash-blonde Swede as she was with him.

'Do you really intend to go to England?' Annika asked her daughter.

'Of course. When we're married and David is ready to return.'

'Married? Huh! Has he asked you yet?'

'Not in so many words. But he will.'

'Oh, you're so sure?'

'I'm sure. He's hinted enough times. It's something I've noticed about him; perhaps it's typical of all Englishmen. He's quite reserved. In my opinion, Swedish men are much more brash.'

'Well, I hope you know what you're doing and don't get hurt if he never gets around to actually asking you.'

'Mother, I *know* he loves me. That's what's important. I'm sure that, when David thinks the time is right, he'll ask me. And I'll jump into his arms and say: "Yes, yes, yes!" before he changes his mind.'

That same evening, David and Mats arrived together at the Tillkvist home. They could be heard before they were seen, the sound of their raucous laughter preceding their physical presence. Ulf threw open the door to the pair.

'What's all the noise? Are you two drunk?'

'Drunk?' Mats exclaimed. 'Drunk? Never! But we're two happy fellows.'

Ulf stood inside the hallway, arms akimbo and, with a puzzled look that turned up the right corner of his mouth in harmony with his raised right eyebrow, said: 'C'mon now, what's this all about?'

'Can't say. But, maybe after David has talked with Birgitta, he'll be the one to tell you.'

David beamed a broad smile while his eyes flitted around the room once more. 'Is she here?' he asked tentatively.

'Birgitta? Yes, she's upstairs,' Annika advised the polite Englishman, normally so reserved but now obviously bursting to tell his sweetheart something of some importance. 'Shall I call her?'

'No thank you. I'll go and knock on her door myself. Is that...?' He hesitated, as if waiting for a confirmed approval before advancing up the broad wooden staircase that led to the four sleeping rooms on the upper floor.

'Of course! You know the way.'

He bounded up the stairs, two at a time, to present himself at Birgitta's door. The door was ajar but his ingrained manners forced him to stand outside and wait until his knock was answered from within.

'Come in,' shouted Birgitta. 'I heard you arrive but I was just putting some things away. What's all the fuss?'

'No fuss. Not at all. But I must ask you a very serious question.'

'Go on.'

'Birgitta, I won't beat about the bush; we've known each other too long for that. But I'd like you to be my wife.'

She smiled wryly back at him. 'That was a statement, not a question. Come along, Walter Raleigh; down on your knees and beg like a gentleman.'

He did. And she accepted, dragging him up and into her arms, drawing him into a long, passionate kiss.

'But there's more,' he enthused. 'The reason for all the hilarity with Mats earlier was...'

'Go on,' she urged, once more.

'I told him what I intended to do and he suggested we have a double wedding. He said he knew you'd accept my proposal.'

'A double wedding? You mean us and Mats and Anna, all in one go?'

'That's the idea. Capital, isn't it?'

'Hee hee, that would be fun. But you haven't spoken with my parents yet. Aren't we being just a little presumptuous?'

The Tillkvists were happy for their daughter to marry David Chettle and were just as happy to agree to their son's proposal of a double wedding. It made sense, Mats had argued, since both of Anna's parents had died when she was in her early teens and she was an only child, having been ushered through her remaining teen years by an aunt. A legacy had supported her Law studies. This way, both couples would enjoy the presence of a large number of family, friends and other well-wishers on their big day.

It was agreed. In April, 1901, the Tillkvists would host a joint wedding on behalf of their son and daughter.

★

As the first month of the new century came towards its end, Soren Branting became more conscious that there remained still a great deal to be done in the time he had left before the big event. Every year, during the first week of March, Ronneby became the focal point for lawyers, solicitors and other members of the legal professions from many parts of the south as they met together in a week long conference. In addition to his regular work as a legal advisor to employers, Branting headed up the Legal Forum, an independent body dedicated to the dissemination of information of interest to the legal profession as well as organising periodic conferences and lectures.

Like his more famous namesake, Hjalmar Branting – leader of the Social Democratic Party – Soren was very much the centre of action and the hub upon which many spokes depended at this time. His was the responsibility for ensuring that all the various facets of organisation for the Law Conference were in place in good time. Again, like his better-known, far-distant cousin, Soren could be described as 'quietly efficient'. Over the years, he had developed the knack of getting the balance right between delegation of certain activities and determination of those that he would take on by himself. As a result, it appeared he could move mountains without breaking sweat. There were no blaring fanfares to accompany his achievements. Things just happened. Like clockwork.

If Branting was the hub, the nut that secured it to its ever-turning axle was Barbro Wallerius, his assistant. Soren had the methodical, almost pedantic, skill of organising; Barbro, the imagination and ideas that made this and other events become the cohesive combination of serious work and social interest that ensured a good attendance on each occasion. Now in her early forties, she had never married. Her erect bearing and no-nonsense approach to life gave the flaxen-haired, bespectacled Miss Wallerius an aura that commanded respect from even the most chauvinistic administrator.

'The meals are all arranged, as you know,' Barbro informed her boss, 'and I'm sure the curator will agree to our delegates visiting the Cultural Museum for the midweek outing.'

'Excellent. The museum is a good choice. I don't know why we haven't used it before.'

'Oh, I've tried, believe me, but it's the new curator who's made the difference. The former incumbent was a boorish man, not keen on large parties visiting. Said he couldn't cope with it. This new fellow seems all fired up with the idea and is refreshing some of the displays in time for our visit.'

'Excellent.' The superlative was one of Soren's favourite words. He liked to use it whenever someone had done the very thing that he, in the same position, would have done. Over the twelve years Miss Wallerius had been privileged to work with him, he'd used it many times in praise of even the most straight forward of tasks she'd accomplished.

'Have we settled on the final numbers?' Branting asked his right-hand woman.

'Forty-three definites and three maybes. Ten have declined for various reasons.'

'All in writing, I suppose?'

'Yes, Mr Branting, and all filed in the usual way. Do you wish to have the file?'

'Not for the time being. I'm still working on the final programme of each day's proceedings. Let's hope this thing at Nybro doesn't erupt into anything more contentious, otherwise some of our delegates may be drawn into it; some of the speakers, too, and that's what concerns me, especially so close to the start of the conference.'

'No, we can do without Union troubles. Hopefully it'll all blow over soon.'

The Nybro sawmill, owned and managed by the bullish Utsi Forest Products Company, was becoming noted as a hotbed of Union activity. Two recent strike actions had been short-lived and inconclusive. Since the tremendous upsurge in timber exporting, the mill had been frenetically busy. But so had the mills of Utsi's competitors. Now, the men were being asked to take a cut in their already meagre wages. It was rumoured that a cut of fifteen per cent was on the cards and Union activists were stirring up the workers into a state of militancy.

'It's getting to be the same everywhere,' said Barbro. 'Sometimes I wonder if we're really any better off with all these big industrial factories.'

'Oh, I'm sure we're better off. As a nation, that is. Hardly fair on the men, though; they have to work just as hard, but for a few kronor less.'

'From what I hear, they're not exactly paid a fortune to begin with. In most cases their wives have to work in the textile factory or the glassworks just to be able to feed their families.'

'Yes, it's a cruel world. "Supply and Demand," that's what it's all about. And competition, too. The more money that the investors sink into these big corporations, the more profit they expect to make. So, when demand is high, they force the companies to make the most of it, driving them to the limits of their production. Trouble is, other companies are competing for the same business so they drop their prices. Even a few ore here and there can mean disaster for any company that's not quick off the mark to reduce prices even lower. Since the investors still want their profits, it's the workers who have to suffer.'

'Sounds to me like a vicious circle. How does it ever stabilise?'

'Breadth of markets usually. Having sufficient customers so that the seller can get higher prices from some to offset low prices from those where competition is fierce.'

'I see. So this is the new way of doing business.'

'Oh, it's nothing new. It's always been that way. The thing that's new is modern communications.'

'You mean, like the telephone?'

'Exactly! Now information regarding supply, demand, stocks and prices can be passed around the marketplace within a matter of hours or, in some cases, minutes.'

'Mmm, interesting. I hadn't thought of the impact of the telephone in that way.'

'Yes, it's certainly changing our lives. Makes *our* job easier, too. Getting hold of people we need when arranging our conferences takes much less time and effort than it used to. At least for those who have the telephone.'

Miss Wallerius brought the conversation to a conclusion by apologising for the interruption. They both gave a quiet chuckle and Barbro returned to her own office. Two days later, she confirmed to Soren that the visit of the conference attendees to the museum had been formally acknowledged and that, of the outstanding delegates, two had accepted and one declined, making a total of forty-five who could now be expected at the forthcoming event.

'Excellent!' was Soren's response.

*

There were three things that concerned Annika Tillkvist, even though all three were a year away from happening. Firstly, the prospect of both her offspring leaving the family home at the same time; secondly, how she would cope with being, in effect, the mother of two brides and a groom at the same wedding; and thirdly, whether Birgitta would be leaving behind not only Halmstad, but Sweden.

Now that the initial euphoria promulgated by the

announcement of the dual marriage had begun to subside, these fundamental realities started to raise discomforting feelings in her mind. She and Ulf would be alone again. Two people, still very fond of each other, but in a house that had grown, over the years, to accommodate a family and all of its peripheral needs. Ulf had been fortunate in finding such a splendid piece of land in the first place and the sprawling house, overlooking the Kattegat beyond which, in the distance, lay Denmark, was as idyllic as any Annika could imagine. The rooms were large, light and airy, and the L-shaped veranda that Ulf had completed only two years ago ran along the south and west faces to gather the sun's rays throughout most of the day. Even before the finishing touches had been completed, signalling the end of the project, the new suntrap had already seen frequent use. It was a beautiful house, but so big. Yet the thought of moving to a small house that would be little more than the size of a *stuga,* or summer house, was something Annika just couldn't bear to contemplate.

The multi-mother role she would play at the wedding was another thing that bothered Annika. As she lay in bed in a kind of pre-dreamtime state before going to sleep, she would try to rehearse the situation. Each night, she seemed to start at the same point but then meander through a different scenario before sleep commandeered her thoughts. The consistent theme was that she would be surrounded by guests, all of whom would be asking questions about one or other of the participants in the ceremony, befuddling her and undermining her enjoyment of a day that was to be a once-in-a-lifetime experience. Was there some way, she wondered, that the *real* day could be organised to be less chaotic.

These first two concerns she brooded over by herself, since she felt they reflected her own, almost selfish, feelings about the respective situations. But the third she shared with Ulf, because she knew that he, too, would find Birgitta's leaving to live so far away in England a hard fact to come to terms with. 'Much as I like David,' she confided to her husband, 'I only wish he was Swedish.'

'What you really mean, my dear, is that you wish Birgitta had chosen to marry a Swede.'

'No, I'm not saying that, nor do I mean it. I like him. I think he's a fine man and I'm not so parochial or nationalistic that his being English represents any kind of problem. It's just that, if she goes, we'll hardly ever see her again.'

'You mean *when* she goes. I don't think there's any *if* in the matter. David was telling me that, should things work out for him this next year, he could be in line for a scholarship or fellowship or something or other at Oxford. Something to do with plant sub-species, I think he said. That'll mean they'll go there for sure.' Then, he surprised Annika by siding with Birgitta: 'In any case, we need to let her be free to carry on her own life. You know what the Good Book says: "Leave and cleave", and all that. It's best we give our daughter our full blessing, wherever she decides to settle.'

'Don't think for a minute you won't miss her. You will.'

'I'll miss her a lot, I'm sure; I'll miss Mats being around, too. But that's not the point. We've worked hard, you and I, and we've done our best for them up till now. The least we can do for them both is to launch them into married life in the best way possible and that means being fully behind them, their spouses and the new life they're setting up for themselves. And for you and me: let's just enjoy life the best we can, too. We have more than we could ever have wished for when *we* were at their stage. It would be sad not to make the most of it now.'

His words were delivered in a tone that spelled a finality to the conversation. No more was said on the subject.

Ulf had thought about the big house and of how it would be with just the two of them there. It was a fine place. Its reddish-brown wooden siding boards could benefit from a new coat of paint, he'd thought, but otherwise it was in good shape. He was caught in two minds: whether to sell and move to something smaller and more manageable and yet, at the same time, unable to bear the thought of leaving behind all the labours of love he'd expended on the place over the years. They'd never find such a beautiful location again, he felt, and that was what convinced him that he and Annika would be happier to contend with the upkeep of their fine home than to move into a smaller one in some place that could be only, at best, a compromise.

At Utsi's Nybro sawmill, things were getting nasty. The men had held a ballot that was overwhelmingly in favour of a week long strike. Extra work they were quite prepared to do, but a cut in wages they couldn't tolerate. The men had already downed tools and were hanging about in groups while their union leaders pleaded once more with the management to reconsider their stance. Soren Branting had been called in to ensure that nothing illegal or unlawful would take place, from the management's point of view. He discussed the seriousness of the matter with Olle Magnusson, the mill manager.

'It's a no-win situation,' Magnusson said. 'We can't cut

the cost of materials any more than we have done and, if we're to remain competitive, something has to be cut. That means wages. It's the only solution.'

'It's not easy, I'll grant you that,' Branting answered, 'but have you exhausted all other possible routes?'

With frustration and exasperation in his voice, Magnusson replied: 'Look here, we know this business. We've spent months looking at the possibilities and there's just no other way.'

'Not by cutting costs, perhaps, but have you looked at other potential markets where prices are holding up?'

'Crissakes man! What are you? Some kind of expert on the industry? We're already exporting all over Europe!'

'I apologise, Mr Magnusson. I'm no expert, as you say. I'm only here to advise you on legal matters and, hopefully, to see that things don't boil over into something that will be out of my hands and yours. If the men stay out you'll lose more than you gain, so we must find another solution.'

'Nei, they can't stand to stay out. Wives and youngsters to feed; they'll soon give up and come to reason.'

'I wouldn't guarantee that. You do know about the Strike Angels, don't you?'

'The what?'

'Then obviously you don't. The Strike Angels, mostly women, are the wives of men working elsewhere who've banded together to promise help to the strikers if they stay out.'

'Bloody hell! What's this country coming to? Don't they realise that, if we can't compete successfully, we'll have to close down! There won't be any jobs to come back to!'

'Really? The whole of the giant Utsi empire will vanish overnight because a fifteen percent wage cut wasn't accepted?'

'Well, not the whole of Utsi, but certainly here at Nybro.'

'Aha! So things are not so bad elsewhere? Only here?'

'We're the second largest mill, after Norrholm, and they don't pay as high as we do to start with. It's not such a problem up there.'

'Then it's worse than I thought. It seems to me your corporate management is badly out of line. Again, as I said before, I'm no expert in these things, but wouldn't it make more sense to try to balance prices and profits across the whole business rather than concentrating on the profitability of just this one site?'

The room went quiet. Olle Magnusson stared out of the window, saying nothing. He withdrew from his pocket a small tin and took a pinch of snuff, wedging it under his top lip. The silence remained for some moments while the mill manager combed his fingers through the thick mop of almost white hair that crowned his head.

'It's not a decision I can take on my own, Mr Branting. Something so far-reaching is a matter for the Board.'

'So? What will you do?'

Again the silence. Magnusson continued to stare out of the window at the gloomy scene of the groups of idle men. Some, who saw him, shook their fists and made vulgar gestures. Thankfully, he couldn't hear the words they hurled in his direction. 'All right!' he said, followed by a tight squeezing of his mouth against the plug of snuff. 'Bring in the union men.'

In the forty minutes that followed, Soren Branting said nothing. He sat dumb, listening to both sides. But, from the way the debate ensued, he took some satisfaction from the influence he'd been able to inject. A third party; almost a neutral outsider; the disassociated conveyor of a fresh idea. Soren had done no more than sow some seeds of doubt to provoke a wider compass of consideration of the impasse. But, at least for now, it was having the desired effect.

'You'll call off the strike then?' Magnusson asked the union leader.

'Under those conditions: yes. Same hours, same wages?'

'That's right. But no guarantees. We'll need to examine the issue in some detail across the board, you understand, and we'll talk with you again in a month's time.'

'Fine. We'll agree to that.'

'Excellent!' Soren exclaimed.

Within the hour, the mill was once more a hive of industry.

*

It was by pure accident that the novice lawyer, Mats Tillkvist, found himself as one of the listed delegates at this year's Legal Forum conference in Ronneby. The untimely illness incurred by his superior had given him the chance. He felt honoured to be included, since most of those who attended were senior practitioners – and some were quite eminent. The detailed letter he'd received from a Miss Wallerius gave chapter and verse on the complete programme of events: plenary sessions, work groups, social events, accommodation and meals, amongst other things. Attached to the letter was a very much simplified map of the location of the Confederation Chambers in which the main sessions were to be held.

This Miss Wallerius must have been a very busy lady, he thought, unless she commands a gang of helpers to prepare all this paperwork for each and every person attending the

Forum. Miss Wallerius had, indeed, been a busy lady. There was no Army of Assistance.

'I can't believe I've been so lucky!' Mats told Anna as they sat at the table in the kitchen of Anna's aunt's small home. 'By rights, it should be years before I get an invitation to the Forum. Just think of it: next week I'll be rubbing shoulders with some of the best in the profession. And, apart from anything else, I'm sure to learn a lot.' As he uttered the words, he could hardly have foreseen just how prophetic they would prove to be.

'Yes, I've heard a lot about these Forum sessions; they're very well regarded in the profession,' said Anna. 'They do seem to be worthwhile and, from what other lawyers have told me, the case studies – based on real, past cases – teach you more than you can pick up in weeks of normal work. Usually, the case studies illustrate some complex issues and tend to bring out some of the implications that you may not even realise were there. I must say, I'm quite envious of you and I'll expect a detailed summary when you return.' She smiled demurely at her future husband as she rose from the table to fetch an inkwell and pen. 'I must jot down a few notes from one of today's cases to jog my memory in the morning.'

'And I must be on my way home. Tomorrow's likely to be a busy day for me, too.'

The couple embraced, kissed tenderly, then parted – Mats making his way across Halmstad and along the broad lane that led to the 'big red house', where Ulf and Annika were preparing supper.

When Mats arrived at the Confederation Chambers in Ronneby he was, at first, overwhelmed by the almost military orderliness of the organisation of the conference. As he mounted the steps of the old building, he felt a mixture of excitement and nervousness. He was greeted by Miss Wallerius, whose face, figure and general deportment shattered the illusions he'd entertained about the personage behind the signature on the letter he'd received regarding the event. He soon discovered, however, that Barbro Wallerius had a most disarming personality and, since he was by far the youngest attendee and a substitute for the intended delegate, she singled him out for particular treatment, shepherding him in a most friendly and charming way into a small group of mature men who stood at the rear of the large room engaged in casual conversation.

'Gentlemen, may I introduce Mats Tillkvist from Halmstad. Recently qualified, I believe; he's attending the Forum in place of Bengt Eklund who is quite unwell at present.'

In turn, the men shook hands with Mats and warmly welcomed him to the gathering. Their open friendliness made him feel at ease, dispelling the lack of confidence he felt when he'd first arrived.

Mats found some of the plenary sessions touched on issues he'd never considered, as Anna had predicted, and his brain was taxed on several occasions to discern the significance of the arguments being put forward. But he found it rewarding. The paper read by Soren Branting on employment law was a new area for him, particularly some of the far-reaching conclusions the speaker expounded. But, if the formal aspects of the conference were treating him to new learning, they would pale to insignificance, from a personal point of view, when compared with the discovery he was to make on the Wednesday afternoon. That was the occasion of the visit to the Cultural Museum, intended as a social distraction from the high-brow intensity of the main conference.

As Mats made his way to the Museum alongside the illustrious company of lawyers and solicitors, he felt the time could perhaps have been better spent in continuing with his learning process. Little did he realise that he was about to learn something that would impact his life even more pointedly.

The delegates were split into four groups, each assigned to a guide who would inform them of some of the background to the relics and displays they would see and Mats was fortunate to be in the group to be led by the new curator, Rolf Arvidsson. Partway through the tour, the visitors stopped in front of a large display case and Arvidsson explained: 'An important part of our heritage in this area comes from the era when Sweden had a powerful Navy and also many private merchant ships plying the oceans.' He pointed out several exhibits, enlightening the visitors on their significance, then pointed to a large, leather-bound book. 'And here we have the diary of one of our famous explorers, Captain Sten Tillkvist. It's not only a remarkable account of his voyages aboard his ship *Peleus*, but gives a great insight into his life as a young man.'

Mats' eyes lit up like signal beacons and he pricked his ears at the sound of his family name. But Arvidsson said no more about the diary and moved on to another exhibit. As the group thronged after the curator, Mats remained rooted to the spot, his eyes fixed on the leather-bound book. He stared at it for a long time, trying to make out the handwriting on the two exposed pages. Sensibly, he contained himself until the tour was ended, but then immediately sought out the curator.

'Excuse me, sir,' he began. 'There was one exhibit that particularly interested me.'

Rolf Arvidsson beamed a smile at the mention of a

particular interest. He was always keen to satisfy the inquisitiveness of a visitor. 'Yes? And what was that?'

'In the maritime section, sir. The diary of Sten Tillkvist.'

'Ah, yes, the old seafarer.'

'That's right. I believe I am directly descended from him; my name is Tillkvist also.'

'Is that so? Then perhaps you would like to examine the old book more closely?'

'Would that be possible?'

'Of course. Anything's possible. I'd be glad to unlock the cabinet and take it out for you. Then, I suggest we go along to my office and you can look through it. Has to be handled carefully, though, as some of the leaves are a little fragile in places.'

The other delegates had, by now, completed their visit and were returning to the various inns in which they were billeted. The curator tucked the book under one arm, re-locked the cabinet and bade Mats follow him to his office. There, the young lawyer began to thumb through the one hundred and thirty year old record written by his ancestor.

'There's a magnifying lens here if you need it,' Arvidsson advised. 'I'll leave you to browse through your family's history as I have a few things to do. I should be back in around twenty minutes or so.'

The diary made interesting reading, annotated as it was by personal insights and, here and there, rough sketches. But it was when Mats turned back to the opening pages and read, word for word, the account of Sten's early life that he became intrigued.

> *...on a farm at Peterlöv, not far from Perstorp. It was called Tilderkvist's Farm, for reasons which I won't*

> *explain, and is there to this day, though now abandoned, for reasons that I will explain, but later in this account. When my brother Bo and I were small, around the ages of...*

Mats read on, his eyes glued to each page, and was still deciphering the old handwriting when the helpful curator returned.

'You find it interesting?'

'It's more than interesting. How did you get hold of it?'

'It was here when I took on the job. Must have been obtained some time ago, I'd say. Probably came from an old house somewhere.'

'It's incredible. Tells a lot about our early family history. Things I never knew. I can't wait to tell my father about this.'

When the conference ended and Mats made his way back to Halmstad, his mind was reeling from the inebriating effects of a cocktail of new facts and guidelines he'd garnered from the Legal Forum, together with the astounding account that had been penned by old Sten Tillkvist. When he reached home, he quickly deflected the obvious questions from Ulf and Annika about the conference and took them straight to the amazing discovery he'd made.

'The curator says it must have come from an old house somewhere. It's like finding a treasure trove. You must get down there to see this book. I couldn't believe it. There I was, standing among this group of lawyers looking at old ships' wheels and the like and suddenly the curator pointed to this old book and mentioned our family name. If we'd been plain old Anderssons, Bergs or Lunds I probably wouldn't have keyed in, but I don't know of any other Tillkvists apart from our own relatives.'

'That really is amazing,' Ulf said, then, turning to Annika, he said: 'Do you remember our cousins from America who came here when we first lived in Halmstad? Must be about thirty years ago. They were going over to Kalmar to try to find out about old Sten. Remember?'

'Yes, vaguely,' she replied. 'They were going to find old Grandma Tillkvist to see whether she knew where Sten's house was.'

'That's right. I'll bet that's where this diary came from: the old house in Kalmar.'

Mats broke back into the conversation, 'And it says there's a farm near Perstorp that was abandoned. I wonder if that means we still legally own it? It was where Sten was born, but he and Tomas, his father, left there to go to Karlskrona after his mother and brother were burnt to death in a barn fire.'

Ulf shot a look of surprise at his son. 'Did you say *Perstorp?*'

'That's right. At least, it's near Perstorp. Someplace called Peterlöv I think it was.'

'But, we always thought the Tillkvists came from around Falkenberg. How can that be?'

'I don't know. Maybe it's explained somewhere. I had only half an hour or so to look through the book.'

'My goodness! This needs looking into!' exclaimed Ulf. 'And you're just the man to do it. Now that you're a lawyer. And Anna, too. Between the two of you, it must be possible to check this out, don't you think?'

'Sure. Let's see what we can find out.'

★

David Chettle was embarrassed. He'd never particularly excelled at sports of any kind, even though his giraffe-like legs would have provided him with some advantage in track events over the longer distances. But, being an Englishman in temporary exile in Sweden was at the root of his present predicament. Two of his colleagues had invited him to take part in a football match to 'show them how the game *should* be played.' To say that he was *invited* disguises the sinister goings on that ensured he would be there. *Coerced* would possibly describe his taking part more accurately.

The English football game was, by now, quite well established in its country of origin. But, in Sweden, it was only just beginning to catch on. The two makeshift teams wore makeshift outfits: white shirts banded by strips of blue and yellow cloth respectively to distinguish the sides. The eight inch wide strips of material were wound around the back of the wearer and slits made according to his girth so that the existing shirt buttons could be used to fasten the strips, making a complete circle of the body. Street trousers sufficed for the bottom half and each outfit was completed by heavy, toe-capped working boots. Thick bars of sandwiched leather, about half an inch wide, were nailed to the soles and heels of the boots to improve the grip on the grassy surface. The playing field was relatively flat and of sufficient proportions to allow a reasonable match to be played. The ball was a genuine English competition grade, with wide, stitched leather panels. In only one other respect had there been no compromise: the goalposts had been formed from stout, four-by-four timbers, bolted together and whitewashed. Nets would have been a luxury.

David had played the game only briefly whilst at college. He was reasonably familiar with the basic rules but, beyond that, he knew only how to kick, run and make an attempt at a tackle. Ball skills, heading and 'dribbling' were foreign ideas to him.

The Blues, boasting they would be fielding an Englishman who would 'show a trick or two,' were confident that their star player would give them at least a two goal advantage. As the teams took their positions to begin the game, the Blues forwards taunted their Yellows counterparts by suggesting the game would be over by half-time. This was serious stuff. These were grown men returning to a kind of gang-warfare childhood.

The game began at a furious pace which was sustained for the first twenty minutes. Neither team had scored, although the Yellows had come closest. Whenever a Blues player gained possession of the ball, his team-mates would shout: 'Pass it to the English!' as if by doing so some miracle would result. There were no miracles. Not even when Mats, Anna and Birgitta bawled encouragement from the side of the field. The threesome had come to support the Blues, and had brought lengths of cloth, about a yard long, of a similar colour to that worn by David and his team-mates. The lengths of cloth were knotted at one end and the supporters swung them around their heads while shouting at the tops of their voices: 'Come on Blues! Stick at it Blues!'

David was beginning to employ a tactic he'd remembered from his college days. He would hang about on the far right and wait for the ball to be played to him. Then he would tap it forward a few paces and gather speed towards the opponents' goal. When one of the Yellows defenders approached him, he would kick the ball far ahead on the outside of the player and go haring after it, rounding the defender on the inside and tapping the ball ahead by a few paces once more. He did this a number of times, quite successfully, but always there was one more defender who got there before David could catch up with the ball he'd kicked so far ahead.

After nearly half an hour, the pace slackened considerably. Sweat poured off all but the goalkeepers, neither of whom had had much to do. Runs became short-lived and most of the players, unaccustomed to the constant activity, were panting noisily. Then the Yellows scored.

The vigour of the opening fury had sorely tried the fitness of most and the game became one of long kicks from one half of the field to the other. In the fifteen minutes prior to the half-time mark, all composure went to pieces. The Blues scored three times and the Yellows twice, making it three apiece when they changed ends.

'So much for your "star player" one of the Yellows teased as they swapped places. Hasn't had a sniff of goal yet, eh?'

'Ja, he's just getting into it. You got two lucky goals. We could easily have been three-one up by now.'

'Huh, we just eased off a bit to make a game of it. Just watch us Yellows go this half.'

Any neutral onlooker would have judged one side to be as bad as the other and would not have been surprised that, with only minutes remaining, the teams were tied at four goals each. Then came the moment of glory for 'the English'. So far, David had made no effort to head the ball, even when to do so would have been the obvious response. But, as a Blues player crossed the ball from the left to where the Englishman stood, almost central to the goal, he swung his head at it. His timing was miserably judged, but the ball flew off his shoulder and looped high into the air beyond the despairing reach of the Yellows goalkeeper to drop just below the crossbar and into the unguarded goal.

As the teams trooped off at the end – the Blues victorious by five goals to four – David Chettle was acclaimed the hero.

'Told you he was just getting into it by half-time,' a Blues forward reminded his opponent. 'Great goal. Great goal.'

David knew his place. And it wasn't on the football field. He became a master of concocted excuses each time the grapevine forewarned him that another game was on the cards.

*

In the aftermath of the conference at Ronneby, Barbro Wallerius was in good spirits. The event had gone well: the contributions from the speakers had had a considerable impact on their audience; the overall organisation and housekeeping had been flawless and many appreciative comments were voiced in respect of the social events, particularly the highly instructive visit to the Cultural Museum.

For Mr Branting, there was little time to rest on the laurels of another successful Forum. Within a matter of days of the event's conclusion, he was called to Nybro once again. His only foreknowledge of the new situation was that he was being called in by Olle Magnusson to vet 'some new proposals'.

'We felt we ought to run our ideas past you,' explained Magnusson, 'just to be sure that we're not stepping out of line.'

'So, what do you have in mind?' Branting asked.

'Quite a tough line, in some ways, but a sensible one as far as our future is concerned. As you know, the arrangements we came to four weeks ago were only stalling for time. Now, we've had the chance to examine our situation more fully and what we propose is this: the workforce here at Nybro will be laid off, *en bloc*, and the jobs will be posted for new applicants at a reduced rate of pay. Of course, the men will be free to apply for their old jobs if they wish. But we will be making the same offer to the men from Norrholm. Since even the new rates will be more than we pay the Norrholm men right now, there's every chance that a good number of them will apply. Replacements can be found quite easily for the Norrholm mill; there's a shortage of industrial work in that area and Utsi pays better than almost anything else they can find. We'll be offering special incentives for the more skilled jobs to encourage some of the Norrholm men to make the move and we'll make some concessions to the best of our own men here. Of course, a little bit of "leaning" by the managers will almost guarantee that we get the right men in the end. That way, we can make the cuts we need to stay competitive and, at the same time, we'll retain most of our good people.'

Soren Branting blanched at what he'd just heard. He sighed audibly and stroked his chin. 'That's a hell of a scheme, Olle. Isn't that what they call "totalitarianism" where the power of the company dominates the will of its employees?'

'Uh-uh, we don't subscribe to that. This is a fair offer. Every job will be posted and open to anyone to apply.'

'For less money than they get today?'

'Depends. Men at the Norrholm mill already get paid less for doing the same work. Why should Nybro be hamstrung by continuing to pay higher rates. Originally, we had to attract labour from the docks and the glassworks.

There was more money in timber then, too. But today's situation isn't like that anymore. You know the score. Either we cut our costs and survive or else we close the mill completely. Then, the men will be forced to find whatever they can, probably for less money than we're offering.'

'Apart from here and Norrholm, what are the other Utsi mills doing?'

'Anywhere else is much smaller. The impacts are not so great.'

'And what do the Unions think of these proposals?'

'They don't know yet. That's why I've called you in. We want you to advise us if there are any pitfalls in what we're proposing before we talk to them.'

'With the present laws, there's nothing to stop you. Not in strictly legal terms. But surely you have some moral obligation?'

'Mr Branting, this is business; we can't afford to be moralistic about it.'

'Can't say I applaud the attitude of your Board in this. It'll bring a lot of hardship.'

Magnusson smirked: 'Isn't that where your Strike Angels come in?'

'I have nothing to do with the Strike Angels but, in any case, their aims are for temporary relief, not wholesale support of the men you're going to put on the streets. Besides, you'll incur the wrath of the Unions and, for that matter, the whole Social Democratic Party.'

'So be it. What we have to do, we have to do. Make no mistake: Utsi will not only survive; in time, the business will expand again.'

When he left the mill manager's office and walked across the mill yard, Soren bit his lip as he watched some of the men hard at work and knowing that, within a few days, they would be faced with the prospect of lower wages... or none at all.

Olle Magnusson drew on all his mental resources and on the toughness that he'd built up from his years of managing men as he steeled himself against the furore he was certain would erupt from the move he was about to instigate.

It was Thursday. Not a good day to show his hand to the Unions. That would give them too much time to reflect on the statement he would make on behalf of the Utsi management.

The men, who were well aware that the future of the mill was in the balance, shouted to him as he left his office that evening: 'Any news yet, Mr Magnusson?'

He fended off their concerned inquiry; 'No. Nothing to say at this stage.' Some of the men continued to press him. 'Maybe next week we'll know something,' he lied and walked briskly away. He slept little that night and did not share, even with his wife, the gravity of the proposals Utsi was about to unleash on the Nybro workforce.

Throughout the day on Friday, he shared his office with two clerks, sworn to secrecy, as they prepared the notices to be posted on the mill's high cast-iron gates on Monday, after he'd met with the Union officials. But, shortly before midnight on Friday night, the matter was taken out of his hands.

To this day, it has never been discovered whether the details were leaked by one of the clerks or whether some 'higher power' exacted judgement on the Utsi Forest Products Company. By the early hours of Saturday morning, an uncontrollable fire raged through the timber sheds and mill buildings, reducing them to blackened piles of smouldering ash. A huge pall of smoke billowed over the town and everywhere people were running towards the doomed mill. By dawn, there remained little that could be salvaged beyond the stark iron gates that were to have been the scaffold upon which would have hung the grim edict. At a stroke, the Nybro mill had suffered cuts far beyond the designs of its management.

When Olle Magnusson heard the news, he was distraught.

When Soren Branting heard the news, his eyes misted over and he gave Barbro a dazed look. He said: 'To them that have much, more will be given; but, to them that have little, even the little they have will be taken away.'

Miss Wallerius looked at him in puzzlement. 'What's that?'

'Matthew's Gospel,' he replied, his voice almost toneless.

She gave a wan smile then, clutching her files to her chest, turned smartly and left her boss's office, closing the door quietly behind her.

*

When Mats made the return trip to Ronneby, this time accompanied by his father, the helpful curator of the Cultural Museum, Rolf Arvidsson, ensured that their visit was well worth their trouble. And trouble it had been. En route, they'd been forced to take a very roundabout diversion because the main road had been blocked by fallen trees. The prolonged delay they'd incurred enforced an overnight stay at a small country inn, so their time in Ronneby was at a premium.

'Of course I remember you from last time. It was the Forum visit, about three weeks ago was it not?'

'That's correct,' answered Mats.

'Mats Tillkvist, wasn't it?'

'Hei, what a memory! And this is my father, Ulf.'

The two men shook hands and the curator took the initiative, suggesting: 'I imagine you'd like to examine the old diary, yes?'

Without waiting for Mats' nod of confirmation, Arvidsson dug into his pocket for the key and headed in the direction of the showcase. Carefully, he removed the aged volume and handed it to Ulf. 'It's an important archive to us, but I know it's even more important to you, so you may take as long as you wish to go through it. I suggest you use my office, as before.'

As the two men sat at the high, sloping desk leafing their way through Sten's account, Mats pointed out some of the paragraphs he'd read during his first visit. Ulf's eyes widened and he felt a tingle of excitement run through him as his eyes scanned the old pages.

'Why do you suppose the Peterlöv place was called "Tilderkvist Farm" and not "Tillkvist" after our own family?' Mats posed.

'I've no idea. Could be just a coincidence. Perhaps the name of a previous owner.'

From the landmarks Sten described, they felt it should certainly be possible to pinpoint the place, even after all these years. They spent the greater part of the day going through the old seafarer's writings.

'Sad, isn't it, that he seemed to turn against his father towards the end?' Ulf said. 'Must have been really jealous of this orphan lad Tomas had taken under his roof.'

Mats made copious notes and, on the journey back to

Halmstad, they talked incessantly about the possibilities.

'We need to get over to Perstorp and try to find this place,' Mats said. 'With what we know, it can't be impossible.'

It was the middle of August and the day was bright and sunny as Ulf and Mats stood on the barren ground that had once been Peterlöv Village. The ruins of the old Lutheran Church, protruding from the overgrowth of long grass and weeds like rotten tooth-stumps fixed their orientation of the old village. They trekked the few hundred yards north to where they believed the farm buildings would have stood when, suddenly, Mats exclaimed: 'Look! The base-stones are still here! This must have been the main house.'

'You're probably right,' agreed Ulf, 'And on either side would have been the barn and workshop, built in the old way to make a hollow square but with none of the buildings touching to prevent the spread of fire.'

Apart from the outlined foundations of the main house, there was nothing else visible to excite them.

'It's enough,' Mats proclaimed. 'With what shows here and Sten's record, I believe we have enough to start making some investigations about the ownership. The main buildings must have stood for some time before someone cannibalised them to re-use the stones, so there must be some record of it somewhere.'

It took more than two months to track down the title to the land. And to convince the Land Registrar that it rightfully belonged to Ulf as the oldest living descendent in Sten's family line. In the process, it became clear that the farm contained more land than either Ulf or Mats had realised. Only the bitter cold and falling snow discouraged father and son from making a further visit to the abandoned farm to examine the physical extent of its boundaries. They would return, they'd decided, once winter was over and would take Annika and Anna with them. Back home in the 'big red house' they discussed their new-found estate.

'It's not quite Halmstad, with a view across the Kattegat, but it's a nice spot,' Ulf reasoned aloud. 'Perhaps we should build a new house there; one that Annika would feel happy with, but not as large as this one.'

'Why not indeed, father,' Mats said in support. 'But, of course, you'd have to give up your ironmongery shop in town... and there's no one around Peterlöv to provide any custom.'

'That's true. But maybe I'll turn my hand to something else.'

'What else? None of us knows very much about farming.'

'Oh, I wouldn't attempt to farm the place. It'd just be a house, that's all. Maybe we'd grow a few things, but nothing that would amount to farming.'

'It's quite an inheritance though, eh? And to think we discovered it only by chance. If Bengt Eklund hadn't gone down with pneumonia, I'd never have gone to Ronneby in the first place and we'd never have heard of Peterlöv.'

'Well, thank God for your Mr Eklund's pneumonia.' Had the lawyer not already recovered, the remark would have been out of place. As it was, both men laughed at the ludicrous insinuation.

'At least thank God for the timing of it,' Mats compromised.

★

As the year drew towards its close, Arne Pahlsson and his wife Sofia, together with a small circle of friends, prepared to celebrate the march of time into a new century. Towards those he termed the 'misinformed majority' who'd welcomed the Twentieth Century a year ago, he bore no malice. In his opinion, they'd simply made a misjudgement based on an erroneous concept of determining dates. The gathering momentum of advancing knowledge that had become the watchword now that the Industrial Age had arrived, Arne felt, would sooner or later confirm that each new century began in Year One and not Year Zero as the majority believed. For the Pahlssons and their friends, the New Year celebrations would take on not only a special significance but would be marked rather explosively due to Arne's intention to signal the moment by the firing of an old cannon he'd arranged to borrow from a friend.

'Should make a fair bang,' Arne enthused to Peter Ekberg, another of the *Year One-ers*. 'We'll stoke it up with black powder and stuff some rags down the barrel. Once it's all rammed nice and tight it'll go with quite a wallop.'

'You sure it'll stand it? Looks an ancient piece.'

'I've no doubts about that. The barrel was cast in 1750 by the Ulfsson Armoury – one of the best in the business in its day.'

'I'll bet it's seen some service though, eh? You know anything about its history?'

'Oh, apparently it came from a merchant ship, the *Tacitus Rex*, which sailed from Karlskrona and was captained by a man called Flemming Hansson. They used to do the Canton run. Probably had to see off pirates a time or two so, who knows, this old beast may have earned its keep by helping blast some freebooter out of the water somewhere between here and China.'

Peter Ekberg thought for a moment, then postulated: 'Made in 1750, you say?'

'So I believe.'

'Then this will be the second new century it's entered. I wonder if it boomed in the last one in 1801?'

When the time came, and the Pahlssons and their friends gathered expectantly behind the cannon, Arne and Peter tended to loading and priming the old piece, mounted on its wheeled carriage.

'Ten! Nine! Eight!' the group counted out while Arne stood alone beside the blackened gun. As the countdown continued, he hoped to anticipate the delay of the priming and as the count reached 'Four!' he applied the taper. 'Three! Two! One!' As the combined voices enunciated the final 'n' sound, the main charge ignited, resulting not in the loud boom Arne had predicted, but in a sharp, flat crack that kicked at the eardrums as shredded rags spat across the snow to land, still smouldering, in a wide arc.

As the heavily wrapped friends cheered and hugged one another, Arne stood scratching his head, looking at the old cannon which was now thrown back several feet and slewed to one side. 'It didn't "boom!" like it should've,' he muttered.

'I imagine it was just that the rags were much lighter than a cannon ball,' Peter suggested. 'But it did the job all right.' He thrust out both his hands, clasping Arne's right hand between them and pumped it vigorously. 'Welcome to the Twentieth Century!'

*

When they weren't being assailed by Annika over the minutest details of the preparations for the double wedding,

Ulf and Mats made time to visit Peterlöv. Surveys were undertaken and materials organised for the building of the new house. On their first visit since the weather began to improve, the men had taken their womenfolk with them. The bride-to-be, Anna, had immediately envisaged the potential of the old farm but Annika, totally preoccupied with thoughts of the forthcoming wedding, had said only, 'It'll do.'

By mid-April, the week before the 'big day' was upon them all, the Peterlöv house was taking shape. The outer walls and main internal room divisions had been framed in timbers anchored to the new foundations.

When the Forum at Ronneby came around once more, Mats could hardly believe that a whole year had passed since he'd first discovered Sten's diary. So much had been accomplished, yet the intervening time seemed to have flown past. At the Halmstad law office where he worked, there was no serious illness this year. Bengt Eklund attended the Forum, as was his custom.

Due to the 'prevailing circumstances' the Tillkvists' project at Peterlöv was put on one side, at least temporarily. Just for the moment, Mats had other things on his mind and Annika reminded Ulf that he ought to have, too.

Annika's continual fussing heightened the already highly charged nerves and emotions in the build-up to the wedding. David and Birgitta were overjoyed, not only in looking forward to the following week when they would become man and wife, but because David had received confirmation that he'd been awarded a 'travelling scholarship' from the University of Oxford, to commence in September. The significant factor was that he and Birgitta would be able to spend some of the following year in England, but would also be able to visit Sweden and other parts of Europe. News of the award allayed some of Annika's fears. On the one hand, she was sad that the award set the seal on the departure of the Chettles to England during the summer but, on the other hand, it did mean that it wouldn't be too long before she saw her daughter again.

The wedding itself was a grand affair and the two brides, Anna and Birgitta, looked radiant. David's parents had travelled from England for the occasion, arriving two days before. They were overwhelmed by the warmth of their welcome and by the hospitality extended to them, so characteristic of Swedish tradition at a time like this. None of Annika's presupposed nightmares materialised and she was enjoying herself immensely. Every aspect of the day seemed to be just perfect. Perfect, that was, until some of David's colleagues insisted on contributing to the speeches at the foursome's reception. One of the players from the Blues football team recalled David's 'wonder goal' that had won them the match against their old rivals, the Yellows. He embroidered the story so much with humorous asides and his account so much distorted the reality that even David could not have recognised the famous goal or its scorer. Then, the goalkeeper of the team told a story that thoroughly embarrassed the more conservative of the guests.

'This couple got married and spent their wedding night at a small, country hotel,' he recounted. 'When the new husband went downstairs to fetch some drinks, he let it slip that he and his wife were on honeymoon. "Why didn't you say so," the manager said. "You could have had the Bridal Suite. In fact, it's not occupied. Would you like it?" "I'll ask my wife," the new husband said, and took the drinks back to the room. "How would you like the Bridal Suite?" he asked his wife. "No thanks," she replied. "I'll just hold on to your ears till I get the hang of it," she answered.' An eruption of bawdy guffaws arose from his team-mates and a more restrained laughter came from some of the more outgoing male guests. Annika was disgusted and apologised to David's parents for the raucous uproar.

Towards the end of the celebrations, as the two couples were about to leave, an uninvited guest appeared at the doorway of the hall. It was Rolf Arvidsson from Ronneby.

'I just couldn't miss this occasion,' he told Mats. 'And I've brought you a special gift, though I'm sure you can already guess what it is.' He handed over Sten's diary.

Some of the guests, standing nearby, craned their necks to ascertain what was going on.

'What do you suppose it is?' one whispered to another.

'Looks like an old Bible or a ledger of some sort,' the other replied.

Mats, clutching the old log, thanked the curator profusely then whirled around, searching the sea of faces for Ulf. 'Father! Look!' he cried, letting go of Anna's hand and hoisting the book above his head: 'It's come home! What a wonderful end to a wonderful day!'

Ulf, who had been reservedly inconspicuous for most of the afternoon, parted his way through the well-wishers to clasp the old diary to his chest. He confronted the curator, 'Mr Arvidsson, there was no need. Surely it's an important artefact for the museum to hold?'

'Indeed. But I redeemed it on your behalf. After your last visit, I didn't return it to the display. I took it home and began to read it. After just a few pages, I began to realise that these were the intimate words of a man about his own family. I could read no more. Nor do I think it has a place on public display. It belongs with you; to remind you of your heritage and of the achievements of a great member of your own family. I have arranged for a small plaque to be made, commemorating Captain Tillkvist, to stand in its place.'

With the wedding over, the Tillkvists and Chettles returned to a less exalted existence. But, for Mats, these were times of unease. The Riksdag had concluded an exhaustive review of the country's defence forces and, in particular, the means used to form its Army. It brought in the Conscription Act and Mats was concerned in case the call to arms would encompass men of his own age. There was no particular threat from any foreign power, but Sweden's relationship with Norway was beginning to become strained. The two countries remained in union, but the seam that bound them was showing signs of weakening. If the matter could not be resolved politically and peacefully, the result might well be akin to a Civil War, Mats thought. The Suffragette Movement was also gathering momentum, since women still had no rights to a vote. This situation, too, gave rise to widespread apprehension.

These political murmurings added to the undercurrents being felt in industry. In a backlash against the activities of the Unions, the country's major employers were formulating proposals to form their own association, the Swedish Employers' Confederation. It would not be long, Mats predicted, until that, too, came into being, bringing a direct confrontation with the Unions, with all of its potential reactionary outcomes.

Just as life for the Tillkvists was on the threshold of new enterprises, the country, at large, appeared to be heading for turmoil.

As the summer months of 1901 marched past, the Tillkvist household reached some monumental decisions. David and Birgitta Chettle had already departed for England, but Mats and Anna had remained at the big red house in Halmstad. This would become their home, while the oldsters, Ulf and Annika, had now determined to claim their inheritance at Peterlöv.

'Probably one more month before we're able to move to the new house,' Ulf announced one morning.

'It'll be sad to leave Halmstad,' Annika said, 'but we'll have lots more trees at Peterlöv to compensate for losing our lovely view of the sea.'

'It'll be more peaceful, too. There are too many people coming to Halmstad now. It's not like it used to be,' remarked Ulf, as if justifying once more to himself the decision they had taken.

Mats smiled across at his parents and said: 'If you don't like it there, you can always come back. Anna and I will take good care of this old place, you can be sure.'

'I should hope you would,' put in Annika, 'There's a lot of your father's life invested in this place.'

For some moments they reminisced, recalling the many happy times they'd spent in the big red house over the years.

'Yes, times have certainly changed,' Mats summarised, 'but we have to have progress. I was thinking exactly that only yesterday. A man brought one of these new *horseless carriages* to town. Quite amazing. Have you ever seen one?'

Annika and Anna shook their heads and Ulf said, 'No, I've never actually seen one, but I've heard about them. Very noisy, they say.'

'True, they're noisy. But I'm sure these clever engineers

in Germany who built this thing will find a way to quieten it down. They're very expensive, too, but I'm equally sure they'll become more affordable in time also. It'll revolutionise the way we get around, you'll see.'

'How does it work?' Anna asked, ignorant of the invention itself and, therefore, completely unaware of the scope her question covered.

Mats, intelligent but by no means equipped with his father's practical leanings, replied: 'By mechanical magic. The whole contraption has something that looks like an aquavit still at the front, filled with a spirit fuel and this drives through mechanical contrivances to turn the wheels. They call it the *engine*. The driver sits on an upholstered seat and guides the carriage with a wheel attached to a long rod instead of pulling on reins. As he turns this wheel, which protrudes from the engine in front of him, so the big road wheels turn in either direction.'

'Sounds complicated,' interjected Anna, 'It must take quite a bit of practice to be able to control it properly.'

'I expect it does. But this fellow seemed to be able to make it go wherever he wanted.'

Mats' introduction of the subject led to a further discussion about the effects of the Industrial Revolution and the women sided against the men when it came to debating the benefits that had come from industrialisation. The women felt that there had been little improvement; the men argued that life had been completely changed, for the better. Except, they allowed, for those who laboured in the big factories to make the many things upon which the economy of the country now depended. They sat in silence for some moments, then Ulf intoned: 'Could be to our advantage. All these mechanical things will sooner or later break down in some way and will need repairing. Since I've always been good at fixing things, this might be the "something else" I could turn my hand to once we're installed at Peterlöv. It wouldn't be difficult to pick up and would surely be more profitable than selling ironmongery.'

'Possibly,' said Mats, ruefully rubbing his chin. 'But, first things first. How is that soup pot, mother?'

'My goodness! I'd forgotten it!' she responded and jumped up to scamper to the kitchen where the large blackened pot bubbled on the stove.

'Hope you all like a thick broth?' she shouted back through the open doorway.

In designing the new house, Ulf had replicated the present one in Halmstad, but on a smaller scale and without the veranda. He'd been careful to make the interior as light as possible by having lots of windows downstairs, together with broad French-style doors to the rear of the lounge, and high-pitched dormer windows in each of the upstairs bedrooms.

'I'm sure Annika will be happy here,' he told Mats on the Saturday before they'd planned to move in. Father and son worked together on the finishing touches that would help to turn the box-like wooden shell into the basis of a welcoming home. Ulf imparted the know-how; Mats contributed both muscle and moral support where and when either was needed.

'Once we get the house itself shipshape,' said Mats, 'I wouldn't mind having a go at getting that long grass scythed down. We might even uncover some relics from the past.'

'Hah! We might, but I doubt it. Anything of any worth would have disappeared a long time ago, so I wouldn't be too optimistic about coming across some long-lost gold.'

'I wasn't thinking of anything intrinsically valuable, father. Just a few old tools or utensils, maybe. Things that would have no value to other folks but, for us, would be a link with the past.'

Ulf gave a short, superficial laugh, then said: 'I don't want to discourage you, of course. Getting that grass down will be a big help. We'll have to dig over a fair piece of it in any case since your mother is fair set on having a vegetable patch.'

As the two men harmonised their efforts to effect the little touches of nicety that both knew Annika would appreciate, first one, then the other, would replay in conversation parts they'd memorised from reading and re-reading Sten's diary.

'Even now, I can hardly believe it,' Mats said. 'Here we are, in a Tillkvist-built house on Tillkvist-owned land. It's all happened so quickly.'

'Yes, thanks to you. We probably wouldn't be here today if you hadn't pulled a few strings.'

'Well, that's what the Law profession is all about. You scratch someone's itch and they'll scratch yours.'

'But how, exactly, did you do it? You've never told me that.'

'Oh, we lawyers play our cards close to our chests. It's best that way. It allows us to operate what we call a *second agenda*, where we can deal with issues that are not immediately obvious from what's being discussed with a client.'

'I don't really follow, but go on.'

'Well, I suppose it won't hurt since you're my own father. Normally, I wouldn't tell even Anna the things I deal with. But, do you remember that night we spent at the little inn on the way to Ronneby? When we had to make a detour?'

'Yes.'

'It was when we were taking a drink that evening. I overheard some conversation from the two fellows who sat across from us. Careless talk. It was to do with the Unions. They were planning to stir up the workforce at a nearby foundry. I made a mental note of what they'd said, but could say nothing to you. What I did was to pass the information to a man called Soren Branting, another lawyer I'd met at the Forum. He specialises in industrial law and I felt he ought to know about it. As it happened, my tip-off was very timely and he was able to act on it to help the foundry prevent the trouble. When he asked if there was anything he could do in return, there was nothing I could think of at the time. Then, when we began to pursue the question of title to this land, I called him to ask if he knew anyone in Perstorp who might be able to help. It was he who put me in contact with the fellow in Hässleholm and... well, you know the rest.'

'That's incredible! You mean, if we hadn't had to make the detour, we mightn't have got it sorted out?'

'Oh, we'd have got it sorted out, but it could have taken many, many months.'

'What a funny world. First we have to thank the pneumonia, then we have to thank the fallen trees. I hope you also thanked your Mr Branting.'

'Sure. Once we'd got it settled, I telephoned him. Typical in these matters, all he said was: "Excellent!" and little more.'

The following week, Ulf and Annika moved into their new house and set to work to make it the more manageable home they'd hoped for.

★

Alfred Bernhard Nobel had been a great man. His development of a blasting explosive, based on nitroglycerine in a stable, dry form such that it could be handled safely and its detonation initiated from a safe distance by a small fusehead attached to long wires, had become, perhaps, his most famous invention. There seems, somehow, to be a strange dichotomy about a man who furthered the cause of agents of destruction yet, when he died in 1896 at the age of sixty-three, left a will that was to devote a major part of his estate to the furtherance of peace.

A few months after Ulf and Annika took up residence at Peterlöv, the first Nobel Prizes were awarded to those deemed to have 'conferred the greatest benefit on mankind' in the fields of physics, chemistry, medicine, literature and, in a special category, the promotion of peace. The Peace Prize was to be awarded for 'the best endeavours towards fraternity between nations, for the abolition or reduction of standing armies and for the holding and promotion of Peace Congresses'. Nobel's will was written in fewer than three hundred words, just a year before he died, and he chose to have the Peace Prize conferred by a committee appointed by the Norwegian Parliament. Little could he have realised that, so soon after his death, relations between the two partners in union, Sweden and Norway, would become tensely strained.

Nobel's childhood was marked by poverty and instability. His father's initial industrial ventures ended in bankruptcy and Alfred, with his two brothers, Robert and Ludwig, moved from one house to another before eventually settling in St Petersburg, just over the border in Russia, where he studied chemistry. Here, his father achieved greater and more sustained success, going on to become a prosperous businessman by the time Alfred was in his teens. The family's new-found wealth enabled the brilliant young chemist to tour Europe and America. He was fluent in several languages and began to turn his mind to problem solving and invention. When he was twenty, he and his parents returned to Sweden, leaving his brothers in St Petersburg to tend to the family's thriving businesses there, particularly the promising oil exploration on the Baku fields.

Alfred Nobel was not only a brilliant man, but a man born in due season. Nobel and the Industrial Age formed a marriage that allowed him to exploit the new materials and technologies to an unprecedented extent. So successful was he in his pioneering and inventiveness that he spawned around ninety manufacturing plants in more than twenty countries around the world.

In marriage within his own species, however, he was less fortunate. He courted a number of women but never married. For nearly twenty years he was in love with a young and unsophisticated Austrian girl. The two dozen years of age gap between them was not the barrier that prevented their legal union; it was more likely their differences in both social status and intellect. The affair must have torn at Nobel's heart on many an occasion for, though he loved her and she returned his affection, he could not bring himself to enter into the permanence of marriage with her.

Further disappointment awaited him as the years went by, for he built a close friendship with another Austrian woman, Baroness Bertha von Suttner. That relationship, too, remained only platonic, since the baroness was not free to marry. It seems paradoxically unjust that a man who bestowed so much on mankind was, himself, often introspective and unhappy. Some have thought that it was his personal unhappiness that spurred his philanthropic benevolence towards others for, indeed, he was not the miserly kind; tales of his gracious generosity are legion. Through his will, Alfred Nobel had ensured that the same generosity that had characterised him whilst he was alive would now do so in perpetuity.

As those first Nobel Prizes were awarded in the December of 1901, the Tillkvists looked back on what had been, for them, a memorable year. While the Christmas season gathered its customary momentum, Ulf and Annika looked forward with mixed feelings to their return to Halmstad to share the festive time with Mats and Anna in the big red house. No doubt the old place would evoke memories of past Christmas times, but it would seem strange and uncanny to have to play the part of guests in the house they themselves had created.

'Don't worry, my love, it won't be the same place without all our own things,' Ulf told his wife. 'You know what these young people are like; they'll have it all decorated in their own style.'

'Yes, but even that'll seem strange. They have their own tastes all right, but I'm not sure I'll like seeing all that they've done.'

'Annika! It's no longer *our* house. Our home is here. The old place is theirs to do with as they wish. I'm sure we'll find it's well cared for.'

'I'm sure you're right. It's just that... these modern ideas of furnishing a home, they're... different. Not quite in character with the rustic charm of an old-style Swedish house. And, after all, that's what the old place is. I can't imagine it with these modern, flashy metal ornaments and wardrobes that look no better than upended boxes.'

It had been some months since the pair had last seen the big red house. As they'd lavished their attention on the new, smaller farmstead at Peterlöv, they'd often speculated on what reciprocal acts were going on at Halmstad. What had Mats and Anna done with this? Had they changed that? The younger couple's letters were newsy, but deficient in description, Annika thought. At no time had either parent shared the thought with the other that Mats would hardly have known many other influences that would have instigated, on his part, some unsavoury revolution in interior design. And had not Anna become, more or less, an integral part of the family over these last few years? Was *she* the one who secretly held some weird ideas that had been unleashed as soon as Ulf and Annika had departed? Hardly. Intelligent though she was, she'd been no Miss Moderne. Her tastes were middle of the road in everything. She was neither plain nor boring, but neither was she outrageous. Had Ulf and Annika reasoned this way, they would have known no surprise when, on their return to Halmstad, they found the decor very much to their liking and felt immediately at one with the new arrangement of their former home.

'Good Gracious! Where did you find those antlers?' gasped Annika, peering at the twisted, bony protuberances on the headpiece that adorned the wall above the fireplace in the sitting room.

'Uh, those?' Anna responded, nodding imperceptibly in the direction of the trophy. 'Mats found them at the taxidermist's in town. They're moose. Typically Swedish, don't you think?'

'They're magnificent. And they look just right there. Needs a big room like this to show them off. Be no good in the new house. They'd crowd the wall.'

'And we bought this, too,' Anna said, pointing to a very much smaller object of the taxidermists' art. 'Do you know what it is?'

'I certainly do,' Ulf butted in, 'It's a lemming.'

'That's right. I'd never actually seen one before we found this stuffed one.'

'Well,' Ulf said, 'you're not likely to see them this far south. They live mostly in Norrland and up in Norway.' Ulf studied the stuffed specimen, turning it over in his hands. It was about the size of a small rat. 'The one you have here must have come from Norway.'

'How do you know that?'

'By his colouring. See. This black patch on the back of his neck and down to the nose. He's known as a Collared Lemming. Also his claws. See these long forked ones at the front? They're for digging through the frozen snow. This one must have been taken in winter. That's when they grow long like this.'

'Mmm, I see. And is it true they form great armies and commit mass suicide by diving into the sea?'

'Not really, as far as I know. Every so often they do congregate in large groups and some believe they follow underground lines of magnetic force so the army does seem to charge along. They'll swim small streams, but not large bodies of water, and they can cover several miles in a day. I've heard about this suicide thing, but I was told by a learned man that it's a myth. It just seems that way. In following the force lines, they go in all sorts of directions. Usually the lines follow valleys and, hence, so do the lemmings. If the valley leads to an open plain, the lemmings disperse over it. But if it leads to the sea, the poor little creatures get drowned trying to swim across what they think is just another stream. As I said before, small rivulets they can manage, but anything bigger generally tires them and, if it's at all rough, the waves will overcome them. That's how the myth got started, I imagine. Someone must have seen lots of lemmings scampering down a valley, then found hundreds of them washed up on some shoreline. It's a simple case of putting two and two together and coming up with five.'

'I'm glad you told me. Now I'll be able to impress our visitors with my immense knowledge of lemming life.'

When Christmas Eve arrived – the time when, traditionally, Swedes exchange their festive gifts – the real surprise was on Ulf and Annika.

There were quite a few parcels, large and small, tied with coloured ribbons, stacked on both sides of the large stone fireplace. Anna and Annika had festooned bunting around the room to add both colour and a fairy tale excitement to the occasion and the huge moose antlers looked down on the scene and presided silently over the present giving.

'First, we have something all the way from England,' Mats announced, placing a small package on his mother's lap. It had been unnecessary to declare that it had been sent by David and Birgitta. The weight of the package was out of proportion to its size, for the parcel wasn't very large but was quite heavy.

'Open it! Quick! Open it!' squealed Anna like a highly strung child. 'We want to see what it is. We've been trying to guess ever since it arrived.'

As the wrappings were removed and a metallic jingle emanated from the remainder, all eyes concentrated on the diminishing object in Annika's hands. Suddenly, as the final shroud was peeled away, a leather belt uncoiled, snakelike, over Annika's knee and four brass emblems attached to it became evident.

'Whatever is it supposed to be?' Ulf questioned. No one leapt to satisfy his probing.

'Look! There's a letter with it!' Anna shrieked in high-toned excitement as the note spiralled to the floor in the opposite direction to that taken by the uncoiling strap.

'It says they're "*horse brasses* which we see often in Oxford decorating the huge Shire horses that pull the brewers' carts through the town. I thought them just so English and hope you will find a suitable place to hang them in your new house." It's obviously been written by Birgitta, but signed by both. How sweet.'

The present unwrapping continued, each couple taking turns until, at length, Mats could contain himself no longer.

'There's one rather special present that's not here,' he beamed. 'It defeated our efforts to wrap it effectively so we've set it up in the drawing room. It's for both of you, from Anna and me.' Then, with a grin that contoured most of his face, he said: 'Follow me!'

Ulf and Annika looked at one another in puzzlement and meekly obeyed his instruction, following their son to the secondary lounge that he and Anna had designated 'the drawing room.' As they filed through, Anna drew up the rear.

'Imported from Germany, especially for you,' he said, waving expansively in the general direction of the stout wooden table on which stood the object of interest.

'My goodness!' gasped Annika. Almost reverently, the older couple approached the table.

'It's a phonograph,' Anna explained.

There, on the table, sat the polished wooden box that formed the base of the machine and, above it, a huge oversized trumpet-horn overshadowing all else to give the whole contraption a top-heavy look. Just behind the narrow, vortexed end of the horn, a round, grooved cylinder lay in horizontal position.

'For the moment, we have just two cylinders,' Mats advised. 'One contains selections from the famous Moore and Burgess Minstrels; the one that's on there at the moment has a variety of beautiful mazurkas. Listen!'

He cranked the mechanism to set the cylinder turning. From the bell-end of the horn came clear, deep-toned orchestral sounds that led into a traditional mazurka.

'Since you both love music, but neither of you plays an instrument, we thought this would bring the music to you. In time, we'll try to find more cylinders for it,' Anna said.

The orchestral strains filled the room and Ulf was helpless to prevent his eyes misting as he listened in wonderment to the beautiful melody and strong rhythm.

'It's the most wonderful thing I... I... don't know what to say.' He dug into his pocket to retrieve a handkerchief to dab at his eyes.

'Thank you,' Annika covered for him. 'We're deeply touched by your generosity. It truly is a most wonderful present. But,' She paused, surveying the phonograph from first one side then the other. 'How will we get it back to Peterlöv?'

Mats gave out an explosive laugh. 'How do you think we got it here in the first place? It dismantles into smaller parts. The horn—'

'Shhh!' Ulf urged, holding up a hand, 'Let the music finish. It's sacrilege to talk above it.' He stood with his head on one side, as if in deep communion with the creators of the sounds that pervaded the air around them. Obediently, all four stood in similar vein, listening to the music until the vibrating stylus reached the final groove.

'Wonderful! Truly wonderful!' cried Ulf. 'Now may we have the other one?'

Mats showed how the cylinder was replaced and the stylus re-set in position. He cranked the mechanism once more and they marvelled again at the reproduction from the big horn.

As the remaining days of the year meandered past, Ulf and Annika declared over and over to each other what an unbelievable year it had been for them. The receiving of the phonograph had been the capstone on a wall of good fortune that had attended them throughout the past twelve months.

'Just one more thing would have made it perfect,' Annika sighed.

'I know,' nodded Ulf, reading her thoughts. 'If only Birgitta had been here with us.'

'You feel that way too?'

'Oh, I would have loved it had she and David been with us, but I'm happy to know that they're both doing well.'

'Her letter says they hope to visit Sweden in the spring. It won't be so long.'

'No, and I'm sure she's missing us just as much as we miss her. I wonder what it's been like, having Christmastime in England?'

They speculated on how the festive season might be spent in other lands and concluded that a Swedish Christmas was best, with the countryside bathed in a light covering of snow to provide a picture of serene tranquillity on the outside, and the gathering of families in one big house providing a picture of love and unity on the inside.

For Mats and Anna, the year had been one not only of great moment, but one of great relief. No conscription call had come for Mats and now, he felt, his chances of being called to Army duty were fading. He could look forward to a constructive year both physically, in keeping the big red house in good repair, and mentally, as he embarked on new aspects of his profession.

*

Soren Branting's office was buzzing with activity. His new appointment to the committee drafting the constitution of the emerging Swedish Employers' Confederation had not only lengthened his working day, it was stretching to the limit his ability to cope with his new responsibilities alongside his normal duties and, with the burden of organising the annual Legal Forum only a few weeks away, would consume all of his available time. In the face of the mounting pressures Soren had known these past few weeks, Barbro Wallerius had emerged as a real champion. She dealt with inquiries, maintained the files, arranged his travel itinerary and, most importantly, kept him amply supplied with pots of tea. As she transcribed his rough notes from the many meetings he'd attended of late, she queried: 'Will there ever be an end to it?'

'Oh, we're getting there. But I'm afraid it'll get worse before it gets better. It's always the same. Eighty per cent of the work seems to be reserved for the last twenty percent of the time.'

'We're breaking new ground here though, aren't we?'

she posed. 'I mean, it's all landmark stuff. Never been done before?'

'True. We're putting the management of our big firms right up there with the Unions when it comes to dealing with workers' rights. Once this is in place, we'll have no more Nybro situations. At least that's the hope.'

The sad debacle at Utsi's Nybro plant still rankled with Soren. He knew that only the mysterious fire had prevented a confrontation that would have sorely tested the management's power over its workers and could have escalated to a scale that only intervention by troops would have restrained before the victimised workers took the law into their own hands.

Miss Wallerius shuffled a sheaf of papers as she prepared to begin another transcription. 'This Martin Erlander must be quite a character. He seems to play a prominent part in many of the meetings,' she observed.

'Erlander? Oh, he's all right. Does sterling work on the committee. He's at his best when he's trying to drive home a resolution. Gets everyone involved and holds the focus firmly on the objectives. It's just that, sometimes, he gets on his soapbox about his *eternal triangle* idea.'

'Eternal triangle? I don't recall ever seeing that minuted.'

'No, you won't see it recorded. Not yet, anyway. It's just his "in-between-times" obsession. Not part of our formal meetings. He has this idea that, once we get the SEC off the ground, there ought to be some three-way mechanism to link the Unions and Employers with the Wallenbergs. Since most of the big companies bank with them, it would make sense in some cases. Unfortunately, as far as his scheme of things would go, that could become restrictive on some of the smaller companies. He argues that, since most worker–management issues revolve around money, those that hold the purse strings ought to be part of the deal, hence his idea of forming a triumvirate.'

'The Wallenbergs are sound as bedrock, surely. You don't think it would work?'

'Yes, it would. In some cases. And especially where a company is strong and healthy. But if things ever started going badly wrong, like they did at Nybro, the Bank might not be so supportive. And, if things like that can happen at a giant concern like Utsi, who knows what might happen to a smaller outfit. Could tempt Wallenbergs into becoming predatory in order to protect themselves.'

'How do you mean, exactly?'

'If the Bank is a major stakeholder by virtue of capital lent to a company and things turn sour, the Bank may call its loans or the collateral that supports them, either bankrupting the company or cutting it back severely. At least with the SEC-Union arrangement, things could be worked out as a last-ditch effort to try to safeguard both jobs and the company's future, albeit both workers and management would have to accept some degree of sacrifice. The concern with having the Bank involved on an equal footing would be that it, too, is a profit-making business and would not be motivated by the same aims as its two partners. I just can't see that Martin's ideas will ever get off the ground.'

Barbro had listened intently to his monologic explanation. Then she said, 'You mean, the already strong companies could become stronger, but the not-so-strong ones could find their position weakened?'

'Exactly!' Soren put on a stern look and wagged his finger at his assistant. 'Miss Wallerius, you're too clever for this job. Too clever by half.'

'Then I ought to be able to make a really good pot of tea. Yes?'

'Excellent!'

Barbro had long respected Soren Branting's opinion. Most of the predictions he was brave enough to voice openly were close to the mark, too. So it was no surprise to her that, by March, things certainly had become worse. With the annual Forum just a week away, their working partnership was stretched to the limit. For the first time she could recall, Barbro witnessed her boss lose his temper. He thumped his palms on the heavy top of his desk and his eyes glared ceilingwards in fury.

'Damn those jumped-up *prima donna* upstarts!'

Barbro ran to the door and peered in, frowning, her mind unable to accept the input her ears had just transmitted. 'Mr Branting! Whatever is the matter? I've never heard you use such language!'

'I'm sorry, my dear. It's Lars Lundell, our speaker from Kristianstad. He's demanding we pay for his wife to accompany him to Ronneby because "it will inconvenience him greatly to have to return to Kristianstad to collect her as he's making an onward journey to Hamburg." I've never heard the like of it. Just who does he think he is? It's tantamount to blackmail, threatening to withdraw at this late stage unless we can accommodate Mrs Lundell.'

'Yes, I can see that something like that would upset you.'

'He's done that all right. I could well do without this kind of thing right now. But tell me, oh repository of all wisdom: what would you do?'

'Now, now, no need to flatter.'

'I'm serious!'

'I'd call his bluff.'

'Oh sure. And lose a speaker with just a week to go.'

'It's worth a try. Lean on his professional integrity.'

Soren called Lundell back, calmly telling him that he'd considered the matter carefully from a number of angles but was unable to accede to his request. The gist of Lundell's response was that he'd 'have to investigate other arrangements and therefore could not confirm his attendance at the Forum.' Two hours later, he called back to say that he was 'not at all happy about the situation but would attend only to present his paper, then take his leave.'

'Excellent!' Soren lied through his teeth. 'I knew we could rely on you to work things out. We appreciate your being able to contribute despite your busy schedule. Thank you.' Then, to Barbro, 'Once again, a triumph for the back office. I should ask your advice more often.'

She gave him a knowing wink.

*

When a change takes place in a person's life, even if it's one of considerable magnitude, it's often the agent of change rather than the change itself that has the bigger impact. Such was the case with Ulf and Annika Tillkvist.

The magnitude of the change was certainly considerable: from a large house on the edge of a busy, major town, to a much smaller house in the middle of nowhere. But they loved it. Most of all, they loved it because it represented a part of their heritage. It was that, more than anything else, that enabled them to adapt so readily to their new situation. This was a Tillkvist house on Tillkvist land, Ulf had said. In some mysterious way, that was much more important than the house, the land, the view, their neighbours – or lack of them – the difference in lifestyles; more important, even, than Ulf's business. It was their inheritance. They had a right to it. They belonged. *It* belonged... to them. Not that these other considerations were not important, but they were less so.

The house soon felt like home. The nearness of the woodland made a refreshing change from the distant seascape. There was enough land to be considered their own small kingdom. They were both fit and easily able to travel into Hässleholm or Perstorp, so the absence of immediate neighbours was not the end of the world. And, aged fifty-seven and fifty-three respectively, Ulf and Annika felt quite up to the challenge of beginning a new life.

David and Birgitta's brightly polished horse brasses hung on their strap in the entrance porch; the magnificent phonograph given them by Mats and Anna took pride of place in the main living room. In various parts of the house were the small, sentimental treasures they'd accumulated over the years. But it was none of these things that set the seal on their feeling truly at home in Peterlöv. That honour was reserved for a coincidental addition to the family.

One day, Ulf had a notion to explore the ruins of the old Lutheran Chapel. He moved some of the fallen stones and dug around at the base of the remains of the walls. As he stood in the centre of what he imagined must have been the main meeting room where the old services of worship were held, he thought he heard a faint noise coming from just behind part of the fallen structure. He walked slowly and very circumspectly in the direction from which the sound had come. Nothing stirred. Then, as he stepped quietly, almost furtively, on to the low line of stones that had once been a side wall, he saw in front of him, unmoving, a tiny kitten.

'Hello little mite. Where's your mother?' he said, crouching to peer more closely at the little creature. His eyes roved around the fallen stones and patches of weed but could detect no movement, sound or sight of any other life form. He straightened up so as to scan further afield. Again, nothing. The kitten looked up at the towering figure of Ulf and blinked a time or two, then gave out again the faint little cry that had first betrayed its presence.

'Seems like you must have strayed a long way from home little 'un. We'd best take you and give you some food.' He picked up the kitten – it was no bigger than hand-size – and strode back to the house. Annika was busily hoeing her vegetable patch when Ulf rounded the corner of the house, the kitten cradled in the crook of one arm.

'Look who's come to visit,' he called out, beckoning Annika with his free hand.

'Whatever have you got there? It's a... a cat.'

'Well, a kitten. Not very old. Eyes are open but it's very small. Found it over by the old church. No sign of its mother or any other cats there.'

'Aaah, then we'll just have to keep it.'

Ulf gave a half chuckle. 'I think we'll have to feed it before we do anything else.' They gave it some dried fish and the tiny mouth worked away at the edges of the small pieces of flaky flesh.

'I suppose we ought to give it a name,' Annika mooted. 'Any ideas?'

'Oh, I don't know what sort of name would suit this little thing. Perhaps... as it's obviously gone off exploring and found itself far from home... we should call it *Peleus*, after Sten's ship.'

'Peleus? Huh! I've never known a cat called Peleus, but I can follow your reasoning and, since it's because of Sten that...' She paused, snapped her fingers, then said: 'Yes, fine. Peleus it'll be.' And it was Peleus who set the seal on their feelings, making them feel like they had a child once more. And making the new house seem like a real family home.

The arrival of Peleus brought a new dimension to the Tillkvist household. Being very young, the kitten would seek out some cosy spot in which to curl up and then sleep for hours. Ulf and Annika appreciated the respite for, when Peleus was awake, there was no escape from the little rascal's curtailment of their freedom and depredatory invasion of their privacy. On the bed; on the floor; under the chair; across the rug. Peleus got everywhere. And in double-quick time. No low-lying ornaments were safe. Even household plants had become fair game. Buttons suspended on twine from the knobs of drawers or door handles provided only momentary satisfaction and were then abandoned. Their usefulness as playthings was limited. They didn't rattle across the floor to go crashing into the skirting or wainscoting the way small bowls did. Nor did they shred like the leaves of Annika's choicest plants. Peleus was afraid of nothing. This was one tiny kitten with a massive ego problem. Anything that came in view and was, within the realms of a cat's imagination gettable, was havable. In just three days, Peleus had gone from being a helpless outcast to become a rampaging, loveable monster. In this case, the contradiction in terms was quite apt.

'That kitten leads a charmed life,' observed Ulf, 'When it plays around, we love it; when it misbehaves, we forgive it.'

'Ja, ja. Just like we did with Mats and Birgitta, eh?'

Ulf shrugged his shoulders, as if to say: 'I suppose so.'

Ulf had set up a sawhorse outside the back door of the house, with a flat, shallow-sided tray underneath. He'd collected a few dead branches of reasonable girth and began sawing them into small lengths. Neither the quality of the wood nor consistency in the length of the off cuts mattered in the slightest; Ulf was interested only in the pile of sawdust he was creating. It had been Annika's idea and he couldn't find a strong enough argument to excuse himself from the task.

'Why don't you saw up some logs to make a nice pile of sawdust,' Annika had suggested. 'We can spread it in the bottom of an old tray. We've got to start getting Peleus house-trained.'

Once into the job, Ulf worked up some enthusiasm and a steady rhythm. Again and again the tray was filled with a grainy, crumbling pyramid of golden sawdust that Ulf tipped into a dried-out old water butt. That night, Annika returned to the role of mother once again – but this time, it was Peleus who was the subject of her lessons in 'potty training'.

At the beginning of April, a letter arrived from England. The Chettles had had to postpone their visit to Sweden until June, but then expected to stay until September. Annika was initially disappointed that their visit had been delayed, but was then elated to read that their stay would be much longer than she'd anticipated.

'Three months! Wonderful!' she exulted.

But, when the time came, it wasn't so wonderful. David and Birgitta had stopped over briefly with Mats and Anna at the big red house, then travelled down to Peterlöv.

During the first few days of their visit, the two women practically talked themselves out. But things were not as they used to be. Birgitta was now very much 'Mrs Chettle'. In the months she'd been in England, and having accompanied David on short trips to the Low Countries and Germany, she'd changed. Either travel or married life had given her a different outlook. She'd become very Conservative – with a big 'C' – and even capitalist, Annika thought. In Sweden, she'd been nominally Social Democrat although no one would have guessed, for she showed little interest in politics. Paradoxically, for one who had developed such apparent Conservative leanings, Birgitta had also become something of a Feminist, frequently extolling the efforts of Emmeline Pankhurst and her daughters.

'It's not before time women had the right to vote,' she said, 'and David agrees with me. In England, at least, Emmy Pankhurst will strive to achieve it. And, when she does, it'll be a lesson the Riksdag should take note of. She'll fight to the end, that woman, and her daughter Christabel won't be far behind her. Compared with England, Sweden has a lot to learn when it comes to political maturity.'

At one point, Annika became quite angered. On the one hand, she couldn't believe how much Birgitta had changed, generally; on the other hand, she was appalled at the seeming anti-Swedish stance her daughter was adopting.

'I can't imagine what's got into her,' Annika complained to Ulf.

'Ach, it's called "growing up". We've all been a bit rebellious in our time. It's plain she's got mixed ideas about things. Living in a different culture, seeing and hearing new things. Give her another year, or until Junior Chettle comes along, then she'll settle down.'

'I'm not so sure about that. She feels pretty strongly about this Suffragette Movement thing. Some of the women here get quite agitated, but not like that outburst we were treated to today. The way she puts it over, I wonder that she bothered to come back at all.'

'Come now, my love, you're getting yourself all steamed

up over something you can do little about. Let it take its course. Tell her you have little interest in politics if she should raise the subject again.'

Whether by design or coincidence, Birgitta hardly mentioned the matter again but, as far as Annika was concerned, the damage was done. A gulf had grown between them and she felt, right then, that things would never be quite the same again. Heritage was precious to Annika. Sweden was precious. How could her own daughter rail against it so. Hardly were there two days strung together without Birgitta, at some point in the conversation, reverting to her rallying cry of: 'In England we do...' or 'Back in Oxford we tend to...' Outwardly, Annika smiled wanly and appeared to accept it all with just an 'Uh huh'. Inwardly, she came close to boiling point on more than one occasion and secretly felt, 'Why don't you go back to England then.' That hurt her. Deeply. As she mentally formed the words, she had to fight them down. This wasn't some foreign waif talking; this was Birgitta. And, in spite of this new persona that cloaked her daughter, Annika loved her. For the time being, she would put on a brave face whenever Birgitta fell into her pro-English or anti-Swedish groove. Time would be a great healer, she felt sure. It was just a matter of coping, for now. Even the coping became harder when, perhaps unwisely in the circumstances, Annika made a light-hearted comment about when they might look forward to the announcement of a Chettle Junior on the way.

'I wouldn't start knitting or crocheting baby clothes on our behalf,' Birgitta said. 'As far as David and I are concerned, having children is very far down the agenda. There's just so much we want to contribute to society from our own lives without getting bogged down with a family.'

The undeclared truce between mother and daughter allowed a superficial calm to exist during the remaining time the Chettles spent at Peterlöv, but served to disguise the real feelings of the two women. Both had so much looked forward to the time they would spend together, but neither felt fully at ease in the other's company any more. It was as if a gift had been given, but with a piece of it missing.

David and Ulf didn't have the same problem. Many were the days they talked and walked in the woods. Sometimes, David became preoccupied with flowers or other plants he spied but, generally, the two men felt comfortable in one another's company. One day, however, Birgitta said to her husband, 'I suppose we've enjoyed seeing old places and old friends again, but I think a month would have been long enough. We must make it much shorter next time. I'll be happy to get back to Oxford, won't you?'

'Oh, to me, home's always best, but I do like to visit Sweden.'

'The countryside's pretty at this time of year but, compared with England, Sweden's a political and cultural wilderness.'

Towards the end of August, the Chettles returned to Oxford – two weeks earlier than planned.

Mats and Anna had visited Peterlöv several times during the Chettles' stay and, on the weekend following the couple's departure, they visited Ulf and Annika once more.

'How did you get along with Birgitta?' Annika asked her daughter-in-law.

Anna threw her a sideways look, then began cautiously:

'All right, I suppose. Some of the time it was just like old times again. But she does seem to harp on about life in England more than I cared to hear, to be honest.'

'Don't I know it. And did you discuss children, by any chance?'

Anna threw back her head and practically blew out a laugh. 'Oh yes. I'm afraid there won't be any, as far as Birgitta's concerned. She's very much into this political thing and seems to think that a woman's place is no longer in the home. Who on earth she mixes with to get these weird ideas I can't imagine.' When Anna thought back to the happiness and harmony evidenced at their shared wedding a little over a year ago, she found it hard to believe that, in such a short intervening time, the two couples had become so disparate in their outlook on life.

'Aha, so it wasn't only me who thought her ideas rather strange. What does Mats have to say about it?'

'Oh, he's probably more philosophical about it than I am. He says that, given time, she'll realise she's making a fool of herself and will calm down and conform to the usual way of things.'

'I'm not surprised. Ulf says the same.'

It became very quickly evident to both women that they shared the same, sad opinions of Birgitta's behaviour. But a brighter note was struck just two weeks later.

Peterlöv, being 'off the beaten track' by some way, was not served by the telephone system. So, when Mats and Anna arrived back at Ulf and Annika's home three weeks later, it was to share with them first-hand the news that they might otherwise have conveyed by means of a telephone call. For, whilst the Chettles had other ideas, Mats and Anna were now quite certain that their first child was on the way.

*

Sometimes an event occurs that, in itself, consumes no more than a moment, an hour, a day, a week. There's a build-up to it, then it happens. The results it bequeaths may be short or long lived. But the event itself is no more. It is never an evanescent thing – hanging, fading, then drifting into anonymity. It comes and it goes; like the beat of a pulse.

When the impact of such an event so affects an individual who has been intimately involved, concerned and in tune with it that, many years later, the same individual can recall, in vivid detail, his or her exact whereabouts and deportment at the time of the event – the year of its happening will ever loom large in the memory of that person as a special year. A real champion in the *Hall of Fame* for Years. For Soren Branting, 1902 was that year. When he looked back, in years to come, it wouldn't be the hours he'd spent at his desk sweating over the correct choice of word or phrase to put into the document that he'd remember. Nor would it be the long hours that he and Miss Wallerius laboured to compile the requisite number of final copies. Not even the lively debates he'd enjoyed with Martin Erlander in thrashing out the statement of objectives nor any of those very few meetings that, genuinely, could have been labelled *productive* would be first to spring to mind. No, it would be, quite simply, that the Swedish Employers' Confederation was founded. All of the endeavour that had brought it into being had been no more than a means to achieve an end; no more than could be rightfully expected of the core of professionals whose integrity and work ethic were beyond question. Now, the SEC would join the ranks of other initialled graduates like the LO, the SDP, the IOGT and many others. And it would incur the same misgivings over whether it should be abbreviated *with dots* or *without dots*. As often as not, the organisations would appear as the L.O., the S.D.P., the I.O.G.T. and, of course, the S.E.C. What really mattered, of course, was that the Employers now had a voice – a formal means of meeting the advances of the Unions to determine, unequivocally, the rights and just deserves of the workers. All the personal sacrifices and hard work had been well worth it, Soren felt.

'At last!' Barbro Wallerius shouted. 'Good for Martin Erlander! He's finally seen his imaginative seeds come to fruition!'

'Yes, good for Martin. And good for everyone else who had to do much of the fertilising,' Soren added. 'Each had a part to play. Now it's there. A real lion with real teeth. Let's hope it lives up to the expectations of all of us.'

'And what about Mr Erlander's idea of a triumvirate? Has it died a death?'

'Died and buried, I'm afraid. Funeral was last week.'

'What do you mean?'

'Wallenbergs themselves saw to that, but let's not go into all of this now. It's a time to celebrate. Will you be coming to the inaugural dinner?'

'I'm not sure, I...'

'Come! I'll take you! Most of the other men will be with their wives but, as we're each on our own, why don't we go along together?'

'That's very kind of you, Mr Branting, I really...'

'Of course you'll come. Good. After all, you never know who you might meet. Ho, ho, ho.' In keeping with his Father Christmas-like appearance, Soren had been endowed with a deep-throated laugh which, when it came out as the *ho-ho* version rather than the *ha-ha* one, complemented his lookalike image of the kindly old St Nicholas very well indeed. Any young children who, by some freak of misdirection, had wandered into the Law Office at that precise moment may well have believed they'd just stumbled on Toyland before Santa Claus had had time to don his red sleigh-riding suit. Miss Wallerius was not so impressed.

'And just who *might* I expect to meet?'

Soren shrugged his shoulders and spread his arms, palms upwards: 'I was only speculating. If you don't come, you won't know. Anyway, I take it you're coming.'

When the Friday evening set aside for the inaugural dinner arrived, Barbro Wallerius accompanied her boss and the pair sat next to one another during the meal. Soren introduced his assistant to Martin Erlander and a number of others whom she had known, only by the number of times she'd typed their names, as having said something or other at one of the lead-in meetings. It was good, she thought, to be able to put a face to these minuted names.

The following Monday morning, as Miss Wallerius received the mail and stood by the worn, wooden table that sat in the entrance hall of the Law Office, slitting open the various envelopes and packets, Soren Branting grinned at her.

'Enjoy it on Friday, then?'

'I had a wonderful time. Thank you,' she replied.

'You seemed to disappear partway through the evening. I was going to introduce you to someone but, when I turned around, you'd gone. One minute you were there, next you'd vanished. You weren't overawed by all those people or anything like that, were you?'

'No, no. I... I...' Her cheeks began to colour and, in moments, she'd taken on a full-scale blush.

'Miss Wallerius! You didn't... I mean... you weren't drunk, were you?'

'All right, all right. I give in. I knew there'd be no way I could keep a secret from *you* anyway, so you may as well get it from the horse's mouth, so to speak.'

'Yes?'

'I... I met a very fine gentleman. At the dinner. A widower.'

Soren looked at his assistant with a twinkle in his eyes. 'Aha! A widower, eh? Do I know this man?'

'I rather think you do.'

'Let me guess.' He paused, his hand over his eyes with thumb and centre finger bridging his temples. 'Yes, of course. It must be, surely. Nils Forsberg?'

She gave him a sheepish look and the slightest nod of the head.

'Excellent! Good gracious, I never thought... '

'Now don't go running off with any ideas. We just got on very well, that's all. Went for a little stroll and talked. Gave us a chance to get to know one another. But I'd prefer if you played it down. For now, anyway. If anything further develops, you'll be among the first to know. I promise.'

He said nothing by way of reply. Just lifted up his hand, with thumb and centre finger touching to form a circle, and gave his wrist the briefest flick as if unleashing a dart.

It had been a landmark year for Soren Branting. And it was turning out all right for Barbro Wallerius, too.

★

Throughout the summer of Annika Tillkvist's discontent over her daughter's untoward behaviour and disturbing views, there had coexisted one sterling covenant of loyalty that had been unwavering. Peleus, the kitten, had been her constant companion.

On that first day, when Ulf had brought the tiny creature into their home – and into their life – they'd noticed, on close examination, that 'it' was a 'he'.

'No matter,' Ulf had declared, '*Peleus* is the sort of name that would suit either gender.' And the name had stuck.

Boldly striped and with only a stump of a tail that compared well with Ulf's middle finger, size for size, the kitten might reasonably have proved to have been the runt of his litter. His head was a little ball and he was truly, in every way except for his paws, a tiny animal. Now, six months on, Peleus showed he was no runt. Well fed and much adored, he'd grown into a fine young cat. His tail, now long and well furred, often featured as the fugitive in a game of chase. Round and round, Peleus would swirl, eventually capturing his own tail and collapsing in a rolled-over heap with the black-tipped prize between his front paws.

'There's not much doubt about you,' Annika told him, softly. 'You're a real Tillkvist. And a real Swede. No fancy ways for you, young man, eh? You're a fighter and a survivor.'

'You treat that cat like he was a human,' Ulf chided her in fun.

'He is! He is!' she countered. 'And probably more reliable!'

Whenever she sat to knit, read or even peel vegetables, Peleus would make an undisguised beeline for her shoulder. It was his favourite spot and, as long as Annika remained seated, she would feel the warmth of the no-longer-so-little body against her neck.

'Funny, isn't it,' she said to Ulf one day, 'we never saw another cat around here. I've often wondered how Peleus got there.'

'We'll never know. He must have strayed from one of the farms on the far side of the old church.'

'But he was so tiny. I'd rather think he was put there by an angel, especially for me.'

'An angel?'

'Of course. Why do you think it was in the church you found him and not out in the fields or in the woods?'

Ulf smiled gently. There were a number of hypotheses he could have advanced to explain why the forlorn little kitten had sought out the shelter of the ruined chapel, but he liked Annika's imaginative justification best.

The relationship between humans and their domesticated pets is not always easy to explain. Sometimes, in the wake of tragedy or emotionally harrowing circumstances, a vacuum occurs which some fill with a deeper spiritual experience. Others fill it through a relationship with an animal that, to them, provides a comfort seldom forthcoming from another human being. In other cases, it's a subliminal feeling of control that forms the bond. A man or woman may take a dog, for example, and train it to become subservient to their own designs. Rarely would such a pet owner examine their own motives or analyse the relationship they'd developed with their pet. Certainly, few would perceive it as having anything to do with control, power, mastery or governing. Unquestionably, the bond between human and animal becomes strongest when the animal, of its own volition, returns the affection of its owner. Peleus was one of those creatures. He was loved, but was equally affectionate in return. He showed his adoration, particularly of Annika, freely and without demand. His was no 'cupboard love' deviously displayed as a means of extracting food or favour. He was, quite naturally, a loving little creature. He showed it, mostly, by licking and cuddling up in close proximity to arms, legs, neck or any other part of Annika's body that was readily accessible. But, as kitten became cat, the natural instincts of his species came to the fore. He became a hunter.

'Oh, Peleus, not again!' Annika squealed. On the doorstep lay the corpses of two mice. At least, one was a corpse. The other still twitched in its last moments of life.

'He's only doing what nature directs,' Ulf rationalised. 'So long as he doesn't bring them into the house while there's still enough life left for them to escape and make a home in our larder.'

'Exactly. It's mice today, it could be rats tomorrow. Who knows what he might catch out there. Heaven knows, the fields and woods are teeming with all sorts.'

'Yes, I can't wait till he starts on some of the bigger stuff. A nice elk will do fine.'

Annika could tell that Ulf wasn't treating this seriously. She wracked her brain to try to come up with some equitable solution, but none came to mind.

'There's no way I would want to ban him from the house,' she told Ulf. 'I love him too much for that. He's my little companion.' Then, to Peleus, 'Aren't you, my sweetie? You'll just have to learn to leave your toys outside.'

As the early harbingers of winter foretold the onset of the colder months, Annika and Peleus shared more and more frequently the well-upholstered, comfortable sofa that faced the large rear windows overlooking the sweep of fields and small copses of woodland. She looked down at the warm, furry little creature that snuggled into her lap and said: 'Oh Peleus, thank God for the angel that brought you to Peterlöv.'

*

During the second year of David Chettle's scholarship, he made frequent visits to Bavaria to conduct field research. Each time, he travelled alone, leaving Birgitta in Oxford. She felt she couldn't possibly go traipsing around Europe when the work of the Pankhursts was at such a critical stage. They would need her support, she was sure, and it would be no fine thing to be on the other side of the English Channel when a number of important issues regarding women's rights were about to coalesce, providing a springboard for the formation of a formal means of representation. This, after all, had been the crux of the movement's endeavours these past eighteen months. Since, to visit Bavaria, she considered inconvenient; to visit Sweden, she considered impossible. Instead, she wrote her parents a letter. Even though she doubted they'd understand, she wrote of her work with the Pankhursts and of the close friendship she'd developed with Christabel, Emmy Pankhurst's older daughter who was just two years younger than Birgitta. She mentioned the protest marches she and Christy had taken part in and the various towns they'd visited to hold meetings whose sole purpose, she wrote, was to evangelise 'on behalf of half of the human race'. Indeed, most of her letter reported on her activities in support of *The Cause*, and she barely mentioned David, other than to tell her folks that he was 'out of the country once again' pursuing his research. She told Ulf and Annika: 'Christy showed me this; Christy told me that; Christy introduced me to...'

'It's all about Christy, Christy, Christy and this *women's rights* nonsense,' Annika scowled. 'At least it's not an England versus Sweden epistle this time.'

She passed the letter to Ulf, who had already donned his reading spectacles in anticipation of deciphering his daughter's hand. He trawled his way through the four pages without pausing to comment then, removing his spectacles said: 'I wonder what David thinks of all this politics stuff? And all her swanning around with this Christy woman? I don't like it, Annika. It's not a healthy state of affairs for a young married woman. And what about David? He hardly rates a mention these days.' He laid his spectacles on one side and let Birgitta's note fall on to his lap then, rubbing his eyes with balled fists, he looked over at Annika and appealed: 'Where have we gone wrong, my love?'

Annika stared through the large rear windows into the undefined distance and said: 'I've been asking myself the same question. I can't imagine what's made her turn out this way. She's not at all like Mats, is she? Yet, we always tried our best to show no particular favours or preferences when they were young.'

'You're right. It's just since she went to England that she's veered off-centre. I keep hoping it's just a passing phase, but there's no sign of any slackening off in her weird ideas.'

'No, she's become so stubborn. We used to be so close, Birgitta and me, but now I feel I hardly know her any more.'

The arrival of Birgitta's letter had brought sadness; all the sadder since Ulf and Annika had been so excited to receive it that morning. In the two years that had passed since the great day of the double wedding, the Tillkvist family was no longer the close-knit, happy union it had once been.

In Halmstad, Anna had continued working in the law practice until three weeks before she was due to give birth. When her time came, the labour was short and baby Helene was routinely delivered. Mats conveyed the news by telephone to Soren Branting's colleague in Hässleholm whom he'd met at the time of the land title business. His fellow lawyer very kindly arranged for the message to be delivered to Granddad and Grandma Tillkvist at Peterlöv. Two days later, they stepped from the train at Halmstad – complete with a small wicker hamper in which they'd brought Peleus – eager to see their new grandchild.

'What a clever pair you are,' Annika enthused, 'to produce such a beautiful daughter.' Baby Helene's tiny head was well sown with tufts of golden hair and, when she was wide awake and lying peacefully, her huge eyes were like glassy saucers set in the silky folds of her pixie-like face.

'Takes more after her mother, I'd say,' suggested Ulf, 'though a bit of a Tillkvist across the mouth and chin.'

'Oh, she's a Tillkvist all right,' Anna defended, 'Likes a good feed, just like her father.'

Mats informed his mother, 'You'll be pleased to know, I'm sure, that we've named her Helene Annika.' Then he joked, 'That gives her the initials "H-A-T" so, who knows, she may break new ground and make it to the Riksdag one day.'

Annika was not amused by his reference to the old Caps and Hats. 'I should hope you'll steer her well away from that. Having one woman in the family mixed up with politics is bad enough.'

The few days the new grandparents spent at the big red house were joyful ones. When they weren't doting on baby Helene, they were toying with Peleus. The two women talked endlessly and their men took long walks in the environs of the town. They visited Ulf's old ironmongery store and chatted with the new owner. Business, he told them, was 'reasonably good'. At other times, the two men walked down to watch the ships, their father–son conversations ranging far and wide, covering myriad topics – most of which would have contributed to putting the world to rights.

When Ulf and Annika boarded the train once more and settled into their forward-facing seats, Annika remarked, 'It's been a lovely time, but isn't it strange: I feel so much closer to Anna than to Birgitta these days; but I know that, if Birgitta was here, I'd want to give her a big hug.'

'Maybe one day you shall, my love. Maybe one day.'

Peleus stirred in his box and Annika slid her hand inside the lid to stroke him gently, her eyes lost in the passing countryside but focusing on nothing in particular. Wearied from the unaccustomed exertions occasioned by the excitement of their visit, Ulf and Annika dozed fitfully from time to time, encouraged by the swaying motion of the railcar and the tuneful clink-clank of the wheels over joints in the rails. Annika's hand remained in the hamper throughout most of the journey, the warmth and steady throb of Peleus' little body inducing its own additions to her feelings of drowsy well being.

The friendship between Nils Forsberg and Barbro Wallerius progressed at a steady rate. Though not without its moments of romance, their courtship exhibited few of the highly passioned characteristics that marked a more youthful liaison. Their cosy dinners and evenings at the opera laid the foundation on which was built a superstructure of intimate lovemaking. On a number of occasions, Barbro had stayed over at the grand, former marital home still maintained by Nils.

'Will we be hearing wedding bells one of these days?' Soren teased his assistant.

'Oh, I don't think so. We're just good friends and, besides, I think we're a little too far beyond our youth for that.'

'Ho-ho-ho! "The older the fiddle, the finer the tune," my old mother used to say.'

'She may well have, but doesn't the Good Book say "don't put new wine in old wineskins" or something along those lines?'

Soren merely shook his head, eyes closed, and muttered: 'Too clever. Too clever by half.' When he opened his eyes, Barbro had already retreated to seek refuge in the confines of her own office.

With the launching of the SEC the previous year, Soren had returned to less elevated work that was, often, bordering on the level of humdrum. Under considerably less pressure, and feeling that his contribution to the formation of the Employers' Confederation represented the pinnacle of his professional life, he found more time to resurrect his one-time favourite pastime... fishing. He seldom landed a catch that was worth a brag, but the solitude of unfrequented river banks and the relaxed nature of his hobby gave ease to mind and body in a way that no other could. In the twilight of his career, he wondered if, perhaps, it would not be too much longer before he felt it time to retire altogether from the profession. He reached his decision quite unexpectedly. Having banished from his mind any notion that, one day, there would come the inevitable culmination of the strong feelings that had grown between his Miss Wallerius and Nils, he was totally unprepared for her announcement that they had agreed, after all, to formalise their bond.

That summer, 1903, Barbro Wallerius became Mrs Forsberg. That summer, too, Soren Branting invited a young man who'd greatly impressed him, Mats Tillkvist, to consider taking on the affairs of a number of his clients of long standing.

Perhaps one day, he thought, he'd land a catch that was worth a brag.

*

Possibly rejuvenated by their celebrations of the birth of Helene, or maybe due in no small way to the pleasant summer weather they were enjoying, Ulf and Annika set about extending what had been regarded, up until now, as 'the vegetable patch'. Ulf ploughed a large field and, together, they sowed a hectare of winter wheat and prepared a further half hectare of ground for planting beet.

'If we keep on like this,' remarked Ulf, 'we'll be bordering on becoming farmers.'

'And what else would we do with the land anyway? It's ours, so we may as well make good use of it,' Annika commented.

Ulf no longer worked, in the normally accepted sense. He tinkered with the repair and re-sharpening of grass-cutting machines and various other implements for a few kronor income but, by and large, he had ample time on his hands. Working on the land was a novelty. And he was beginning to enjoy it.

Over the past few months, Mats had managed to find a

small number of additional music cylinders for the phonograph and, in the fine, balmy evenings, the couple listened to the reproduction of some of the world's finest music – an experience they thought remarkable. When they allowed themselves to become locked into the insular envelope of their own little world like this, the Tillkvists felt happier than they'd been for many years.

Peleus had developed a human time clock. He roamed freely for most of the day, catching mice and voles, but faithfully returned each day before nightfall to spend the night indoors. Occasionally, he would appear during the day, bringing with him his latest victim. His catch would still be full of life and he would toy with it for some time, letting it loose then recapturing it, before the hapless creature became yet another morsel in his free-range diet. The sight never pleased Annika, but she'd learned to accept that it was nature's way of control in the microcosmic food chain that ended with Peleus. God forbid, she thought, that anything bigger would continue the chain. Luckily, for the Tillkvists and for Peleus, that was not to be.

Only when they talked of their own offspring was their bubble of happiness deflated. They were justly proud of the great strides Mats had made in his profession. And they adored Anna and baby Helene. It was whenever they thought and talked of Birgitta that they felt a sadness. Her latest letter once again eulogised on the work of *The Cause* and declared, triumphantly, that, 'We've cleared our first hurdle. Now we'll be a force to be reckoned with. Emmy has inaugurated the *Women's Social and Political Union* and, from here on in, the only way is up. We'll show the way to the rest of the world's women.'

'She's becoming blinded to life outside this damn

movement,' Ulf said, the tone of his voice betraying the bitterness he felt. 'She seems to think England is the only country in the world where women are seeking a fairer deal from their government. Look at what that Bremer woman got started here. I shouldn't be surprised if our Swedish women are given the vote before the English. She's just besotted with Oxford and London and, it seems, everything that's English. I can't believe David just stands aside and lets her spend all this time campaigning and travelling around with these Pankhurst women. I know Mats wouldn't stand for it.'

'Yes, I must say, David's turned out to be something of a disappointment. Even so, I suspect that, if he'd stayed on in Sweden, this would never have happened. Anna, for one, would have put Birgitta right on a few things.'

'Maybe so, maybe so. I'm coming to the conclusion there's only one thing we can do.'

'And that's...?'

'Go to England. The two of us. Find her and try to talk some sense into her.'

'Ulf! You're dreaming! How could we ever afford the passage?'

'I don't know. Not at this moment. But we should talk to Mats. Maybe he would...'

'Unthinkable! Go cap in hand to borrow money at our age?'

'Not exactly *borrow*.'

'Then what?'

'Well, don't forget, we let him have the house at a very good price. He might consider...'

'No, Ulf! That's almost like blackmail.'

'Bah! If he hadn't already got the house, then maybe.

And I wouldn't consider it. But we're talking about his own sister. His own flesh and blood. Besides, he once told me how he managed to get the title to this place sorted out so quickly. Something about "I'll scratch your itch and you scratch mine" or, in other words, co-operating with those who help you out when you need it most.'

Annika's defences weakened as she began to consider the gravity of the situation and the mess she felt Birgitta had got herself into.

When Mats and Anna had listened to all that the older folks had had to say, they nodded to one another and, far from showing any reluctance, Mats positively encouraged his parents to carry out their wishes. He generously offered to underwrite their expenses and look after Peleus while they were gone, but warned them, 'Birgitta can be a stubborn little so 'n' so when she feels like it. So, don't be surprised if she's not at all receptive. We didn't like to say so at the time but, when she and David were last here, we noticed how hardened she'd become. Not at all like she was when we were growing up together. She's changed. Don't ask me why. I have no answers. But she's changed in lots of ways.'

'That's right,' interrupted Anna, 'We couldn't believe she was the same person who'd shared in our wedding. She's lost her old warmth and seems to like to play her cards close to her chest these days. When she was here, I tried to share close things with her. You know, the way we used to before we were married. It just didn't work. She wouldn't reciprocate and I gave up. It won't be easy for you over there. She's surrounded herself with this hard political shell and her closest friends don't sound to be our kind of people at all.'

'Don't take all of this the wrong way,' Mats interposed. 'We're right behind what you're trying to do. All we're saying is that it won't be an easy matter talking her into turning her back on this Women's Rights thing.'

'Should we talk to David, do you think?' asked Annika.

'David!' Mats almost spat the name out. 'He's a Botanist! Lives in his own little world with plants and things. I doubt he even realises the half of what Birgitta gets up to.'

When Ulf and Annika arrived in Oxford, neither David nor Birgitta could be found. A neighbour informed them that David was away on a field trip and Birgitta was in London. She was due to return in two days' time.

The couple took lodgings nearby and waited. Late in the afternoon on the second day, Birgitta returned to the small house to find her parents awaiting her arrival. At first, the Tillkvists hardly recognised their daughter. She'd lost a great deal of weight and her face appeared drawn and scrawny. Her once beautiful blonde hair hung in long, lank strands. Birgitta treated them almost casually, as if they were near neighbours she hadn't seen for a few days. But she welcomed them inside the tiny terraced house that was her home. Posters, proclaiming the doctrines of the Women's Rights Movement and announcing forthcoming marches, were hung at intervals on a number of the walls. A rolled wad of hand tracts gospelling the same subject lay on the table.

'What a pity David's not here. He won't be back for another two weeks,' Birgitta informed them. 'You've come at a bad time. I'll be here tomorrow, but then I must go to Northampton. We're holding a march there.'

Showing no emotion of disappointment, Ulf played

down the affront. 'That's fine. Would you mind if we came with you? We'd like to see for ourselves what your cause is all about.'

'Why... yes... if you really want to. But I'll be involved with the marchers for most of the day. You might—'

'We understand that,' Ulf interrupted. 'But, in your letters, you talk so much about it. We're interested. It would mean more, perhaps, if we saw it for ourselves.'

Ulf had intended to disarm his daughter to make her feel unthreatened by their impromptu visit. Perhaps, he reasoned, she'll be more open to talking about it if we don't take an offensive stance from the start. It was a mistake.

If the Tillkvists were surprised by the large number of women who assembled to take part in the procession, they were more surprised by the multitude of authority-challenging placards the women carried and, not least, by their strange attire. Many wore ropes and chains around their wrists and upper arms. Some trailed chains from their ankles, depicting the bondage they felt had been placed unfairly upon them by the male dominance of official offices and their lack of voting privileges. But it was the loud-mouthed, coarse language that offended the Tillkvists' sense of propriety most of all. When some of the women began to chant in unison, their faces contorted with a vehemence that aligned them more with Amazonian warriors than with the graces one expected of women, Ulf and Annika felt sickened to think that Birgitta was a part and parcel of this rebel-rousing they were witnessing.

Mats and Anna had been right. In none of the lengthy talks her parents had with her did Birgitta yield an inch of her ground. She was more than stubborn; she was obsessed with what she claimed to be *her calling*.

Two days after the Northampton march, the Tillkvists

began their homeward journey. Bravely and stalwartly, Annika held back her tears in her daughter's presence. Only when the couple had reached the sanctuary of the station was all inhibition abandoned and Annika's tears flooded on to her husband's shoulder. Saddened; almost heartbroken with despair, they returned to Sweden. Birgitta, they felt, was beyond redemption. When they kissed her goodbye, Birgitta could not have failed to notice the hollow sadness in her parents' eyes. But she gave no clue to any recognition of their feelings for her. A powerful opium had imprisoned her, controlling her emotions... and her life.

The homecoming was an occasion of mixed feelings. The far-travelled Tillkvists were happy to see Mats and Anna again. Baby Helene seemed to have grown enormously and Peleus had led his temporary carers a merry dance with his lively antics but, when Annika related the substance of their talks with Birgitta, a cloud of gloom descended on the gathering to dilute their joy of reunion.

'It was just as you said,' Annika recalled. 'She's become very hardened and is so blinded to anything outside of this... this cult. Make no mistake; that's what it amounts to. She's been sucked into this thing and nothing else matters. David was somewhere in Germany and we didn't see him at all. I shouldn't be surprised if their marriage falls apart. They're just two people travelling on entirely different paths.'

'Yes, it's a sad affair,' concluded Mats. 'We just have to hope and pray that, one day, she'll see the folly of it all.'

'We're so glad we've got you two. You're both very special to Ulf and me.'

*

The progress wrought by the continuing momentum of the

Industrial Age had changed Sweden. In neighbouring Norway, the change had been even greater and the spiralling increase in prosperity had brought a new awareness of national identity to the Norwegians. The King of Sweden, Oscar the Second, claimed the allegiance of his neighbours through the two countries' union, but the bond that cemented their relations was beginning to weaken. With increasing fervour, the people of Norway pressed for their country's independence and, in 1905, the old union was dissolved. Oscar relinquished his dual regency and Norway became an independent country.

Twentieth Century development and exploitation of the inventiveness of the last decades of the previous century led to a greatly enhanced lifestyle among the Swedes, at least in the southern part of the country. Electrification of the towns had given people 'glow bulbs' to light their homes and the sight of 'horseless carriages' on the streets of Stockholm, Göteborg and Malmö, whilst by no means commonplace, was no longer the novelty it had been just a few years before. Even the smaller towns had their share of the new *motors*. Mechanisation had changed work patterns in industry and people now dreamed of a time when man might possibly join the birds of the air in vehicles that could rise above the earth. In America, Orville and Wilbur Wright had already taken a 'heavier-than-air' machine into the skies. Great steamships now plied the oceans, carrying Swedish goods and produce to play their part on a world stage. Those same ships returned from foreign ports laden with goods that brought a new dimension to the lifestyle of many Swedish homes.

In back-of-beyond Peterlöv, the great national and international happenings had little impact. The Tillkvist homestead was slowly transforming to become the Tillkvist

Farm. Ulf and Annika were emerging from the almost leisurely lull they had known when they first moved south from Halmstad to find themselves working as hard as ever, sometimes harder, as the land drew them closer to releasing its potential and they rose to the challenge of returning it to its productive origins of times past.

'We'll need to think of building a barn,' Ulf announced one day. 'Our grain yields are better this year.'

'Yes, the beets are better, too,' added Annika. 'Fewer deformities and no sign of any yellows. We should be able to get a contract for this lot.'

'We could do with some help, too. It's becoming more than I can manage. If we can find a trustworthy worker it'll make life much easier. The seasonal helpers are fine, but they're not around the rest of the time. Let's face it, we're not getting any younger. One day, when Mats inherits this place, he'll need some experienced help to keep it running.'

'If he wants to. I can't see Mats and Anna ever doing what we're doing. They're not that way inclined.'

'Perhaps not. They may wish to sell off some of the land, or lease it. In any case, that'll not be for a while yet, we hope.'

Annika laughed at his optimism. 'All right,' she said, 'Best put the word around that we're looking for a good labourer. And, while you're at it, don't you think it's about time we put a proper sign at the bottom of the lane?'

'I was thinking the same thing just the other day. What shall we call the place? I don't think *Tilderkvist Farm* has much meaning anymore.'

'No. But we don't want anything too pretentious. Why not just *Tillkvist Farm*?'

Ulf shrugged his shoulders. 'Fine. I'll find a good piece of planking and make the sign. *Tillkvist Farm* it'll be.' They smiled at one another and Annika suggested it was time for another cup of tea.

With some justification, the Tillkvist family might have regarded the year 1906 as a year of mixed blessings: a year when, like a partly read book, one chapter ended and another began.

In February, Ulf and Annika received a letter from David Chettle. It was short and to the point. One day, he wrote, he'd returned to Oxford from a visit to Gloucester only to find a scribbled note telling him that Birgitta had left him. Her note contained no clue as to where she'd gone, nor did it elaborate on any explanation for her decision other than to say, 'It seems we are no longer fitted for one another.' She never returned to Halmstad, nor did any of her folks ever discover her whereabouts.

In March, Mats formed his own law practice, building on the fine reputation he had established. He was particularly gratified that, almost without exception, all of his clients transferred their allegiance to the new business.

In June, Anna gave birth to her second child. Little Helene, now three years old, was happy that, 'God had sent her a baby brother.' They named him Tomas, after the father of the old sea captain, Sten.

Ulf, who'd celebrated his sixtieth birthday the previous November, was overjoyed that his new grandchild was a boy. 'At least one more generation of Tillkvists can be assured,' he declared.

In September the new barn was completed and put immediately to use. Henrik Holmgren, Ulf's labourer, had worked at the farm for almost exactly a year. He was proving to be as hard-working and trustworthy as Ulf and Annika could have wished. They were confident that they'd found the right man to help build on the simple foundations they'd laid. Where, only a few years ago, wilderness weeds had obliterated the once productive fields, there was now new growth. Between them, Ulf and Annika had created what they themselves called 'a gem of a place'. The entrance to their little paradise, in what was once Peterlöv village, was marked by a simple sign painted on stout, neatly sawn planking. It read: Tillkvist Farm.

Part Seven
The Reconciliations

For Mats and Mia

A fool sees not the same tree that a wise man sees.
                                William Blake

The telephone rang three times. Loudly. Deafeningly loudly, it seemed to me, as the strident sound reverberated around the small motel bedroom.

'Hello, Walt Kirkland.'

'Ah, Doctor Walt, it's Berthe.'

I'd become used to the form of address for, like her husband, Berthe Tillkvist always referred to me as 'Doctor Walt.'

'Is everything all right?' I asked, taken a little by surprise; it was only five minutes short of eight o'clock on Monday morning.

'Yes, all right. Only it's Bertil; he asks if you can come to the farm today?'

'Of course. After breakfast? About nine thirty? Fine, I'll order a taxi for then. Bye bye.'

During these past few weeks, since Bertil had been discharged from hospital, I'd felt it best to keep a low profile as far as the Tillkvist household was concerned. It had been a traumatic time for all concerned and I'd busied myself digging into some research on the family's background, following the few clues Berthe had given me.

As the cab driver swung his big Saab into the Tillkvists' driveway, I noticed that no other cars were parked alongside the house.

'Ah, Doctor Walt, come right in,' Berthe beamed from the doorway as she characteristically wiped her hands on her apron. Bertil was slumped in a well-padded armchair and straightened into an upright position as I entered the now familiar lounge. We greeted one another and swapped comments on his well being.

'Berthe has told me you are making a research about our family, huh?'

'That's right,' I answered, cautiously. 'Is there some problem?'

'About what you are doing? No, no. It's very good that you should find out about our history and our heritage. That's why I wanted to talk to you now. For the moment, it's not about the old gun.'

I was conscious that I was throwing him a quizzical look.

'I have something to show you. It has been what you English call a "prize possession" I think. More important to me even than the gun.' He reached under a cushion by his side and withdrew what appeared to be an old book. 'Here is written about our family since many years. It is from my ancestor, Sten, who was captain of his own ship. He was the son of Tomas, the same one who made the rifle.' With a proud glint in his eyes, he handed me the ancient diary. 'It is in the Swedish, of course, but you can have it translated. It tells many things about us Tillkvists that you need to know.'

Slowly and carefully, I thumbed through several pages. The writing was plain enough but none of it was understandable to me. Even so, I realised that what I was holding was a family treasure; as Bertil had put it: a 'prized possession'. I studied it, silently, for some moments and then, as if to authenticate the value of Sten's diary, Bertil added, 'It's almost as old as the gun.'

'It's incredible. I just wish I could read Swedish.'

'No matter. Someone will translate for you. I'm giving it to you for looking after, Doctor Walt. I trust you with it.'

'But Mr Tillkvist... it's... no! I can't take it. It's your family's heirloom. Surely you wouldn't want to part with it. Wouldn't Mats...'

That did it. I'd put my foot right in it. The old man's face pulled into a stern look that turned his facial lines into deep crevasses of contorted displeasure. I'd obviously said entirely the wrong thing.

'Not Mats! He will never have it! He is my boy and I suppose I must love him, but he has let me down. He has let all the Tillkvists down. I have tried and Berthe has tried, but he won't listen. He wants only that we should sell this land and give him a share of the money. Then what? Will he look after us? No! He is selfish only for money. Berthe and me, we wanted only that he should find a good girl and marry. He needs to marry. And have a son, who will go on with the Tillkvist name.'

I was beginning to make sense of his attitude towards Mats and Mia. If things stayed as they were, in one more generation the family name would disappear. That's what irked him. All the wonderful heritage that was no doubt spelt out in Sten's diary would fizzle into nothingness.

'And this land,' he went on, 'is Tillkvist land. We cannot just sell it as he says. Our spirit is here. Our blood is here. What is money against these things?' He was fairly tensed up now and his clenched fists shook as he pressed his arms close to his side and down against his thighs.

'I'm sorry, Mr Tillkvist. I didn't realise...' I was struggling to find a satisfactory way out of the mess I'd got myself into. But he was riled, and there seemed no stopping him. His tirade against his son continued.

'It's the same with the gun. It should go to Mats, but I know he'll only sell it. Doctor Walt, I don't know what is best to do.'

He winced and held his side. The painkillers that made what was left of his life bearable for him were obviously not coping with the peak of added stress brought on by his strongly vented feelings. Seeing his sudden discomfort brought me back to earth. And to the realisation that poor old Bertil had already used up more than half of the time the doctors in Malmö had given him in their prognosis. I was witnessing, perhaps, not only the demise of this once stalwart Skånian farmer, but of a family with a tremendous heritage.

'Is there anything I can do to help?' I ventured.

'Not for the moment, Doctor Walt. Perhaps I have said too much already.' He smiled thinly and his eyelids dropped involuntarily to half mast. I suggested he take a short nap and excused myself, taking the old diary with me to join Berthe in the kitchen.

'I'm sorry, Doctor Walt. He gets quite upset sometimes,' Berthe said defensively, keeping her voice just above a whisper.

'I understand. Seems he has some justification though. I gather he doesn't care too much for Mia.'

She flashed her eyes ceiling-wards. 'Nor do I. She's no good, that girl.'

It was not for me to judge but I had my own misgivings about Mia, conjured from the few times we'd met when Bertil had been in hospital. She was petite, with a cute, almost impish, pale-complexioned face set below a mop of thick, witch-black hair that was severely chiselled at the back and, at the front, completely masked her forehead, ending in a sweep that was barely above her eyes. Each time I met her, her eyes were ringed with a heavy liner and she sported an almost black lipstick. Her clothes, too, were almost always black and she often wore a broad, studded belt around her ultra-slim waist. I judged her to be in her mid-twenties, but her appearance suggested that she was going on seventeen. It wasn't her looks that had made me feel uneasy in her company; it was more to do with her manner. And her attitude. When she and Mats were together, it was clearly she who 'wore the trousers' and was the dominant partner in their relationship. I'd wondered then if, perhaps, most of Mats' ambitious ideas had not been seeded by Mia. Mats had told me they had no intention of having children; just looking at Mia, I couldn't imagine her as a mother.

'They've been together for quite a while, haven't they? Why don't they just get married?'

'Huh. They don't see the need. It's not the thing to do anymore, they say. But maybe it's for the best; they think only of themselves. Mia is not good for Mats; she brings only bad things for him. Drugs... and her other business.'

'I see.' I didn't see at all. Perhaps naively, I'd taken her *other business* to mean their plans for setting up a marketing enterprise. It would be another two weeks before I found out what Berthe had really meant.

Our low-volume conversation was interrupted by a sharp shout from Bertil.

'Berthe! My pills! I need my pills!'

Instantly, Berthe rose from the kitchen bench; she poured a glass of water and hurried to administer Bertil's pills. I felt a little awkward, almost as if I was intruding in whatever precious time was left for the pair to enjoy together. After ensuring that Bertil was all right, I suggested that it might be best if I returned next day. On my insistence, Berthe ordered me a taxi.

'Please, I don't feel that I should take the old diary with me. Perhaps another time.' I handed it to Berthe and she just nodded. By the time the taxi arrived, Bertil had fallen into a deep sleep.

When I arrived back at the motel in Hässleholm, the receptionist informed me that Mats Tillkvist had telephoned and asked if I'd return his call. He would be in the apartment in Hälsingborg all afternoon, he'd told the receptionist. I already had his number.

'Hei, Doctor Kirkland, thank you for calling,' Mats said when I phoned him. 'Mia and me, we would like to talk to you. May we meet you this evening?' I had no good reason to object.

Mats and Mia arrived promptly at seven thirty as arranged. On their suggestion, we headed for a quiet bar on the other side of town. Our conversation during the few minutes in the car between motel and bar was confined to superficial small talk but, once ensconced in a corner of the low-lit bar, our round of drinks before us on a small, round beaten-copper table, Mats wasted no time in beating around any bushes. He got straight to the point.

'What we want to talk to you about is the old gun. We've been asking around various antique dealers and so on, trying to get a figure on its real worth. Without seeing it, and going just on my description of it, the best price we've been quoted so far is only thirty thousand SEK. Now, we know—'

'Just a minute! I don't understand! What are you trying to do? As far as I'm aware, your father has no intention of selling it.'

'That's probably true. But he won't be around for ever and we have to—'

'Whoa! You can count me out. I'm not in the business of

getting involved in a family's affairs. Besides, aren't you being just a bit presumptuous?'

'Listen, we have to be realistic. Father will not live much longer. When he's gone, mother will not be able to stay on at the farm forever. It'll have to be sold. And she has no interest in the old gun, either, so that will have to be sold. It's only a matter of time.'

'You seem to have it all worked out, eh? Cut and dried. It seems you just can't get your father into his grave quick enough.'

'We're not saying that,' Mia cut in. 'But Mats is right. We have to be realistic. *We* have no interest in the farm and Berthe could live in Ystad with Britt. Her share of the money will be enough to keep her.'

'And the gun,' Mats continued, 'could be sold now. At least then we'd have some money to invest in something useful. It could take months before the farm is sold.'

I was speechless. I found the couple's attitude despicable and wanted to hear no more of it. I'd tried to steer clear of any involvement in the matter but, heck, I *was* involved. I had no qualification to support my role as 'moral policeman' in all of this but I couldn't just sit back passively and let these two ride rough-shod over Bertil and Berthe.

'Okay, I've heard what you have to say,' I began. 'But I don't think things are as clear-cut as you seem to think. I have no intention of helping you find a buyer for the gun because, right now, it's not yours to sell. I suggest you discuss that with your father, Mats. As for your other ideas, I think your mother might want to have some say in the matter.'

They looked at one another and Mats merely shrugged his shoulders as I drained the last of my beer.

'Thank you for the drink. Can you take me back now?'

We returned to the motel, the journey marked by a stony silence that was broken only when I bade the couple goodnight.

I felt awful. Did I dream the whole conversation or had it actually taken place? It was as if I'd been insulted. Or betrayed. Or something. Whatever it was, I just couldn't get to sleep. Time and again, I replayed the scene in the bar. Why hadn't I said more? Why hadn't I taken the bull by the horns and told them both, in no uncertain terms, how selfish and callous they were. I must have led a sheltered life, for I'd never come across two human beings so consumed with avarice.

The following morning, I had to exert a resolute act of will to get out of bed. My broken sleep left me feeling drained. But I had to get back to the farm; I'd promised the Tillkvists I'd be there.

Bertil was in better spirits and very talkative. I decided to ask him about the old gun.

'Mr Tillkvist, what do you intend to do with the rifle? I think I have enough to be able to write the article for my publishers now.'

He didn't reply immediately, but sat back in the armchair and pursed his lips while digging out his little snuffbox. He scraped a plug of snuff from the tin and wedged it under his top lip. When he began to speak, his words were slow and measured.

'It is more than just an old gun. It is a memory of the old Tillkvists. So it must stay.' He sighed, audibly, and worked his gums on the snuff. 'When I am gone, Doctor Walt, the Tillkvists are gone. Here, in Sweden, there are no more. Only in America. And those, we have lost touch with. Maybe, with your research, you can find them one day. For now, the gun should go to a museum or someplace that will keep it safe.' Then, steeling himself, he said vehemently, 'It must not go to Mats! I have told that to Berthe, now I tell it to you. Not to Mats!'

In a way, I was glad that he felt so strongly about it and wondered if he knew of his son's scheming. It was then that I felt I ought to tell him about the things Kerstin Berg and I had found out at Kristianstad, at the home of Siegfried Wersel.

'Did you know that your old rifle over there is just one of six? All made by Tomas.'

'Six? What are you saying?'

'It's true. I have seen them myself. In a private collection in Kristianstad. Each one has Tomas's mark and the Greek letters next to it.' I explained the whole thing in detail.

'And this is the missing one?'

'It seems so.' I avoided mentioning the inscription on the card I'd seen at Siegfried's. *Tilderkvist* or *Tillkvist*: we'd been through all that before. Somehow, it didn't matter anymore.

He rubbed his eyes and sat forward in the chair. 'Can we go there? To see the Tomas guns?'

I was taken aback. It was something I hadn't expected.

'It might be possible. I'll talk to Kerstin to see what we can arrange. I'll call Mrs Tillkvist on the phone once I've spoken to Kerstin.'

It was Friday evening before I managed to get hold of the elusive Miss Berg. I'd had no response from her mobile phone, but now she was back in her apartment in Lund. Almost in diary-fashion, I brought her up to date with the happenings of the past week.

'I don't imagine it should present a major problem,' she replied, when I told her about Bertil's request. 'It's more likely to be just a case of catching Siegfried Wersel and agreeing to some convenient time. But are you sure Bertil will stand the ride over there?'

'Oh, I should think so. He seems to tire quite easily but, most of the time, he's okay.'

'Fine. Just leave it to me; I'll see what I can arrange.'

'There's just one thing. Assuming Siegfried will see us again, would you ask him if he would remove the inscription card before we arrive. Just temporarily. You know, the one that refers to Tomas Tilderkvist. I'm sure it would upset Bertil. In any case, perhaps we ought to try to persuade our Mr Wersel to change it to *Tillkvist* – permanently.'

'Good point. I'll see what I can do.'

'Thank you, Kerstin. You're a star. By the way, how's the bridge project going?'

'Oh, they're having a few problems but, from my point of view, it's going well. I'll tell you all about it sometime. Perhaps after we've been to Kristianstad, if that works out.'

It did work out. Siegfried Wersel was not unhappy about our making another visit to view his collection and Kerstin agreed on Sunday afternoon as the best time for all concerned.

A surprise awaited Mr Wersel. A surprise that was going to make him very excited, for Bertil insisted on taking along the *pi delta* gun – 'to check that these others really are authentic.' In the event, no bets were placed. But it was difficult to judge who showed the greater excitement: Siegfried or Bertil. When the antique weapons were placed side by side, both men exhibited eyes like the proverbial organ-stops, set in faces that were, in each case, a sea of glee. They gabbled away in very animated Swedish and became lost, for some moments, in another world. We spent close on an hour in the Wersel's basement. When it came time to leave, Bertil stood for a moment looking at the line-up of Tomas's six flintlocks before he reached forward to retrieve his own and return it to its coverslip.

'Seems a shame to take it away,' he said, with a half smile.

'I was thinking the same,' Siegfried countered. 'Perhaps, if the price was right?' He cocked an eyebrow towards Bertil, but the old man let the moment pass unacknowledged.

As we made our way back to the car, Siegfried tried one more olive branch. 'I'm so happy to know about the rifle. I'd never realised the significance of the Greek letters before, so I never thought there might be another one around. I'd like to keep in touch, Mr Tillkvist. Perhaps, one day; who knows.' As the two men shook hands, little did Siegfried realise that his visitor would very soon be living on 'borrowed time'.

*

Kerstin was in a chirpy mood and I began to realise how much I'd missed her company over this past two weeks.

'Hei, I promised to tell you about the latest developments with the bridge. Would you like to go for a meal? My treat?'

'That sounds great. But *I'll* treat *you*.'

'No way. I got in first with the invite.'

'Yes, but... oh, well... go on, then. Nowhere too expensive. I'd be happy to be your chaperone.'

'Oooh, that sounds *awfully* English.' She made a pathetic attempt at taking off an English accent that set us both laughing. Yes, it was good to have Kerstin around again. I knew our meal together would be in stark contrast to my last outing... with Mats and Mia. Her choice of dining establishment was little more than five minutes away. Its name-board proclaimed it simply as *Mo-Jo*. It didn't look expensive.

'So! What've you been up to this past two weeks?' I asked.

'Oh, it's been hectic. I'm preparing a series of feature articles to promote the concept of the Øresund Region. Basically, looking at it from a number of different points of view – like the cultural side, business, transportation, leisure activities, the environment and, of course, the effect on Stockholm. I've been talking to—'

'Whoa! Hold on! You've lost me already. Are we both talking about the same thing? The bridge?'

'Uh huh, the bridge, of course. But there's much more to it than that. The bridge-tunnel is important in itself, of course, but that's really just the catalyst. It's the final product that's *really* important: the new region.'

'I'm sorry, I still don't follow.'

'Okay, let me explain. As we discussed once before, the bridge-tunnel link across the Øresund will drastically cut the journey time between Copenhagen and Malmö, right?'

'Right.'

'But that's not the end of it. Just imagine: apart from the two big cities, other places on both sides of The Sound such as Hälsingborg, Landskrona, Lund, Elsinore, Hillerod and Roskilde, for instance, will all be pooled together. I mean p-o-o-l-e-d, not p-u-l-l-e-d. The new Øresund Region – that's what everyone's calling it – will have as big a population as many of today's major European cities. And there's a great fear in some quarters that it might become more influential than Stockholm. The potential is enormous.'

'My goodness, I hadn't thought of it like that.'

'Oh, yeah. It's a far-reaching concept.'

'But, those various towns you mentioned. Aren't they already closely linked on their respective sides of The Sound?'

'Not in the way they will be in a few years' time. The project is not just for the cross-water link, it includes new town and city bypasses, tunnels and rail links. That's what'll really bring the places together. And, of course, it'll form a gateway into mainland Europe. Make no mistake, the twenty-first century will see a new Scandinavia.'

'And all this will be in place by the year 2000?'

'Well, that's the aim of the Øresund Consortium but, you know what it's like, these big projects usually overrun.'

'Don't I know it. Like the Channel Tunnel, I suppose.'

'Hopefully not that bad. The Consortium is a real multinational affair. They've drawn from the best consultants and contractors in France, Holland and England as well as from Sweden and Denmark. But it's no mean feat, that's for sure.'

'Sounds fascinating.'

'Oh, it is. The landworks on the Danish side are already quite advanced, near the airport at Kastrup.' She lit up a Marlboro and blew out a streamer of smoke, then continued: 'I've met so many top professional guys while doing all these interviews to collect data for my articles. And that includes some of the high-flying consultants. They have a beautiful scale model of the whole bridge-tunnel link at the Consortium's offices. Would you like to see it sometime?'

'Sure. Can you arrange that?'

'Possibly. I'll put out some feelers and see if there's a chance.'

The conversation went on for over an hour. I couldn't truthfully say *our* conversation – it was mostly Kerstin doing the talking; I just listened, fascinated. Eventually, my turn came, and I was able to share my distaste at what I'd been subjected to from Mats Tillkvist and his girlfriend.

'Yeuk! What a pair.'

'Yes, it's funny how things have turned out. When I think back to that day when you first took me out to the farm, it was Mats I liked. Old Bertil seemed like a real old grump. Now, the old man treats me like his closest buddy and I find myself only just able to tolerate Mats.'

'Weird, isn't it? Must be one of the most unusual commissions you've ever had, huh?'

'Certainly is.'

'Will you be returning to England quite soon?'

'That's a strange thing, too. I've more or less got what I came for. And a lot more, besides. But, somehow, I don't feel in any hurry to leave right now. I've become so involved with these folks and I've developed a real soft spot for Bertil and Berthe. At the same time, I've heard nothing from CHP for some time; I think they must have given up on me. I guess I'll have blown it with Don Wade.'

'Oh, I don't know about that. Don's a good sort. If you can come up with the goods in time for his publication I'm sure he'll forgive you. After all, you're freelance, like me. You don't *actually* work for him.'

'No, but don't forget, he paid for my initial trip over here. I owe him that.'

'And what will he get in return? More than just the one

article he was looking for, I'm sure. I'd bet you could write a book with what you've found out.'

'I might just do that, who knows.'

We let it go at that. This meal had turned into a marathon.

'I won't forget about trying to arrange your visit to the Consortium,' Kerstin piped up as she dropped me off at the motel. 'I'll try to get something in the next week or so. I assume you'll still be here?'

'In the next week or so? Oh, I'll be here. You can bank on it.'

*

Mats Tillkvist didn't know when to call quits. In the past ten days, since our last little 'episode' at the bar, I'd neither heard nor seen anything of him. Then he rang. He began in a conciliatory mood, apologising profusely for the remarks he'd made. The essence of his call was that he wanted to meet me again to discuss the whole matter in a more constructive way. I agreed. But this time, *I* called the shots. I agreed to talk with him on his own, without Mia, and here at the motel.

When the receptionist called me to say that Mats had arrived, I had to consciously remind myself that I was going to *discuss* the matter with him; not give the man a *lecture*. We met in the reception area and made our way to the small coffee shop. I'd prepared myself mentally for this. I would be straight with him. It was essential, I felt, that I take charge of the conversation, right from the start.

'Look, Mats; I'll say again what I told you on the phone. After our last meeting, I was very angry. *Very* angry. And I don't want to hear any more of the kind of comments you made last time. Understood?'

'Of course. I was wrong to say those things. I know that.'

'Perhaps there are some things you ought to know,' I began. And for the next twenty or so minutes, I told him exactly what I knew and how I felt about the situations concerning his parents, the farm and the gun. Intentionally, I made no mention of Sten's diary.

'I just have this feeling,' I told him, 'that, sometimes, you're driven more by Mia's ideas than your own.'

When he looked up at me, silent for the moment, I thought I detected a sadness in his eyes.

'I think you're right.' Again, a few moments of silence passed. 'She's very ambitious, you know. And works very hard to build up our savings. It's a problem for me.'

'In what way?'

'Her money. At the paper mill I work as a backtender on the machine. It's okay, but the money is not so good. Mia is doing well now in hairdressing and... and she... she has her other business. It pays very well.'

It was the way he enunciated 'her other business' that reminded me of Berthe's comment. 'She has another business?'

'Yes. We don't talk about it with Bertil and Berthe. They disapprove and are ashamed of it, but they don't understand.'

'Go on.'

'Mia does glamour photography. You know, for magazines. It's the only way we have been able to build up our savings. One day, we both want to give up all these things and have our own business; I told you before. I know it's not very good, but she's very popular. The photographers are always calling her.'

Later, when I thought about it, I could have kicked myself for being so naive. 'Sounds good to me. Surely, in this day and age, it doesn't matter if your partner earns more than you do. Why do your parents have a problem with that?'

'Oh, it's not that. It's the work; the people. They've seen some of Mia's pictures in the sex mags.'

'Sex mags? You mean, she...'

'Only soft porn, nothing too bad. I see all the pictures; they're okay. It's no big deal here in Sweden.'

This was a new twist. I began to picture Mia, as I knew her, and tried to imagine her in the role of a centrefold. I'd always thought she was a little unusual, but I couldn't get my head around Mats' latest revelation.

'And you're quite happy that she does this?'

'No, not happy. That's why we want to get out of it. But we need the money to get started. That's why we thought... well, you know our feelings.'

I had to forcibly remind myself that I was a writer, not a counsellor. Whatever my own morals, I had no right to impose them on anyone else. Besides, I would be back in England soon and, hopefully, on with another commission. I couldn't afford to get into this thing any deeper.

'Listen, Mats, I feel you really ought to talk this through with your father. I know that won't be easy, but it might help, in the long run.'

I changed the subject at that point and began asking Mats about his own job. At first he dismissed it but, as I pressed him further, he made it sound more and more interesting. I'd never been in a paper mill so it was all new territory for me.

'Would you like to come to the mill one day? I could show you around perhaps.'

'Hei, that's the second visit invitation I've had in a week! Yes, I'd love to come, if you can arrange it.'

'I'll discuss it with my supervisor. It should be okay. I'll let you know.'

We parted on better terms than before. On reflection, I thought that maybe it was not so much anything *I'd* said as his being able to open up about Mia. Strangely, somehow it had brought us closer.

Bertil Tillkvist didn't look like a man who was dying. In truth, I'd never seen him look better. He was bright-eyed and, were it not such a contradiction of reality, appeared to be full of life.

'I was telling to Berthe about the collection at Kristianstad. Isn't it wonderful? How can one man have so many things collected? His basement is like a museum.'

'Yes, I must say I was very impressed when I first saw it. And he's made a good job of all the display cases, too. But I just wondered: what is it for? He has no public showing of his collection and seems very guarded about it. Must be just his personal obsession.'

'Maybe so, maybe so. But it is important for someone to care so much about our history.'

'Yes, he's a real enthusiast. It all seems to mean so much to him.'

'I think so, too. I liked him. He's a good man. And I've been thinking, Doctor Walt, perhaps he should be the one to look after Tomas's gun.'

'Really? You mean you'd consider selling it to him?'

'No, not selling; just giving.'

'Giving?'

'I think it's best. How much money can I ask for such a

thing? It is a memory, not goods like you sell in the shops. You called it airlom, yes?'

'Heirloom? That's right. It's a treasure handed down through your family.' I laughed at the thought of it. 'In this case it was handed down in a rather unusual way but, even so, it's still an heirloom.'

'So. How can you make a price for a memory? I know Mr Wersel will take good care of it. Also, he has the other guns from Tomas. It will make a full collection.'

'I can't disagree with your thinking, Mr Tillkvist. You're a wise man. If only more folks would think like that about their family heirlooms, there'd be fewer squabbles and arguments in families when these things are handed down. Have you told Siegfried Wersel about this?'

'No, not yet. Berthe and me, we have talked about it only last night. We, together, think it would be the best thing to do.'

'Would you like me to speak to Siegfried about it or will you do it yourself?'

'The both, together. We do it together. Can your girl take us there again?'

I smiled at his reference to 'my girl' although I wasn't sure that Kerstin would find the description quite so apt.

'She's usually very busy during the week, but maybe we could organise something for the weekend.'

What an amazing contrast, I thought; Bertil prepared to just give away the valuable antique while his son countenances his girlfriend working for a sex magazine to earn some extra money.

Kerstin was having lunch when I contacted her on her mobile phone. She wasn't at all surprised when I told her of Bertil's intentions. She just laughed: 'That's a Swede for you. A Skånian Swede. He may be old, dying and grumpy sometimes, but he's no fool, that one.' We agreed to repeat our Sunday afternoon visit to Kristianstad. On this occasion, I would make the arrangements myself.

Siegfried was flabbergasted. He'd discussed the possibility with his wife, Ursula, but they'd come to the conclusion that there was no way of raising anything like the sum he'd imagined he'd have to pay for the missing flintlock. It was out of the question, they'd decided, and he'd dismissed the idea of pursuing it with Bertil Tillkvist.

'Just one thing more,' I told him on the phone: 'You really must change the inscription card to read *Tomas Tillkvist*. Is there any chance you could do that before we arrive?'

'Changing the card is a small matter, but is it correct? I have to think of the Bergengrens, too. Is there any way you can substantiate that the gunsmith was *Tillkvist* and not *Tilderkvist*?'

'Yes, I believe I can.' I told him about the diary of Captain Tillkvist and suggested I'd ask Bertil to bring it with him. He may or may not agree, of course; I wasn't sure on that.

'That's good enough for me,' Siegfried replied. 'As long as you're sure it's right, the card will be changed before you come.'

It was a fitting reunion. I've always admired the old flintlock rifles of a bygone age and have seen hundreds, over the years, in the course of my research and writing on the subject. But the picture of those six Tomas Tillkvist rifles, together again as they must once have been in his little workshop at Peterlöv, side by side and arranged in order of their maker's mark, will always live with me. As we seated ourselves in Kerstin's car once more to make our way back to the farm, there was a just detectable misting in Bertil's eyes, betraying the mixed feelings he must have had over what he'd done.

*

I'd just come out of the shower when Kerstin rang. In a state of undress, I dodged around the bed-end towards the phone to take her call. She'd managed to arrange my visit to the Øresund Consortium offices in Malmö for Thursday. That was in two days time. She would meet me at the rail station in Malmö. By coincidence, Mats called me that same evening to say that he'd okayed it with his supervisor for me to visit the mill in Klippan on the Friday. Two days of 'jollies' – that would make a change from my usual routine.

'Hi!' Kerstin called out, as I made my way from the station platform. 'Good journey?'

'No problem. Quite straight forward really.'

'Good. Everything's arranged for today. A man called Arne Svensson will be looking after you this morning and I've arranged for Martin Chelford to join us for lunch. You know, he's married to Mats Tillkvist's sister.'

'That's right. You've told me about him and I've seen some photographs of him. He's the chap from Kanootsford, right?'

She laughed and threw me a pretend punch for reminding her of her embarrassment over the name. 'Knutsford, Knutsford. No "K" okay? I've learned it now.'

The Consortium's offices were no less plush than I'd imagined; appropriately representative of the prestige attached to the Øresund project. Arne Svensson was awaiting my arrival and appeared promptly at the reception desk. Kerstin made the introductions and we took the elevator to the third floor.

'You'd like some coffee first?' Arne suggested.

'Yes, I'd love one. Just black, please, with no sugar.'

The dark-panelled coffee room was furnished in what I'd come to recognise as typical Scandinavian style. Everything smacked of quality. On the wall hung a picture that showed soldiers from a previous century marching across what appeared to be a frozen lake. I noticed that, on a small brass plate underneath, it was titled in both Swedish and English. The English read: 'A Daring Raid – by a German artist.' The picture itself carried an inscription in the bottom right-hand corner, along with what I assumed to be the artist's initial. It was an undistinguished 'U' in red.

'This was the old way of crossing the water,' said Arne, smiling, as he caught my interest in the picture. 'It is depicting the time when the Swedish army crossed the ice in 1658 to defeat the Danes. In those days, the place where we are now belonged to Denmark. Ever since the battle pictured here it has been a part of Sweden. The painting is a copy of one that used to hang in one of our finest mansion houses, the Tido Slott, which belonged to one of Sweden's High Chancellors.' I smiled. Six months ago, I knew nothing about any of this, but now the date was engraved firmly in my mind. 1658. A pinnacle date in Swedish history. I'd come to know the story well.

'The best place to start is with the models; just upstairs,' Arne suggested. 'Kerstin is leaving us now, but I will look after you until lunchtime.' He turned to Kerstin and said something in Swedish. For my benefit, she replied in English: 'Yeah, twelve o'clock. I'll meet you in reception, okay?'

'Fine. See you then.'

There were two models, set on large, heavy tables and taking up almost half of the room. One was of the bridge-tunnel complex itself; the other was a three-dimensional relief map of both the Swedish and Danish sides of The Sound.

'We will look first at the map model so that you will have a good idea of the plan for the Øresund Region and the impact of it, then we can look at the construction model to see some of the problems we have to deal with.'

We positioned ourselves at one corner, next to Trelleborg on the Swedish side. I could see, near Malmö, what appeared to be a lake.

'What's that?' I asked, pointing to the lake.

'Ah, yes. It's a leisure complex. Today, it is a large quarry owned by Euroc. Before, it was run by Cementa. For many years they quarried limestone there, but its future is for a large leisure facility. That's all part of the project. And here, close to Malmö City, you can see we are providing a fast-flow traffic bypass with the city tunnel and the ring road.'

We must have spent over half an hour at the map model. Arne Svensson knew his stuff. The whole project, as he outlined it, was much more all-encompassing than I'd imagined. I began to see how Kerstin could make an almost full-time job out of keeping track of all the various developments and writing about the different impacts the project would have.

'It's phenomenal,' I gasped, as I tried to take it all in. 'How much will it all cost and who will pay for it?'

'Huh, the cost? I think it's what you might call *megabucks*. But, in fact, the whole cost should be borne by the users and made good within twenty-five years. At least that's the aim. Mostly, it will be the road traffic who pay.

Probably something like seventy percent from the road users and the rest from the railway system. You can see, on the other model, how it will be arranged.'

We moved to the second table to look at the construction of the link.

'You can see that what we will have is a mixture of tunnels, low bridge sections and one high bridge section. Some of the reasons for that are from the practical point of view and some are environmental considerations. It's best if we move around to the Copenhagen side to begin with. That's the logical starting point. It's also the point where we are at today. Did you see the landworks when you landed at Kastrup?'

'No, I didn't. But, then, I wouldn't have known what I was looking at. I've learnt about the project only since I've been here in Sweden. You folks must be keeping it a secret from the rest of Europe.'

'Nei, it's no secret. But maybe the rest of Europe don't take us so seriously. That'll all change once the Øresund Region comes to pass. Sweden and Denmark, even Norway, will become major players in the European economy in the next century. Maybe by the time I retire.'

'Retire? Huh, you're only a youngster.'

'Ja, ja. Thirty-five. Another thirty years and everyone in Europe will know about Øresund. Stockholm may be our capital city, but what you're looking at will be our future.'

It had been an absorbing morning. Arne Svensson had highlighted the major civil engineering challenges to be faced in the construction of the link: the artificial islands that had to be formed, just off the Danish coast; the 'no-residue' dredging compliance; the decongestion of Malmö City by the tunnel and ring road. I thanked him for his time and hospitality as we made our way back to the reception desk. My two and a half hours with Arne had simply whizzed past; it was almost twelve o'clock.

'Miss Berg should be here in a few moments so I will say goodbye now.'

'Thank you, again. It's been a real pleasure.'

'You're welcome.'

I'd no sooner subsided into the upholstered depths of a large leather-covered sofa when Kerstin arrived.

The lunch was excellent. And Martin Chelford was not at all as I'd imagined from my recollections of seeing his photographs although, admittedly, in the shots I'd seen he was bundled up in skiing gear. Martin could best be described as 'casual' – in every way. His dress; his speech; his manner; his outlook on life; everything about him was casual. His eyes bore a permanent mischievous twinkle as he joked and fooled around like an overgrown schoolboy. Neither of the two waitresses who served us escaped his teasing wit. He could have lifted the spirits of the most disconsolate soul and raised the tempo of many a flagging party. In all probability, he'd done just that on past occasions. He began to tell us the 'Kanootsford' story, but both Kerstin and I recognised the direction he was heading and, practically in unison, cut him off. 'Heard it!' we chorused.

Not to be outdone, Martin looked at the two of us, shifting his twinkling gaze from the one to the other, then said: 'Okay, so you two are the experts on the English language; how about this: can you come up with a sentence that contains the word "and" five times in succession? You know, "and and and and and" but still making sense?'

'I'm sure I've heard this one somewhere,' I replied, 'but it doesn't jump to mind. Sorry.'

Kerstin, too, admitted defeat. 'Sounds a bit contrived. I'd be here all day trying to work that one out.'

'Ah, it's simple,' Martin explained. 'It was on the signboard of a Fish and Chip shop in Manchester. The signwriter had made a poor job of it so the spaces between "Fish" and "and" and "and" and "Chips" weren't equal. Simple as that!'

We groaned, audibly, but probably both of us had secretly stored it away in memory for recycling on some other occasion. Certainly, it brought to mind a similar example once promulgated by one of my schoolteachers.

'Very good. But now I have one for you. Similar kind of thing, only this time it requires a sentence with the word "had" used consecutively not five, but six times.'

Kerstin merely shook her head and reached into her handbag for a cigarette. Martin, meanwhile, mumbled away with his eyes closed – obviously trying to conjure up the answer.

'Okay. You couldn't get mine; I can't get yours. I give in.'

'Well, it's all to do with a teacher who was marking a boy's essay and, although the boy had had "had", "had had" had his teacher's approval.'

'Nice one! I'll remember that.'

Having got to know Martin a little bit, I reckoned that, most likely, the conundrum would be trotted out to challenge his colleagues in the office that same afternoon. At any rate, it seemed to be the means of toning down the relentless hilarity that had accompanied our meal for, as the coffee arrived, Martin took on, for the first time since we'd met, a more sober approach to the conversation.

'You were impressed with our little project, then?'

'It's amazing. Not only as a visionary enterprise, but it's a marvel of construction.'

'Oh, it's that all right. Sixteen kilometres of fixed link across The Sound that'll carry passenger trains travelling at anything up to two hundred kilometres an hour and cars at up to one hundred and twenty. They reckon it'll save nearly ten million travel hours per year.'

'You're kidding.'

'Nope! Come back in the year 2000, Walt, and you'll be able to get from downtown Copenhagen to downtown Malmö in less than half an hour.'

'That's incredible. Makes you wonder why they didn't start building this link years ago.'

'Oh, they tried,' Kerstin burst in, 'but each time the issue was raised the plan was ditched for one reason or another. In recent years, it was part of the Gyllenhammar plan, but that, too, got squashed. It wasn't until June '94 that a decision was finally made to push ahead with it. Since then, it's been all go.'

'It's certainly the largest project *I've* worked on,' added Martin. 'And probably the most significant, too.'

'In what way?'

'Well, did you realise that Copenhagen and Malmö were once "sister" cities? Years ago, they were both Danish and monopolised access to The Sound, exacting passage tolls on the traders and freight shippers. Now they'll be joining forces once again. Quite a reunion, eh?'

'Yes, it's a curious twist of history.'

'For a neutral Brit, it's nice to be part of it.'

'Uh-huh. And I suppose you'll see it through?' I asked.

'Guess so. Annika has no particular wish to live in England permanently and I like it here, so I guess I'll become a Swede. Besides, with Bertil's condition, it's likely we'll have to keep an eye on mother.'

It had been an extended lunch hour for Martin but, as he reminded us, 'there was work to be done.' He called for the bill and raised his cup, with what remained of his coffee, declaring, 'Work is the curse of the drinking classes. Skål!'

The brain-stretching morning, followed by the jaw-aching, laugh-a-minute lunch, had left me feeling as if I'd done enough for one day. On the train ride back from Malmö, it was all that I could do to prevent my eyes from closing. I knew that if I gave in to my feelings I'd drift off into a deep sleep.

It was nearing six o'clock by the time I arrived back in Hässleholm. When I collected my key from the motel reception desk, the young lady on duty handed me a note along with my key. Don Wade had telephoned and his message was asking me to return the call: urgently. With the one hour time difference, it would be only five o'clock in England; Don would be almost certainly still at Crown House.

It was good to talk to Don again – but his news was disturbing. A large publishing house, Greenshield Press, had made a bid for CHP and, although the takeover was not a *fait accompli*, Don felt that it would be only a matter of time. He wanted to know if I could get back to the UK within the next two weeks to discuss the aspects of the likely deal that might affect my current obligations. I told him I'd make the necessary arrangements and would see him in two weeks time, complete with a feature-length article. And almost enough material to outline a book. It all may or may not be relevant anymore. That's what he told me. I'd have to wait and see.

Over dinner, I reflected on some of the commissions I'd worked on for CHP and thought of the many times I'd visited Crown House to discuss my work with various editors – and Don Wade, himself. If this Greenshield thing went ahead, it would never be quite the same for me. Over the years, CHP had become a part of my life. And my return to England, too, I'd face with mixed feelings. In some ways, I was looking forward to being back in Lichfield; in many other ways, it would be as if I'd be leaving behind some unfinished business. I thought, particularly, of the Tillkvist family and of what might happen once the old patriarch Bertil passed away.

In one day, I'd packed in so much. Or so it appeared. The fascinating time with Arne Svensson; the fun-filled lunchtime; the train journeys to and from Malmö; and now, just one more aquavit to round it all off. Ah! It was the stuff of dreams.

I was quite glad Mats had suggested I catch the train at a reasonable hour. It was due to leave Hässleholm at 9.36. He met me, as planned, at Klippan station and took me directly to the mill. It was one of his off-shift days and I expressed my appreciation for his taking a 'busman's holiday'. He'd seemed rather sullen when he met me from the train, but brightened up as we spoke.

'That's okay. I sometimes go into the mill even when I'm rostered off if we've had some problems during my shift. There's no definite rule about it, but it's more or less expected that we either stay on or follow up if there's been a problem in meeting an order.'

'How long have you worked at the mill?' I asked him.

'Since I left college. I've worked nowhere else; only here.'

We began our tour of the mill at what Mats called 'the

stock preparation' area. Huge bales of compressed sheets of pure white pulp were fed into large tanks that he described as 'pulpers' where they were thrashed around in water to form a porridge-like stock.

'From here, the stock is diluted and pumped through various screens. You can't see much, because the pressure-screens are all enclosed. We'll walk over to the cyclone cleaners; that's a bit more interesting.'

He pointed out the way the dilute stock swirled around at high speed inside the cone-shaped cleaners to create a vortex. The good, lightweight pulpstock was carried upwards through a pipe in the top of the cone and the heavier particles of dirt and other unwanted material were carried downwards with the spiralling vortex to be treated as 'rejects' in another tank.

'And is this where the pulp becomes paper?' I asked, now looking at what appeared to be no more than dirty water spewing out of a long slot on to a speeding wire mesh that ran over large rollers. It was about four metres wide and, Mats assured me, was speeding along at almost fifty kilometres an hour.

'Yes. Here, the water is drained off, helped by these ceramic blades pushing against the wire and by suction applied to these pipes.'

The machine-house was quite warm, and it was getting very humid as we walked farther along the machine.

'Now we come to the part where the paper is dried almost completely. The part you have just seen we call the "wet end" but now we're going to the "dry end" which is where I normally work. See, the sheet is supported by felts as it goes through the press-rolls. Then it goes into the banks of drying cylinders. They're heated by steam.'

Just being beside the machine gave me a wonderful feeling. It was as if this huge mechanical beast was alive. The sense of speed and the power of these rotating masses aroused within me the same kind of feeling that had once thrilled me when I stood on the footplate of an old steam locomotive. To these papermakers, it was all taken for granted as part and parcel of their working environment. To me, it was awesome.

'What's going on here? The warning signs say it's radioactive.'

'That's right, but you're quite safe. This is the scanner. As you see, the head travels forwards and backwards across the sheet. Inside, it has a Krypton 85 source for measuring the weight of the paper. It's all very well shielded, of course.'

I was amazed at the size of the massive reels of paper accumulating at the end of the machine. Mats explained what his job as a backtender entailed then we headed in the direction of the testing laboratory to see how the quality matched up to requirements.

In a little over an hour and a half, I felt I got a good insight into how paper was manufactured. It also gave me a good idea of how Mats spent his working life. I'd been enthralled by what I'd seen and the things he'd told me but, personally, I wouldn't want to do it day in, day out.

'We can have some lunch in the canteen,' Mats informed me, 'then I'll drive you back to Hässleholm.'

'Lunch I can manage, but there's no need to drive me back; I have a return ticket.'

'That's okay but, since last time we met, some things have happened. I think you should know. I'd like the chance to talk with you.'

I wondered, then, if he already knew about the gun. I hadn't told him, but perhaps he'd heard from Bertil. If that was the 'something he wanted to talk about' there wouldn't be much to say. It wasn't. We'd no sooner pulled out of the mill car park when Mats began to pour out his troubles.

'First of all, I can tell you this: I no longer care about the old gun. It doesn't matter any more.'

'That's a bit of a turnaround, isn't it? Why the sudden change? Does Mia—'

'She's the reason,' he cut in, 'I should have seen it coming but I guess I was blinded by thinking so much about the money for our business. For the moment, at least, Mia is no longer living with me.'

I was stunned. From my incredulous look, Mats must have realised he'd just dropped a bombshell.

'I think she has been lying to me for a long time. When she started doing the pictures with the glamour mags it was only to be for a few sessions to put some extra money in our savings. Now, I find out she has been making hard-core porno movies and they wanted her to go to Hamburg for some kind of special filming. We had a big bust-up, night before last. She said she was going to Germany whether I liked it or not and I told her to go to hell. She said: "I'll see you when I get back from Germany" then just left the apartment and slammed the door. I haven't seen or heard from her since.'

'Good gracious! Has she done this before?'

'Never. But since she started this glamour thing, she has sometimes stayed away. Each time, she told me it was a long photography session and the magazine put her up in a hotel. She always got good money for the sessions so I just accepted her explanations.'

'You didn't become suspicious?'

'No, it's so stupid. That's what I mean when I say I should have seen it coming. I trusted her too much.'

'What will you do?'

'I don't know, exactly. I have no idea when she'll get back but, in any case, I don't want her back. Not after she's been screwing around with all those guys.'

I just shook my head and muttered the occasional monosyllabic word. I couldn't get to grips with what he was telling me. It was like something out of a Hollywood movie. I wanted to console him; to sympathise; or even just to show my concern, but nothing I could have thought of saying would have come out right. We drove in silence for several minutes, then Mats broke the impasse.

'Perhaps now you can see why I'm not so interested in the old gun anymore, eh?'

In view of his comment, I realised he had no inkling of his father's visit to Kristianstad. I felt it best to put him fully in the picture. Surprisingly, he showed little reaction to what I told him. He just uttered a quiet 'hmmph' and continued his tale of woe.

'Mia and me, we've been together a long time. We both had very ordinary jobs and we wanted so much to have our own business. In Sweden, you probably know, the tax situation for individual persons is not good; with a business, it would be much better. But, even if I took her back, how could I ever trust her again? Stupid whore!'

He called her a few other unseemly names and spent the next couple of minutes lambasting her character. He mentioned the drugs, too, but was insistent that they'd only dabbled in the vice; neither of them had become dependent on any of it.

'Quite a mess, Mats. And with your father barely clinging on to life, it's not leading up to a happy Christmas.'

When he dropped me off at the motel, I shook hands with him and looked him in the eye. 'Go and see your father, Mats. He needs you. And I think you need him.'

*

On the Saturday morning, I went to the travel agents. Tuesday, November 26th. I was booked on the SAS morning flight from Copenhagen; that gave me just fifteen more days in Sweden. I'd stay the Monday night in Malmö and leave first thing on the Jet Cat for Kastrup. I called Kerstin to tell her of my plans. And to tell her about the threat to CHP's future, if she hadn't already heard. She had.

'There's one thing I'd really like to do before I go back to England.'

'What's that?'

'Well, I've travelled far and wide around this part of the country, but I'd love to see a bit of Stockholm. Any suggestions on what I might see and do there for a couple of days?'

'Sure. But you must be psychic.'

'Why's that?'

'I was going to call you a little later to suggest that very thing. You see, a group of us from the project will be going to Stockholm next weekend. It's a social outing. We've got tickets for the Pavarotti concert at the Globe and I wondered...'

'Luciano Pavarotti? Wow! I'd love to come. How much are the tickets?'

'Special deal the Consortium managed to pull; we have a block booking at nine hundred kronor each. Interested?'

'Of course I'm interested. How are you getting up there?'

'By coach. We're leaving at eleven o'clock on Friday. It would mean you'd have to get the train to Malmö in the morning; I could meet you again at the station.'

'No problem then; count me in.'

'Wonderful! Martin and Annika will be coming, too, so we'll make it a real send-off party for you. We'll be booking into Frey's Hotel. It's quiet, but very friendly, and we get a good rate there. We have all day Saturday and also Sunday morning free to do some shopping or sightseeing or whatever. Then we return at midday Sunday. Oh, and don't worry about getting back from Malmö on Sunday night; I'm sure the Chelfords will give you a bed. I'll check with Annika, just to be sure.'

With the excitement of our inchoate plans for the following weekend now behind us, we reverted to our more normal 'catch-up-on-the-week' conversation. I told Kerstin about my visit to the paper mill and of what transpired afterwards.

'You're right,' she acquiesced, 'it's a real mess. Poor Mats. In all honesty, I'm sure he'll be a lot better off without Mia. And I agree with you; he and Bertil need each other right now. If he *does* go over to the farm, I'm sure it'll work out for the best.'

I needed some time by myself again. With the various arrangements that were now in place for my last two weeks in Sweden, I had to be sure that I'd got everything I considered important down on my portable PC and edited, near as dammit. Once I was happy with it, I'd make double back-ups on disk – one set to be put in a jiffy bag and mailed home. I smiled to myself as I thought about all the mail that would have accumulated in my absence. My housekeeper, Mrs Samuel, would need the whole dining-room table to stack it on, I was sure. After all, my intended two week trip had turned into a four month escapade. I'd missed getting my monthly injection of worldly wisdom from *National Geographic* but they'd all be piled up waiting for me when I got home – still enveloped in their familiar, recycled yellow covers.

By the Wednesday afternoon, I felt I was well on top of everything. Tomorrow, I'd visit the old Peterlöv farm to see how Bertil was progressing.

As the taxicab pulled into the Tillkvists' driveway, I noticed the red Volvo parked outside. I hadn't expected Mats to be here. Even as I counted out the taxi fare, my mind was recalling Mats having told me he would be starting an 'eight days on' stretch, as from last Sunday. I waved off the taxi driver and turned towards the house, beginning to feel anxious about what I might find. I was hoping that nothing serious had happened to Bertil to bring Mats here during his scheduled work time. It was Mats who answered my knock.

'Hello! Come right in! This is a surprise!' he said, clearly taken aback by my unannounced arrival.

'Likewise. I thought you were on shift today. I just came over to see how your father is doing.'

By this time, I was already in the lounge and answering my unspoken inquiry with my own eyes: Bertil was sitting in his favourite chair and his face was wreathed in smiles as he acknowledged my presence.

'I'm having a few days off,' Mats said, by way of answering my other inquiry.

'Yes,' added Bertil, amplifying the answer, 'and he has

taken his old room again. The one he had when he was a boy.'

I looked from one to the other. Both were grinning.

'It's true,' replied Mats, 'I've moved in here for a week or so. I've still heard nothing from that runaway bitch so I'm not sure what will happen with the apartment. All our things are still there, or most of them; I've brought what I need for the time being.'

'So, you've moved back home?'

'Just for now. It's about the same travel time to Klippan as from Hälsingborg, so perhaps I will, as you say, move back home.'

Bertil raised his hand as if to indicate that it was his turn to speak. 'And he's quite happy that Tomas's old gun is now in the museum. We have talked many things, me and Mats, since he is here. It is good. He will never be a farmer, but we have talked another way to do it. It's possible, we think.'

I looked at Mats, consciously raising a quizzical eyebrow.

'Let's get you a coffee first, then we'll tell you what we have discussed.'

Just then, Berthe wandered through from the kitchen. 'Hei, Doctor Walt. It's good to have Mats here to stay for a while, eh?'

'Yes, I... I suppose it's... like old times?'

'Ja, ja. *Good* old times,' the homely, good-natured woman beamed back at me.

As father and son shared with me the ideas they'd juggled with during the past two days, I felt almost that I ought to pinch myself to confirm that this was real life. Perhaps the kinky little miss who'd run off to Germany had done more of a good turn to the Tillkvist family than any amount of money she might have contributed from her seedy, erotic adventures. There was just one thing that crossed my mind as I listened to the dying man and his prodigal son: whatever happened to the old sea captain's diary? Unknown to Mats, yet so important to Bertil; would that be another family heirloom that would find its way back to some museum?

*

It was going to be a long day. With the prospect of an hour and a bit's train ride to Malmö, followed by umpteen hours cooped up in the coach, I felt tired before I'd even left the motel. At least, on the train, I could have a snooze for most of the way, I thought.

I recognised many of the landmarks as the train sped towards Malmö. I could hardly tag them as 'familiar' – I'd made the journey only once before – but they offered sufficient distraction from any tendency I might have felt that the journey was boring. I made a game out of guessing what was coming up next, replaying from my memory the various buildings and land formations I'd seen before. I checked my watch to review our progress. We were spot on for time. The Swedish railways ran like clockwork; that was something I was going to miss when I returned to a reliance on the British rail network.

Kerstin, Martin and Annika had already met up by the time I arrived. I was introduced to Annika and saw immediately the family resemblance that declared she was a Tillkvist – and Mats' sister. I observed, too, that even with his wife present, Martin was still the effervescent character I'd come to know.

'Good morning Doctor "had had" Kirkland,' was his opening salvo. Just then, a covey of pigeons flapped noisily in a low swoop from the station roof. That was it; he was off.

'Hei, did you hear about the old couple who were driving through Macclesfield one day, when a pigeon dropped its mess all over their windscreen?'

'No. Go on.'

'The woman turned to her husband and said: "Quick, George! Wipe it!". "I can't," he replied, "It's flying too high!"'

Annika slapped his arm, but the story set Kerstin off in a fit of giggles. I smiled, shook my head, and said: 'Martin, you must have been your teacher's worst nightmare at school.'

The high spirits, presumably heightened by the expectancy of the forthcoming coach trip, brightened an otherwise dull morning. Weatherwise, it was grey and cold, with a significant chill factor. If Martin's jovial mood was indicative of what was to come, we were in for quite a party on the way to Stockholm.

'How many are going?' I asked Kerstin.

'Twenty-four, at the last count, I think. Enough to make a good coachload anyway. Come on. I'll introduce you to some of the crowd.'

They all seemed a nice bunch. Mostly, they were Swedes, from what I could tell. Two couples were from Holland... then, of course, there was Martin from good old Blighty. Just like the railways, the coach ran strictly to time. At precisely eleven o'clock, we pulled out to join the flow of traffic. Martin and Annika had taken up seats halfway along the coach; Kerstin and I sat directly behind them and the Dutchies filed into the four seats opposite ours. We were on our way to the 'City of Islands' and I reflected that, most likely, I was the only one on the coach who'd not been there before. The six hundred kilometre drive would give me ample opportunity to verbally explore the potential kaleidoscopic treasures that would await me in the nation's capital; quite apart from the anticipated delight of listening to Pavarotti once again. I could hear the gently rolling melody of *Nessun Dorma* begin to build up in my head and hoped the famous tenor would include it in his repertoire. His other renditions from Puccini, Rossini and Verdi were always a delight, but his inimitable performance of Puccini's aria from *Turandot* remained my favourite.

Sooner or later it had to happen. It took a little longer than I thought. But then it happened. We'd been travelling barely more than half an hour when, as if triggered by some sudden flashback to a deeply engraved memory of youth, Martin spun around in his seat and bellowed at me from between the headrests: 'Hei, Walt! Do you remember the "Four and twenty virgins who went to Inverness"?'

I wagged my index finger at him, schoolmaster-style. He grinned and pulled a comical face. But at least he didn't strike up with the bawdy rugby-bus ballad.

It took almost eight hours to get to Stockholm, with just three 'comfort breaks' that allowed a brief stretching of the legs and the intake of food, drink and the chilly outside air. It was a long journey, but by no means tedious. Kerstin clued me in on the best of the tourist attractions that would be within easy reach of our hotel. The Dutchies were charming; Jost Boersma, Jan van Leeming and their wives chatted on and off throughout the trip and told me of their separate experiences during visits to England and Scotland. From time to time, our conversation was interspersed with one of Martin's 'funnies' and Annika elaborated on some of the landmarks we passed.

My first glimpses of the Stockholm Globe were awe inspiring. It reminded me of a time when, a few years ago, I was working on an assignment in Tampa, Florida. One Friday night, I caught the plane to Orlando to take in Disneyworld over the weekend. I was seated on the right-hand side of the aircraft and, as we descended into Orlando airport, my first view of the Epcot Centre's huge, floodlit globe had given me that same feeling of awe-inspired anticipation.

The massive auditorium was a buzz of expectant excitement as we took our seats. We filed into our designated block and I took my place between Kerstin and Hendrika van Leeming. I'd already paid for my concert ticket and, as I mentally reckoned up the likely cost of the whole weekend – with hotel bill, my contribution to the coach hire and incidental meals – it was beginning to look like it would make quite a hole in my pocket. True, it was a one-off social event, but I was coming to the conclusion that these Øresund project people were either highly paid or the cost of living in Sweden was even higher than I'd become accustomed to in the past four months. And that was taking account of the concessionary concert tickets we'd secured through the good offices of the Øresund Consortium. But, to hear Pavarotti again, it would be worth it, I reasoned. I wasn't disappointed.

Backed by a full orchestra and a very competent chorus, the ageing tenor performed majestically. The precision-engineered acoustics of the Globe seemed to enhance his crystal-clear high notes and added a resonance to his lower spectrum. It was a delight. His repertoire for the evening included all his well-known favourites, including my much-loved *Nessun Dorma*. For his encore of the Puccini aria, he performed a special reprise version that had the whole audience on its feet. What a voice! What a performance! We could have listened to him all night, enraptured. The majority of the audience was far removed from any alignment with sedate opera-goers; there was a party atmosphere throughout and, as we stood applauding endlessly while the maestro took his final bow, one section off to our right began a repetitious chant accompanied by the now familiar, arm-swinging 'Mexican wave'. Never again would I allow the assertion that Scandinavians are undemonstrative to go unchallenged.

Sweden is a magnificent country: a star-spangled crown of natural beauty and tranquillity. And Stockholm is, undoubtedly, the jewel in the crown. The city's culture revolves around its doorstep abundance of water – and its old buildings. In Gamla Stan, the old town, there's a sense of 'time warp' as the latest fashions are paraded against a backdrop of the fine old architecture of the past. The Gamla Stan precincts may be old but, from the cobblestoned streets to the intimate alcoves, everything was spotlessly clean. No graffiti, no tawdry bill-posting, no accumulation of litter. Everywhere was the same; I was forming the opinion that cleanliness was an inborn obsession of the Swedish mind.

Our long coach trip and fortuitous choice of seating had created the platform that brought about the bonding, at least for this weekend, of our own foursome with the two Dutch couples. On Saturday afternoon, having exhausted the more immediate sights around Gamla Stan, we decided to reconstitute our respective foursomes, the men banding together and the womenfolk likewise. *We'd* do some more sightseeing; *they'd* follow the pull of the price tickets and trawl the major stores. So it was that Jost, Jan, Martin and I headed for the Djurgarden.

While the girls were wearing down their heels trailing around the shops, we menfolk spent a more leisurely time. From the pier near the old town quarter, we took the ferryboat across the harbour to the former royal deer park, Djurgarden. During the brief crossing, Martin pointed out a beautiful castle, Kastellholmen, proudly flying the blue and yellow of Sweden. It is now used as an army station, he told me. In a little over ten minutes, we disembarked alongside signs for 'Grona Lund' which, my hosts assured me, I'd probably have enjoyed thirty or more years ago. Its collection of Ferris wheels, giant roller coaster and other amusements certainly smacked of a young man's paradise. It was relatively quiet now but, they defended, in the height of summer it was always thronging with the young 'good time' set.

We walked through some areas of mixed woodland where myriad species of birds fluttered around and generally ignored us. Climbing terraced steps, we came at last to Skansen, on the crest of a mound. This was what I really wanted to see: the oldest open-air museum in the world, with more than a hundred traditional Swedish buildings of all sorts, depicting the country's lifestyles down through the ages. There were cottages, workshops and little cabins where men had carried on their crafts. It was delightful. So late in the year, many of the craft demonstrations were no longer running, but we did visit the bakery to take our fill of the local, old-fashioned spiced biscuits they call *bullar*.

For me, time just flew. Our few hours at Skansen and Djurgarden were over much too soon. If ever I was fortunate enough to return to Stockholm, I'd allow myself at least a full day, and preferably in summertime, to visit this place again.

When both sexes came together for dinner at the hotel, the evening turned into a lengthy and hilarious affair. Totally unpredictably, Jost Boersma emerged as the star entertainer. Not given to telling jokes, as such, he drew, instead, on a stream of real life anecdotes in which he, his family or his close friends had become the hapless victims of some mistake, mishap or miscalculation. It was a hoot. Perhaps to our relief, no international football matches were taking place in Stockholm that weekend for, from the facial expressions of some of the other diners, we may have been taken to be football hooligans living it up on the town.

Any aspirations we may have harboured for further exploration of the locale on Sunday morning had dissipated in the wake of the full day we'd had on the Saturday. We were no sooner done with breakfast, it seemed, before it was time to re-board the coach for our return journey, a little more subdued than when we'd left Malmö. I was happy to know that I'd be spending the night with the Chelfords in Svedala. After another eight hours in a coach seat, albeit most comfortably upholstered, it would feel good to be horizontal again. And bed would be but a short hop away, once the coach deposited us at Malmö station.

*

Bertil Tillkvist was one of those guys who just wasn't going to lie down and die. Inexplicably, over the past ten days his pain and discomfort had eased to the point where he'd coped without painkillers for over forty-eight hours. Berthe was the first to tell me about it when I called at the farm on Tuesday after lunch.

'It's good, ja? Two days, he has had no pills.'

'My goodness, Mr Tillkvist, you'll be confounding the doctors next,' I called across the room. I was pleased for him and my comment was intended to be light-hearted but, as the words left my mouth, I wanted to retract them. How could I be so insensitive? The old man's dying! But I got away with it. Maybe Bertil's English wasn't quite good enough to discern the implications behind my use of the word 'confounding'.

'Ja, Doctor Walt! Two days, hei? It feels good. But Berthe has not told you all the truth. Something more: this morning I sat again in the tractor. It takes time to get in the seat, but it feels good.'

'You did *what*? You sat in... in the driving seat?'

'In the driving seat! Ja!'

Berthe placed a tray of cheese biscuits and coffee on the small table, glancing up at me as she did so. 'He knows he won't be lifting beet anymore, but he wants to feel like he could do it if he decided to try. Next week, he and Mats will be interviewing for the new manager. On Thursday and Friday when Mats is off.'

'Aha. So, you're going ahead with the idea? Mats will take over the financial side of the farm and an experienced man will run it?'

'It's the best way,' replied Bertil. 'Maybe after some years Mats will also see the best way to run things.'

'Is he moving in here permanently?' I asked, directing my question to Berthe.

'We think so. He says he has heard no more from Mia. He doesn't know when she will come back but, in any case, he is finished with her. He told me that himself.'

I wasn't at all sorry that the manipulative little sex kitten no longer figured in his plans for his life. It crossed my mind that, perhaps, it was Mats' returning to the farm and his splitting with Mia that had given Bertil this new lease of life, even if it should prove to be only a short-term respite.

'Doctor Walt, we will miss you when you go back to England,' Bertil suddenly intoned, the change of tack in our conversation appearing almost to be a diversion tactic.

'Yes. And I'll certainly miss you folks. I feel as if I've become like one of the family.'

'That's also what we think,' he returned, 'So, we want to make a special party for you on Friday. Berthe will tell it.'

I was, I must admit, quite taken aback by the out-of-the-blue announcement. For that's what it was. There was no hint of suggestion about the matter; it had already been decided.

'We would have liked to have made it a surprise,' Berthe began, 'but that was too difficult. So, now we are telling you all about it instead. Mats will be here and we have invited Annika and Martin. Also, we asked Martin to be sure to invite Miss Berg. I think she is coming.'

'My goodness!' I responded, 'You've got it all planned already.'

'Ja, it has been planned,' added Bertil, 'because you are a good friend, Doctor Walt. We want also for it to be a special party for Mats coming home. And we are having a secret that you know about.'

'A secret?'

'The diary from old Sten! At the party, we are giving it to Mats. Berthe and me, we decided.'

Hearing of their 'secret' brought a flood of warmth to my soul. Not from any emotional attachment I held for the writings of the old sea captain, but for the significance of the old couple's intention. Bertil and Mats had obviously made up more than just their differences. The break-up of Mats' relationship with Mia had put in motion a chain of events that had, evidently, begun the bridge-building that was to traverse the gulf that had grown, over the years, between father and son. Bertil's boy had come home.

'He has learned a hard lesson,' Bertil went on. 'Now he has escaped. He has the chance to become like all the real Tillkvists. That's why we give him the book.'

Berthe smiled, wiping her hands across her apron. 'More coffee, Doctor Walt?'

I spent the rest of the week digging around to see what else I could find out about the Øresund project. Kerstin had given me copies of two of her articles which were in English and Martin had been helpful, too, in pointing me to a number of sources of English language information concerning the venture. In particular, I homed in on two aspects of the development that interested me: the City Tunnel and Euroc City. Although considered integral parts of the main project, these represented major undertakings in their own right.

Take the City Tunnel: to be bored out of the rock below Malmö City, and running to more than five kilometres long, it is destined to become the main artery through which trains will carry the bulk of the region's passenger transits in the early part of the twenty-first century. Not only Malmö–Copenhagen trains will pass through the tunnel; there will be Euro-City Express trains and special Øresund Region trains, making Malmö one of the major travel crossroads of Europe.

I learned that most of the future freight traffic was to be targeted at the new twenty-five kilometre orbital motorway. The region's travellers of the future would have many incentives to use the rail systems by preference. At least that was the vision held by most of the planners in 1994 when the project began.

Euroc City, the conversion of the old limestone quarry into a combined business and leisure zone, would also make a significant impact on the lifestyle of the area by the turn of the century. I was intrigued by some of the suggested uses for the surrounding areas and thought it incredible that so much co-operative spirit had been generated by the regional concept that was being promoted here. I couldn't remember detecting the same degree of optimistic harmony amongst the general public along the south-east coast of England when the Channel Tunnel project was underway. Clearly, the Nordic attitudes were much less insular and parochial than those of the southern Brit. Being a part of Europe seemed important to Scandinavia's businessmen and women, and the Øresund link, to them, would become the gateway to the marketplace.

There was a lot to digest from the reading matter I'd accumulated on the subject. I marked up the photocopies of the material I'd been given by Kerstin or had obtained from the library here. The enormity of the project and the ethos behind it had sparked off a special interest within me. I was keen to find out as much as I could. From time to time I would recall to mind images of the models Arne Svensson had shown me and I tried to envisage the construction in real life, with ships making their way up The Sound and super-fast, streamlined trains flashing across the bridge in either direction. It was a satisfying picture.

My last few working days in Sweden sped past at a whirlwind rate. On the Thursday evening, Kerstin telephoned to tell me not to bother with a taxi to the Tillkvist's the following evening; she would collect me from the motel. I was looking forward to my farewell party with mixed feelings; the joy of being surrounded by folks I'd come to know so well would be diminished by the thought that, in a matter of a few days, I'd be leaving them behind. Almost certainly, I'd never see Bertil again. The others? Who knows? Maybe one day.

Kerstin was her bright and breezy self when I met her in the reception area. And she looked even more stunning than when I'd first met her, four months ago, in the bar at the St Jorgen.

'All set for the big send-off?' she chirped.

'Well, I hope we'll all have a good time, but I'm not so sure about the "goodbyes" when it comes to that.'

'Have no fear, Sir Galahad!' she bounced back, 'You're not exactly going to be "treading where angels fear to tread" are you?'

'No, it's just that I hate goodbyes at the best of times. You folks have all become really special to me, so that part I won't enjoy.'

Almost as if by design, we pulled in to the driveway just as Martin and Annika were making their way into the house. Obviously, they'd arrived less than a minute before we did. Wherever the gregarious Martin went, noise was sure to follow. And tonight, he was noisy. Standing in the porch as we made our way from the car, he bellowed a loud fanfare through bunched fists.

'My lords, ladies and gentlemen!' he shouted, 'Pray silence for the entrance of the most esteemed Doctor

Walter Kirkland and his most highly ornate dish of the evening, Miss Kerstin Berg!'

I caught Kerstin's arm and pretended to doff the hat I wasn't wearing, playing along with his revelry. As we made to step inside, he didn't move. Instead, he threw his arms around our shoulders and began to circle round in a boisterous jig.

'Martin! Behave yourself!' The reprimand was from Annika, standing in the doorway to the lounge with arms akimbo and shaking her head. She was smiling in a way that said: 'He'll never change.'

Berthe Tillkvist will never win any blue-rinse beauty contest. That's a safe prediction. But she had a way with food that turned the ordinary into the magnificent. From the wide assemblage of hors d'oeuvre and starters, arrayed like an artist's palette on the large, heavy table that normally occupied the kitchen, I tried several. All were delightful, but my favourite was the pickled herring, marinated in honey and coarse-grained mustard. The main courses were no less imaginative. She'd worked culinary wonders with both mixed seafood and guinea fowl. My taste buds responded with an effuse salivation. I had no option but to try some of each.

'You are used now to our Swedish food?' Bertil smilingly inquired.

'I could always get used to Mrs Tillkvist's cooking,' I replied, raising a forkful of guinea fowl, plums and raisins to emphasise my meaning.

'Took me a bit of getting used to at first,' Martin remarked, 'but now I love it.'

Apart from the enjoyment of the food, I was surprised to see how well Mats and Annika got on together. This was the first time I'd seen the brother and sister together socially. The only other time had been when Bertil was in hospital and, then, the atmosphere had been quite strained. Now, they were like two frolicsome teenagers. How Mats had changed, I thought.

Presently, Mats called us to attention and Annika appeared through the kitchen doorway with a tray of aquavit glasses.

'We're going to drink a special toast to a special friend,' he announced. I was, of course, allowed to partake of the Skåne aquavit, but it was the others who raised their glasses in my honour.

'And we have some little gifts for you to take back to England as a memory of us,' Mats went on.

I'd felt slightly uncomfortable at being the object of their toasting. I wasn't used to being the centre of attention. But now, I was overwhelmed. Their 'little gifts' included a leather suitcase, a bright red Mora horse and a beautiful solid glass sculpture.

'This is too much. I don't know what to say,' I somehow got out as my voice began to waver. 'Thank you all very much. I shall always treasure the memory of my time here...' Then, almost as an afterthought, I added, '...at Peterlöv.' Everyone applauded and Martin let out a loud, thigh-slapping whoop.

Bertil held up his hand, indicating that he wanted to say something.

'This is not the end of the gifts. We have two more to give.' He walked slowly to one corner of the room and brought out a white plastic bag. He placed the bag on a chair then, dipping his hand into it, he produced the old book that I immediately recognised.

'Some will remember it from before,' he began, 'but Mats, you have seen it only when you were very small. It is the true diary from Captain Sten Tillkvist. In his writing, he tells many things about our family. Even our family here at Peterlöv, many years ago. Tonight, Berthe and me give it to you for you to be the safekeeper of it.' He handed his son the old book with his left hand and, grasping Mats' right hand in his, shook it earnestly. A lump came to Mats' throat and he swallowed hard, saying something in Swedish as he opened the diary and began to scan the ancient record.

'And now, we have the last,' Bertil said, dipping his hand into the plastic bag once more.

'Doctor Walt, this is for you. Berthe and me, we have made it with the photocopy machine. It is also Captain Sten's book. Berthe has made a translation of some first pages. Maybe you can get more pages translated in England.'

I took the replica diary from him and hugged him, then kissed Berthe on the cheek. They'd made an excellent job of binding it between stiffened leather covers. Quite apart from the photocopying, it must have taken many hours of patient effort to stitch and glue it all together. Bertil and Berthe were making quite certain I would never forget this evening... and my times with the Tillkvist family of Peterlöv.

*

It felt like a million years since I sat here in this bar, enjoying my first experience of Swedish beer, looking at the unusual perspective of my reflection in the mirrored ceiling tiles and smiling inwardly at some of the handwritten wall signs. Tonight, I drank alone. This time around, I had no pensive expectations of meeting any intriguing foreign correspondent. There was just me. And my thoughts. My recollections of those past million years swam around in my head, cresting the waves of my Starkol beer as I lingered over each draught. Familiar faces came and went, sometimes drifting silently past, sometimes accompanied by snatches of long-ago conversation. One face, one voice stood out above the others. 'Do you have enough kronor left for one more beer?' It was Kerstin Berg. And she was real. Her voice had carried too much of a timbre for it to have come from some mere memory.

'I... I'm sorry... I was miles away. What on earth are you doing here? I didn't expect to see *you* here tonight.'

'And I couldn't let *you* spend your last evening in Sweden on your own.'

She slid elegantly into the chair opposite me and I signalled to a passing bar attendant.

'Oh, just a beer. Thank you,' she smilingly told the waiter.

She removed her heavy wool coat and folded it on to an empty chair, then ran her fingers loosely through each side of her hair, tossing her head to throw the bulk of the strands behind her shoulders.

'I know we said our "official" farewells on Friday, but it really didn't seem right, somehow, knowing you were back here in Malmö, to let you just fly off home to England without this one last chance to get your conclusions on the whole scenario. I suppose I feel responsible, in quite a big way, for your coming here in the first place and it's all turned out quite differently to what we first thought.'

'Yes, it's been an amazing four months. So much has happened and I've met so many people; been to so many places. My *Arms and Armour* article has quite a different slant to it from what I thought I was going to write when I first arrived. Whether or not it'll ever be published is another matter, of course, with all of this uncertainty hanging over CHP's future.'

'But it was worth the trip, even so?'

'It would be hard to put a value of any kind on a trip like this. Some of my experiences over these past weeks have been priceless.'

Kerstin's Starkol arrived. The waiter had barely released his grasp on the tall, concave glass when Kerstin replaced his hand with hers and took two quick sips. In a way that I thought cute, she flicked her tongue in a circuit of her lips to remove the frothy head that had momentarily added a glistening sparkle to her lipstick.

'And what, would you say, are your most striking memories?'

'Most striking? Well, that's an interesting way of putting it. Let's see now. I suppose I'd have to say it's been the theme of reunion.'

'Reunion?'

'Or restoration, or reconciliation. Think about it: we've seen old Tomas's antique gun reunited with Siegfried Wersel's other Bergengren guns; we've seen Mats reunited with his father, and with the land that's so important to the Tillkvists; and, of course, we're witnessing perhaps the greatest reunion of all in the conception of the Øresund link, bringing Zealand and Skåne together again after three hundred and fifty years.'

'That's a very succinct summary and, yes, I can see exactly what you mean.'

'Have you thought: the schoolchildren of 2010 may learn not about the Nordic lands, but just "Northern Europe" and with a different map of Scandinavia to the one we know today, in 1996.'

'It's possible,' she agreed. 'We're all so busy, wrapped up

in our own little worlds, that we don't realise just how much formative change is taking place around us. Europe, certainly, is going through major change in these closing years of the century.'

'And talking of change, I must say I've seldom seen anyone change as quickly as Mats has done. I wonder if he ever will meet some other woman and get married. They're so proud of their heritage, the Tillkvists. I'm sure he won't be allowed to forget that. Unless he marries and fathers a son, the family name will just disappear.'

'Oh, I think Bertil will be preaching that particular gospel even on his deathbed, God bless him.'

At that point, we heard, wafting through the open glass doors that led from the reception area, the soft, jazzy chords that were unmistakably from a grand piano. Kerstin suggested we relocate to the Piano Bar to continue our conversation in the more subtle ambience of the mezzanine lounge. Toni, an American girl, was tinkling the ivories and asking for requests. When we first entered the Piano Bar there were only four or five other people there. They looked like business types, spoke in German, and were probably recently arrived from Copenhagen – and, before that, from some metropolis in Germany, Austria or Switzerland.

I strolled over to the piano and Toni looked up with an all-American smile that said, either: 'Wasn't I lucky to be born with perfect teeth,' or 'Daddy always paid top dollar for our dental insurance.' To give her some encouragement, I asked if she knew the old jazz favourite *Lullaby of Birdland*. She nodded. 'Long taam since ah plied it, though.' Even so, her rendition of the piece was quite acceptable.

Just as on Friday, when the time seemed reasonable for

us to terminate our conversation and prepare to make our separate ways, Kerstin clasped my hand warmly and kissed me on the cheek.

'Have a good trip back to England. Oh, and give my best wishes to Don. I'll call him in a couple of weeks to find out what's happening. That is, if he hasn't called me first.'

'Goodnight, goodbye and thanks for all your help. You have my number so, please, if you get over to UK next year, do give me a call.'

The taxi driver gave me a thumbs-up sign as he pulled away from the Malmö Harbour terminal, leaving me to manage my luggage through the check-in point. The bright new leather suitcase I'd been given by the Tillkvists was already in use and I trundled my three pieces to the check-in desk before sorting through my tickets, passport and a few remaining Swedish currency notes.

From my window seat on the big catamaran, I recognised the huge Kockums crane as we manoeuvred towards the open Sound. The dark patches of Saltholm Island I could only just make out as the Sea Cat throbbed its way across the slightly choppy waters. By what would have been my normal breakfast time, I was wandering aimlessly around the duty-free area at Kastrup airport. The next hour and ten minutes melted away and I was feeling just a little jaded as the big SAS jet taxied in readiness for take-off.

The engines roared and we belted along the runway, misty spray lashing past my window. There was a dull thump, followed by a flat-sounding 'blap' and we were airborne. I could feel a lifting sensation while the plane fought as if to free itself from the clutches of the earth. We began to bank and I could see the Danish-side landworks for the Øresund crossing. This time, it was no model.

These were for real. I thought of the picture I'd seen in the Consortium office 'by a German artist' and how, in just a few years from now, the Øresund link might well bring about the reunion of Denmark and Sweden. Then, as we were swallowed up in spray-filled clouds that obscured my view of anything below, I recalled Martin Chelford's words: 'Come back in the year 2000, Walt, and you'll be able to get from downtown Copenhagen to downtown Malmö in less than half an hour.'

Yes, Martin, I might just take you up on that.

Part Eight
The Incident

...we cannot dedicate, we cannot consecrate, we cannot hallow this ground.

                                           Abraham Lincoln

Unlikely though it may seem, the key incident around which the storyline of *Reunion* revolves – the concealment and later discovery of a rifle in a hollow tree – is based on a real-life occurrence. It happened like this:

During the *War Between the States*, often referred to as the *American Civil War*, the turning point in the struggle between North and South was reached during the first three days of July, 1863, at the Battle of Gettysburg.

On the second day of the fighting, as the Confederates of Hood's Division swarmed through a gorge between the low hills known as the Round Tops, they engaged, amongst others, the Pennsylvania Reserves. One Pennsylvanian, severely wounded in the exchange, withdrew to seek shelter in a small grove of trees. Uncertain of his own future, but thinking, perhaps, that he might be taken prisoner, he hid his much prized rifle in the narrow, hollow part of a forked tree. The rifle was simply propped in position; it was neither covered nor protected in any other way. As things turned out, the wounded man was not able to retrieve his weapon as he became very weak and was carried off the field of battle to be treated in a makeshift hospital.

Some years after the War had ended in 1865, surviving soldiers from both sides visited the sites of the major battles in organised reunions. It was during just such a reunion, in 1885, that the Pennsylvanian veteran walked the field between the Round Tops and recognised the tree where he'd propped his rifle. The hollow between the forks was, by then, completely closed up to form a tree of substantial girth. Convinced that the peculiar growth pattern had been caused by his concealed rifle, he requested that the tree be taken down and sawn open. As the wood was stripped away, it revealed his rifle, still in the position in which he'd stood it exactly twenty-two years before.

In this true-life incident, the gun was no longer in serviceable condition. Nonetheless, it is reasonable to postulate that, if wrapped and protected *and* if cocooned loosely in the tree rather than becoming almost a part of it as it grew, the gun could have survived for a very much longer period of time and still functioned. In the fictional incident at the Peterlöv farm, it is suggested that this might possibly have been the case.

Records of the strange incident concerning the Pennsylvanian soldier are detailed in the columns of the *Gettysburg Compiler* and in a commemorative book by Herbert Grimm, Paul Roy and George Rose, entitled: *Human Interest Stories of the Three Days' Battles at Gettysburg.*

THE PETERLOV FAMILIES

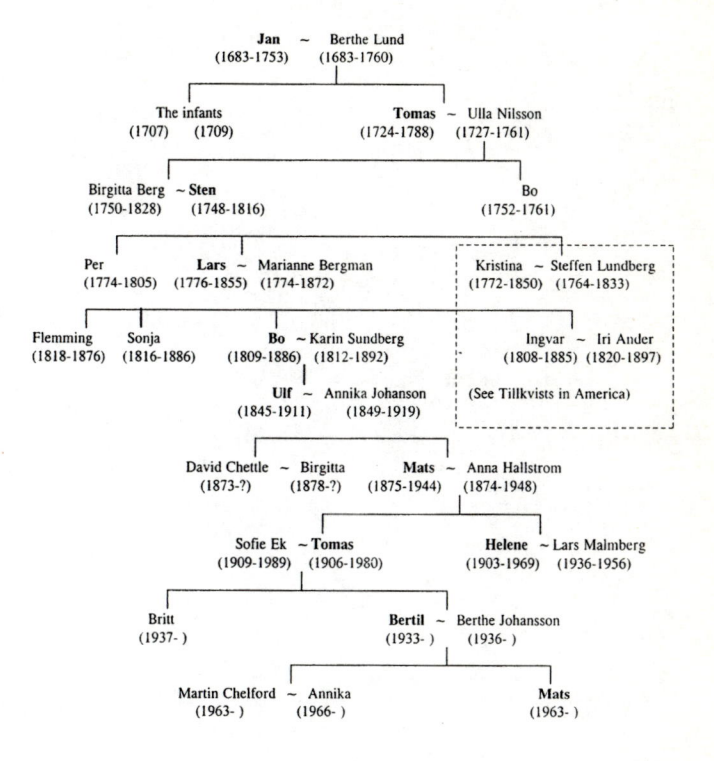

- **Jan** (1683-1753) ~ Berthe Lund (1683-1760)
  - The infants (1707) (1709)
  - **Tomas** (1724-1788) ~ Ulla Nilsson (1727-1761)
    - Birgitta Berg (1750-1828) ~ **Sten** (1748-1816)
      - Per (1774-1805)
      - **Lars** (1776-1855) ~ Marianne Bergman (1774-1872)
        - Flemming (1818-1876)
        - Sonja (1816-1886)
        - **Bo** (1809-1886) ~ Karin Sundberg (1812-1892)
          - **Ulf** (1845-1911) ~ Annika Johanson (1849-1919)
            - David Chettle (1873-?) ~ Birgitta (1878-?)
            - **Mats** (1875-1944) ~ Anna Hallstrom (1874-1948)
              - Sofie Ek (1909-1989) ~ Tomas (1906-1980)
                - Britt (1937-)
                - **Bertil** (1933-) ~ Berthe Johansson (1936-)
                  - Martin Chelford (1963-) ~ Annika (1966-)
                  - **Mats** (1963-)
              - Helene (1903-1969) ~ Lars Malmberg (1936-1956)
      - Kristina (1772-1850) ~ Steffen Lundberg (1764-1833)
        - Ingvar (1808-1885) ~ Iri Ander (1820-1897)
        - (See Tillkvists in America)
    - Bo (1752-1761)

THE TILLVISTS IN AMERICA

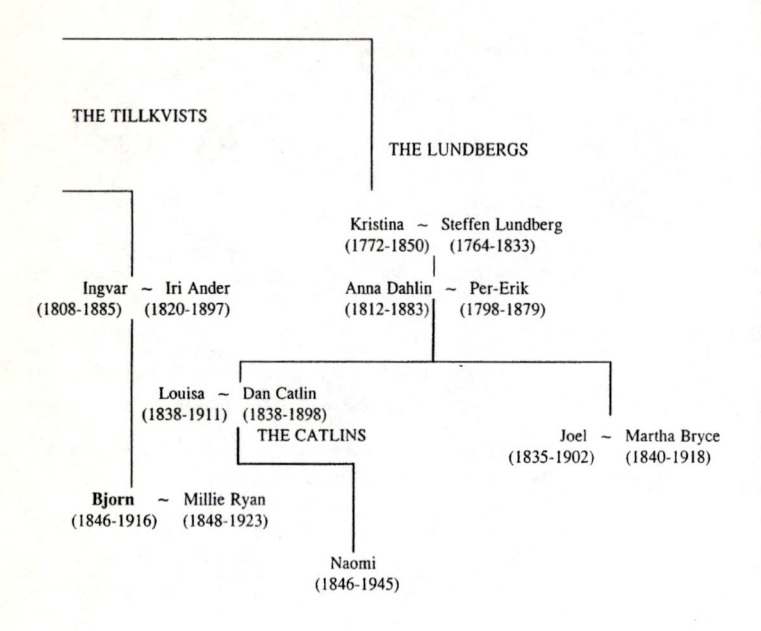

THE TILLKVISTS

THE LUNDBERGS

Kristina ~ Steffen Lundberg
(1772-1850) (1764-1833)

Ingvar ~ Iri Ander   Anna Dahlin ~ Per-Erik
(1808-1885) (1820-1897)   (1812-1883) (1798-1879)

Louisa ~ Dan Catlin
(1838-1911) (1838-1898)
THE CATLINS

Joel ~ Martha Bryce
(1835-1902) (1840-1918)

Bjorn ~ Millie Ryan
(1846-1916) (1848-1923)

Naomi
(1846-1945)